P9-DNA-925

DARK
WARRIOR
RISING

Tor Books by Ed Greenwood

Dark Warrior Rising

BAND OF FOUR NOVELS

The Kingless Land
The Vacant Throne
A Dragon's Ascension
The Dragon's Doom

The Silent House

DARK
WARRIOR
RISING

A Novel of Niflheim

ED GREENWOOD

TOR®

A TOM DOHERTY ASSOCIATES BOOK

New York

This is a work of fiction. All of the characters, organizations, and events portrayed in this novel are either products of the author's imagination or are used fictitiously.

DARK WARRIOR RISING: A NOVEL OF NIFLHEIM

Copyright © 2007 by Ed Greenwood

All rights reserved, including the right to reproduce this book, or portions thereof, in any form.

A Tor Book
Published by Tom Doherty Associates, LLC
175 Fifth Avenue
New York, NY 10010

www.tor.com

Tor® is a registered trademark of Tom Doherty Associates, LLC.

Library of Congress Cataloging-in-Publication Data

Greenwood, Ed.
  Dark warrior rising : a novel of Niflheim / Ed Greenwood.—1st ed.
    p. cm.
  "A Tom Doherty Associates Book."
  ISBN-13: 978-0-7653-1765-0
  ISBN-10: 0-7653-1765-6
  I. Title.
  PR9199.3.G759D37 2007
  813'.54—dc22

                                            2007017375

First Edition: September 2007

Printed in the United States of America

0 9 8 7 6 5 4 3 2 1

To Abby,

For all of Taerune's good qualities,
and none of her bad ones

Acknowledgments

Brian Thomsen, for enthusiasms shared.
Gary Gygax, for mapping the road to this branching.
Jenny, for the tea and the patience.

Dark
Warrior
Rising

Little is known of the Dark Below in the years before the Great Doom, but from the writings and testimonies of the few Niflghar and humans who came up into the light in those times, some truths can be told.

The two most numerous races of the lightless lands were then the Niflghar or dark elves, called "nightskins" by most humans for their obsidian-hued bodies; and the brutish gorkul or "grayhides," whom some have called "orkhs" and worse.

The tusked, hulking gorkul were of greater physical strength, but spent their lives in rages, fighting among themselves whenever they weren't raiding others, or wandering the Dark Below in nomadic clans.

They were easily enslaved by the agile, swift-minded Niflghar, who mastered fell sorceries, tamed lizards of the lightless lands to be their pack-beasts and the deadly darkwings to be their flying steeds, and raised great cities in the largest caverns of the Dark.

Most Niflghar followed one of two faiths: They either worshipped the Ever-Ice at the heart of Niflheim, the all-seeing source of the greatest magic, or they cleaved to the goddess Olone, whose beauty was matchless. To achieve physical perfection was to so ascend in Her holy favor as to join Her, and know true power and fulfilment.

Niflghar saw the Ever-Ice as something greater than Nifl themselves, an everlasting Silence that perceived all, spoke to Nifl in dreams, and granted mastery over, and new knowledge of, sorcery to those who served it best and so made all Niflghar stronger. Many of these wizards, called "spellrobes" by Nifl, were male Niflghar, and they ruled the cities that worshipped the Ever-Ice, such as Ouvahlor, Arnoenar, and Imbrae, taking advice from the priestesses of the Ever-Ice and seeking their interpretations of events and holy signs.

Olone was the mother and future of all Nifl, the ultimate Nifl-she, and her priestesses enacted all justice and kept order in cities that venerated the Goddess, such as Uryrryr, Nrauluskh, Oundrel, and the greatest of all, Talonnorn.

The cities were ruled by councils of the greatest Nifl houses or families, a nobility dominated from within by the elder Nifl-shes, or "crones," family shes beyond birthing age, who sought power and respect among the Consecrated priestesses of Olone by their furthering of the church's aims and influence—and who in turn ruled their families using the might of the church. The crones of every house were led by the Eldest of that house, but every house had a ruling Lord, a war commander and public face of the house who kept his throne only at the pleasure of the crones. Whereas in the cities of the Ever-Ice male Nifl spellrobes were great lords, they were little more than useful house weapons in the cities of Olone.

Otherwise, the cities were socially much the same: the priestesses on top, a dominant house among noble houses, each having a nobility ruled by a Lord but truly ruled by the crones (the unmarried shes of the house), overseeing many servants and warblades (the warriors). Beneath the houses were Nifl merchant traders, shopkeepers, crafters, and laborers of no house, deemed "the Nameless," who dwelt outside the fortified compounds of the houses in a central cluster of homes and hovels . . . and beneath all were the slaves.

Slaves in the Ever-Ice cities were prisoners of war, and tended to be few and well-treated. Slaves in the cities of Olone were constantly expended necessities, for the pursuit of the perfection made necessary non-Nifl hands to do all work that could scar or maim, and the cruelty of crones and others caused the deaths of many slaves. Moreover, one road to greater power among houses was the ability to build more weapons, fortifications, trade goods, and finery, and do so faster than rivals—and one way to accomplish such things was through ever more slaves.

Hence, the Niflghar cities of Olone took to raiding surface lands, coming to the surface through mines and caverns to seize humans first by the score and then by the village, by thousands upon thousands, and drag them down into the Dark to lives of cruel, dangerous work.

In both sorts of cities, the Houses made constant and covert war on each other, striving for supremacy. These struggles were tempered by the churches of the Ever-Ice and Olone, and often twisted into open warfare between rival cities, warfare that never truly ceased.

The churches carefully balanced House against House, moving to let a

House be brought down only when it had truly offended the authority of the church or the power of its city. Their weapons were knowledge, church aid, slayings, and the bestowal of magic items, notably the powerful enchanted swords of many powers, known as "spellblades," into the hands of those not gifted by the gods with mastery of magic.

Those who offended against the laws of the church and the authority of the houses were slain or exiled—or escaped out into the Wild Dark. Most such perished, but some banded together to dwell in small roving bands, raiding the caravans and fighting the patrols of the cities, the Nifl they called the Haraedra or "Towered Ones." These outcasts were known as the Ravagers, and in time they became the chief slave-takers raiding the surface, and the slaves the trade goods they exchanged with Nameless Nifl merchant traders operating from city to city.

With others doing their drudge work, the dominant cities of Olone rose to ever-greater power over time—and ever-greater decadence. Riven by constant strife between houses and raids between rival cities, they were societies of vanity above all, where murder was a mere means to an end, and cruelty the way of life—as their non-elven slaves from the surface all too often found out.

–from *Dynasties of Darkness*,
penned by Erammon the Elder,
published the Sixth Summer of Urraul

$\mathcal{P}$rologue

A sword can do great ill, but the lands hold many great
ills, so better, it is, to wield a sword than to have none.
—saying of the priests of Thorar

This was it. The moment of punishment he'd been marched to the holy hut to receive.

Orivon stood trembling in the darkness, his bare feet on the cold dirt aching to turn and flee. He might be as tall and as strong as many of the men in the village, but he was still a boy. And right now, here under the hand of the god, he felt very young and very alone.

All he'd done was smash a stick across Aldo's sneering face for calling his mother "old widow." And then called the stick a sword, and warned Aldo one day it would be. Nor was he sorry for saying that. For, aye, one day *it would be.*

In the wavering candlelight, the shadow of the armored warrior loomed over him, nearer and nearer.

Orivon clenched his teeth and shut his eyes. This was it . . .

"Strong! Aye, you're strong, Orivon Ralla's son. That is good. Ashenuld will have need of you."

The voice was stern. "Look at me!"

Orivon swallowed and opened his eyes. As always, the gaze of the old bearded priest in the cracked helm and battered armor seemed to thrust right through skin and bone, right through Orivon's own eyes to see inside his very head.

Which made Orivon Ralla's son flush bright red. There were a lot of things he didn't want the Eyes of Thorar to see. His spying on the youngest village wives as they bathed in the Deep Stream back in the woods . . . trading two fresh-killed tratha to Dahlma the Widow for a long look at and swift, blundering caress of her deliciously curved bareness, down as far as her hips, as she winked and chuckled . . . sneaking into the Nightskins' Caves that every grown Ashenuldar sternly said were forbidden . . . stealing almost-ripe brimmun from Old Larthor's fields . . .

Unexpectedly, Old Eyes laughed, and swept out a hand as swift as a striking viper to clap Orivon's shoulder. "Grow stronger, Orivon. Thorar has seen you watching the women, and approves. The women of Ashenuld are fair, and more than fair."

Orivon's face burned, but he knew better than to look away from the priest's gaze. Those ice-blue eyes were like two dagger points thrusting into his, but they were smiling.

"Stay here, work hard, grow strong, and you'll become great in Ashenuld. There will come a day when all Ashenuldar look to Orivon as they look up to Dargar."

Dargar? Tall, laughing Dargar, whose shoulders were wider than most doorways and whose arms bulged and rippled with his brawn? Dargar who kissed any woman he willed, leaving their men grinning rather than glowering? Dargar who could snatch on a rein and drag a running, snorting lowhorns to a halt from sheer growling strength?

Hah! Not prancepaw likely! Not when—

The priest of Thorar stiffened, and his eyes became two leaping blue flames. His hand tightened on Orivon's shoulder, fingers digging deep like talons.

It hurt, and Orivon tried to twist away, but the old priest was gazing past him at nothing, and starting to gasp, now.

"Blood!" he said hoarsely. "Blood and . . . much darkness, and the fire of a forge. Great hammer blows, sparks on steel, and . . . a lash, scourging as hard and as often as the forgehammer! In a cavern so large that castles stand in it! And—nightskins, nightskins everywhere!"

The priest's arm was shaking so violently that Orivon's teeth were chattering as he shook, too, helpless in that steely grip.

And then the Eyes of Thorar coughed, his hand fell away from Orivon, and his eyes were flaming no longer. Clouded and empty, they stared at nothing from above a shaky smile.

"Heh," the priest said vaguely, sounding old, his voice now as kindly and empty as those of the old aunts who dozed all day by the cauldron in the Moot at the heart of Ashenuld. "Heh-hem. Aye, there will come a day when all Ashenuldar look to Orivon as they look up to Dargar. There will come a day when they will need to."

"They"? Not "we"?

Orivon frowned at that. The old man didn't seem to notice. He turned and shuffled away, mere bones in ruined armor, leaving the boy staring after him and frowning.

Silence fell. After standing alone in the dimness of the dying candle-light for a time, Orivon turned to leave the hut.

And froze, fear racing icy fingers up his spine.

Floating in the air behind him was a stick. His stick. The one he'd hit Aldo with, and wished was a sword.

For a moment he trembled before it, wondering if it would start to move, and strike at him with no one wielding it.

No. It did nothing, not even when he dared to reach out and take it from the empty air.

Aye, this was his stick. He thrust it back through his belt. His sword.

Feeling somehow stronger, Orivon strode toward the light of day, still frowning.

Truly, holy punishments were strange.

"Holy Olone, that reeks!"

"It will be worse before it's done. Be ready to use your blade; the smell draws the worst beasts of the Dark."

"Then *why* not have slaves mix it—in the Outcaverns, say? Instead of here, on the very brink of the Blindingbright!"

"It must be fresh, or it avails us nothing. Now stand away, unless you want to help soak the hoods."

"Phaugh; I do *not*."

"Oh? You fail to surprise me."

His mother had been surprised to see the stick in his belt, but awed and pleased when Orivon had told her about how it had returned to him, and what the priest had said.

He did not mention, to her or anyone, what the Eyes of Thorar had said about the hammer and castle and Nightskins. Somehow he knew the old priest wouldn't remember having said those words. Which meant they came from the god to Orivon Ralla's son, and were for him alone.

He had to remember them—all of them, in the right order—and try to find out what they meant.

Blood! Blood and much darkness, and the fire of a forge. Great hammer blows, sparks on steel, and a lash, scourging as hard and as often as the forgehammer! In a cavern so large that castles stand in it! And nightskins, nightskins everywhere!

Orivon knew what nightskins were: cruel and evil monsters, though they were more beautiful than the fairest maid of the village. They had soot-black skin and lived in caves—and what was that great cave full of castles, but a cavern behind and beneath the Nightskins' Caves he was forbidden to go near? The nightskins came out of their caves only once or twice in a lifetime, to slay and to snatch Ashenuldar. Many of the cauldron-aunts said they ate humans, and "came up" only when they were hungry enough to dare seeing the sun.

"Dark elves," the priests called them, and said they called themselves something like "Naefell," but to the Ashenuldar and folk all around in the land, they were nightskins. The Murdering Ones.

Tall they were, these nightskins; as tall as the tallest men of the village, but thin. As sleekly curved and fine-featured as the most delicate young maids, both their hes and shes. Their swords were as long and curved and thin as they were, and they wore leather armor that clung to them more like tavern dancers' costumes than real war-plate. They moved like tavern dancers, too, the tales all said, swift yet always graceful, like the shiny-winged darters in the air above ponds on warm evenings: here and there, leaping eyeblink-swift, over there, as soft and as easy as drawing breath.

And when the dark elves came, those who fought them died, and young humans disappeared.

The nightskins gnawed on human bones as they sat in their caves full of jewels, some in Ashenuld said. Bah, other villagers disagreed, there were no jewels—and no human bones, being as evil sorcerers turned all the lost humans *into* more nightskins, to be their servants . . .

The tales couldn't all be true, and villagers swiftly got red-faced over who was right and who was wrong.

Frowning, Orivon went out after sunset, to the dying fire at the Moot-cauldron, to talk to the old aunts about nightskins.

"The noise you hear is my warblades being sick. Must this—this stink continue? I—"

"Have them arm themselves, over on the ledge there, by the ward-shield. It won't be long now."

. . .

Old Aunstance shrugged her shawl more tightly around her, for the night had turned sharply cold, stars glittering overhead in a clear sky. The dew was dripping from the kettles hanging beside her head, far from the hissing, dying fire under the cauldron. "Nay, Dertha, you've got it wrong!" she snapped. " 'Twasn't the year they took Arblade Fletcher!"

"Oh, now, Aunstance! Just when was it, then, if your mind is so bright and clear on the matter?"

" 'Twas the year they carved up old Piers Gaunt!" Aunstance replied triumphantly, wagging one wrinkled finger.

Orivon sat as still as a statue just beneath it, not daring to stir or say a word for fear the aunts would remember him, and retreat to their usual guarded mumblings. They'd been talking like this for a long time now, remembering bygone nightskin raids of fading years, voices rising and eyes catching fire as they remembered the dead and gone, lost loves and foes and rivals. Rocking back and forth in their shawls for warmth, getting louder as they came alive again, recalling younger years and feuds long laid by.

Orivon listened, learning much—and becoming stone-hard certain that he'd learn more about nightskins while they talked on freely than if they remembered he was there. Some of it might be fancy, of course, but . . .

So nightskins called themselves "Nifful," or something like that, and they were elves—dark elves—who had black skin and white hair, could see in darkness, and lived underground. *Deep* underground, in cities that stood in huge caverns.

In a cavern so large that castles stand in it! And nightskins, nightskins everywhere! Y-yes. Orivon shuddered, seeing again the flaming eyes of the old priest.

They took humans as food, or slaves, or both, raiding out of their caves to do it. They were the reason the men of Ashenuld all had swords, and practiced using them, and they were the reason every stump-and-stone fence in the village had prickly redthorn growing in it: the thorns and berries were deadly poison to nightskins, and made their flesh melt at a touch.

Dark elves had raided Ashenuld more times than the old aunts could agree on, and—

"Those weren't old rags on Dunstan Ghallow's gate, Maraude!

They were nightskin hides—all shriveled and not much to look at, aye, but skin he'd cut off dark elves with his own sword before his dogs ate the rest!"

"Aye, ate the rest and died!"

"Ho, now! *Ho,* now, Maraude Gyntly! Died they did, yes, one after t'other, over four-and-ten years following! Of old age, they went, not of eating elves!"

"*Hah!* A lot *you* know, Dertha Bucklebody! Why, those dogs gobbled and tore like I don't know *what* all! Worst he'd ever seen them, Nars said, and then lay down whimpering and just died!"

"Oh, Nars *Boldwood*! He'd lie about his own name to his own mother, he would! Don't be heeding a word Nars Boldwood says; not a *word*!"

Several of the old aunts cackled agreement, wagging bony fingers at each other.

Something moved behind Orivon, a shifting as soft as a shadow. Then Dertha Bucklebody's hoarse chucklings ended in an abrupt, solid *thupp* sound, a wet and heavy thud that made Orivon look up.

In time to see old Aunt Dertha's head, withered jaws parted in a look of staring surprise, leap from her shoulders.

Behind her shaking, spasming—and now headless—shoulders, Orivon saw a face.

A face—liquid dark eyes in a face that was blacker than the night around it. A *pointed* face, with features as fine and as beautiful as anything he'd ever seen, that looked back at him, over the bloody sword that had just beheaded Dertha Bucklebody.

. . . and grinned cruelly.

A man started to shout nearby, but it twisted into a scream—and the night all around Orivon was suddenly full of shouts and screams. Men were running, a sword clanged on something, and a falling lantern exploded and caught a line of washing alight.

Orivon sprang up. In the flare of flames black figures were darting everywhere. The old aunts were sprawled and butchered, and men of Ashenuld were running, too—most of them fleeing into the night.

That was all he had time to see, as the grinning dark elf finished killing old women and came leaping at him like a fox in a hurry.

Orivon dodged away, and ran hard for the nearest trees.

A great roar erupted behind him—a voice he knew.

He twisted around, not slowing, and saw Dargar, the great warrior of the village, burst into view from behind a wagon, sword flashing in hand.

The nightskin chasing Orivon turned and sprang at Dargar, who snarled defiance and swung his blade viciously, its edge shimmering back firelight. Dark shadows were leaping at him from all sides.

"For Ashenuld!" he roared.

"For Ashenuld!" Orivon shouted back. "Dargar! Kill them, Dargar!"

He was still shouting as four shadows lunged with contemptuous ease, four long and dark blades met in Dargar's body, and the great warrior of Ashenuld reeled, wide-eyed, and started spewing blood and dying.

"No!" Orivon shrieked. "No!"

And then something that stank of spring flowers, odd nose-prickling scents, and something sour all at once, descended over his head and blotted the night out. The something was thick, coarse cloth that pulled tight across his face, sawing at his nose . . .

And the starry night went away, and true night came.

Darkness.

Just darkness.

1

The Towers of Talonnorn

Drink, drink down the juksarr,
Let none now moan nor mourn,
For we fare forth fast and far
At last to bright Talonnorn.
—**Niflghar way-chant**

*I*t was as long as four large wagons, yet looked like a tiny insect flitting among the stone fangs of the Outcaverns. Silently it flapped and banked, dodging through the great columns of rock with smoothly scudding familiarity. It was batlike and black, and held its long neck as straight as a lance, baleful eyes burning in the darkness.

It was afraid.

So was its rider, Naraedel of Oondaunt, glancing all about warily and often, crouching low and wrapped in a half-cloak to hide the house targe on the breast of his leathers. For this Niflghar was an envoy of one house, skulking home expecting trouble from others; not a loud, wildly laughing blade of the Hunt cavorting in the air with many well-armed fellows. In lone, swift silence the messenger sped homeward.

Suddenly empty air in front of the batlike beast flared into a warning glow—but the Nifl sat back in his saddle, sighing with relief, as the dark-wings under him left that brief flare of magical shieldings fading in its wake, and glided serenely out into the great cavern beyond.

The spires of proud Talonnorn awaited, many lights glowing among six soaring castles, and twinkling here and there in the broad dark swath of lesser dwellings sprawling between them like a flung-down cloak.

Everywhere was beauty and elegance, for the greater glory of Olone demanded such, and all Talonar Nifl worshipped the Kiss of Beauty. Or died.

A spellrobe—young Ondrar, his cruel face raised to watch Naraedel intently—was standing watch in an ornately curved turret on the highest walls of the fortress of Har Vigilant, home to the rival House of Rask-shaula. He gazed steadily at Naraedel as the envoy flew overhead, but did nothing. Nor did the warblades standing around him, bannerpoints in their hands. Custom was all in Talonnorn, and where there were gaps in custom, pacts had been woven long ago to bridge those gaps.

The envoy guided his mount lower, banking over the crowded central Araed, where the Nameless lived. Its winding streets were choked with scurrying servants and slaves, heavily-laden pack-snouts and wagons. As usual.

Everyone in haste, but no one getting anywhere all that swiftly. As ever.

Lower still Naraedel scudded, trusting in his wardshield to protect him from darts or things hurled up out of malice or mischief, wanting to see what he could of whatever was unfolding on the streets.

Whips cracked yonder, where overseers—Nameless Nifl wearing the rival targe of Evendoom—were lashing a trudging line of newly arrived slaves to a sale pen. Weak, hairy, repulsively light-skinned humans, all of them stumbling along in drugged obedience in their stinking capture-hoods. Hairy Ones, tamed but not trained.

Then the envoy was past, too soon to properly see and know the pattern of the colored scarves knotted along the rope that bound the necks of the slaves together in their long line, that would tell him which slave-takers owned that rather pitiful brawn.

Not that it mattered much; humans were slow-witted and seldom lasted long, being both weak and lazy. Thank Olone that the Blinding-bright seemed to hold an endless supply of them.

The next street held rather better slaves: a gang of great muscled and tusked brutes, the gorkuls of the mountains. The weakest of such could match the straining strength of three large humans—and Talonar needed many slaves to do all the things that might otherwise scar them, or make their sleek selves bulge overmuch and mar their strivings to be ever more beautiful—and so please Olone, and rise in Talonnorn.

Some among the Nameless went masked—as the ruling crones of the six ruling Houses did, while all Talonnorn pretended not to see their wrinkles and sagging withering—but the truly maimed or deformed were slain and burned, or driven forth into the Wild Dark beyond the Out-caverns, so as not to offend Olone.

Naraedel sighed inwardly. Talonnorn was a vain and ruthless place, but it was home.

In truth, he liked most the scheming traders and struggling shop-keepers of the Araed, who mumbled prayers to Olone but spent their lives seeking to stay alive and a few stones to the better. He understood them, even if every alley bristled with knives and every tavern housed a waiting succession of brawls, with only the rogue priests and potion-brewers who healed for stiff fees getting rich.

It was the murderous whims of life in the house compounds that made him shiver.

The envoy sighed again, casting a regretful glance at a particular roof below: the tavern called the Waiting Warm Dark, where he'd much rather be heading.

Perhaps later . . .

Then he straightened and unwrapped his cloak to proudly display the Talon of House Oondaunt, and used his spurs almost gently; his steed was already gliding, banking sharply and sweeping its wings back so as to dart through the narrow, waiting opening between the two guardspires.

Home again.

The tingling of the inner wards was still raging through Naraedel when the first brutal probes of the Oondaunt spellrobes' magics flooded into his mind, sending him reeling back in his saddle, eyes rolled up in his head and lip bitten through.

A gentler homecoming than usual.

"Voices *down,*" Urgel muttered warningly, leaning forward over his drinking horn and pointing warningly at the feeble flicker of the hear-not shield on the table in their midst. It had been old when he'd bought it, and that had been long enough ago that Urgel's hair had still been lush and thick. "What we speak of is as much treason as if we were invoking the Ever-Ice with every breath!"

Tarlyn rolled his eyes in disgust. "Gel, this is the Waiting Warm *Dark,* not a Kissers' temple. I mean, look around you! Who here would dare go to any High House to tell them about us? Hmm?"

The subterranean tavern around them was quiet just now, which meant that most of the loungers on its stools—as opposed to the Nifl decorating the floor—were gowned pleasure-shes, winking hopefully at the handful of Nameless clustered around their usual table. Beneath those gowns were the brandings, piercings, and deep body sculptings—holes right through sleek bellies and torsos—that drove most Nifl rampants wild. Those charms would, however, stay hidden until tally-stones enough—rather more than the rampants around the table had to spare—were proffered.

The shes knew Tarlyn and the others, of course, and weren't really expecting these particular rampants to pour out gems enough to tug at nipple rings or ring rows of little bells set into flanks, but a pleasure-she has to keep in practice somehow . . .

Most of Talonnorn knew Tarlyn, if only by reputation. He was handsome even among Talonar Nifl, the very elegantly smiling image of a "prancing rampant." His pair of two tiny horns that all Nifl males have at their brows were exquisitely twisted and arched—and polished to a high sheen, with his hair sculpted back and away to display them. His eyes and jaw had the strength of command, and yet his mouth was as soft and sensual as that of the most yieldingly desirable Nifl-she. His wits might be a trifle thick, but that mattered not a whit to the lusty Talonar shes he was so skilled at "servicing," from alleyhips here in the Araed to ladies of the grand Houses. He almost never stopped smiling.

Many in Talonnorn knew Urgel by sight. A maker of masks for aging crones—every one of them beautiful, and most of them magically augmented with the minor glamors he could cast—he never took off the mask he was wearing now. He took care that as few Talonar as possible knew it had been magically bonded to his skin, after his face had been ravaged by magical fire hurled by a spellrobe hired by a rival. He hoped no one knew that his knife had slashed out that wizard's throat, diced the mage's brain, and burned it in a back alley brazier. The spellrobe had been a prominent member of House Dounlar—and all of the Houses were more than accomplished in matters of vengeance.

The other three at the table didn't want Talonnorn to know or notice them. Tall, slow-tongued, amiable Munthur was their "strongfists," whose punches could break necks or bestow senselessness in an instant. Wry-tongued old Clazlathor was a rogue spellrobe—something none of the High Houses liked to think existed in Talonnorn, or wanted to see visit their city for even a single breath, given how swiftly some spells could be hurled. Handsome and soft-spoken Imdul was the sort of viper the Houses wanted cleansed out of the Araed, so they alone could control certain vices; he was a poisoner-for-hire, a forger, and a buyer and seller of stolen items. Just now, the goblet in his hand should have been adorning a table in the private chambers of the Lord of House Maulstryke, which was one of the two large and secret handfuls of reasons why he was smiling.

"Nifl have always pondered great changes in Talonnorn aloud around tables like these," he murmured. "So long as we plot nothing specific against any House, I see nothing wrong. Why, even Lord Evendoom has spoken of turning to coins, as some cities do, and away from gemstones as currency. The metal's sturdier."

"Yet, so?" Clazlathor growled. "Gems I love the feel of, gems I know the worth of; tally-stones I trust. Any fool can set slaves to stamping out endless coins, making mine worthless—but he who sends slaves gemmining is a *fool*."

"A murderous fool, aye," Urgel agreed. "Or a slaver with too much brawn in his pens to be able to feed them all."

"Some have done just that with slaves," Imdul murmured, "so as to be able to heap up gems enough to buy themselves a name."

"Huh," Munthur grunted. "More fool them. *Willingly* stepping into all that sneering and poisoning—beg pardon, Imdul—and daggers up backsides?"

"All of that very rarely goes on within Houses," Imdul told them, "unless the family is already doomed, and collapsing. Houses have too many foes outside their own ranks not to stand together. A Nameless who marries into them, if not personally useful, may well be allowed nothing more than a place inside the door—but some Nifl spend their lives striving for such advancement. If they find meaning and worth in it, who are we to cavil?"

"We're the smarter Nifl who waste no time at all on such hollow achievements," Urgel replied, draining his horn and looking around to find a serving-she to bring more aehrodel. The tallspout on the table seemed to have gone empty. Again.

Clazlathor cradled his goblet in both hands, shook his head, and snorted. "Can't see a House that'd be willing to let you join them, Gel. Or me. Or any of us."

"Be not so sure," Imdul purred. "Some crones play long games indeed, assembling skills and bloodlines among their servants and well nigh ordering matings. After all, an oriad can always meet with a convenient accident after the breeding's done."

"Quite so, quite so," Urgel said soothingly, for smiling Naersarra was at his elbow, holding up two full tallspouts with a questioning smile. "Both," he told her gently, and by way of thanks received a warm and almost bare bosom in his face as she leaned forward to set them on the table. Inhaling her warm, faintly musky scent, Urgel grinned to himself. There were worse taverns in the Araed than the Waiting Warm Dark, to be sure.

"Me," Munthur rumbled unexpectedly, "*I* worry about Raskshaula's tamperings with yeldeth. I don't want to end up eating poison, with one of *them* smilingly holding out the cure—in small doses that I have to pay and pay and pay for!"

Tarlyn chuckled. "Have you ever *seen* a yeldeth cavern? Hot and damp and all aglow, walls thick with the stuff—yellow-green growths like fried *brains,* look you—dripping with sticky rose-blue slime! It'll put you off yeldrau and dethen for a while, I tell you!"

Clazlathor regarded the plate by his hand, well-sprinkled with dethen crumbs—and they'd been round, firm, good loaves, too—rather sourly, looked down the table to where Imdul's empty bowl of yeldrau stood, and then asked, "And just where, Tarlyn, did you discover what fried brains look like? Or taste like? And were they Nifl brains, or gorkul wits, or . . . ?"

"I believe I'll have another bowl of yeldrau," Imdul observed unconcernedly, and Clazlathor recalled that the poisoner had finished his first bowl of the soup with swift and eager enjoyment.

Tarlyn laughed. "No, I'll not say! Yet, Munthur, you I will answer: If ever what you fear comes to pass, I'll do what many will, I'm sure: turn only to eating meat, and drinking beast blood to slake my thirst."

"Oh? Saving the Nifl-she breast milk for late dining?" Clazlathor asked the low ceiling overhead slyly, and the table exploded in laughter.

Vaeyemue stretched, the ever-present whip in her hand slicing the air with a soft sigh that would have passed unheard elsewhere in Talonnorn.

It was always quiet in the yeldeth caverns. The edible fungi muffled all sounds, and grew so fast that slaves had to be sent out when weariness slowed their picking; only fresh fingers could keep up with the sprouting blooms. Slaves were fed raw yeldeth, but probably ate it with no more enthusiasm than most Nifl would if what ended up on their platters had been kept from wines and sauces and the cooking brazier. Amraunt, now; even raw, *those* mushrooms were pure pleasure on the tongue, and rare and small of course—and as far as a Nifl belly could get from soft, nourishing, yet nigh-tasteless yeldeth.

Hmm. Up in the Blindingbright, she'd heard, the Hairy Ones dwelt amid a bewildering variety of edible plants, and ignored most of them. Oriad-witted creatures!

Or perhaps, as Vaeyemue had thought more than a few times before, they were simply so stupid as to not realize the plants could be eaten—and never think of exploring or experimenting with what grew so abundantly at hand. She looked down the cavern at scores of them intently plucking, twisting, and peering—seeking blooms of just the right hue—and shook her head. They *seemed* intelligent enough. But then one could never tell with humans.

Ugly and hairy and pale, yes, but they could imitate Nifl speech and gestures and even—albeit gracelessly—mannerisms.

"So they watch and hear us," she murmured aloud, "and remember. And are clever. Yet such imitations have their limits. After all, it's not as if they're *Niflghar*."

"Is *this* the best the raiders could find?" Brylyaun's lip curled as he watched the line of sagging humans being unhooded and lashed by bored Nifl overseers; most of them toppled hard to the ground after only a stroke or two. "Every run it seems worse! Is the Blindingbright running out of Hairy Ones, that our take is such . . . dregs?"

Orellaun chuckled. "I recall your grandsire saying almost those exact words, while standing looking out this window. I think we all believe slaves were bigger, better, and stronger when we were young—and must have been roaring monsters before that! Yet Talonnorn manages to struggle along, as Houses rise and Houses fall, and slaves beyond numbering work and perish and are devoured and replaced, ov—"

"Over and over and over again," Brylyaun interrupted, in perfect mimicry of Orellaun's grandly declaiming tones, and they chuckled together.

The younger Nifl stopped first, shrugging and turning away from the window. "Well, *all* the Houses would fall—and Talonnorn itself dissolve into a brawling, lawless way-market of slavers and traders—if ever we ran out of slaves. Thank Olone they're mindless, endlessly replaceable fodder."

"Yes, but *are* they endless?" Orellaun said, still at the window. "This seems a matter no one bothers to debate, when it should concern us all!"

Brylyaun frowned. "Well, they certainly *breed* fast enough, up in the Blindingbright!" He strolled back to the window. All of the slaves were down, now, with the overseers bending and untying their throat collars from the line, and retying them to floor rings, for the drenching to come. "We raid and we raid—and there they always are, grubbing the earth of their 'farms' and living one day much as the next, making no effort to improve their ugly bodies, or even to keep themselves *clean*!"

"Well, why would they? They know not Olone; they can have no inkling of devoting themselves to the Holy Way. Not that their grotesque bodies can ever achieve much beauty, no matter how they strive—but the reward of ascending to Olone is not only unknown to them, it's not offered to them!"

Brylyaun's frown deepened. "Indeed. Sometimes I forget that Holy Olone reveals Herself to Niflghar, not to all. It must be strange indeed, to be a gorkul or a Hairy One, and not know the Kiss of Beauty! Do they feel Her radiance, do you think? Or *can't* they feel Her?"

Orellaun shrugged. "I know not, but offer this point: There are Nifl who do not worship Olone. Even here, in the Araed—to say nothing of entire *cities* who cleave to . . . other worship."

Brylyaun shuddered. "Evil, perverted Nifl, the priestesses say."

"No doubt." Orellaun's voice was wry. "And all of them delicately reared shes who've seldom ventured into the Araed, let alone outside of Talonnorn—so that they know so much of the world."

"But surely their holy teachings . . ."

" 'But surely' *nothing*. Do your elders tell you all, or just what they think you should know, and no more?"

Brylyaun blushed, his obsidian-dark skin going pale. "Well, I am young—as they constantly remind me."

"And I am older," Orellaun said dryly, "and have . . . seen more of what is out in the Dark."

The younger Nifl turned, so sharply that it was almost a challenge. "And if I saw all of those things, right now, it would change me how, exactly? Spare me the claims it would drive me mad, or kill me outright. I hope you know me better than that."

"I do." Orellaun turned away from the window, where hot oil was dousing the slaves, and their frightened screams were rising. "So they would probably just make you weep, and tremble, and wet yourself as you stopped believing in Olone, and the Holy Way. There is more to life than the endless pursuit of beauty—or should be."

Brylyaun started to tremble, and suddenly snatched at the hilt of his sword.

Only to discover it missing.

It was in Orellaun's grasp, and raised warningly against him—as was the older Nifl's own blade, in Orellaun's other hand.

"Blasphemers move faster," came the dry explanation.

"Why is this one walled away from the rest?"

"On various occasions, six other slaves have been put to work alongside him. All ended up in the Rift."

"*What?* So why not hurl *him* in, and be done with the trouble? A rebellious slave is the start of—"

"Yes, but *this* rebellious slave is the best forgefist in Talonnorn. Olone spew, he's the best *firefist* in Talonnorn!"

"Oh. So worth the six, and more besides. I see. 'Forgefist' I know, but what's a 'firefist'?"

"Forgefist is anyone who can work metal, firefist is one who can create new things with it, knows metal through and through, can temper and taper and make tiny and intricate things—and make it all seem easy. This one works fast, and it's superb work. House Evendoom has the finest swords and locks in the city because of him."

"Hmm. So, can we see this wonder?"

"From this side of the Rift should be safe enough."

The Master of the Forges led the way through no less than three magical barriers that flared and faded into tingling slumber at his approach, and along a narrow track between the glowing heat of the Rift and tall heaps of ores. When he came to a certain height of rock, he stopped and looked across the river of molten rock. His gaze was cold. "There: Orivon Firefist. As good a firefist as there is."

The Nifl trader looked, crooked an eyebrow, and said slowly, "Well . . . he's a bit of a brute, now, isn't he?"

The Master nodded. "Watch."

"Who are those two?"

"His owner, the Lady Taerune Evendoom, and the overseer assigned to that part of the Rift: a gorkul slave we call Grunt Tusks."

"He's glaring at them like they're hated enemies he's about to carve up in battle!"

"He always does. Watch."

The trader chuckled. "Ha. That look earned him a taste of the lash, of course."

They watched the slender, graceful Nifl-she wield her long lash with skilled viciousness, slicing deeply into the rippling shoulders and arms of the human slave. His glare never wavered, even when she spun the lash across his face, slicing it deeply as well.

Unflinching, the human kept his burning gaze on her, ignoring the gorkul's heavy studded goad—and the burly, snorting tusker wielding it—completely. Through the dripping blood, his eyes bored into those of his owner, even when she spoke sharply—just what she said was lost in the clangs and crashings of forgefists at work, up and down the Rift—and struck him across the face again and again.

The gorkul moved in to join the relentless whipping, clubbing heavier blows onto the firefist until at last the human was driven to his knees.

Whereupon the Nifl-she, obviously tired, let her lash fall and stood gasping and trembling, obviously struggling to regain her temper. They glared at each other, owner and slave—until she abruptly took something from her belt, threw it to the blood-spattered stone in front of him, and turned away.

"Healing magic," the trader said. "Repairing the valued possession she's damaged."

The Master of the Forges, who had seen this so many times before, merely nodded.

The gorkul lingered to watch the slave seize the means of relief, but Orivon Firefist made no move to take it up. On his knees in his blood, unbroken, he glowered at Grunt Tusks until the overseer shrugged, spat, and turned to follow Lady Evendoom.

The human slave glowered after them. Defiant.

2

Leisurely Unfolding Doom

Olone is perfection.
Olone is beauty.
Olone is all.
Be like unto Olone, and rise in her regard.
—**Niflghar chant**

Taerune was in a hurry, excitement building in her—and when Taerune was excited, she used her whip.

The sharp cracks of the lash, and the shouts of startled pain it caused, turned heads up and down the busy street.

She strode purposefully, viciously slashing everyone in her way aside—fools, surely they should have learned by *now?*—as she went. No business in Talonnorn came before Evendoom business, and none of House Evendoom's many schemes could be so urgent, so thirsty for the soonest moment just now, as this.

The crowded street was clearing as lesser Nilfghar hastened to be elsewhere, snapping commands to hulking gorkul porters and waddling pack-snouts. A whip scar across the face brings no one closer to Olone. Taerune of Evendoom quickened her pace, gleaming boots clacking on the damp scorchstone.

She could have used the family tunnels, of course. The Eventowers and the Forgerift were both within the House grounds, and the work crew of House servants behind her—Nameless Nifl, all—could have traveled much faster within the Evendoom gates. But marching openly through the city, thrusting lesser Nifl aside, was the whole point of this journey. Making a show is what ruling Houses *did*—and Taerune of Evendoom loved to be seen.

She had always loved to be seen, from the first admiring or amused glances her infantile preenings had drawn, long ago, to the open throat-swallowing admirations Nifl—and even less-than-Nifl, the beasts like gorkul and the hairy humans—gave her now.

They warmed her like deepfire. And why not? Every admiring glance is, after all, a prayer to Olone. Taking care to let not the slightest hint of a wry smile touch her set and perfect lips, Taerune of Evendoom slashed her way toward the waiting fires.

Nifl take heed: House Evendoom strides first, and all Talonnorn gets out of its way.

In the gleaming depths of the watch-whorl, the sleek and breathtakingly beautiful Nifl female strode imperiously down the street, her black whip cleaving a path through the crowds.

One of the watchers bent intently over the whorl-glow growled softly, deep in his throat. It was a growl—almost a purr—of admiration and idle lust.

He never took his eyes off what the whorl showed him: ears that were ever so finely pointed, and big, tilted-teardrop eyes filled with the cold fire of cruel contempt. Graceful curves and limbs, a slender waist and flat stomach that scanty dark emerald leathers did little to cover and nothing to hide. So much skin these shes of Talonnorn left bare to watching gazes . . .

Ah, but *what* skin! Obsidian black, a supple, rippling darkness broken only by stark-white hair at brows, lashes, and—long and swirling—on her scalp. And by leathers that clung to her like a second skin: snout-hide bracers and matching boots of deep emerald green, the leather buffed to a gleaming sheen, straps studded with gems hugging jet-black hips tightly as she moved . . .

"My, my. If she lives, after we smash Talonnorn, I'd not mind *her* on my—"

"That is *not* what you're here to think about, Aloun." The cold voice from the far side of the watch-whorl held every last shard of ice Aloun had expected it to. Any straying from the task at hand always made Luelldar curt.

The elder Watcher of Ouvahlor leaned forward over the shifting glows of the whorl, the chill of the Ever-Ice in his eyes. "Those lost in the pursuit of Olone may have fixed their eyes on outward show and lost their wits in so doing, but take care you don't drift to the same doom."

"Luell, Luell! Rest easy! I'm not loins-lost nor gone oriad, I'm but admiring perhaps the most beautiful Nifl-she I've ever seen! I—well, *look* at her! Dark One, did you ever *see* such beauty? Yet I doubt not that she's as vicious and empty-headed as the next Olone-lover! By the Ever-Ice, Ouvahlor shall triumph!"

"Ouvahlor shall triumph, indeed. Seen enough of the show? Good!" Without waiting for Aloun's disgusted nod, Luelldar bent his will to turn what the whorl viewed elsewhere, and waved down at its flaring, whirling silence. "So, keen watcher-of-shes, tell me: What are we seeing now?"

"House Dounlar's gates," Aloun said, a little sullenly.

"And you know that because?"

"The oorth skull carved into the arch."

"Which is remarkable as a House targe *why?*"

"The fools of Talonnorn worship Olone, who represents physical perfection, so Talonar adornments—even House emblems—are symbols of beauty. Save this one."

"Name the six Houses of Talonnorn. And their targes."

"Evendoom—the she we were just watching is one—are foremost, and use the Black Flame. Or the Hand of Flame, or whatever it's supposed to be."

"The Black Flame, they call it, but yes, it's shaped like an open hand, cupping nothing. The others?"

"Maulstryke, the Three Black Tears. Cluster of three vertical teardrops, touching, center one lowest. Wants to be First House, so are haughtiest, swiftest to feud. Drain the lives of their slaves daily to—"

Luelldar made the circular finger wave that every Ouvahlan knew meant "Get *on* with it! Right now!"

"Dounlar, the Grim Skull," Aloun said hurriedly. "Raskshaula, the Arc of Eyes; Oszrim, the Glowgem; Oondaunt, the Talon. There!"

"There," Luelldar agreed wryly. "So many to remember. Six, and only one brain to hold them all. However do the Moaning Crones manage it, I wonder?"

"Deepspew!" Aloun snarled, his temper slipping. "Narl and worms take you, Luell! *I* stoop not to mocking *you*! Just *how* am I like unto a crone of Olone?" He leaned across the whorl in clear menace.

The older Ouvahlan sat unruffled. "Well, you've survived this long, despite a habit of letting your over-clever tongue ride riot when others cloak themselves in more prudent silence and obedience. They of Olone manage much the same trick."

"They'll find it hard to go on doing so, when we start butchering them," Aloun said savagely, "and that'll be soon enough!"

"Not soon enough for some, I take it." Luelldar's voice was as dry as old stone. "You sound as blood-mad as the youngest of our warblades. So tell me, Butcher of Crones: say we are to strike now, as swiftly as you can arm and make ready, and you will command our warblades. I ask you: What are the weaknesses of Talonnorn? What answer have you, for me?"

Aloun stared across the watch-whorl at Luelldar, his eyes reflecting back its glows as their glare went from anger to thoughtfulness by way of resentful malice. Then he said slowly, "Their worship of Olone is their weakness."

"How so?"

"Why . . . well, they breed for beauty, work spells for more beauty, and try to make themselves and their offspring ever more beautiful, so they'll Ascend to join Olone in some sort of mindless, endless joy. Which makes them not want to be scarred, so they leave fighting and hard work to slaves and beasts and Nifl who are already maimed, or who are 'Nameless' and held of little account. Those who become imperfect— except the crones—are cast out, to become enemies of the faithful of Olone; and even if they do not, the city loses their prowess. So we and any other foe of Talonnorn fight inferior defenders."

"And?"

"And these defenders are poorly commanded. Again, because of the crones."

"So you *have* thought about this. Good. No, no, Aloun, save your curses; I mock you not! How are crones a battle weakness, in cities who worship Olone?"

"Such cities are ruled by conclaves of ruling Houses—six or so families—and every House is headed by a Lord," Aloun said slowly, thinking aloud. "And the crones—all the females past birthing age—are his envoys, spies, poisoners, advisers, and even his lawmakers and keepers.

If he displeases them, he meets with an accident. So they truly rule, and let him see and hear and do only what they want him to."

Satisfaction crept into his quickening voice as he added, "So where *our* warlords are warblades whose mistakes are born of old habits or not understanding the newest spells, those who defend and go to war for any city of Olone are weighed down by crones who care nothing for the fate of others, and lie to them, and let them not even *know* about some magic they could wield against foes."

Luelldar nodded. "You see things rightly. It makes one wonder how they've lasted this long, yes?"

Aloun's glare sharpened. "Perhaps, about that matter, *you* can inform *me*."

Luelldar nodded, and waved one long-fingered hand at the whorl. "Look you there—and there! What do you see?"

The scene of distant Talonnorn glowing in the spinning silence between the two Ouvahlan was now of a bustling street—a meandering way of smooth, dark scorchstone, winding between many stone spirals of Nifl homes, across the floor of the great main cavern of the city. The stone floor of the cavern, fissured like the parallel fingers of a massive stone hand, rose in gentle humps behind the close-crowded homes—but no spirals stood on those humps, and no side streets meandered up them. Aloun peered at where the whorl's glow was rising eagerly, sparks swirling, to meet its caster's fingertips, and saw something in the scene beneath that spot flicker and glimmer. A roiling in the air, a radiance seen only for moments, here and there. Half-seen flickerings that traced a line behind the homes.

Aloun frowned. "Some sort of magic. Looks like a barrier."

"Looks like just what it is: a barrier, part of the outer wards of House Dounlar. A wall, but of flesh-rending magic rather than forged war-spikes or stone. Keeping unfriends out, and lesser Nifl from building their homes on that stretch of bare Dounlar rock. Rock that House Dounlar may find a pressing need for, in some moment or other to come. Such magical fields are why cities of Olone have lasted this long. When you do your part in the storming of this one, take care not to touch them, or you'll die—*and* warn all Talonnorn of our intrusion."

Aloun's frown deepened. "So just how are we supposed to surprise them, if breaching their wards—?"

"We shall not breach them. Klarandarr's spells will take our warblades past the wards without disturbing them, like a wave in the Dark Ocean rolling a long way ashore, that leaves something behind on the rocks when at last it ebbs. We'll appear *inside* the wards, strike hard and fast—and then the worms will come."

"But what of *their* spells? Their Hunt—"

"Are young and overconfident fools, who rely overmuch on their spell-armor and the speed of their swooping darkwings. Their whipswords are pain-gloaters' toys, not weapons to wield against a *real* foe. We've all heard that the Hunt of Talonnorn 'never misses,' yes? Well, they never taste defeat because they never fight anything more formidable than fleeing slaves or Maimed Ones!"

Aloun sighed. "So you and the Elders always say. Yet we have nothing to touch them in battle! No spell-armor! No flying steeds! No whipswords! What if they snatch up the Talonar crones who *can* humble us with cavern-collapsing spells, and whisk them past us, to land and work their magics up our backsides? What then?"

His voice had risen; he flinched and fell silent in the wake of his own bitter words, half-expecting Luelldar to lash out at him.

Yet no snarling outburst came.

The older Niflgar stared at him, nodding slightly, face unreadable, as the whorl spun in slow silence for what seemed to Aloun a very long time.

"I am heartened," Luelldar said at last. "You see beyond the hungry point of your blade—and dare to question what the Elders say. You may well be ready for a first taste of command."

"A 'first taste' of command?" New-flaring anger made Aloun's voice sharp. "What—"

"*That,*" Luelldar snapped coldly, his voice suddenly as loud and hard as a sword ringing on stone, "is why a taste is all you're ready for, yet."

He held out one hand, fingers spread, and the whorl flickered and died, its sparks flowing back up into his fingertips. "Temper and pride rule you," he told the younger Ouvahlan, "and you cannot even command *yourself* sufficiently to curb and hide them. All that makes you more useful to Ouvahlor than the merest youngling is your strength and reach with a sword—and that you strive and struggle a little longer against adversity than a drooling babe ere you start to cry."

Aloun half-rose, face darkening and eyes afire, gaze locked with

Luelldar. His lips twisted—and then froze. Eyes still fierce and hard on Luelldar's, he sat back down and said nothing.

Luelldar nodded as if satisfied, and said calmly, "The Talonar tactic you anticipate has been pondered by others. Ouvahlor is ready if such attacks are attempted."

The last of the whorl's glow died away, and Luelldar added softly, "More than ready. Klarandarr's spells are mightier than anything Talonnorn can manage. Klarandarr—and so, all of Ouvahlor—is closer than any Talonar to what lies within the Ever-Ice you so glibly swear by. He knows how to reach closer to the cold heart of Niflheim, harnessing deeper magic than any crone of Olone."

"And so?"

"And so they are doomed."

"In my admittedly limited experience, brother, staring at nothing doesn't make it become something. At least, not at any speed one might deem 'enlightening.' You will probably crumble to nothing yourself first." Jalandral's drawl was playful, even affectionate, but Ravandarr flushed. As usual.

"I was merely—"

"Of *course* you were. Picturing what the dread 'Door of Fangs' will look like in that doorway, where nothing but a curtain now keeps us from striding right into the sharp edge of Taera's loving tongue—and closets enough of gowns for even the biggest of our gorkul to get lost and smothered in. Pretty things, but I doubt they'd fit either of us."

Ravandarr flushed again, and said stiffly, "I—Dral, I have no intention whatsoever—"

"Of *course* not. You flinch back from touching gowns—and the fair shes inside them—as if they're made of fire. Olone look *down,* brother, can't you take things more easily? Laugh, wink, even *smile* a time or two; I can't even remember if you know *how* to smile!"

Jalandral's bright teeth flashed as he struck a grandly heroic pose, long arms crossed elegantly, one hand gripping the hilt of the wickedly slender sword at his hip. He wiggled his eyebrows, winking exaggeratedly, and broadened his smile into a parody of a leer. "See? A smile, and it cost me nothing? Olone will be *so* pleased!"

Ravan regarded his older brother with the usual hot flare of envy.

Jalandral was handsome, elegant, and debonair, his flippancy somehow charming—even, it seemed, to the oldest masked crones of the House—and his reputation as a deadly duelist and acid-tongued wit outshone even his standing as the heir of House Evendoom.

Whereas Ravandarr Evendoom—he made himself try to smile—was younger, taller, heavier; a shy, gorkul-clumsy younger brother standing always in the shadow of his brother's shining fame. Hesitant and heavy-tongued beside Jalandral's drawling elegance, slow-bladed and slower-booted against Jalandral's almost careless agility, overlooked where Jalandral drew every eye—

"That's a smile?" Jalandral rolled his eyes. "Or *have* you lost the knack?"

Ravandarr grimaced. He was rough dark stone where his older brother shone like a gem, terse where Jalandral was glib, plodding where—

Jalandral slid out of his pose like an uncoiling snake, and was suddenly gripping Ravandarr's shoulders. "Brother," he murmured, "we are what we are, not what we long to be. Be yourself, and be content, and wait. I'll probably soon get myself killed in some oriad prank or other, and you'll be heir, and—behold! House Evendoom will suddenly discover the worth of someone thoughtful and methodical and mostly silent, rather than dazzlingly annoying! Oh, our crones love you more than me right now, believe me!"

"Because they see me as too witless to be more than an trudging tool," Ravandarr said bitterly. "I've not your looks, your—"

"Ravan, *enough*. Learn your own way to be happy—ordering Nifl to go out and get themselves killed, as Father does; or manipulating we rampants, as the crones do; or playing pranks and wenching, as I do—and *do* it. Glowering and glooming will get you noticed, yes, and deemed dross to be hurled away in battle and forgotten as if you'd never been. Then poor Father would have to get busy and sire more of us, and you *know* how he *hates* such work!"

Despite himself, Ravandarr chuckled, and a moment later they were laughing together. Lord Erlingar Evendoom's appetites were as legendary as what Olone had endowed him with, and the subject of many Talonar tales and jests. Some of the nastiest, told in other Houses, were the funniest, though Ravandarr never thought of them when his father was looming over him, cold-eyed and dominating every chamber he entered, seething rage never far behind that chilly smile. Lord Evendoom had eyes like two drawn and waiting daggers.

With distaste Ravan thrust thoughts of his father away, as he always did, and found himself gazing, in his mind, on a far dearer member of his family. The closest thing he had to a friend, closer and more trusted than his laughing brother—who, after all, always thought first of Jalandral, and cheerfully said so.

Taerune, cruel-tongued, as keen-witted as Jalandral, and oh, so beautiful. Taerune whom he ached to have, but never could. Taera, eldest of his many sisters, who'd mothered him when they were younger and who still lashed him with advice when she saw the need, leaning against this very wall with her arms crossed languidly and barbed words darting from her mouth, a crone in time to come but a formidable warrior and envoy of House Evendoom right now, who . . .

"Dral," he blurted out suddenly, "how does Taerune find happiness?"

The heir of House Evendoom rolled his eyes. "Rampants, sometimes—"

Ravandarr flushed, swallowed, and muttered a wordless protest that he'd *not* meant—

Jalandral still had hold of his brother's upper arms, and shook Ravandarr a little to silence him, so as to add, "And scheming for her inevitable cronehood, when she'll be able to order such as we hither and thither to all manner of dooms for her entertainment and sometimes for the profit of House Evendoom—"

And then he let go of Ravandarr and thrust him away.

The younger brother staggered back, still embarrassed, and saw Jalandral lose his easy smile.

The heir of House Evendoom concluded quietly, "And toys. More than any of us, Taera loves toys. Not gowns and jewels, but toys: coffers with hidden compartments, buckles with poison fangs, things that do one thing but can also secretly be used thus-and-so to do something else; that stone-headed firefist she's been teaching to talk as we do; toys."

He waved at the empty doorway. "This Door of Fangs? It's a toy, no more, to be nigh forgotten by her come next Turning—but toys keep Taerune happy."

"Why toys, do you think?"

Jalandral shrugged. "She had to find her own way. She was *not* going to use Mother's way."

Ravandarr could not remember his mother, beyond a tall, sharp black shadow that strode through his dreams cloaked in more fear than Father ever evoked. "And what was Mother's way?"

There was something twisted in Jalandral's sudden smile. "Killing her children in slow, creative, and painful ways. I once had six older brothers. Didn't you know?"

3

The Door of Fangs

There is Olone, and the pursuit of Olone.
And there is diversion.
Olone gives life meaning.
Diversions make it bearable.
All hail diversions!
—**Niflghar drinking chant**

*A*nger grew in Taerune with every step: dark, surging, *alive*. She could taste it; as always, it thrilled her. She lashed the scorchstone of the street beside her restlessly as she stalked forward, growling under her breath in quickening eagerness.

Her way was slowed again, blocked by Nifl who were all standing watching something yonder. In another moment she'd be among them, whip slicing deep into flesh, hurling screaming Nifl aside amid spraying blood . . .

Blood. Should she call up her wardshield? It would take only one drawn dagger or frantically clawing hand to mar her, and so in an instant thrust her far from Olone. Yes, best—

Best hold, as her shield flared into flickering life around her, and watch what the knot of standing Nifl were craning to see. Their murmurings had told her what it was, now, something she never tired of—and why should she? This should be good.

If the Hunt were swooping over the streets, it was to parade trophies and proclaim their victory. They'd be—

A long, high bellow of exulting laughter came swooping out of distant stone-fanged darkness, swept around the eagerly murmuring Nifl standing shoulder-to-shoulder in front of Taerune, and tore past, air humming over taut black wings.

Another and another, the air snarling in their wake. As heads turned and the watching Nifl in the street laughed in delight, the racing riders made their mounts loop in the air high overhead, and swoop down and past again.

The darkwings they rode were like weirdly twisted, gigantic bats—bats with long, snakelike necks and small, baleful-eyed, triangular heads. Like petulant vipers they hissed and tossed their heads, chewing on the bits in their mouths, as the laughing riders on their backs—young warblades of House Evendoom, whipswords gleaming back the shifting rosy glows of their spell-armor—brought them rushing lower still, long black talons scudding past within easy reach of upturned Nifl faces. Riders leaned down and shook their gory trophies: the severed heads of human slaves who'd tried to flee Talonnorn.

Slaves were always escaping. If they were strong and desperate, it was easy enough to drag the ore- or offal-sledge they were chained to into a river of rockfire until it melted away. They cooked their manacled limbs trying it, usually, but then . . . they were dead anyway. The Hunt never missed.

Still laughing, the warblades made their flying steeds climb, great bat wings beating, to soar high over the city and jeer victory from a safe height, high above the towers of Houses less than friendly to Evendoom. Along with every other Nifl around her, Taerune watched them go—but then looked down again and snapped her whip, thrice as long as she stood tall, causing it to undulate and then bound up from the scorchstone and crack across a Nifl's back and shoulder.

He turned with a startled roar that held more anger than fear, hand going to sword hilt.

So did the four other Nifl standing with him.

Three black tears were clustered on all of their chests. Maulstryke. Taerune's glare caught fire.

She brought the whip back to her shoulder, still smiling tightly. Her wardshield would sear them to the bone if they caught and tugged on the whip to pull her within reach, and then tried to use warsteel on her within its silent might.

They knew that—how could they not? All Talonnorn had tasted Evendoom wardshields a time or two, in the brawls every Arkklar if at no other time, but these were young rampants, five to her one—and they were Mauls.

And all Mauls are fire-tempered fools.

As their blades sang out, Taerune brought her arm down and sent the whip leaping out.

With a crack that echoed off the scorchstone it shattered a sword arm and sent that blade flashing and clanging away, striking sparks off stone as it rebounded off a wall and fell.

The Nifl she'd struck reeled and shrieked, his eyes wide in shock and disbelief, and fell. His four fellow Mauls scattered with purposeful speed, moving to come at her from all sides. They hefted their swords like veteran warblades, faces flat and eyes deadly.

Behind Taerune, some of her darmarch murmured in alarm. She lashed the street behind her, to make the whip crack back in their direction and remind them just who they should be fearing the most. The last thing she wanted was them fleeing through the city streets like frightened younglings, chased by happily hewing Mauls.

"You are overbold, foolish she," the nearest Maulstryke rampant said icily, lifting his sword.

In reply Taerune gave him her coldest smile, and raised her whip again.

"Daughter of the Ice, it is time for you to learn more than chants and holy sayings and the teachings of the Way. Sit."

"Revered Mother?"

"*Sit,* child. Sprawl. Lounge on the table. Scratch yourself. Be at ease. Awe and solemnity end at that door. This chamber is for plain speech. There are no secrets here."

Utter bewilderment was clear on Lolonmae's open-mouthed face. The wrinkled old priestess chuckled.

"I'll make wind if you like, to completely shatter your reverence. Don't stand there gaping, little one—you look like a sacrifice, all wide-eyed dismay! Sit down!"

Lolonmae's lip trembled. "So . . . so there *are* sacrifices?"

"Of course, but not in the way you're thinking. We don't slay needlessly here; we persuade recreants to take the shapes of beasts useful to us, and serve for a time as guardians or hunters-of-intruders. It's a punishment some grow to enjoy."

Hesitantly the young novice went to one of the chairs at the table and sat in it, drawing her legs in under her. She crossed trembling arms over her breast, still staring at the Revered Mother of Coldheart with confusion and fear brimming in her eyes. "Am . . . am I to be punished?"

"No. Enlightened. And yes, there *is* a difference."

"Oh. What . . . what are you going to tell me?"

"Answers to whatever you ask. So think of something, or you're going to be rather bored, sitting there in silence watching me eat slaarworms." The Revered Mother lifted a jar from her lap, plucked off its lid, and smiled down into the faint glow. "I *love* slaar-worms."

Lolonmae managed to quell her shudder completely. "Ask about . . . anything?"

"Anything. The Ravagers, my undergarments, why Nifl worship other gods, or gods at all—anything."

Lolonmae blinked as she tried to picture what a Revered Mother might wear under her robes, decided she did not want to know, and then sighed, fought down the fears still flooding her, and blurted out, "All right: the Ravagers. Why are there Ravagers? Are they all oriad?"

"No. Most are unpleasant and desperate—they have to be, to survive in the Wild Dark—but they are not mad. They are outcasts."

"Murderers? Lawbreakers? Darksins?"

"All three, some of them. Others choose to go out into the Wild. Most aren't guilty of much more than being ugly."

"Ugly?"

The Revered Mother sighed, dipped a hand into her jar, and munched. The child knew nothing; this was going to take longer than she'd feared.

"Lolonmae," she asked quietly, "what do you know of the worship of Olone?"

"A false faith," the novice said promptly. "The foolish Nifl who follow it strive ever to become more beautiful, so as to ascend to Olone, whom they see as . . . well, as beauty. They spend—waste—their lives trying to become ever more beautiful."

The Revered Mother nodded. "What do you think happens to someone in a city of Olone worshippers, someone who is not beautiful—or becomes less so?"

"They . . . they are killed?"

"Often. Yet just as often they are driven forth into the Wild to die, or flee to avoid being slain. The 'Wild Dark' is called that for a reason: many beasts that devour Niflghar lurk there. If Nifl outcasts don't join the Ravagers, they seldom last long."

"So the Ravagers *aren't* butchers, infant-eaters, and rapists?"

"Some may well be. Most are ugly or disfigured, or maimed or infirm in some way. They raid and hunt, as the tales you've heard describe so bloodily, but mainly up in the Blindingbright where humans rule. Look at the table beside you."

Lolonmae blinked, peered into the gloom, and gave the elder priestess a puzzled frown. The tabletop was bare.

The Revered Mother sighed again. "Regard the bare stone more closely, child."

This time the novice noticed the faint markings.

The Revered Mother quelled another sigh, swallowed a last mouthful of slaar—ahh, both sweet and roast-meat juicy; *how* she loved good slaar!—and bent her will.

Obediently, one little mark on the tabletop suddenly glowed, making Lolonmae jump and exclaim.

"Ever-Ice *preserve*," the elder priestess snarled under her breath. Were all the younglings this slow-witted? "That," she announced calmly, "is the city of Talonnorn. You've heard of it, I believe."

If Lolonmae heard the biting sarcasm in those words, she gave no sign of it, but turned wide eyes to the Revered Mother. "This is a map?"

By way of reply, the elder priestess pointed silently at the tabletop. Lolonmae looked there again.

A handful of other points of light glowed, amber to Talonnorn's emerald. "Ways to the surface we know of," the Revered Mother explained. "The table between is our local Wild Dark."

"Local?"

The elder priestess *did* sigh this time. Heavily. A ruby light, brighter than the rest, blossomed not far from Talonnorn's emerald glow. "Us," she said, and waved her hand.

Seven brown-yellow lights glimmered into life, scattered across the table. "Ouvahlor, between here and Talonnorn. Ouvahlor and Talonnorn love each other not at all. Over there, Uryrryr. There, Imbrae and Nrauluskh. Beyond them, Yarlys and Oundrel."

"And in far Yarlys I met my doom," Lolonmae murmured, a snatch of song so old that the Revered Mother had sung it as a child.

The elder priestess wondered if Lolonmae knew any other words of that tune, or why it had been composed at all. The young these days seemed so *asleep,* so unaware and complacent, accepting the ways of things without understanding why things were thus-and-so, and who had fought to make them that way. She waved her hand again, ere dipping it once more into the jar.

And the table grew a shimmering tangle of lines, a chaos that linked all of the cities and ways up to the Blindingbright, in routes so meandering and entwined that it was hard to trace them, even peering hard and close at the table.

Lolonmae frowned and squinted, but at least she was trying to follow routes, here and there. "These are . . . the underways? The passages from city to city the raiders take?"

"And traders. More often, traders."

That made Lolonmae turn, eyes wide. "*Trade?* We *deal* with the cities of Olone?"

"And the Ravagers," the Revered Mother told her calmly. "They bring us plants, and their berries and juices, for our alchemies. In return for magics and healing ointments."

The novice was frowning. "What do they trade with the cities of Olone for?"

"More magic. Good weapons."

"And what do Talonnorn and Imbrae get in return?"

"Slaves."

"*Slaves?* Nifl enslave *Nifl?*"

"Humans, child. Strong humans. Plucked from where the Hairy Ones dwell, up in the Blindingbright."

Lolonmae's lip curled. "And what do they of Olone need humans for? Food? Surely not breeding for beauty? Or are they all so indolent that they need slaves to do everything for them?"

"Indolence, yes, though they see it not so. Their need was born of fear. Fear of being cast out due to disfigurement—and fear of such marring befalling them in cooking over hearth fires, fighting with blades in the cities, mining, or smithywork. So they have slaves to do such things for them."

The novice shook her head. "Truly, they are worthy of our contempt," she said, disbelief and amazement strong in her voice.

"The Ravagers sneer at us and the cities of Olone about equally," the Revered Mother said gently, gazing into the slaar glow in her jar in contented satiation. "They think us both oriad and lazy, ignorant and doomed."

"Doomed?"

"To stagnation, decline, and eventually disaster when some foe or cataclysm we are entirely unprepared for rises and smites us."

"Really?" Lolonmae was too aghast to be deferential. "And in just *what way* are we as contemptuous as those of Olone?"

The elder priestess put the lid back on her jar and set it on the table, which promptly became plain dark stone again. "To the Ravagers, we are all Haraedra."

Lolonmae frowned and looked her question.

"Towered Ones," the Revered Mother explained. "Nifl who dwell in cities. The Ravagers see that as decadence—and the constant need of Haraedra for slaves as proof of that judgment."

The novice looked disgusted. "Can they not see that we of Arnoenar are no softlings who need slaves?"

"Ah, but we are."

"What?" That word was almost a shriek. *"We* take slaves?"

"All Nifl take slaves, child. If we weren't so cursedly indolent, we'd not need them—but we *are* indolent. It's part of our charm, some say."

" 'Some say'? What of the others?"

The Revered Mother's wave of dismissal was languid. "Ah! They are of no account."

"Overbold? Foolish? Perhaps," Taerune said softly, making her whip crackle with racing lightnings. "And perhaps your judgment is mistaken. Maulstryke reasoning usually is."

Anger warred with fear in the rampant's eyes. He—and the other Mauls, one of them still down on the scorchstone, groaning over his shattered arm—knew very well how that whip would sear them, bone-deep, if it touched their blades.

"House Evendoom holds erroneous opinions regarding all Houses of Talonnorn," he said icily, "including House Evendoom. Your supposed supremacy is but an empty pose, and you overreach yourselves. That will prove fatal . . . perhaps much sooner than you think."

"Perhaps and perhaps," Taerune said coldly. "Yet 'perhaps' cries of wishes and assumptions. Care to taste a little truth?" She made her whip rear and roil menacingly, its crackling arcing to her wardshield and back again, making her hair stand out straight and her breast tingle and stiffen.

"Your arrogance demeans your House," the Maulstryke hissed scornfully, growing a sneer the other Mauls matched in an instant.

"Whereas your mouthings are as empty as ever," Taerune told them calmly, cracking her whip as she strolled forward—and they all hastily gave way, the wounded Maul whimpering in his gingerly clambering haste.

They all hissed scorn at her, swords held up and ready, as they stepped aside in ever-increasing haste. Taerune gave them a wintry smile and cracked her whip as she turned, herding them. For a moment she feared they'd rush the wincing Nifl at the rear of her darmarch, but the Mauls were eager to be away from their humiliation, and ducked between laden, slowly trudging gorkuls and through Nameless Nifl, jostling and striking with the hilts of their blades to get gone in haste.

Watching them go, Taerune discovered she was trembling in excitement. "Icy defiance fades before icier dismissal," she murmured, "as usual. A pity they didn't dare more. Ah, well, perhaps *next* Turning." And she spun around stylishly, one hand on hip, to stride onward, satisfaction a cold mantle about her. She'd known a moment of fear, facing the five of them with her Orb back in her chambers, but they'd proved as craven as she'd expected. She might or might not be an overbold, foolish she—but she was of Evendoom. *Tremble, Talonnorn, tremble,* as the saying went, *for Evendoom is risen and a-prowl.*

Ah, yes, prowling; what she sought was but a little way ahead now, and no other obstacles or defiances awaited her. Taerune barely had time to quell the lightnings and gather her wand back up onto her shoulder before the last pack-snouts and goad-waving Nifl porters parted before her—and she was facing the gates of the Forgerift.

Tall and stark black those doors were, two massive forged slabs as tall as four Nifl. Onto each had been bolted the Black Flame of Evendoom, great cast metal representations that stood out from the doors more than the thickness of a large Nifl's body—and below them were descending rows of black metal runes, also standing forth from the door boldly, that crackled with restless power. Of fabled ordauth, the only metal that could have held so much magic, they were the largest spellrunes ever forged in Talonnorn. Their snarling power—an endless muted thunder Taerune could feel as well as hear, even this far from the doors—was a standing boast of the might of House Evendoom.

They were grander even than the Great Gates before the Eventowers, and it was common lore in Talonnorn that their forging had cost hundreds of lives—Niflghar finesmiths and forgehammers as well as slaves—though House Evendoom never spoke of such things. And if whispered rumor grew such tales in their retellings, what of it? Rumor did as much with all its whispers touched. ·

Touch. Though she was still a dozen strides from the gates, Taerune stretched out her hand, feeling her wardshield sing and surge eagerly toward them—and the flare of deadly power that responded, shouting silently in her mind. To all but the most strongly warded Nifl, unless they were of Evendoom, merely touching the Forgerift doors meant death. Yet they and the tall gate arch around them were guarded by no less than six warblades of the House, who now grounded their drawn swords and raised open hands to her in salute.

They were expecting her, of course, and at her nod stepped back to open the gates, revealing the angry, ever-present red-orange glows of deepfire beyond. The Forgerift was House Evendoom's greatest treasure, and even if the runes and warblades had both been thrown down and swept away, flitting fireghosts of the spellbound Evendoom dead guarded the Rift itself from intrusion and seizure by others. Only those of Evendoom, and bound to Evendoom, could pass through the gates and live.

Head held high, Taerune of Evendoom strode through the opened gate. In perfect unison, heads lowered, her darmarch followed her, the House sigils painted on their bared shoulders flaring into wary life as the gate-magics probed and clawed at them. They would bear her Door of Fangs hence, and up through the Eventowers to install it, under the watchful eyes of two House spellrobes as well as her own—and though they knew it not, they would be seared by it, deep enough to leave scars they would bear to the ends of their lives.

For the door, promised ready for her, was to be all of ordauth, grandest of metals, smelted from the blackest veins of ore in the deepest rifts closest to the Ever-Ice at the heart of Niflheim. The ore whose mining slew so many, and so kept it scarcer than any wanted it to be. Ordauth the Bearer-of-Magics, the metal that can hold more and mightier spells than any other.

Oh, and spells her door would have! Taerune had commanded the best spellrobes of the House—save the crones, to whom she dared not reveal the full extent of her schemings—to work spells upon spells, melding their castings into the unfinished doors even as the sweating forgehammers, led by her Dark Warrior, did their louder, cruder work.

Taerune smiled, as she always did, at the thought of him: her loyal mountain, the one creature in her life that did her bidding without cold looks of challenge. The only being in all Niflheim she could trust. More than any other, the door was of his making.

Not the enchantings, no. Slaves worked no spells. She had thought and dreamed of what she wanted, and told the best spellrobes of the House—and they had argued and experimented and argued anew for a very long time, ere they finally managed to enspell the door as she wanted it.

Many staring eyes had been torn from living creatures and embedded in the door while still warm and working, so the finished door could "see" intruders approaching. Many fangs had been dissolved in spell-slake and been mixed into the smelting vats; intact, gore-dripping, enspelled jaws had been ripped from living beasts and melded into the formed but unfinished door.

The spellrobes had worked their magic, and assured her that her will had been fulfilled and all was in readiness.

Which meant that once her Door of Fangs was in place guarding the way into her chambers high in House Evendoom, unauthorized hands that dared touch the handle of the door would be greeted by a many-fanged jaw thrusting forth out of the smooth metal to close on and sever them.

The very thought made her smile. And this beautiful thing was her conception, so she'd shown herself worthy of cronehood while still—

It was waiting for her, black and gleaming, lying flat on stone plinths before her. Fire flared as she drew near, and the door reflected its reaching greed toward her.

Her Dark Warrior at the forge was silhouetted against that flame, a broad-shouldered black figure with steady tongs that looked small against the gout of flame—and then, as the fire fell back and he turned in her direction, looked large.

Very large, as he came hastily toward her, a sword blade angry red in his tongs, his bulging, sweat-slick upper arms twice as thick as her waist. He set it on a blackened stone side table, drew off the black cloth mask he'd bound over his eyes—a bit of one of her old cloaks, that she'd given him when she'd first broken him to her will—and went to his knees, lowering his gaze to her boots.

He stank, of course. All humans did. Yet it was a smell she was getting used to, that clung to beautiful things he fashioned at her command.

"You," she whispered, so softly that he'd have no chance of hearing her, "are *mine*." With a fond smile she brought her whip forward, cracking it across his back with a stroke that rocked him. Slaves need to taste the lash often.

Yet it was a gentle stroke, that drew no blood, and she drew back the whip without giving him another. Too gentle a stroke, her sisters would say—but then, this was probably the best firefist in all Talonnorn, he was *her* firefist, and just now she was very proud of his work.

"Orivon, tell me of my door," she commanded, using his name rather than her more customary "Slave." By the looks of the gleaming dark door at her hip, he'd earned that, and more.

"Highest, it is ready. Its last oiling sinks into it. If you tarry long enough to look at it before the darmarch lay hands on it, it will be ready."

That deep, soft voice. He might be a Hairy One, a stinking, muscled brute who just happened to be a superbly skilled smith, but her Orivon Firefist had the voice of a pleasure-dancer.

"And its magics?"

"Highest, the spellrobes have been, and pronounced all well."

Taerune smiled down at the scarred back of her Dark Warrior. He wasn't dark at all, of course, but repulsively pale, except down his back where she'd marked him.

He bore many brands—she surveyed them now, smile widening—and she'd ground his own forge ash into the raw, freshly burned flesh of each one, to blacken them permanently. Even when floggings laid his back open, the healing scars stayed black.

"I am pleased, and more than pleased," she hissed. "You have won yourself a new brand, Firefist! Expect my return two Embers from now!"

"Highest, I who am unworthy am yet honored," he replied, soft voice carefully and slowly—reverently—saying the words she'd trained him to say, with more lashes than she cared to remember. Yet was there, this time, the faintest hint of eagerness in his rough, quietly rumbling voice?

She shrugged. Humans are so hard to read, so . . . *brutish*.

Taerune tossed her head by way of reply, turned her back on the brute, and cracked her whip sharply on the floor in an imperious signal to her darmarch to take up the door and bear it back through the streets to the Great Gates, so that all might see.

She did not look back at the kneeling slave. Her Dark Warrior was her favorite toy, but he was just a toy.

4

Schemes and Servings

Look ahead into darkness. Waiting dooms should be greeted properly.

—old Nifl saying

F ire flared again behind him, a brightness that warmed his backside.

As if that had been a cue, the kneeling man rose slowly to his knees and then stood, watching the door move steadily away from him between two lines of marching Nifl.

At their head he could see that slender, familiar, now tiny figure, the whip that had visited so much pain on him riding her shoulder.

Bitch. He uttered that savage naming in his mind, not with his lips. Yet he thought it with dark amusement, not rage; he was pleased at her delight in the door, despite his hatred.

Just as he was her favorite, and she was pleased to watch him, own him, and give him pain.

For which, one day—he remembered days, the sunrises and sunsets, and had long ago vowed he'd one day see them again—he'd give her death, slow and terrible.

And preferably involving floggings.

He knew better than to let any of what he was feeling show on his face, even here in the Rift, with the fires the nightskins feared so much spitting and flaring around him. You never knew when they'd be watching.

Silently spying from afar with their spells, of course. Craven fear not all that far under their oh-so-supreme pride, to be sure.

"To be sure," Orivon Firefist murmured slowly, watching his hated tormentor disappear back into the busy streets of Talonnorn. He stood like a statue, watching as the great doors closed in her wake—and only when they stood like an unbroken black wall once more, blocking his view of the city beyond, did he turn back to the fires and the blade that would need to be heated again.

There would come a day of death, and he would be at the heart of it. And on that day more than those doors would fall, and more than one impossibly beautiful, vicious elf-bitch would die.

Oh, yes. I'll be her Dark Warrior, all right. And it will be her turn to learn how loud and long she can scream. Yes.

"Kiss of the *Goddess,* how she preens and prances! Like a silly little just-weaned *brat!*"

"Ah, but that's just it: she's young, Maharla! We were all young, once."

"Oh? We never taunted Mauls in the streets in one breath and drooled in open lust over hairy human slaves the next! At least *I* didn't, Klaerra. Perhaps things were more lax in *your* time."

"Then our House must plunge into, and rise out of, decadence as swiftly as you don and doff that favorite cloak of yours. As I recall, you *were* a silly little just-weaned brat when I was about the age our Taerune is now."

Maharla's hiss of fury was as sharp as a knife. She liked to think of herself as the senior crone of House Evendoom—and, of course, of all Talonnorn—not the third eldest.

"Behave, Maharla," the oldest crone said sharply, startling everyone around the watch-whorl. Orlarra never spoke; her voice was thick and raw from disuse. "Or be still. Your snarlings and spittings demean us more than the youngling you decry so."

Seething, Maharla held silence, knowing that the chamber held more than a few inward smiles just now.

So it was one of the youngest crones—Galaerra, one of those she'd coached—who dared to voice what she'd been going to say. "Yet is it wise, this value Taerune places on the human firefist?"

"A good tool has value," Orlarra replied. "It is unwise not to see the value of what we can make use of. You may be sure that Maulstryke and Dounlar envy us our Forgerift, and the skills of our slaves there. Rask-shaula often sends their spellrobe Ondrar to openly watch the work at the Rift—*openly,* when he could easily use his spells to farwatch without anyone being the wiser. And Oszrim only has *gorkul* firefists."

"Oh, *Oszrim,*" someone said dismissively, amid a general murmur of wordless derision—and out of it Maharla spoke, daring to challenge the eldest crone openly.

"I fail to see how humans can be valued so much more highly than gorkuls at our forges. Both are witless, stinking beasts, after all, fit only to be slaves."

"Not food? Not breeding fun?" someone asked mockingly, in a voice deliberately pitched high and childlike, so as to escape being identified.

"How *dare*—"

There were many dry chuckles around the flickering glow of the watch-whorl, and Maharla fell abruptly silent again. It seemed her long-ago experimentations had become more widely known than she'd thought.

"Yet, sisters," Galaerra said a little timidly, "is there not danger as well as wisdom in valuing a human slave? Taerune entrusts more and more knowledge of House plans and intentions to this . . . this animal. What if he should—"

"Fall into the hands of Maulstryke or another House? And just how will that happen, when our spells can make the Forgerift itself spit its fire at intruders? Nifl turned to shrieking bones make poor captors of anything!"

"That was *not,*" Galaerra said with unaccustomed fire, "what I was going to say. I am pondering what damage the human she so fondly calls her 'Dark Warrior'—as if he's a *pet,* look you!—might do if she tells him too much. What mischief *he'll* think up, to harm us all."

Maharla saw her chance to seize her accustomed verbal dominance, and firmly took it. "Humans?" Her laugh was half a sneer. "Hairy, stinking beasts—with wits and malice enough to ape what we do, yes—but they can't truly *think.* They've nothing in those lust-ridden heads with which to reason! Remember that."

The hammer rang, rose, and rang again, the blade under it flowing and thickening like a living thing.

Orivon worked without thinking. He didn't need to, after so many thousands upon thousands of such blades. The hue and smell of the metal told him all he needed to know.

It was other knowledge he hungered for: everything he could learn about House Evendoom, and about Talonnorn beyond it. About the city—beyond Evendoom sneerings and boastings—he knew all too little, but he'd seen a lot of House Evendoom over the years since he'd been brought to Talonnorn. Many years, it must have been, though there were no seasons in the Dark to help him mark the passing years. The Nifl spoke of something called "Turnings," but he'd no idea what a Turning was; it didn't seem to be nearly as long as a year, or even a season. Yet in this dark and endless time of forge work, while plying his hammer, he'd grown large, and sprouted hair on his face long since.

Taerune came to see him often, to indulge her taste for whipping slaves raw, and had taught him much of how Nifl talked—yet she'd avoided, time and again, telling him anything *useful* about the wheres and hows of life in Talonnorn.

Not often, but more times by now than he could easily count, he'd been chained and led through back tunnels—never the city streets—from the Forgerift to the huge, sprawling castle of House Evendoom. "Eventowers," they called it, though the one time he'd been up high enough in the gigantic cavern that housed Talonnorn, and had tried to count its many towers, he thought there'd been an odd number.

He'd managed to snatch only a few glimpses out of the windows when inside Eventowers, and never on the city side of the castle. Yet in the other direction, gazing at the tunnel-riddled walls of the great cavern that held Talonnorn, he'd seen several interesting things—among them some small but deep clefts in the rock, in a little area littered with rubble. An area the Nifl seemed to avoid. It might serve to hide things, if ever he needed to hide something.

Always he'd been brought to Eventowers for the same task: shifting furniture around the grand rooms of the castle, as changing fashions demanded high seats and tables be dragged into attics, to be replaced by the latest sculptings. There were no trees in Talonnorn, and Niflghar made most of their furnishings, it seemed, from stone sculpted and melted to smoothness with magic. So the larger pieces—tables and the round bases of beds, mainly—were cursedly heavy. That meant strength, and far more deftness than pack-snouts dragging things with ropes, or tusked gorkuls snarling and straining, could manage.

Wherefore, to keep breakages to a minimum, Evendoom stripped its forgefists, brought them up from the Rift in chains, surrounded them with the cruel hooded Nifl wizards called "spellrobes" and even more warblades wielding lightning-whips, and set them to work sweating furniture from one chamber to another—under the sharp eyes of the impossibly beautiful female Nifl of the House.

Some of the nightskin shes were interested only in seeing the furnishings moved safely to just here—or no, perhaps over *there*—but others (he could tell by his fleeting glimpses of their faces, and the weight of their gazes) wanted to see the naked slaves work, sweat glistening on their straining muscles. Daring to look up at the shes brought instant punishment—and so did any visible arousal that such looks might evoke—so the forgefists kept their faces down unless ordered otherwise.

From time to time a forgefist got taken away, and once or twice that had been Orivon's fate—to be flogged to weak helplessness, chained down tightly, blindfolded . . . and then caressed by wandering Nifl fingers, while excited nightskin shes giggled and sighed and made playful or wonder-struck comments over him. Sometimes they bit him, though older female voices gave sharp, swift orders quelling any cruelty that might maim or do lasting harm.

A very young Taerune had been one of those who'd handled him on one such occasion, he was sure; on her first visit to the Rift, she'd looked at him with familiar recognition. That had been the first time she'd flogged him, so long and viciously that he'd almost fallen into the flames. As he'd groaned and writhed, she'd hissed to him that he now belonged to her, and such pain was nothing to what he'd taste whenever his service displeased her.

Wherefore he'd learned very quickly to please her, and—

But no. Enough. He was *not* going to delve into those memories again now. Rather, he was going to see once more every detail he could remember of House Evendoom and the city around it, and everything he'd heard of the Wild Dark between it and where he'd come from.

The village where he'd been born. The place he'd get back to, if he had to butcher every last cruelly sneering nightskin to do it.

Ashenuld, it was called. Ashenuld. Farms and forests and a wide, muddy wandering cart lane. The smell of green growing things, and the sun hot on his face, and buzzing flies, and . . . and mud, lashing rain-storms, and great green forests he'd run and hidden in, laughing with his friends, laughing with—with . . . *no!* The names were gone, all gone long ago, and now even the faces were fading! It was all fading! Thorar *damn* these nightskins for that!

His hammer came down so hard the blade under it shattered, hot shards ringing and clattering off the stone walls around him. One seared his arm, just by the elbow, but he cared little, shaking off its sizzling pain almost absently.

With the stink of his own cooked flesh strong around him, Orivon frowned and reached for the next raw forgebar.

One of the darmarch stumbled on the fourth flight of steps, and disaster nearly ensued. Whereupon the tall, languid Jalandral Evendoom elegantly uncrossed his arms, from where he'd been lounging against a pillar watching the slow upward progress of their precious burden, and remarked pleasantly to Taerune's sweating, grimacing Nameless Nifl, "Drop it and die."

"*Dral!*" Taerune snarled, whip stirring in her restless hand out of sheer habit. "They *don't* need your needlings!"

"Ah, forgive me, sister dearest. I quite forgot that after you're through needling your toys, they need no more needlings—ever." In mournful tones, head bent as if in shame, he added, "I stand chastened, drowned in the dark abyss of utter remorse."

Taerune snorted. "Jalandral, you're impossible! Now get you gone—right out of this tower—until the door is up! You can drop by and wag your over-clever tongue just as you wish, then."

"Sister, I *always* wag my over-clever tongue just as I wish. Did I not, this castle would never hear a single plain or direct word that wasn't one of us giving slaves orders!" Jalandral Evendoom didn't look as if he was going anywhere. He crossed to the wide stone stair rail and settled himself on it at ease, the picture of handsome indolence.

"Jalandral," his sister said warningly, her voice far more glacial.

The heir of House Evendoom evidently took this to be a polite request to examine the backs of his long, sharp fingernails—and began to do just that, taking his time about it.

"Dral," a another voice chided him, from another direction. Ravandarr Evendoom stood in a door that was rarely opened, looking apprehensive. "Father's unpleased. Shoan Maulstryke has been making threats again."

Jalandral rolled his eyes. "And this is news? It's about all *charming* Shoan knows how to do, is it not?" With a sigh he unfolded himself from the stone rail and strolled to join his younger brother. "And tell me:

Shoan's father added some oh-so-subtle adornments, didn't he? House Evendoom is to be destroyed six sneezes hence, that sort of thing."

"Yes," Ravandarr said heavily. "Ohzeld did say that sort of thing, and is continuing to do so. At length."

"He'd make a good House crone," Jalandral mused, "if he didn't happen to be a rampant." He arched an eyebrow. "Of course, we could amend that trifling oversight of Olone. Is your knife sharp, brother?"

Ashenuld.

Just how far away was it?

He'd been a child, and the raid had been at night . . . and to the Niflghar of Talonnorn, "the Blindingbright" was ever so far away. There was always fear and distaste in Nifl voices when they said that name.

But then, there was fear and distaste in many Nifl voices when they gave orders to him, too.

So, yes, some of the nightskins feared him. Good. They were wise to do so.

He wished he could remember more of Ashenuld. Some of what he'd known had faded the moment they cast the darksight spell on him, that let him see down here in Talonnorn, so that the faint spell-glows seemed like soft but bright lights, and he wasn't lost and blindly helpless whenever he turned away from glows and flaring fires. Sometimes they punished slaves by reversing the darksight casting, to bring down utter blindness. It never took such "Blinded Ones" long to start screaming.

Which led him once more to a certainty he'd settled on long ago, and returned to many, many times since: He'd only have one chance to escape.

One.

So make it *work,* Orivon Firefist.

He plunged a finished blade into the hissing, bubbling oil of its last tempering, thinking hard. He'd gone over all he knew of House Evendoom a thousand, thousand times, but he went through it all one more time.

As he had so many, many times before.

Jaw set, Orivon cast the finished blade down on the cooling slab and strode to take up the next, the ever-present leaping heat of the Rift hot on his face.

His longing to be free of this place and back home burned within him just as the Forgerift burned—and just as strongly.

Yet the long years of whips—he'd long since lost track of time in this place, but by the scratches he'd made from time to time along the back edge of the cooling slab, it had to be about fifteen years—had taught him patience. He'd probably only get one chance to escape, and failure would mean death. Right now they fed him, gave him work to do, and his skills meant the only abuse he got was the whips. So he did the only sane thing he could do: He schemed.

He plotted, considered all he'd seen, and plotted some more, alone and silent amid the clang and clatter of the Rift as he hammered and slaked and hammered some more. Among the firefists, he kept to himself because he could do nothing else: as Taerune's favorite and the most skilled Rift slave, he was kept apart from the others by stone sidewalls unless he was needed elsewhere, and taken there in chains by the surly, much-scarred gorkul overseer the firefists called "Grunt Tusks."

The gray-skinned overseer was lurching past right now, peering narrowly at Orivon's work and trailing his usual sour stink. A rather disapproving grunt rolled out from under his broken brown tusks—but then, the gorkul never said anything else. He went on along the edge of the Rift without stopping, and little wonder: His worries were farther along, among the younger firefists. Orivon Taerune's-Pet never made any trouble.

Ashenuld . . . he'd often wondered just what he was wondering now: how he'd find his way there, once free of Talonnorn and out into what the Nifl called "the Wild Dark." Monsters roamed there, horrible things that made sneering Nifl shudder when remembering them . . . and then there were the Ravagers. Did the Nifl have maps of the surrounding Dark? Such things would be treasures, well-hidden or guarded or both, surely . . .

There were other Niflghar cities out in the Dark: Orivon had overheard the names Uryrryr and Imbrae and Ouvahlor, though their names were all he knew of them. The Nifl of Talonnorn hated the Nifl of other cities. All other cities.

Now that he thought about it, the Nifl hated many things. Hatred seemed their daily drink, their slakethirst.

Orivon reached up his jug of slakethirst and drank deep, frowning. At the thought that always made him frown: He had to get out of Talonnorn first. And Talonnorn was home to the Hunt.

He had to find a way to survive the Hunt.

· · ·

Batlike blackhide wings flapped loudly as squalling darkwings landed, dark talons skittering on stone and long necks undulating in anger at being chokingly reined in. There would be later patrols, but the full-mustered Hunt of Talonnorn had hunted—and, as always, had failed to miss its quarry.

Laughing together as loudly and freely as those who are drunk on bloodlust and excitement are wont to laugh, the warblades of the Hunt tossed reins and writhing, over-long whipswords to the waiting Even-doom hostlers, and stalked off the High Ledge, their spell-armor pulsing sapphire, emerald, ruby, and amethyst as they went.

Servants were waiting to take their bloody battle trophies and wash the gore from their war-harness with ewers of scented water. As always, the warblades strode on, not deigning to notice them, forcing them to hop and scurry to keep pace with the triumphant warriors as they worked.

The warblades knew the young Nifl-shes who adored them would be waiting, and they strutted in their glowing magnificence, masters of the moment and eager to taste eagerly offered flesh. Crones might snap cold orders at them later, but now younger, far more magnificent shes surrendered all to them hungrily, submitting to their every demand.

"Ha-ha!" one of the eldest of the young Hunt warblades roared, "let us sport with our beauties once more! By the Burning Talon, bring me wine! And not just any quaff, but icefire—and mind it's smoking in the flagon!"

"At once, Rolaurel!" cried a tall, long-maned she whose breasts were both pert and—aside from a sprinkling of glued-on gems—bared to him.

The warrior spread his arms and roared his exulting laughter to the unseen roof of the great cavern overhead—and by the time he lowered his head again, she was back before him, holding out an empty flagon and a huge decanter with icefire sparkling up into its very neck.

With a roar of pleasure Rolaurel backhanded the metal flagon out of her grasp, sending it clanging away across the Ledge. Snatching the decanter from her, he emptied it in one long swig that made the watching shes gasp in awe.

On the wings of another bellow of laughter he whirled around and flung the great decanter to its shattering destruction against the nearest wall, sending a roar after it: "So shall we serve *all* foes of Talonnorn!"

.   .   .

Luelldar was contemptuously amused. "The last time I saw such empty strutting revelry, I was up in the Blindingbright, watching humans around a campfire. Just before we burst forth and began our slaughter."

Aloun nodded, tight-lipped in unsmiling disgust. "Their boasting and preening is unworthy of Niflghar. I doubt even their eldest crones are so swaggering in their overconfidence."

Luelldar turned away from the watch-whorl. "Well, let them drink and rut—and so be far from the saddles of their darkwings when we strike. It won't be long now."

"As the fools of Talonnorn laze and strut, all unsuspecting," Aloun murmured, slowly growing a smile that was less than nice, "they'll never know their doom until their city is shattered forever around their ears."

Luelldar was now casting swift spells on small clear crystal spheres that sat in individual carved cradles on the desk beside him. As he finished each spell and touched each orb with a finger, it floated up into the air, spinning gently, to float at the level of his mouth. They moved as he moved, awake and ready to carry his commands, observations, and warnings to distant warblades of Ouvahlor as he watched the fighting unfold.

He waved at Aloun to relinquish his seat and go across the chamber, to sit at a distant desk.

The younger Ouvahlan rose reluctantly, frowning. "Already?"

"The moment a single speaking-sphere is active, I am at risk from Talonar magics. You can hardly replace me if I fall, if you're sitting right beside me and fried by whatever blasts me. This is not a game, Aloun."

"Yes, but Talonnorn *sleeps*! They won't know what—"

"War is . . . war. Nothing unfolds as intended. *Nothing*. Remember that, if you learn nothing else from what we are about to unleash. More than that: Not all the crones of Talonnorn are petty fools or blinded by Olone or gone oriad. There's a reason they alone, when age ravages them, are allowed to hide their wrinkled and withered ugliness behind masks—'holy masks of the Goddess'—and continue to lord it over their city, rather than being cast forth into the Dark to feed the prowling beasts and entertain the Ravagers."

"But you said Klarandarr's spells are stronger than anything they can cast!"

"I did, and meant it. Yet he's but one, and risen not so long. *Think,*

Aloun. Why did you think Ouvahlor has prepared so long for this if the Nifl of Olone are as decadent, oblivious, and overconfident as all that? We have Klarandarr—and Talonnorn has had thousands of crones, daughter after mother, time and again, and each one of them casting spells, to await the time when Talonnorn is threatened."

"Unholy . . . melting . . . Ever-Ice," Aloun whispered, hoarsely and slowly, his jet-black skin slowly going pale.

"*Now* you're beginning to understand. At last. Hurts, doesn't it?"

5

All Our Ancestors Undefended

It is for this reason that ineffectiveness in battle pro-
fanes Olone, despite the ugliness and imperfection of
such strife: that to leave all our ancestors undefended,
by the loss of so many they have handed down memories
to, is to weaken the shared understanding of beauty that
is Olone. In the knowing of Olone, Olone gains grace
and holy power—that Her reach extend to more Ni-
flghar, so that they know salvation, and Olone knows
greater dominion. Praise be to Olone!

       —The Book of Olone

S o will the slaves rise up when we strike, and make our victory easier?" Aloun was struggling to regain confidence with an eagerness Luelldar could almost smell.

Ouvahlor might need Aloun's confidence in time soon to come, wherefore the older Ouvahlan hid his sigh and replied calmly, "Some may, perhaps, though the daring to lash out has been flogged right out of many—even most. Yet I very much doubt such risings will make our conquest any the easier. Rage-driven slaves will see all Nifl as foes, and hamper our warblades more than anything else."

"With all the magic they command, and the Forgerift and all, why do they need so many slaves? Surely a minimum to guard them against blemishing tasks would be easier to feed and house—why, there must be more than a score of slaves for every Talonar Nifl!"

"There are. Yet consider: the work of that feeding and housing is done by slaves. Slaves of some races they cook and eat, as delicacies, and so must be replenished. And then there is status."

"*Slaves* have social standing?"

Luelldar did sigh, this time. Was Ouvahlor so weak that such a one as *this* was only one dying mind away from overseeing its swords?

The dying mind would, of course, be his. Well, perhaps it was best that Aloun was too dull-witted and craven, for all his tantrums, to have ambition enough to kill a bitter old Nifl hight Luelldar.

Yet to serve Ouvahlor, it was his task to forge the blade that might one day slay him.

Aloun of Ouvahlor, shrewd and swift to see consequences and wise about the world. *Hah.*

His snort was loud and emphatic, but he kept the words, "Ever-Ice, scourge us all!" unsaid. Ouvahlor did not need the young fool's anger just now.

"Slaves do *not* have social standing," he said patiently, "in and of themselves." Luelldar lifted his hand to point at a speaking-sphere, and slowly turned in his seat, arm outstretched, to point at each in turn, feeling the linkage, feeling its readiness. "Yet they do enhance the rankings of families in Talonnorn—except for the Evendooms, of course. *Their* standing is due to their size and long dominance and what that dominance is rooted in: control of the Forgerift. They could have no slaves at all, and yet be the first House in that city."

Satisfied as to the state of the spheres, he turned to lock gazes with Aloun. He hoped the youngling might just pay attention enough, if he made these oh-so-obvious matters sound grave and important enough, to *remember* them.

"Consider now all Nifl cities of Olone, and dismiss local rifts, past history, and this or oriad or stone-witted dupe among Niflghar. Well, then: The prestige of Nifl families is linked to the size of their pureblood ranks; the beauty—that is, physical perfection, the very long limbs and sleek curves you were so admiring earlier, when you gazed upon Taerune Evendoom—of those purebloods; the efficacy of their magic; and the wealth (in gems and metals) their slaves bring them. So, now: More slaves can do more work, and so reap more—and so, having more slaves creates greater status."

Aloun nodded. "So whenever I see a House with the most slaves—"

"No. Even if magic and rifts were distributed evenly from House to House, across all of Niflheim, a mere body count will never tell you anything. All powerful Nifl Houses share at least this one habit: They keep some slaves hidden away, in various distant caverns and castle dungeons, for experimentations and in endeavors they'd rather rival Houses not know about."

The younger Watcher of Ouvahlor frowned. "So how will we know, after Talonnorn lies awash in blood and our warblades stand triumphant, that we've got them all?"

"We won't get them all."

"*What?* But I thought—"

"That we were here to 'see all,' and direct the warblades of Ouvahlor to every last Talonar throat?"

There was a brief silence, in which Aloun blinked at the older Watcher several times, ere mumbling, "Well . . . yes."

Luelldar passed a hand over his own brow. *Ever-Ice give me the cold strength!*

"You are mistaken," he said wearily. "So listen, now, and *heed*. I do *not* want you plunging that boot knife you think I'm unaware of into my back when battle is raging high, bellowing that I'm some sort of traitor to Ouvahlor!"

Aloun paled again, and his lips moved as if he wanted to say something, but didn't know what.

Luelldar leaned closer to him, and said slowly, loudly, and firmly, "Ouvahlor does not intend to conquer Talonnorn. Now or in time any of us are likely to see."

"You . . . you mean it," the younger Watcher whispered. As he saw Luelldar roll exasperated eyes, he snapped, "Swear this is truth! Swear by the Ever-Ice!"

Luelldar reached into the front of his robes, drew out the blue-white shard that he wore glimmering against his breast, and held it up on its chain so Aloun could see it well.

Then he closed the fist of his other hand on it and said formally, "By the Ever-Ice that sears all falsehood, I swear: Ouvahlor does not intend to conquer Talonnorn. Now or in time any of us are likely to see."

Aloun's mouth hung open as the older Watcher calmly restored his Ice shard to its customary place. When he found the use of it again, it was to splutter, "But—well—why then—?"

"While you speak, you are slower to listen." Luelldar quoted the very old saying in an almost droll voice, and waited for the younger Watcher to blush, find silence, and get over his emotions. Something the young fool would not have time for in battle; he was far from ready for this duty yet.

When Aloun was truly listening once more, Luelldar said gently, "We've discussed trade among Nifl cities more than once—and recently, too. Yes?"

"Yes." The youngling said that one word and then stopped. Good; he was learning at last.

Luelldar made him wait, just to see if the flood of questions would burst forth . . . and almost smiled, when it did not.

"Talonnorn destroyed," he explained almost gently, "benefits Ouvahlor little. We gain greater loot, if our warblades don't destroy overmuch in the fighting, and lose more of our warblades, just to win two things: the enmity of a few surviving Talonar, who will be death-sworn to avenge their city and so willing to do *anything* to work us harm; and the fell regard of all Nifl cities—not just those of Olone—who will see us as too great a threat to be allowed to survive."

"They'd ally in arms against us?" Aloun's disbelief was clear. "Even *two* Nifl cities can't trust each other enough to rise in arms together, to say nothing of three or more, and Olone and—"

"They would. A Pact exists to prove it."

"The Darksway Pact?"

"Is more than just an empty phrase we chant as infants, Aloun. If invoked, it will be answered. And, sooner or later, Ouvahlor will fall. Probably later, but it will be a long and wearying fight that consumes all of our lives, leaving us no time for laughter or pride or lording it over anyone."

Aloun was going pale again. Luelldar hid his smile. After all, this might be far from the last shock the attack on Talonnorn would deal this young Watcher.

"But let us turn away from such grim contemplations, and consider how Ouvahlor benefits if we shatter Talonnorn, and then withdraw. We are seen to be merciful—or at least, not so wantonly destructive as to be worth trying to eradicate. Any call for the Pact will go unheeded by city rulers mindful of the cost. Yet we stand no longer in the shadow of mighty Talonnorn, fast rising to be powerful enough to seriously threaten Ouvahlor with conquest. Rather, we hold the dominance, and the riches to come."

" 'Riches to come'?"

By the Ice, but the youngling was a simpleton! "A weakened Talonnorn will see its rivals close around it in the Dark, rivals they've given ample cause to hate them. They will fear these rivals, and seek to rebuild their defenses and their trade. So they'll turn to the same Forgerift and ores that enrich them now, and enrich *us* by offering payment in magic and weapons and coin for the slaves, food, and goods our traders will offer them, purporting to be risking much by doing so illicitly, and therefore demanding much higher prices! Then we shall have Ouvahlor on high, and Talonnorn in its shadow."

"So will they not scheme and plot in turn attack us, and win back their dominance?"

"Yes," Luelldar said sweetly. "Yet we shall work to delay that attack for as long as possible. First, our attack will fall most heavily on the foremost ruling House of Talonnorn, the Evendooms. If they are nigh—but not quite—eradicated, the struggle among the various Houses to establish a new local order will occupy the Talonar for the longest time we can hope to cause. This delay will be aided by specific damages we seek to inflict in this attack: the magic we seize, the crones we slay—and the eradication of the Hunt of Talonnorn. Those are the true goals of this strife we're launching: the slaughter of as many crones and darkwings as we can manage. All else is adornment."

"Adornment?"

"A little less incredulous disgust, please. Remember, you are a Watcher of Ouvahlor, and a Watcher—"

"Has no use for incredulity, yes," Aloun said heavily. "I remember *that* lesson."

Luelldar smiled. "Well," he said gently, turning back to the watchwhorl, "that's something."

Grunt Tusks lurched past again, but Orivon kept his eyes on the red-hot bar he was hammering, raining swift blows along its edges to flatten it out into what would soon be another blade. You'd think every last Nifl in all Niflheim would have a dozen swords by now, but *someone* kept buying them from Talonnorn's traders, so perhaps Nifl *were* "numberless in their rightful might," as that longest chant of Olone claimed.

Well, all the more to slay, then. Starting with those hated most: the Nifl of House Evendoom, the she-elf who thought of him as her pet first of all. It would be a pleasure to dismember her slowly, listening to her screams and smashing her down whenever she tried to struggle.

He might well have to slaughter a lot of other Nifl first, though, to win himself leisure enough to make Taerune the Whipping Bitch's death slow and fittingly painful. And she might well use that time to flee, or gather magic to use against him that he'd have no shield against. So perhaps she needed to lose her hands and feet as swiftly as he could manage it—oh, and her tongue, too, to keep her from snarling out spells—so she'd have no choice but to just lie there and bleed while he dealt with the *rest* of House Evendoom.

Not that he'd take all that much delight in maiming a female—even a female Nifl. Nor, come to think of it, would he enjoy striking down the heir of the house, the one who laughed so much—Jalandral, that was his name, aye. Though he tasted no whips, and sweated over no Rift, he felt as trapped as Orivon Firefist, Taerune's pet Hairy One. Or so he'd seemed, at least, on every one of the handful of occasions when Orivon had seen him in the Eventowers.

"Oh, aye, that one prowls as restlessly as I do," Orivon told the nascent blade he was hammering so deftly, as his sweat rained down around him and the Rift raged, bubbling as it flowed past. He took care to keep that comment under his breath, even in the clanging, ringing heart of a flurry of hammer blows. The nightskins had magic that let them spy and listen from afar—and who knows when they might use it?

The Whipping Bitch probably spied on her big brute of a pet often. It was not out of whim that Grunt Tusks checked to make sure he never tried to cover any part of his body except his eyes—and came growling to drag him back if he strayed too far or too often from the area lit by the ring of braziers. Braziers that were not only burn perils, but utterly unneeded heat and light, here on the lip of the Rift. All they served to do, aside from lighting him from shoulders to nethers to any magically unseen eye, was make him glisten with sweat all the while he was working. They also made necessary the slakethirst that Grunt Tusks provided so grudgingly—but attentively, clearly under orders.

Oh, yes, Taerune was watching. Perhaps not this particular moment, but often. She'd pounced on his every trifling carelessness, insolence, and defiance—even those he'd done when he was certain he was quite alone—when he'd first come under her sway, training him well with her whip to behave as the perfect slave.

Often, in those early days, when he'd roared curses and hauled hard on his chains, she'd flogged him bone-deep, used a dagger to slice muscles into uselessness, and even hurled handfuls of salt into his open wounds—only to revive him and heal him with magic.

It had been a long time since she'd cast such spells on him—but then, it had been long indeed since he'd offered her the slightest defiance, either. She liked it more when he seemed eager to receive punishment—and in her delight, dealt out less pain.

They'd come to know each other, far more than he was sure other Evendoom even noticed their slaves, and . . . well, she had spirit, he'd grant her that. A certain reckless tossing aside of fear, a defiant "well, what of it?" that he admired. She was a fool, but a magnificent fool.

Aye, magnificent—that was the other thing. She *was* beautiful. Achingly, exquisitely beautiful—by Thorar, they *all* were, these Nifl, for all their cruelty and sneering. Sleek, rounded where they should be, with . . . with . . .

He shook his head, trying to banish memories of velvet black flesh he'd glimpsed when Taerune and her sisters wanted the thrill of revealing themselves to a slave. Orivon growled as he held up his blade to sight along it. Straight and true. Of course.

He could barely remember what human women looked like. He'd seen none in the Eventowers, and from talk among the gorkuls and nameless Nifl he'd overheard, he knew how short a time human "playpretties" were likely to last when dragged to Talonnorn. They were called "screamers" by most Nifl for good reason.

He might share their fate, in time to come, if ever he displeased Taerune or her fellow Evendooms sufficiently. House Oszrim was reputed to prefer male slaves for bedchamber play, and he'd seen hunger in the cold eyes of the Oszrim brothers when they'd encountered Taerune in the streets and exchanged smoothly cutting insults—or as Taerune termed them later, "the usual pleasantries."

He *had* to escape Talonnorn, had to get away from these cruel dark elves and back to sunlight and green growing things and . . . *forgedark,* why couldn't he even remember their *faces?*

There'd been women in Ashenuld, women he'd scampered after and spied upon when they stole off into the deep forest to bathe in the streams. Long, wet hair, curving over drenched, dripping breasts as they murmured pleasure at washing away the stink and grime, standing up in the stream to toss their heads back and—why couldn't he remember their *faces?* Thorar *damn* it!

He brought his hammer down so hard on a new, red-hot forgebar that it shattered, shards clattering everywhere and making Grunt Tusks, even at a safe distance, belch and stagger aside in startlement. Disappointingly, the gorkul didn't fall into the Rift. Kicking the largest shards aside with complete disregard for the burns he'd acquire—mere adornments on the battered and much-scarred things that his feet had become—Orivon reached for another bar.

Oh, he had gauntlets for handling red-hot metals, and even boots and breeches at the back of his forge floor, near the gates, for wearing on his rare chained journeys through the streets. He was never ordered into them if he was going to the Eventowers through the Evendoom back tunnels, and could barely remember the last time he'd put them on.

Breeches. Boots. What did such fripperies matter, when he lacked freedom?

Just running away, if he smote down Grunt Tusks and somehow avoided the fireghosts and warblades—probably by leaving through the tunnels and then up and out through Eventowers, not trying to win out past the Rift gates—would be futile. The Hunt would pounce on Orivon before he'd drawn a dozen breaths. Even if the Hunt itself was busy elsewhere, gleefully plying their whipswords to slice up and behead some other fleeing slaves, aspiring to join the Hunt was the heartiest pastime of many young, reckless Talonar he-Nifl, and some of them had cavegaunts and even darkwings of their own to ride, and were aching for a chance to prove their worthiness to fly with the Hunt. So how to elude them?

His hammer fell on the bar. And again.

No trader would dare hide him in a pack-sledge or manywheels wagon, no matter how much he offered. Their lives were worth more to them than any payment—and after all, what was there to keep them from taking the fine blades or gold and then straightaway betraying him, and keeping it?

Bahhhrang . . . bahhhrang . . . another blade-to-be, shaping up nicely . . .

Oh, yes, he had some gold. He'd managed to collect soft gold as forgesplash over the years, and work it together into a lump about as large as both his hands, that he kept coated with pitch and stuck down a crack in the stone floor, under his side tables.

Not that he had anything to spend that gold on, or any chance to buy anything.

Bahhhrang.

The only other wagons that regularly left Talonnorn were the dung carts that took daily loads of excrement out to distant caverns, to be devoured by giant dung-worms: blind, mindless deepserpents that were thankfully too large to fit through the tunnels to reach the city and gnaw on Nifl—and Nifl slaves—instead.

He'd pondered this possible way out many a time, but it seemed desperate slaves had tried to hide in wagonloads of dung in the past; the wagons and their loaders were guarded at all times by armed and armored Nifl who were both watchful and belligerently suspicious of anyone and everything, probably out of anger at drawing such duty.

Talonnorn had something worse than the Hunt, too, but he doubted they'd unleash it for one fleeing slave. A handcount or more, yes, but not for just one. Once the raudren were loosed, they had to feed—and he knew, from talk he'd overheard, that even the Nifl feared the raudren. He'd only caught a fleeting glimpse of one, frozen by spells and caged, but he knew what they were: flying hunters even deadlier than the darkwings, creatures whose entire bodies were a great leathery wing—a wing with a razor tail and even sharper jaws and claws.

Not knowing any spells, let alone how to cast one that would freeze a swooping raudren, he'd just have to take the chance he'd not have to try to outrun one. Or more than he could count of them, sleek and silent and deadly.

Orivon sighed, gave the cooling bar one last deft tap with his hammer, and held it up to peer at it critically.

Slave tales always claimed it was easy to swarm a Nifl guard, don his armor, and fool everyone thereby—but words were easier to spin than finding any Nifl large enough to have armor that might even begin to cover the shoulders of Orivon Firefist—let alone fooling anyone into thinking this pale muscled mountain of a human was actually a sleek, black-skinned Niflghar. Even saying airily that he was a Nifl trying out a magical disguise would mean having to speak convincingly like a Talonar Nifl, and answer swift questions well enough to satisfy suspicious dark elves who would no doubt have sharp swords ready in their hands.

Moreover, most Evendoom Niflghar—and probably the warblades of all the other Houses as well—wore bracers or amulets that turned away cinders, shards, small missiles, stinging insects. To even touch one he'd need a determined, full-strength attack with a weapon. Tossing rocks or even daggers would accomplish nothing.

Orivon sighed sourly, and turned to put the shaped blade—flawless, as always—carefully down on his sidetable.

It was then that he saw it.

The tall, rune-adorned gates of the Forgerift stood alone in their arched frames, flanked on either side by apparently empty air. As every Talonar who'd blundered too close to them knew, however, that air was alive with invisible piercing spikes and crawling lightnings, a treble barrier of unseen magics that meant sure death even to the most powerful Nifl spellrobes—unless they had the leisure to stand and work spell after spell, exhausting themselves just to fleetingly breach those mighty spell-walls. The Evendoom warblades who guarded the gates wore something—Orivon knew it was their belts, but only because he saw something he hadn't been meant to see—that made the spikes and the lightnings nonexistent for them, but even they were stopped by the third barrier: the solid, invisible unbroken wall of pure force that soared from the very solid rock underfoot up through the air to the lost-in-darkness cavern ceiling, so high above. More than once, Orivon had seen darkwings shatter themselves against that solid air and tumble down in dying ruin, spilling their riders to lesser dooms.

Just now, and suddenly, as he stood staring, the air outside the gates was flickering. Closest to that stirring, the unseen lightnings of the wall-spells were becoming visible, gathering and crackling viciously, like a guard-wolf baring its fangs and leaning forward, straining to strike. The gate guards drew their swords and approached warily.

Those flickerings became a sudden flare of orange flame, out of which stepped a Nifl in dark armor unlike any Orivon had ever seen or had a hand in crafting. There was a sword in his hand, and in brisk, calm silence he stepped forward to lunge at the nearest Evendoom guard.

The warblades charged him—which was when orange flames flared behind them, and more unfamiliar armored Nifl burst out of that roiling air, swords thrusting. Some of the guards were dying even before they turned.

Orivon stopped watching the newcomers viciously sword the Evendoom warblades just long enough to snatch up a red-hot pair of forge tongs, so he'd have a weapon against whoever these fools were.

He was hefting the long tongs in his hand—reassuringly heavy they were, too—when the very stone under his feet trembled. The solid stone of the cavern floor.

"Thorar!" Orivon breathed. Anything that could shake the great cavern of Talonnorn was—

The trembling became a real shaking, a long and rolling thunder that threatened to hurl him off his feet.

Orivon strode hastily away from the edge of the Rift, as dust and stones started to rain down on him. He tried to peer past the Great Gates, out into the city proper, but saw only that dust and stones were falling on all of the city he could still see. Which wasn't much, and would have been less had the runes on the gates not been blazing up bright and angry.

The mysterious attackers were gone into the gloom, slaves were screaming up and down the Rift, Grunt Tusks was cursing with more amazement than anything else in his rough deep voice—and as Orivon watched in growing awe, something reared up *under* the stone before him, forcing the gates open from within.

The runes on the tall dark doors became white blazing beacons, hurling light into the tumult that Talonnorn had become.

In their radiance he stared at what now was bursting up out of the solid stone cavern floor, to rear up beyond the gates of the Rift, even taller than they soared: a huge dung-worm, tall and dark and malevolent as it peered about.

Thorar, if it noticed *him* . . .

That fear was still kindling in Orivon as he stared at the distant Eventowers, now brightly lit by the awakened white glows of their wards, and saw three—*three!*—more dung-worms, truly giant deepserpents that seemed now not sluggishly mindless but full of keen-witted malice. They were rearing up over the towers and turrets of the proud Nifl castle, surging forward.

And then they were crashing down, jaws agape, gnawing and slamming at stone. And the Eventowers were rocking and crumbling, one turret leaning out to begin the long, rumbling plunge to oblivion.

Orivon shook his head in astonishment.

Thorar, it seemed, had answered his prayers at last.

6

War Comes to Talonnorn

We'll drown in hot blood and leave widows forlorn
Earning bright glory when war comes to Talonnorn.
—from the ballad
"War Comes to Talonnorn"

They were well into the chant, face-down and shivering as they embraced the great dark slope of ice, when Lolonmae threw back her head and screamed.

It was a scream that broke off into wild, uncontrolled shakings and tremblings, so that the scandalized disgust of her fellow novices and underpriestesses turned to alarm—and for some, swiftly hidden delight at an excuse to rise from the frigid ice, all bare, wet, blue, and shivering as they were, and bundle the moaning, unseeing, still-writhing Lolonmae down the long, dark hall to a certain door.

A door that wasn't answered, even when their tentative knockings turned to fearful hammerings—until Exalted Daughter of the Ice Semmeira dared to do what was never done. She flung the door wide, and led the way in.

Temple spells that had been old before the Revered Mother was born made the darkness glow blue-white around the wet, anxious priestesses as they hurried, bare wet feet slapping on smooth stone. Down a shorter, narrower passage to a small round room where the Revered Mother should have been kneeling alone before her private altar of ice . . .

But was instead sprawled spiderlike on the floor, writhing in the same manner as the stricken novice Lolonmae.

"Revered *Mother*?" Semmeira cried, rushing forward.

Pain-filled yet wryly amused eyes looked back up at her from the floor, and then past her to what swayed in the grasp of a knot of priestesses. "Ah," the aged high priestess croaked, her voice raw from screaming. "Lolonmae. Of course."

Semmeira knelt to help the still-trembling Revered Mother to her knees. " 'Of course'?" she dared to ask.

"She felt it, too. Great magic, unleashed—spells strong enough to shake the Ice itself."

"Are we . . . under attack?"

The Revered Mother shook her head. "No. At least, not yet. The spells are too distant for that."

She thrust herself up to her feet, swaying, as the priestesses stared at her. "Yet not so far off that we should not be gravely concerned."

Semmeira swallowed. "How concerned?"

The Revered Mother gave her a long, thoughtful stare. "We should probably all be wetting ourselves. Not that doing so will be much help."

A watch-whorl burst into an inferno of whirling sparks, hurling a headless, blackened crone back in her seat, to slump into eternal silence. Someone screamed, and Maharla and Orlarra snarled in unison, "What's *happening*?"

"Olone preserve us," Galaerra whispered hoarsely, staring into the watch-whorl she'd hastily backed away from, but hadn't dared flee—nor, to tell the truth, had been able to resist staring into. They could all see what she was staring at: the great heads of dung-worms rearing up to overtop the lesser towers of the very castle they were sitting in.

And plunging down, like great living rams, to smash through ancient stone walls and shake the chamber around them. Dust and tiny stones pelted down on their heads, and all over the room crones of House Evendoom started screaming.

Every watch-whorl was showing the same scene: the Eventowers beset, three dung-worms—no, *more*!—rearing their heads once more to strike, lesser towers slowly toppling or gone already, and Talonnorn beyond a scene of devastation, with plumes of smoke billowing up, distant deepserpents undulating and rising up to crash through buildings, and Nifl fighting Nifl everywhere.

"We're all going to *die*!" an elven crone shrieked.

Another burst up out of her chair, her watch-whorl collapsing into falling, fading motes in her wake, and raced for the door, crying, "They're coming! They'll be breaking into *this* tower next!"

Orlarra raised a hand, face cold and set, but Maharla was faster. Fires flared from her fingertips, tiny beams of flame that streaked across the chamber—and the running crone shrieked suddenly, clawing at a door that would not open, as her personal ward suddenly flared into visibility around her, beset around its edges by Maharla's flames . . . and already shrinking visibly.

Desperately the crone struggled with the door, her hands flaming with emerald fires of her own—but though it burst into roiling green flames under her touch, it held firm.

Crones all over the chamber stared at their eldest, Orlarra, who was standing with one hand raised, palm out in a "halt" gesture. Whenever emerald magic flared across the door, Orlarra's eyes went emerald too, and her face slowly creased in pain—but the door held, and it was the crone fighting with it who suddenly screamed in agony as her wards collapsed and Maharla's flames claimed her. She reeled, sobbing, ablaze all over, and then sagged to the floor, becoming her own pyre.

Orlarra winced, but turned to Maharla and said, "That was well done."

"Yes," Maharla hissed, "and so is *this*."

The gestures she made then were small and swift. The eldest crone easily repulsed her flames, rage rising to join pain on her face—but Maharla's spiteful smile never wavered, and a jet of flame rose from the burning crone on the floor to race across the chamber and stab the eldest crone of House Evendoom in the back.

Orlarra stiffened, crones gasped and half-rose from their seats all over the room—and a deepserpent head slammed through a nearby wall. The chamber cracked and reeled in a slow thunder of grinding, falling stone and suddenly swirling dust that hurled shrieking crones this way and that.

Orlarra gasped, Maharla's crimson flames gouting from her mouth—and then her eyes burst into spitting, stabbing lightnings. "Olone!" she whispered, wonder joining sobbing pain in her voice. "Oh, Perfect One!"

Her body flared into golden flame that sent Maharla staggering back in surprise and alarm, and she whispered, "Of course. Use me, please!"

And she was gone, only empty air and silence where golden tongues of fire had swirled a moment before.

A sudden hush fell upon the tower, even as dung-worm heads reared up again, looming large and darkly terrible in the watch-whorls.

That golden calm held as dark, mottled monster heads larger than the crones' lofty tower-top chamber raced right at every watch-whorl, the crones frozen at them slack-jawed in terror, watching death rushing to claim them . . .

They heard the blows of those great heads, faintly, but felt nothing.

And in every watch-whorl, dung-worms writhed in agony, rearing back into the air trailing plumes of golden lightning, twisting and shaking from side to side, seeking to be rid of the pain they could not escape . . .

Vast and sluggish they fell back, coiling and thrashing, their great loops crushing loping pack-snouts and running servants and flattening the walls of the Eventowers gardens—and then the gardens, too.

More than one crone laughed in triumph, peering into her watch-whorl, but that mirth was short-lived. The golden glow in the room faded slowly, bringing down a darkness lit only by the bright eyes of the whorls.

Eyes that were now showing other, larger dung-worms surging out of ruined Talonnorn into the Evendoom grounds, swaying and slithering, gliding through wards that should have crisped them . . . wards that no longer seemed to be there.

"No!" Galaerra gasped. "How can Olone let this happen?"

"Fool!" snapped old Baraule. "Forget never: Olone tests us always! Those who prevail win brightness in Her eyes!"

Maharla stood alone in the center of the chamber, watching these new menaces, ruby fires dancing and flickering around her clenched fists.

Over the feebly moving coils of the burned dung-worms the new deepserpents came, purposeful, moving forward together. Heading straight for this tower, *this* chamber . . .

"All of you!" Maharla snapped. "Look at me, think of me—*open your minds to me*! I need you with me!"

And she spread her hands and whispered a Word.

The air itself tingled, every hair in the chamber standing on end, sword-stiff and straining.

Maharla said another Word, and the tingling air went very dark, only the frightened faces of the crones glowing faint and pale as they stared at each other. More than one of them looked enraged.

"How *dare* you! That, Maharla, is only to be used when all else has failed, and the end of our family is upon us!"

"I'm glad you remember the rules so well, Klaerra." Maharla's eyes glittered in the gloom like two dark flames, blazing without brightness. "A pity you're too wan-witted to understand that all else *has* failed—yes, just this swiftly!—and if I don't use it, you and I will be sharing in the extinction of House Evendoom!"

It was a sickening feeling, this jostling of minds. Suspicions and dislikes seethed like acid, searing, and more than one crone moaned or mumbled prayers to Olone.

Deepserpent heads towered dark and massive in the lone watchwhorl that was still bright, the one floating nearest to Maharla.

"*Now,* sisters of Evendoom!" she snapped. "Work with me now, or we are all undone! *Strike!*"

Her own mind was full of roaring flames—a flood of conflagration that plucked at those of the other crones, seeking to tug them into the quickening flow, bearing them along to . . .

"*Raaaaaah!*" Involuntarily they cried out together, wordlessly, shouting their rage and fear and pain . . . and, slowly unfolding, their exultation as bolts of flame snarled out, searing the air, to strike dung-worm after dung-worm, darting into parted jaws to cause great heads to burst, or splashing over snouts and sending fire raging around serpent heads.

The huge monsters flailed about, headless and convulsed, or swayed and burned, seeking to scream but managing only a vast, wet hissing.

Crones slumped all over the chamber, weeping or clutching at their heads. Maharla stood triumphant, arms crossed, watching the dung-worms die.

It had cost the wits of several in the chamber—and she had seen to that. It had stripped the Evendoom wards of much of their power, snatched away from within; even now, she could feel wards all around Eventowers fail and fall in tatters.

Yet the deepserpents were all gone—and so was Orlarra. And anything that left Maharla the foremost crone of House Evendoom, no matter what else happened, could be counted nothing less than a great victory.

The senior Watcher of Ouvahlor turned from his whorl with a gleeful hiss. "They've done it!"

Aloun had never seen Luelldar this excited; his eyes glittered like sword blades catching firelight. "Their wards are down! Send in our blades!"

For once in his life, Aloun sprang eagerly to cast a farspeaking spell.

As she left the balcony behind, Taerune's mind was awhirl. Down the stair she sprinted, scabbarded sword in hand, the buckle of its belt flailing her arm at every step, and plunged into the mad tumult of the armory hall.

It was every bit as crowded as she'd expected, as she ducked and dodged her way through the hastily arming Nifl of House Evendoom, furiously snarling warblades, aging uncles, and young Hunt braggarts among them.

Jalandral was laughing, of course, when she caught sight of him, clapping warblades on their shoulders and spitting swift orders into their ears, directing them to this gate and that hall in a manner that could only be deemed gleeful.

"Ha-ha, little sister!" he cried, catching sight of her hurrying toward him. "Blood! Blood at last!"

"And much of it Evendoom blood! Our walls are breached, Dral! *Breached!* And this makes you *laugh?*"

"But of course!" Jalandral's eyes danced with delight. "I've something to do at last! Something important! Something that *matters!*"

"Your *death* will matter to Ravan, yes, and no doubt please more than a few crones, but—*Olone forfend!*"

Taerune's angry words rose into a shout as she pointed. At the far end of the hall, gorkul were lumbering forward, sweating, fearful humans, right behind them. Nifl were at their backs, urging them on with whips and goads. Weapons bristled in every hand, and some of the goads crackled with angry lightnings that shed flickering light enough for Taerune to see eye patches and scars among the Nifl. No disfigured dark elf rampant of Talonnorn would be commanding warriors; these were strangers—Ravagers, or Nifl of a city that did not revere Olone.

With shockingly casual ease the foremost gorkul thrust their long-claws deep into Evendoom warblades, hurled the dying Nifl aside and shook them free, then stuck their bloody blades into the next House defenders.

Taerune wasn't the only one shouting and pointing by then, and warblades alerted in the din spun around to fight no matter how little harness or blades they had ready.

"How did they get *this* far?" she snarled, to no one in particular. "Who's guarding our gates?"

It was then that a heavily armored Nifl came reeling down a side passage, drenched in blood. Not recognizing him, Taerune drew her sword and almost slashed open his face before she saw it was Ravandarr.

"Brother!" she shrieked. "What—?"

He struck her sword aside wearily with one armored forearm, and stumbled past, gasping, "The East Tower's down, and all the rest back to the Hall of Helms is lost to us! Hansur's dead, and Doualaur, and Malavvan . . ." He shook his head. "So many coming at us . . ."

"Ho, Ravan!" Jalandral called cheerfully. "I need you here—can't let them seize *this* hall, and use all our weapons against us! To me!"

Ravandarr shook his head, face a loose mask of despair under all the blood, but turned and started back across the room, hefting a notched and bent sword as he staggered.

"They're pouring in from the back tunnels!" a warblade shouted, bursting out onto a balcony above.

Jalandral looked up, nodded eagerly, and turned his head to snap, "Ryskraun! Naernar! To the Long Hall!"

Raising his blade to the warblade on the balcony, he roared, "Wait for me, Orsyl! I'm coming!" Taerune saw him run three steps before he spun around, pointing with his sword back across the room and almost slicing open Ravandarr's breast in doing so, and bellow, "Laskal! Take all of the Hunt you can find and get down to the front, to rally our House blades there! Evendoom forever!"

"Evendoom forever!" rampants roared, up and down the hall, and suddenly everyone was rushing, helms and weapons clanging and clattering in dropped haste, and the enemy gorkuls and humans were shrieking and dying, a flashing forest of Evendoom blades thrusting them through. The Nifl who'd commanded them fell back, and with a ragged roar the Evendoom warblades pursued them.

The armory hall emptied with astonishing speed, leaving Taerune momentarily alone with the sprawled dead. She could hear someone— Raskulor, by the sound of the voice—shouting orders in the inner armory.

No one, of course, had given her any orders. She was of the blood Evendoom, and she was female; in most Houses only rampants fought, and the shes cowered behind guarded doors deep in castles during battle, or attended the crones in the innermost, highest, most heavily guarded chambers of all. Her sisters were probably shut away somewhere right now, well supplied with sweet treats and wine, gasping and giggling over old tales of Evendoom victories. Maelree always "adorned" the stories she told, every time—and Nalorne always wanted to hear the gory moments over and over again. The others just giggled. On cue.

Lip curling at that thought, Taerune ducked behind a pillar long enough to avoid being sliced open by errant blades as Raskulor burst out of the inner armory and sprinted off in the direction of the Hall of Helms, Evendoom warblades streaming in his wake. Buckling on her sword scabbard, Taerune hoped they weren't all racing to their deaths.

Evendoom had never been defeated—or so the crones liked to claim, though she remembered asking once what had caused deep grooves in a wooden sculpture deep in the upper bedchambers, and being told by a low-voiced servant that they were sword scars from "one of the strifes," and must never be mentioned by her again.

Hmm. Ravandarr had just named three of their uncles dead, which left four, including her favorite, Faunhorn, and the one she loathed, who in turn despised her: Valarn. Would any of them survive this battle?

Would House Evendoom survive this?

Yes, enough dusty history; who was attacking *now*? Not a rival city House, by what she'd seen of Talonnorn from a high tower window, though then again, a craven House like Oszrim or Oondaunt might be behind this; how else could dung-worms—*dung-worms!*—have gotten in, without many spellblasts to open a way for them, that would have warned everyone and had the Hunt flying?

And where was Lord Evendoom, who should be leading the veteran warblades and spellrobes of the House in a calm, all-capable defense of the Eventowers? Or was he—were they all—dead?

Olone *spit!*

Taerune ducked into the inner armory, to see if they'd left anything that might aid her. Amid the warning glows of deadly ward-fields she could see helms—she hated the things, and they were always too large for her, deafening and blinding metal buckets she'd just as soon do without— and . . . aha!

A field chimed and retreated before her enspelled bracers, letting her reach a fistful of daggers unscathed. Simply scabbarded, with push-home hilts, hefting nicely . . . Nodding, she dropped a pair down either of her boots, inside and out, trotted a few steps to make sure they'd not hamper her, and then ran back out of the room, seeking the nearest stairs down. If no one was guarding the tunnels that led to the Forgerift . . .

No one needed to, she discovered a few panting descents later. The inner gates of the tunnels were twisted and buckled to the floor, a pool of Nifl blood spreading from underneath one of them. Something had brought the tunnels down in collapse, spilling rock rubble half across the chamber. No foe would be charging or skulking into the Eventowers from here.

So what had become of her Dark Warrior, and all the weapons he'd been crafting?

"Spew of Olone," she muttered, turning back. Well, either she'd have ample time to discover that later—or no time at all, and it would matter to no one important, if House Evendoom fell or Talonnorn itself was lost.

And lost, Olone damn all, to *whom*?

Who was attacking, and why? Talonnorn was the mightiest, proudest city of Olone, and Evendoom the greatest House at the heart of it! Which meant many unfriends, yes, but—

Warsteel clanged and skirled on warsteel, and Taerune ran toward that sound of fighting. The clamor led her up some stairs, around a corner into growing light, and along a passage into—

Alauntagar's Hall, she was standing in now, blade in hand and pausing uncertainly, but it was an Alauntagar's Hall much changed from the last time she'd seen it.

The smallest of the grand vaulted halls of Eventowers—it could be fitted into the glossy-tiled Long Hall seven times over, but then, the Hunt could find room to fly around the Long Hall!—Alauntagar's Hall had always sported a row of soaring, glossy-polished pillars sculpted into sinuously exquisite representations of the rising Rapture of Olone. Until now, however, those pillars hadn't risen out of a floor decorated in sprawled fresh-slain Evendoom warblades—and the hall itself hadn't lacked a front wall.

Through that huge smashed opening, and the heavy cloak of stone dust still swirling around it, Taerune found herself gazing—no, gaping in disbelief—out at what had been the central garden of the Eventowers.

It, too, was much changed.

"How can so much," she whispered incredulously, "be swept away so *swiftly*?"

The many-hued glowing fungi she'd seen flourishing all her life were largely flattened or gone, familiar curving paths and benches gouged and heaved aside in great scatterings of earth—or buried under the huge dark coils of dead deepserpents. Corpses lay everywhere, most of them Niflghar in Evendoom livery.

One of the gate towers now stood alone, blazing like a torch, and intruders were pouring into the Eventowers past its billowing flames and smoke.

The enemy.

Mainly terrified slaves, by the looks of them, urged ánd goaded on by Nifl rampants in motley armor, many of them scarred or even disfigured. Just like those she'd seen in the armory hall—only there were more of these, far more, and they just kept coming!

Olone spit, what could one defiant daughter of Evendoom do against so many?

Well, *not* run and hide, that much was certain. Before Olone and all the Elder Gods, she'd not—

One lone Evendoom-she *still* without her Orb, damn it! Not that it held many battle spells, but still! Why did she never remember it, in her rush to snatch sword and get into battle? It was back in her chambers with her whip and her armor, secure behind her gleaming new Door of Fangs!

Well, she'd soon see just how much use she could be. How long she'd last, to put it more bluntly. There were so many of them that surely some would come running in this direction, into the opening that was so large that they could hardly help but see it. It might look more deadly than an unscorched door—but then, if Taerune Evendoom had been running into an enemy castle, she'd prefer a way torn by recent battle over a possibly trapped and guarded door, every time.

Yet these were gorkul and human slaves, with a few Nameless Nifl, not Taer—

As she watched, Evendoom castle guards in full, gleaming battle armor came trotting into view, hastening along the outer wall of the castle to form a line across the front of the breached hall. The air flickered and flared where their personal wardshields grazed each other, arcing where they intersected. They were making a living wall of defenders, two Nifl deep, to meet the enemy gorkul and Hairy Ones.

Taerune smiled grimly. These were veteran Evendoom warblades, and some of them hefted spellblades that were igniting, as she watched, with baleful radiances of their own. This should be good.

The foe sent up a ragged roar as they rushed to meet the warblades, and Taerune took two swift sideways steps to where she could see better, sheathed her sword, and folded her arms across its pommel in satsifaction. And now for the slaughter.

Gorkul and humans were both so *clumsy* when they fought, so frenzied and graceless, limbs and blades jerking and slicing the air wildly, nothing like the fluid grace of . . . dying Nifl . . .

She couldn't breathe. She couldn't make a sound. This wasn't happening. They couldn't . . .

They could. With shocking ease the shouting, grunting, staggering invaders were hewing down senior Eventowers guards, who were lunging and fencing and slicing out throats and eyes in their usual dances of death—but being overborne and hurled down, or transfixed by enemy blades or casually hacked and hewn by gorkul blundering past, or humans leaping and rolling in and under their guards and—

This *shouldn't* be happening! Even as she watched, a half-naked human—still wearing manacles at his wrists and ankles, with a few ragged links of chain flailing the air at his every movement—rushed forward, ducking under a warblade's elegant slash so that it sliced away half his scalp, in a gory spray of blood and hair, and tackled the Nifl, hurling him down and back to the heaped rubble of the fallen wall. The human punched the dark elf's throat viciously and then wrestled against the Nifl's failing strength to get his longblade. The warblade's back was broken and his shattered throat left him no way to breathe; it took the bleeding, maddened Hairy One less than one of Taerune's disbelieving gasps to wrench free the Nifl's longblade and turn and hurl it at the backs of the knees of the nearest Evendoom warblade who staggered, driven off balance, and got a sword slash across his face from the human he was fighting.

Evendoom Niflghar were suffering similar fates everywhere she looked; Taerune swallowed—it was closer to a sob—and peered up and down the line, trying to see how many defenders of her home and family were left.

How few . . .

Seven—no, six, now, and the last few were beset by dozens and would be overwhelmed in another breath or two. Trying not to weep, Taerune snatched out her sword again, and—

There came a great groaning sound, so loud that it set her teeth to chattering against each other and shook her to numbness, a mournful rending of stone that seemed to be above her and behind her and all around her, echoing off stone walls everywhere.

Those echoes were shattered by sharp crackings, so loud and fierce that Taerune fell to her knees, sobbing and trying to cover her ears.

And then, with a shriek that deepened into the loudest cry of agony she had ever heard, half of the Eventowers tore free and came crashing down to bury the intruders.

7

Battle and More Battle

I see no bright future for our House.
No immortal ballads, noble statuary,
Innovations or marvels of garb.
Just battle and more battle,
And the same bloody deaths
As all other Niflghar seem so eager to greet.
—words of the character Lord Vorth Drear,
from the play *Bright Houses Fallen*

*I*n the shattered, sagging ruin of the smithy, cloaked in thickly coiling smoke from the fiery deaths of things that had half-fallen into the ever-hungry Rift, Orivon Firefist worked frantically by the angry glows of the gate runes, sorting out and snatching up the best weapons he'd been working on. Armor that might fit him was farther along the Rift, well beyond the side walls that had shut him off from the other slaves, but there had been more than a few screams and shouts from that direction—followed by some horribly loud biting and munching sounds.

If Talonnorn was truly shattered, this might well be his chance. If it was conquered swiftly, new captors might crush his hopes of freedom in their gauntlets. Yet if, as he expected, House Evendoom recovered itself and hurled back this attack, he might have only a little time to achieve just one thing.

Hiding some weapons and tools in those clefts in the cavern wall, in the area the Nifl shunned.

Of course, they might shun it for a reason that would be deadly to him, too . . . but then, he was little better than dead anyway if he willingly undertook to live out his entire life just hammering things, here on the hot lip of the Rift.

He had to work fast, and trust that no one would see him in all the tumult and fighting—or if they did see him, be slain, so no one would come to torture or flog him, slay him outright, or spell-scour his mind to uncover what he'd been doing.

And he had nothing at all to carry things in but his hands. Then again, that might well be all he would have at a later attempt to escape.

That escape might happen right now, if he reached the clefts unseen and battle was still raging fiercely enough that a pursuit by the Hunt—or the raudren—seemed unlikely.

The breeches and boots still fit him, but he needed something to cover his shoulders for warmth; the Wild Dark wouldn't be nearly as warm as the ever-raging Rift. A cloak snatched off a Nifl corpse, one of those tabardlike garments some of the spellrobes wore—Thorar, even a gown! The tight jerkins and hose male Nifl wore would never fit him. Shards and rockfall, he didn't even know the Nifl names for those garments!

And with that little exasperation making him shake his head and smile, Orivon Firefist filled his arms with a few choice weapons and tools, wrapping them in his breeches, and hastened along the edge of the Rift, trusting that Grunt Tusks wouldn't be trudging his usual rounds along that narrow, well-worn way.

He'd have to watch out for any and every beast that might come charging out of the smoke into him, of course—one staggering step in *that* direction and he'd be greeting the flowing rock face-first, in a first kiss that would also be his last.

He slipped once or twice in blood, feet a little clumsy in his unaccustomed boots, and passed a lot of tumbled tables and anvils—and once, a long ankle manacle that ended not around an ankle but in a churned and talon-raked puddle of mud and blood—but met with no foe, thank Thorar.

And then he was at the end of the Evendoom forge, and feeling the warning prickling and tingling in his limbs that meant the ward-wall was still strong. Barring his way, and forcing him to turn back and dare to duck out the open, crackling-with-leaking-power gates.

He did not waste his breath on a curse—a curse that might well alert someone or some*thing* in this accursed smoke to his presence—but felt his way along the unseen barrier as quietly as he could with a bundle of un-scabbarded tools, swords, and daggers in his hands.

Sudden fire flared ahead of him before he got to the corner where the invisible barrier would turn to run back toward his forging ground, parallel to the Rift.

Orivon halted, crouching low, trying to see what was causing the sudden blaze. Something dark was waving wildly in the heart of the ra-diance. Something—

Blackened gorkul arms, waving in wild agony, as their owner—who must have blundered into the wall—died in eerie silence. When the torso was crisped, the arms fell off and tumbled their separate ways.

Orivon's stomach heaved. He stayed motionless in the restored darkness of roiling, evil-smelling smoke, warsteel bundled in his arms, and waited. That gorkul had died because it had ended up off balance, falling through the very magic that seared and pierced it, impaled and helpless to win freedom. Had it just stumbled? Or had something forced it forward, into the wall?

He heard faint sounds from the smoke-shrouded darkness ahead, the other side of the wall. Hissing, gasping . . . no, someone was sobbing. Short, sharp, tremulous sobs, born of pain and not grief.

"May the Ice deliver me!" a voice moaned faintly. It sounded like a Nifl, but the speech was subtly different in accent from the Talonar Orivon was used to hearing. "Ah, but that hurt!"

A new glow kindled, and Orivon was glad he was crouching down. The radiance was faint and wan yellow in hue—and it was centered on two long-fingered black hands. Black fingers, black nails; Nifl, without doubt. Those hands were weaving air, cupping emptiness in smooth ca-resses that shaped and outlined a sphere. A sphere of nothingness that suddenly held tiny twinkling lights of its own, many of them, dancing and swirling as the Nifl muttered words over them. They changed hue, going a sudden vivid blue-white, then a rich amethyst.

As they changed once more, spinning back into gold, the Nifl raised them in one cupped hand and hurled them right at Orivon.

Jalandral Evendoom shook the last enemy Nifl body off his blade, Nifl blood smoking down its dark and slender length—hmm, smoking; that meant this foe had recently downed a powerful potion of some sort—and turned to call, "Well, Orsyl, that's the last of them! Shall we seek elsewhere for more sport? Hie ourselves back to the front, so to speak?"

Weary warblades stared back at him, but Orsyl made no reply.

"Orsyl?"

"Dead, Lord," one of the Nameless Nifl said reluctantly, stepping back to point with his spellblade. The faint glow from its tip showed Jalandral the features of a severed head lying among tangled limbs of the fallen. Though they were twisted in pain, eyes wide in disbelief, the heir of House Evendoom knew them. Orsyl would cry warnings no more.

He shrugged, smiled, and told the warblades around him—and how had they become so few?—"Olone greets us all, sooner or later. It's merely a matter of when, and how we please Her, before and at our passing. Or so they tell me."

"Or so they tell me," a veteran warblade echoed, sounding bitter.

Jalandral shrugged again and waved his sword at a passage that led to the front of the castle. "Come! This way is as good as any, and better than most: there's a guest chamber along it that should be crowded with decanters I haven't emptied yet! Care to join me?"

"Ah. Bribery," an aging Nifl—an Evendoom, one of Jalandral's half-forgotten uncles, Presker by name—growled. "I like that. First thing that's gone well since the worms came. Heh. If we drink enough, perhaps we'll all stop seeing worms!"

Jalandral wagged a finger. "One decanter each. I want you to fight like raudren, not stagger about as half-blind, helpless targets!"

Presker snorted. "You chose the wrong House to be born into, then. Right now, we're all targets here."

The hurled motes of the Nifl's spell struck the unseen wall and scattered right and left along it, racing wildly, their movements making the barrier glow; a light that grew and grew with astonishing speed. Spreading more slowly in their wake was a darkness, a flame-edged darkness where the magic of the barrier was melting, or burning away. So it was that increasing darkness shrouded Orivon and the Nifl spellrobe, as the golden glow of the revealed barrier retreated to right and left.

Still silent in his crouch, Orivon could hear the spellrobe stepping forward, loose stones clattering underfoot.

"Now," the Nifl murmured, "we'll see what treasures await! Surely—"

He spun sudden handfire, a palm-sized sphere of soft white light that he tossed into the air ahead of him to light his way.

And promptly showed him Orivon, crouching almost at his feet, staring silently up at him.

"Icefire!" the Nifl cursed, hands flashing into frantic patterns of casting, an incantation bursting from his lips that sounded cruel and vicious in every syllable.

Orivon did not want that incantation completed. He surged to his feet in a lunge that brought him hard into Nifl knees, toppling the spellrobe over him with a startled shout. Warsteel clattered loudly as he flung his bundle aside, snatching one blade out of bouncing hilts to whirl and drive it deep into the ribs of the struggling spellrobe.

The dark elf screamed, stiffening around the cold, cold sword through his side, clawing at it in a vain frenzy that ended in a sudden slump, gusty sigh, and slow sag forward to greet the stones.

"Where are you from?" Orivon asked, tugging his sword forth. The Nifl jerked under his hand, moaning as the blade came free, and gurgled, "A human! Slain by a Hairy One . . ."

"Where are you from?" Orivon snapped, digging his fingers deep into a robed shoulder and shaking the spellblade hard.

A face that spat blood lolled over to look at Orivon with watering, clouded eyes.

Eyes that went staring even as they met his.

Orivon shook the dying Nifl again, and the spellrobe slurred "Ouvahlor forever!" and turned his head away, in the last deliberate movement he'd ever make. Much blood had drooled out around those words, but they'd been clear enough.

So Ouvahlor was smiting Talonnorn, city invading city, in a battle blow strong enough to shatter the Eventowers. *Well,* now . . .

Whatever day or night this might be up in the Blindingbright, it might well be the day Orivon Firefist escaped from Talonnorn.

Now, if he could only slaughter a few Evendoom dark elves on his way . . .

Such as a certain whip-wielding Taerune.

They were crowding in at her now, the gorkul, their bulk and strength numbing her arm at every parry. Her blade bent more than once under the force of their sword slashes, and she'd been lucky to slice open the arm of the one who'd been hewing with an ax, so that it had fallen useless, leaving his neck open to her well-bloodied point. Axes she could *not* handle.

Alone she stood against them, fighting grimly against endless foes who'd come charging at her out of the dust-shrouded gloom at the rear of Alauntagar's Hall. It seemed a falling castle had failed to crush all of them.

The humans had fallen quickly. All males, they gaped at her curves—especially after she undid three buckles and let the front of her leathers fall to her belt, so they were staring at her bared and sweating self from her hips up. Astonished and distracted, they gave her an instant of hesitation here and a moment of gazing there—enough, time and again, to dart her blade in and slay them.

The gorkul cared much less for Nifl flesh, and pressed her, heavy and slow but too strong to fight snarl for snarl. So she danced, ducked, sprang this way and that like a scurrying cave-rat . . . and somehow stayed alive. More than once she'd ducked to pluck up a fallen blade and toss it into the face of a foe—following it with her own steel, thrusting hard. More than once she'd thought herself cornered and dead, with the tusks of some scarred gorkul or other snapping triumphantly in her face as his stinking strength bore her down—but she knew better than to try to keep hold of her blade when it meant certain death, and had more than once hurled herself away wildly, leaving a foe to overbalance and sprawl clumsily, only to dance back in and dagger him in an eye, pluck up her blade again, and tackle the next gorkul.

Yet there could only be one end to this battle. One increasingly weary Nifl-she against so many brutes. Sighing shudderingly at the end of one fray that had left her leathers sliced and too much of her blood streaming everywhere, Taerune found breath enough to shrug. They were driving her back anyway; why not seek a place she could better defend? A narrow door, a passage that bent sharply . . . such cramped quarters were found only in servants' passages. And among the huge adorned chambers of the ground floor main Eventowers, all around her, such service passages existed only around and about the grand guest chambers.

Taerune fled, grunting and derisively snorting gorkul lumbering after her, seeking the dim and deserted guest chambers at the heart of the ground floor. The largest, grandest rooms in the Eventowers were all around her now; surely she'd see *some* house guards.

Jalandral had been crying jaunty orders to scores of Evendoom war-blades back in the crowded armory hall. And most of those warblades were well-trained, experienced in battle, and eager to win—through battle-prowess, how else?—formal membership in the Evendooms rather than remaining expendable, ill-treated Nameless servants . . . they couldn't *all* be dead!

She saw her first guards. And her second, third, and swiftly more, beyond counting: bodies lying crumpled and still, here and there. Even-doom bodies.

Lots of Evendoom bodies. Even if Talonnorn survived this attack, Evendoom would be a handful of Nifl in a ruined castle, the haughty foremost House of the city no longer.

And the Niflghar of Talonnorn had a cruel way of reminding fallen ones that they were no longer mighty, and no longer deserved to be treated as such.

Not that any of that would matter in the slightest to a dead Taerune Evendoom.

She ran on, too many hulking gorkul close behind her.

The Rift and its fallen spell-wall well behind him, Orivon was out of the smoke now. He could see a lot of carnage, but not much fighting. Yon-der, a darkwings hung from the spire of one of the towers of the Even-doom castle, impaled and dripping. Far below it, at the base of that tower, lay several bodies; its rider was probably among them.

Over here, the stones were scorched by some fiery but spent spell that had left bones and ash in some spots, and heaped cooked corpses in others.

A few wounded Niflghar were crawling over distant stones, feebly seeking aid they'd probably never find. No one was standing in his path, waving a sword or anything else.

For which Orivon gave heartfelt thanks to Thorar, as he hurried over a canted stone floor he'd gazed at from afar more than once, toward the clefts he'd seen from the Eventowers.

He was almost at the cleft when someone came out onto one of the ledges high on the cavern wall. A Nifl, in robes, with two more behind him. There was no telling which of the more-than-a-handcount of tunnel mouths they'd come from—particularly as he was now lying as flat as he could, awkwardly cradling some very sharp steel. He was half on his back, so he could at least see anything that approached, and had a clear view of the long and intricate casting the spellrobes on the ledge were weaving.

It went on for what seemed a very long time, as Orivon watched and hoped by Thorar they hadn't seen him, or just didn't care about one lone human slave.

Then the trio let their arms fall and stood watching, obviously waiting for something to happen.

Their wait wasn't long. A high, eerie singing sound arose from the Eventowers—and then dropped into the thunderous roar of much of its rear, tower upon tower, slumping down into tumbling rubble.

Thorar's Thundering Fists! Orivon stared at the destruction, peering through billowing, rising dust into the depths of suddenly-torn-asunder chambers that had been deep in the center of the Eventowers moments ago. Half the castle, or more, had come crashing down in ruin, just like that!

A moment later, a bright bolt of sizzling magic sprang out of a surviving upper turret of the Eventowers to serve the ledge the same way, blasting it to flying rubble.

Yet all those towers lay as they'd fallen, and the dust was still rising. Orivon stayed where he was for quite a while, letting it billow and drift higher, before daring to roll stiffly over, find his feet and his bundle, and trudge carefully on.

His shoulders tingled, as if expecting to taste a bolt of magic at any moment—but then, if they did, he'd be too fried to feel it, would he not?

The cleft hadn't been far off when he'd cowered down, the curving, overhanging cavern wall already looming above him. Long, tumbled stones rose to meet it; Orivon picked his way cautiously between and over them, slowing as he saw sprawled, just-slain Nifl and fallen weapons ahead, and smelled blood and death.

There was a cave or tunnel mouth in the nearest cleft! Clambering cautiously up a rock slope slick with fresh blood—the little scuttling things the Nifl called "suripth," but slaves called "rock maggots," scattered and scurried at his passage—Orivon peered at the dark opening. Was that a door within it, standing open? Or . . .

Gaining the lip of the cleft, he peered cautiously this way and that, seeking a foe. There were Nifl bodies aplenty here, heaped in front of the cavern, most clad in familiar Talonnorn war-harness. Evendoom armor, and—Maulstryke!

"Yes," a voice that held a lot of cold malice and a little cool amusement agreed with him, from somewhere above. "Maulstryke, indeed. And here I thought you were their second wave of attack!"

Orivon sprang back, almost tumbling back down the slope, and had to claw wildly at rocks to keep from falling. Swords, a smallwork-hammer, and a pair of small tongs clattered out of his bundled breeches, as he craned his head to wildly look up and all around.

A spellrobe wearing the Black Flame of Evendoom on his breast was lounging at ease on his side with his head propped on one elbow, as if he were reclining on a guest-chamber couch with slaves attending to his every whim—but there was no couch under him, only empty air. He was smiling a cold smile, and waggling two of his fingers.

In response to those gestures, two gleaming swords were gliding forward through the air, points first, flying by themselves with no warblade gripping their hilts.

Ever so slowly, they were gliding at Orivon.

"Hairy One," the spellrobe said pleasantly, "I am the guardian of the Hidden Gate. Which is obviously far better known than any of us suspected. I don't know what you *thought* you were doing, slave, clambering up here naked with your arms full of obviously stolen swords and whatever else you could snatch, by the looks of it. But I do know what you *will* be doing: dying. Forthwith."

Smiling that cruel smile, he waved his hand dismissively—and the two swords swooped, points glittering.

Right at Orivon, who hadn't even time to curse. Darting his hands down into his bundle, he came up hefting a sword in his left hand, and his favorite smallwork-hammer in his right.

The spellrobe laughed.

"Huh!" Taerune Evendoom gasped, bringing her blade down hard on the gorkul's helm, and sending him staggering.

"Hah!" she added, driving her sword up between his legs from behind, and twisting to make sure it didn't get caught on anything. The gorkul obligingly added the shriek of crowing agony, as his own stumbling rush tore him off her steel and onto a pain-wracked face-first landing on the smooth, hard tiles of the passage floor.

Grinning wearily at the shocked faces of the rest of the gorkul, Taerune turned and ran, shouldering a wall painfully in her own tired, wounded reeling. She was through the narrow places—they hadn't been narrow enough—and out into a long passage that ran right through the Eventowers, from back to front.

There was a room a little way along here that had a down-stair opening off it, for servants to carry drinkables up from cellars below . . . yes, here it was, with its door standing open.

Thankfully Taerune ducked through the doorway—and found herself face-to-face with a House spellrobe gaping at her, the fire of a risen slaying-spell raging in his hand but his eyes fixed on—

Oh, yes, her bared breasts. Well, they'd obviously saved her from being blasted once more . . .

Taerune raised an eyebrow and snapped, "*Don't* hurl that magic at me, or your life will be forfeit. You can, however, use it on the gorkul right behind me."

It was taking the young spellrobe a long time to find something—anything—to say. Staring at her with similarly astonished delight, over the spellrobe's shoulder, were her brother Jalandral, her uncle Presker, an older spellrobe, and almost two handcounts of warblades, most of them growing broad grins. "By the Burning Talon," one of them muttered appreciatively.

"*Rampants,*" Taerune told them in disgust, ducking under the spellrobe's arm and into their midst. "Dral, Uncle Presker," she greeted her kin casually, buckling up her leathers.

"My, my," Presker observed, "Olone seems determined to provide us with *every* form of entertainment just now. Something to drink, my dear?" He proffered a decanter, one of many that stood ready to hand.

"Don't mind if I do," Taerune replied. "Trust you to think of your thirsts, in the midst of all this."

"Sister," Jalandral drawled, holding out a half-empty dish of fried amraunt in sauce; the smell was making stomachs rumble on all sides, "we merely sought some spellrobes to bolster our next assault—and found them here. And once some of these have been unstoppered . . . well, you *know* they won't keep!" He saluted her with an almost-empty decanter. "Nice, ah, *display,* by the way!"

Taerune sketched a parody of a coquettish Nifl-she's formal dance salute, and claimed a decanter of her own.

Which was about when the young spellrobe at the door cursed, his spell roared into full flame, there were several deep, gurgling screams, and the room was suddenly full of the unlovely reek of cooked gorkul.

"Olone *spew,* Alandalas!" Presker coughed. "*Must* you?"

Whatever reply Alandalas the spellrobe might have been planning to make was lost forever in his ragged scream, as the long-claws of two gorkul met in his shoulder, plucking him off his feet and thrusting him back into the room.

"Kiss of the Goddess, Taera!" her uncle snarled, as the warblades cursed and rushed forward, hurling decanters into the faces of the foe. "How many tuskers did you bring with you?"

"Enough, Uncle. More than enough. I've grown very tired of killing them—alone."

Then they were all too busy fighting for idle converse. The gorkuls overmatched the warblades greatly in size and strength, and were pushing into the room, forcing the Nifl back. Even a tusker dead with six swords meeting in him has size and weight, and when shoved from behind, as a shield, forces a way onward ere he falls. There had been three such shields already, and Evendoom now held less than a third of the small room, Jalandral cursing fervently because he had no room to ply his blades in the increasing crush.

Nigh the back wall, the senior spellrobe slapped Presker's arm and snapped, "Shield me! Lady Taerune?"

Taerune nodded and joined her uncle, bracing arms with him in front of the spellrobe—whose name she recalled now: Raereul—as he worked a swift spell.

And the room was suddenly full of lightning.

8

"Laughing, I Put My Sword into Him"

And that, I fear, is all he had time to say
For, laughing, I put my sword into him.
—from the traditional Nifl ballad,
"How the Old Lord Died"

Orivon parried one sword with his own—it wasn't much different than deflecting a blade tumbling at him after a Rift-burst—and smashed the other aside with his hammer, the flying blade ringing like a bell.

Then he was racing forward, charging over bodies and rolling loose stones alike. His only hope was to slay the spellrobe and trust that the flying blades died with the Nifl.

The spellrobe abruptly stopped laughing and scrambled from his indolent lounging up to his feet to begin fleeing in a scampering run on empty air.

Orivon sprang as high as he could, slashing with his sword.

Nifl grunted, all over the room, as the breath was snatched from them and every hair on their bodies sprang out as stiff as spikes. A decanter toppled and shattered loudly, in the singing instant of silence that followed—as lightnings raced everywhere, arcing from Evendoom wardshield to Evendoom wardshield, and gorkul shuddered helplessly, their eyes going dark, as the air filled with the smell of their roasting.

And then the lightnings died away, and gorkul all over the room sagged to the floor, their eye sockets trailing little plumes of smoke.

"Neatly done, Raereul," Jalandral drawled. "You could save the House much time in the kitchens during feasts . . . though somehow I believe it will take even House Oszrim a long time to grow truly fond of roasted gorkul."

Then the heir of House Evendoom frowned, peered, and pounced on a dead tusker, snatching aside a baldric. "Everyone—look you here!"

Beneath his pointing finger, seared deep into gorkul flesh, was a brand they all knew.

"The fair city of Ouvahlor," Presker murmured. Taerune saw where the brand was, strode to another gorkul who was sprawled the right way up, and tugged aside the broad leather of its baldric.

"This one was a slave of Ouvahlor, too," she announced calmly.

The warblades looked at the Evendooms and each other, frowning.

"They must really hate us," one offered.

Jalandral, Presker, and Taerune Evendoom all stared at him—and burst into mirthless laughter.

"We're winning!" Ravandarr Evendoom cried triumphantly, waving a gauntleted fist in the air as an enemy Nifl slid off his blade, slack-jawed and dead. "Winning!"

"If by 'winning' you mean we're beginning to hurl these motley attackers back out of what's left of our ruined home," his uncle Faunhorn—an Evendoom rampant so beautiful he outshone most of the young and daringly-gowned shes of the House—said bitingly, "then I suppose that, yes, we are winning. Myself, I'd call it something less."

Ravandarr flushed, his obsidian cheeks going pale, and turned away—only to find himself meeting the mocking gaze of another uncle: the dark and dashing Valarn, who in his youth had led the Hunt so valiantly that Olone's priestesses had healed him of disfiguring wounds thrice. "Your first real taste of battle, youngling?" He sneered. "Mind you don't wet yourself when they come back at us." He pointed down the passage with his blood-drenched sword at a distant chamber where someone was using a whip viciously, making many gorkul snarl.

Ravandarr blushed again, turning even paler. "Has . . . has anyone seen Taera?"

Valarn chuckled. "How touching. The little rampant wants his elder sister. Tell me, how often do you usually run to the loving warmth of her arms? And, ahem, her 'more loving' parts?"

Ravandarr raised his blade. "Do you *dare*–?"

"Obviously," the most hated Evendoom purred, giving Ravandarr a dark smile. "Of far more momentary import is what *you* dare, bladder-wet youngling: Do you dare to cross blades with Valarn Thrice-Blessed?"

"Valarn," Faunhorn snapped, "while we all stand in danger, such baitings are treason to this House."

Valarn smiled lazily. "Matters of honor are never treason, brother. And I believe you've just insulted mine. I'll deal with you after I end this pewling unworthy's babblings. Forever, of course."

Smile widening, he strolled toward Ravandarr, the legendary spell-blade in his hand winking as it shed more of its wet mask of fresh gorkul blood.

"Much as it pains me to speak seriously," Jalandral Evendoom told everyone in the room, "I must ask you to hear and heed these my orders: It just might turn out to be vital that the crones of our House learn that this attack comes from—or at least involves, and I intend to examine more dead if we get the chance—Ouvahlor. Which means some of us *must* survive, at least long enough to carry word to the crones. So, if we're reduced to two, both of you break off fighting and try to get to the crones' tower, avoiding frays if possible." Placing a hand on his chest, he added grandly, "I have spoken!"

"Hearken to the will of Evendoom," Presker intoned solemnly, bowing his head in the manner of a novice of Olone.

Jalandral's swift grin was echoed by most of the warblades. "Right," he added, "now let's charge out of here and find more foes to slay!"

Swords held close to chests, the Evendoom rampants—and one she—rushed out of the chamber.

Raereul ran nowhere, but knelt beside his wounded fellow spellrobe. "Alandalas?"

The sprawled Nifl moaned a little, and moved not at all. The elder spellrobe reached out a tentative hand, not knowing what to do. There was so much *blood* . . .

"Leave him." Presker's voice was firm, but not unkind. "He's beyond fighting, and House Evendoom has urgent, present need for your spells."

Raereul looked up at him, shocked, and then down again at the silent Alandalas. "But he'll die!"

Presker shrugged. "Olone gathers, as usual. Come, and bring a decanter. We'll probably all need it ere long."

The tip of Orivon's sword caught one of the spellrobe's boots, biting deep. The Evendoom wizard shouted in pain, hopping awkwardly in midair—and Orivon sprang high again, swinging his hammer with all his strength.

He felt the spellrobe's knee shatter under his blow, even before the Nifl's shriek of pain smote his ears.

Abruptly the wizard fell out of the air, that spell broken, his meeting with the ground swift and heavy. He mewed in agony as he bounced, shattered bones jarring—and then stopped his whimperings forever when a hard-swung hammer shattered his skull.

Orivon pounced on the dark elf, broke the spellrobe's neck with a quick twisting tug of a Nifl jaw, then rolled hastily away from the dying wizard.

He was in time to see the two flying blades that had been streaking at his back plunge down to the stones, to skirl and clatter to harmless stops.

"Beard of Thorar," he growled, "but that was . . . too near a thing, by half." He rubbed at his knuckles where he'd rolled on rough stone, found his feet, and looked around warily, murmuring, "Aye, too near by half."

No more foes seemed to be lurking in the cleft. Not behind rocks, not inside the tunnel mouth—where there was an old, massive metal door, standing open and with a plentiful supply of corpses to hand—nor in the air above.

So, should he just keep going, out into the Wild Dark right now, while Talonnorn was still in an uproar?

In the air above . . . the Hunt, or even raudren . . .

Orivon shuddered at that thought. No. Not yet. Not without something he could carry to drink and eat, and at least a Nifl cloak, perhaps a helm . . . as he stood right now, anyone could see from afar he was a human; that had to change.

But one chance, Orivon Firefist, so do it *right*.

With a sigh, he retrieved the tools and weapons he'd dropped and went along the narrowing cleft to its end, far from all the bodies, to hide them. He put on his breeches but added the sword to the cache, leaving himself just the smallwork-hammer, which could be carried thrust through a belt if he found one suitable among all the battle-fallen.

Orivon was surprised at how hard it was to heap stones over everything and make the heap look natural rather than a deliberate cairn; he was sweating before he was done.

Aside from rock maggots swarming over the bodies, gnawing busily, the cleft was as he'd left it. He found two baldrics that would serve him as belts, buckled them both on, and stripped the robe, with its Black Flame of Evendoom, off the wizard he'd killed—who considerately hadn't bled on it.

It tore a little down the back as Orivon pulled it over his head, but, well, would have to serve.

Feeling heavily covered indeed after so many years of living naked, Orivon went again to the tunnel mouth with the open door. It looked as if it led back to the Eventowers, to the heaped ruin that had recently been the oldest part of the great castle. So it might well now end in a collapse.

Yet the alternative was to clamber back up onto the bare stone of the cavern behind the Eventowers, and head for one of the many tunnel mouths yonder. A journey during which he could well be seen by half of Talonnorn, if half of Talonnorn were still alive.

Orivon sighed, hefted his hammer in his hand, and went through the door.

"Man," a weak Nifl voice husked, from just ahead. "Do you believe in Olone?"

"No," Orivon said shortly, backing away hastily and straining to see. Spell-given darksight took some moments to adjust to great differences in light, whereas darksight one was born with . . .

"I am far beyond hurting you," said the voice, and a faint glow kindled.

Frowning at it warily, Orivon soon saw that it was coming from the bracers on the forearms of a war-armored Nifl lying on his back in the tunnel, a black puddle of melted flesh where his legs should have been. The breast of the warblade's harness bore the Three Black Tears of Maulstryke.

One long-fingered Nifl hand was resting on the hilt of a long, slender sword. As Orivon watched, it closed feebly on that blade, tried twice to lift it, and on the third straining attempt waveringly brought the blade up—and threw it, back over the Nifl's own shoulder to bounce and clatter just beyond the warblade's head. "See? I am unarmed, man."

"There's a dagger at your belt."

"So there is," the weary voice agreed. "I had forgotten that. I doubt I can reach it any longer. Man, I mean you no harm. Olone comes to claim me; I am beyond all loyalties and causes."

"So why did you speak to me?" Orivon asked curiously. "Why not just lie still, and let this hairy human slave walk past and leave you in peace?"

"I'm lonely," the warblade sighed. "Never talked to anyone much, beyond curses and orders and grim grand denouncements of Evendoom. Are you in a hurry to get yourself killed, as I was?"

"I . . . Can I do anything for you?"

"Stay a bit. Talk. When I die, walk on. Perhaps we'll both see Olone. They say She's so beautiful—"

"It drives Nifl mad, or blind, or both, aye," Orivon growled, "unless they be Her anointed priestesses."

"You don't look like a priestess of Olone," the dying Nifl said, and chuckled—or tried to; it became a wet, blood-filled choking that faded into whimpering.

"An Evendoom spellrobe did this to me," he added suddenly. "Called himself the guardian of the Hidden Gate. Said he was a better spellrobe than Ondrar of Raskshaula."

"I killed him," Orivon said. "Just now."

"You *did*? Good. Ah, good! Man, you've done me a service."

"Good," Orivon growled. "So tell me: What is this Hidden Gate? Here, aye, but who made it? Where does it lead?"

"A back way into the Eventowers. The oldest and best of six or so hidden ways; it goes deep, down to the Evendoom dungeons. Lord Maulstryke called us together in haste, to go in this way and do as much damage as we could. This attack on Talonnorn was none of our doing, but Evendoom seemed hit the hardest, and in great disarray. A grand opportunity."

Orivon nodded. Everyone knew Evendoom and Maulstryke were hated rivals. "Does all Talonnorn know this tunnel is here?"

"Yes." The voice was noticeably weaker.

"Then why but one door and one spellrobe to keep other Houses out? Why not a tower? It's not as if the Evendooms don't like to build them!"

That made the Maulstryke warblade try to laugh again, a convulsive, alarming choking that almost finished him. "Well said, well said," he gasped at last. "No pureblood House Nifl will build such, here, or bide in such a turret if you built it for them. The magics here in these clefts make their bracers burn, and would force them away."

"Their bracers? That turn aside shards and forge cinders?"

"Yes, and arrows, flung stones, and the like; those bracers."

"What magics?" Orivon looked hastily about. "I feel nothing."

"Magics are down, now. We broke them to get here." The Nifl's voice had faded to almost a whisper.

"What magics?"

"Ever wonder why dung-worms don't thrust their snouts into Talonnorn every Turning? And the packs of wild darkwings and raudren—and all the other beasts that maraud out there in the Dark—don't come raiding through our streets?"

"There are wards."

"Yes, wards. Well, the biggest ward in all Talonnorn is—or was—anchored right here. The beast-ward, that keeps all such at bay, unless or until they start wearing those bracers or carrying in their jaws Talonar corpses who wear them."

"So you broke this ward, and let the dung-worms in?"

"No, they were almost as much an unwelcome surprise to us as they were to the Evendooms. Someone else sent them in—and that took powerful spells, to get them past the beast-ward. The beast-ward circles the city, and turns. Always." The Nifl's whisper was becoming slurred, and Orivon hurried forward to hear better. "Very slowly, but it's always moving. Something—I'm no spellrobe, mind—to do with denying some sort of spell-attacks on it. It turns, and once around Talonnorn is a Turning, see? To you—d'you remember the Blindingbright, man?—that'd be about a month. I think."

"*You've been to the Blindingbright?*" Orivon shouted. "You know the way there?"

"I've been," came the weak whisper, sounding apologetic, "but I know not the way. They cast spells on warblades to keep us from knowing the passages through the Wild Dark, and lead us when we go. So we can't so easily go rogue and join the Ravagers, see?"

"So *spellrobes* know the way?"

"I . . . guess," the warblade said very slowly, his whisper wet and rattling.

"Who knows the way?" Orivon snapped. "Are there maps?"

There was no reply.

"Damn you," Orivon snarled, bending close to pluck at the breast of the Maulstryke armor. "*Live!* Live long enough to *tell me!*"

The Niflghar turned his head, gave Orivon a beautiful, welcoming smile, and gasped, "Olone . . ."

Then he went still. Orivon shook him, shouting, "Where are the maps? Who knows the way?"

Smiling happily, the dead Maulstryke stared at nothing. Orivon threw back his head and roared out wordless frustration.

And then he let go of the dead Nifl and said gently, "My thanks, warblade. May Olone find you worthy."

"Much as I dislike hampering the fun of *any* of my kin," a deep, familiar voice came from behind Ravandarr, making him stiffen, "this particular pewling unworthy happens to be my son. And Secondblood heir of this House. Harm him in any way, Valarn, or by your neglect or deliberate action cause him to be harmed by another, and I shall personally remove your organs—one at a time, and slicing them *very* thinly—and fry them in your own blood, and feed them to you. Several of the crones of our House have offered to provide recipes and assist in the cooking, so long as they get a taste, too. No less than three of our spellrobes have offered their services to keep you alive and fully conscious throughout, so you'll miss none of the fun—or the pain."

"L-Lord Evendoom," Valarn said stiffly, "I was but jesting."

"Ah, good, good. Valarn, I'd hate to think you were doing anything else with your carelessly chosen words to my son and to our honored kin Faunhorn. It is my personal opinion that you become steadily more unloved, and that is both regrettable and dangerous. Oh, and one more thing."

Lord Evendoom fell silent, until Valarn was forced to ask, "Yes, Lord?"

"There's a battle unfolding. *Try* not to waste my time."

And with a flash of the ring that whisked him from place to place in an instant, the Lord of House Evendoom was gone as abruptly as he'd arrived.

It was almost as if he could listen to words from afar.

. . .

"By the Burning Talon, *die,* Ouvahlan scum!" Jalandral Evendoom shouted jovially, driving the sword in his left hand through a Nifl throat and slashing a gorkul across the eyes with the blade in his right hand.

They'd reached the Long Hall before meeting with any of the foe— but the Long Hall could hold hundreds, and right now those hundreds happened to be warblades and fighting slaves of Ouvahlor, conferring and gathering loot and laughing over their kills.

Until Raereul's best spell lashed through them, and sent them howl- ing up the stairs to the handful of armed Evendooms.

Raereul's second magic slew only a handful, and it was his last battle-spell.

"Well," Presker said, kicking a gorkul in the face and driving his sword over its shoulder right down the snarling gullet of the one behind, "we're just going to have to kill the rest of them the old way."

"Uncle, stop killing *my* gorkul," Taerune told him happily, plying her warsteel at his elbow.

"Pray pardon, Lady Evendoom," he replied in formal tones. "I re- gret to inform you that my regrettably aged eyesight has caused me to mistake one of yours for one of mine. Again."

"No doubt you tell all the shes something similar," she laughed, causing the warblade on her other side to chuckle before an Ouvahlan long-claws thrust through his throat, and he died.

"So a Turning is about a month, perhaps," Orivon muttered, turning over corpses. "Would you happen to remember just how many Turn- ings you've had Orivon Firefist as your slave, Lady Taerune Even- doom? Aye? Well, speak up!"

He shook a dead Evendoom warblade by the shoulder until slack jaws in a lolling head clacked and clattered—but still it wouldn't meet his gaze or answer him.

Grinning wryly, Orivon let it fall and went on searching.

He'd found four corpses—no, five, now—he was certain were of House Evendoom. He even recognized one face: a guard who'd often accompanied Taerune of the Whips.

From them he took the three best pairs of bracers, strapping them to his upper arms, his forearms, and his calves, hoping their magics wouldn't react with each other and harm him in some strange way. He wasn't go- ing to risk Maulstryke bracers in the Eventowers, in case the strange magic raised alarms—or even unleashed waiting spells left ready by spell-robes. He knew just enough about magic to know that he knew nothing that could be trusted, noth—

A shadow fell over him.

Orivon looked up, froze—and then sprinted for the tunnel mouth faster than he'd ever run anywhere in his life, one half-buckled bracer flapping.

Overhead, a raudren was gliding.

Like a huge black living arrowhead, it looked—a sleek, leathery arrowhead as wide as the Rift itself. Peering up from the tunnel mouth that was thankfully too small for it to enter, Orivon saw its many-fanged under-slung jaw, wide enough for about five Orivons, several fanglike claws set in trios along the edges of its body, two rows of liquid black eyes that were gazing back at him knowingly, and a long, sinuous tail studded with razorlike projecting bones. Lots of them, lashing back and forth with slow, sinuous lassitude as it drifted through the air. Hunting.

There was another raudren behind it, and another. Large and silent and relentless, hunters of Talonnorn's foes and fugitives, and so guardians of the city. Unleashed, they'd hunt at will until called back with horns—but each raudren would return only after it had eaten.

A Talonar had become desperate enough to release them, a menace to Niflghar and Ouvahlan alike. Probably they were intended to harry the invaders well out into the Wild Dark—but they were proferring a starkly simple fate to Orivon Firefist: If he tried to escape now, he'd be devoured, swiftly and messily. Raudren liked to tear their prey apart in midair, wheeling and darting—in pairs and trios, or more—to bite off pieces as the bleeding meat fell.

Bleeding meat. Orivon's smile held no mirth at all as he stepped through the door again and started down the tunnel. Either he was going to find the way blocked by fallen rock, and try to hide here or somewhere in the clefts until the raudren were called back in—or he was going to the Eventowers dungeons, and up through them to back storage rooms he dimly recalled, and thence by the servants' stairs to the only relatively safe place in all the Eventowers he knew to hide, *if* spellrobes were finished hurling down towers: the attics of the older part of the castle. There to await the best time to take his plunge out into the Wild Dark—unless he could make his way unseen amid the chaos, with so many Evendooms dead, to one of the Eventowers libraries, and somehow find a map of the

Wild Dark. Preferably one with a bold and clear marking on it that read "Ashenuld."

"The one with the eye patch is *mine*," Taerune said grimly, hacking aside a squalling human with a greataxe. "Dral, *get that door open!*"

They were now only seven, and there were still hundreds of Ouvahlans. Wherefore they'd retreated to a corner of the Long Hall where an ornate pillar held a secret door all of the Evendooms had used countless times before to duck out of boring feasts or slip into meetings without having to endure the tedious greetings of disliked guests or Talonar officials. Unfortunately, it seemed Jalandral was having great difficulty in getting the door open.

Of course, the dozens of blades he was acrobatically fending off while trying to do so might have had some part in that difficulty. Or perhaps it was the scarred elder Ouvahlan Nifl with the eye patch who seemed to know exactly what they were trying to do, and was ordering his forces to their deaths with a ruthless precision of attacks designed to keep Jalandral Evendoom from ever accomplishing anything.

"No," Presker gasped, between furious rounds of parrying, "I've never seen him before. He's not some former slave or servant, as far as I know. Perhaps he came into the Hall in the past posing as some trade envoy or other. It's one of the few rooms we've always let them see. *Ha!*" His sudden thrust caught a human by surprise—and in the crotch. Trying to scream and weep at the same time, the man doubled over and fell, clutching himself. His fellow Ouvahlans trampled him and finally kicked him aside.

Taerune threw herself at the ankles of the pair of clumsily thrusting humans in front of her, bowling them over. She came up lunging, sharply putting her blade right into a hurrying Nifl behind the humans: her quarry with the eye patch.

He screamed and hopped his way off her blade, howling, his leg collapsing under him the moment it touched the floor. He fell sideways with a speed that took half a dozen Ouvahlan Nifl by surprise, as he came crashing into them and they all went sprawling. The warblade beside Taerune sprang forward to thrust at throats and mouths and faces, despite her snarled, "*No*, you fool! *Don't break our line!*"

She was still shouting that when four Ouvahlan blades met in the warblade's ribs. He stiffened, spitting blood, reeled—and fell dying atop the Ouvahlans he'd just killed. Leaving Taerune to face both the two gorkul pressing forward at her from behind the humans she'd felled—and those four Ouvahlan warblades now whirling to strike at her side.

Blood pounding in her ears, Taerune suddenly finds the whirling moments of bloody battle slowing to a crawl, with her own heartbeat thundering in her ears . . .

She strikes aside the first Ouvahlan blade, managing to steer the first gorkul's long-claw with it, into a tangle with the second seeking sword. Which leaves her unprotected against the other two blades—and the second gorkul, who is swinging a greataxe with savage disregard for his fellow Ouvahlans in such a cramped affray.

Taerune takes the only way left to her, hurling herself into a rush to embrace that gorkul, whose eyes have time to start widening in amazement as she thrusts her breast forward into the path of his onrushing ax—and then goes to her knees at the last possible instant, so his rising knee almost shatters her face, brushing her cheek instead, and the ax sweeps over her, slicing off a lock of her hair ere it slams into the third blade with force enough to break it.

And it does break, with a shriek of its own that no one will begin to hear until Taerune is shrieking, too.

The last Ouvahlan Nifl is smiling ruthlessly as he twists his way through this rushing press of combatants, every bit as adroitly as Taerune has ever done in battle. He manages to avoid both the lumbering gorkuls and the blades of his fellows, and yet find room enough through it all to thrust his blade at her spine.

Desperately Taerune twists around, seeking to strike his blade away with her left arm no matter how badly she gets cut, hoping the now-toppling gorkul will both knock his blade down and shield her in its helpless, roaring toppling of tusked flesh.

The gorkul obliges, so the blade meant for her vitals instead cuts deep into Taerune's arm, driven in and in by the entire weight of the gorkul falling past, shearing muscle and sinew and bone alike, in a pain so coldly intense that the breath is forced out of her, in a shriek like a sword point slicing down a metal shield.

She's never felt such pain before, and wonders if this is the end, so swift and sudden, and death has reached out for her before Lady Taerune Evendoom has managed to make any of her big dreams real . . .

9

The Gloating of the Crone

There is no more cruel sound, I own,
Than the slow gloating of the crone.
—from the traditional Nifl ballad,
"Houses, Houses Over Us"

C ome," Exalted Daughter of the Ice Semmeira said curtly, dragging Lolonmae to her feet with hands on her shoulders that were
like talons. "The Revered Mother has need of you."

"What?" the novice gasped, wide-eyed, as grim-faced priestesses
half-marched, half-dragged her down passages. "What *now*?"

"I was hoping," Semmeira said icily, "that *you* could tell *me*, Little Favored One. Behold!"

The Revered Mother stood unmoving before a watch-whorl that
was as large as she was, staring fixedly into its depths. Out of which pro-
truded a thick black leathery arc of flesh that rippled and shuddered and
gave every evidence of being alive.

Alive, angry, and trying to thrust its way forward, through a whorl
that was too small for it. The cruel fangs of a vast maw beneath it could
just be seen through the whorl's radiance, as could the glistening half
spheres of eyes atop its . . . snout, if that's what it was.

"W-what is it?" Lolonmae gasped.

"They're called raudren. Flying predators that some Olone-loving
Nifl are foolish enough to cage—and uncage!—as defenders of their cities.
The Revered Mother called this one here, or it sought her out, we know

not which. She's been like that—and *it's* been like that—for quite some time now."

Lolonmae blinked at her, on the trembling edge of weeping. "But I am the least among us! You *know* that! What has any of this to do with *me*?"

"Before she . . . went like that," Semmeira said grimly, "the Revered Mother called the raudren by name: Lolonmae."

The novice found herself encircled by accusingly glaring priestesses.

"Now, Lolonmae," the Exalted Daughter of the Ice asked her softly, "is there anything you should be telling us?"

The attics were far more cluttered and dusty than Orivon remembered them. He'd managed to find a scrap of cloth and an old, long-forgotten, dripping tap to wet it at, and tie the whole thing around his face to quell his sneezes—and by Thorar, he was glad he had.

He had no idea how many human centuries the Evendooms had been living in this castle, but they'd evidently been here a long, long time. Time that had been spent replacing the furniture often—without ever getting rid of any of it, by the looks of these crammed, rafter-heaped rooms. Up to the attics, always, went everything. To stay. Even the cave-rats had moved in, and fought their battles with each other and anything that might taste good to gnaw on, for generation upon generation.

Through their dusty corpses and heaped excrement Orivon Firefist trudged, as quietly as possible, ducking between shelves that held a bewildering variety of seating, and shelves that held carved wooden coffers of all appearances and sizes—though, like all the Nifl coffers out in the rooms of the Eventowers right now, they all had rounded-off corners. He'd heard spells had been cast up here that prevented any flame from igniting, but he could see no glows and feel no tinglings.

This winding way, and now this one . . . no, a dead end, heaped with—what *were* those, anyway? No, later, if ever in his life he had idle time to come back here and waste it sorting out Evendoom leavings—ha!

Orivon was searching for a room he'd seen only once, and fleetingly. Wherefore he barely remembered it: a sumptuously furnished meeting chamber, its floor covered in long-furred beast hides; its center occupied by a grand oval wooden table around which stood many, many tall, spire-backed chairs; and its walls sheathed in wood panels that were the doors of long rows of closets that *surely* would hold a cloak or three for him to snatch, for his journey out in the Dark.

It had been in one of the larger, central towers, this chamber, and indeed it was only in that core of sixteen or so largest, oldest towers of the Evendoom castle that the attics were joined, to form the vast and cluttered labyrinth he was wandering through. So it was somewhere here, and close, though finding it might take seemingly forever—unless some fool of a crone had taken it into her head to change things. Even then, surely, he'd find evidence of rebuilding and recent shiftings.

Just so long as the bracers he was wearing didn't awaken any ancient slaying magics that had been left to greet any warblade poking around where he shouldn't be . . .

That chamber had been important, once. A place of secrets and important discussions, where crones met with the Lord of the House, and . . . yes, there *had* been a hole in the center of the table where a watch-whorl could be cast, and everyone around the table could peer into it. So, the place, too, from which the Evendooms had spied upon Talonnorn around them, and the wider Dark beyond that. Perhaps even Ashenuld, and other villages in the Blindingbright, choosing where to raid and what to seize.

A place from which the Evendoom crones could watch a fleeing slave wander in the Dark, and direct the Hunt and raudren and warblade patrols just where to find him.

Did he dare take a cloak, or anything beyond his own forgings—that had never left the Rift, that he *knew* no spellrobe had handled and enspelled? Could they trace everything else?

Could they trace *him*? He wore no collar, and knew of nothing they'd thrust into him, under his skin . . . but he'd been branded and enspelled many a time, and the crones alone knew what they'd done to him. Or was he but one slave among many, scarce worth such trouble despite his forge skills? Were slaves beneath all but passing notice?

He turned another corner, nose prickling despite the wet mask he wore, picked his way carefully over something fallen and rotten that had tumbled out of coffers that had collapsed, and spread his hands in a shrug.

No matter what fancies he spun, and traps he thought up, there wasn't a single Thorar-damned thing he could *do* about any of this. Just stay alive from moment to moment, and do whatever it took to get away—and stay away. Whatever it took, from hiding up here for Turning after Turning, to pleasuring Lord Evendoom himself.

That thought made him snort in dismissive mirth—which was when he turned a corner and found what he'd been seeking.

He saw no dust and clutter from where he stood beside a cracked, life-sized statue of a Nifl that was missing its hands but had acquired a stray collection of old, moldering war-harness, draped and hung over the sculpted stone, to a grand door that was outlined by a faint glow. On the other side of that door, if scant traces of memory served him right, was a landing, the top of a stair leading down into the rest of the castle.

And just over *here,* there should be a similarly grand door, and behind it was the meeting chamber.

Orivon approached it cautiously, looking all around for guards or watching Nifl or stirring magics. Nothing, and the silence seemed empty, not tense or watchful. He was alone.

So he shrugged, strode up to the door as if he belonged in this place, closed his hand on its pull-ring, and drew it open.

Still but not stale air greeted him. The great table with its chairs stood just as he'd remembered, neat and clean and quite free of dust.

So the room was still used. He should move quickly.

Leaving the door just ajar behind him—no bolts of lightning, no sudden flare of spells or Nifl shouts—Orivon strode to the nearest panel on the left, and pulled it open.

The expected closet greeted him, but it was empty. As was the next . . . and the next. The fourth held cloaks, hung on shaped frames that descended from a metal bar, but when he held them out on an angle to peer at them, he could see at a glance that they were much too small: ornate half-cloaks, with feminine trim and adornment; garb for young Nifl-shes. Orivon closed that panel and patiently opened the next, and very soon the next after that.

More cloaks, and they were larger. Yet not large enough; they'd cover his shoulders like an old Ashenuld woman's shawl, if he found nothing better, but they'd hardly *hide* anything. Well, this was still better than rummaging through all those coffers in the dim dust of the attics behind him, hoping to find something suitable.

The next closet was a surprise. It ran along beyond the next several panels, a longer—and deeper, too, with a tilted mirror-glass, table, and stool crowded into it—space that held a long bar hung with many cloaks. And caps, and *hoods*!

Well, now! Orivon held one up, spreading his fingers inside it to ape the size of a Nifl head, so as to get a good look at it. Eyeholes, a pointed chin, feminine trim again . . . but it certainly offered concealment. Yet did it have some ritual meaning or represent some ancient fashion or now-shunned custom, so that wearing it would draw more attention than the sight of his own human head?

Well, he'd just have to chance it, assuming he ever found one large enough, in all this, for his head. Nifl were surprisingly small, sleek, fine-boned things when they weren't standing tall and grand and sneering in front of you, with whips in their hands! Orivon set the hood he'd plucked up carefully back where he'd found it, and selected another. Yes, this was bigger, perhaps big enough—

Voices!

Yes! Nifl voices, very near! *Thorar preserve!* Orivon sprang into the closet, pulled the panel to—it had little finger-holds on the insides, thank Thorar—and pulled a huge handful of cloaks down off the bar, sitting down and burying himself in a slumped heap of them. He had just time to check that his boots were covered, drape the last few cloaks over his head, and settle into stillness before he heard a cruel, gloating female Nifl voice say clearly, "Galaerra, cast the whorl!"

"Yes, Highest," a softer voice—another she—replied eagerly.

"Baraule," the first voice commanded, "sit you there, on one side of Taerune. Klaerra, take the seat on the other side of her."

"This is my seat, Mah—"

"It *was* your seat, Klaerra, in Orlarra's time, but *I* am eldest of House Evendoom now, and it is my will that you shall sit there, where I've directed. I believe you are familiar with the extent of my authority."

"Yes," came a reply that was as icy as it was soft, "I believe I am."

Then radiance kindled in front of Orivon's cloak-veiled eyes, and he froze, scarcely daring to breathe. The glow took on the slowly turning shape of a watch-whorl! *Thorar!* The swift fury of his cloak work must have whisked the door panel ajar again, leaving him visible to everyone in the room! For if he could see out, albeit in a narrow column, it followed that the Nifl crones could see in!

"Eldest Maharla, the whorl is ready," the soft voice of Galaerra said suddenly.

"Good. Show us all Talonnorn, as if from the highest spire of the Eventowers."

After a moment, there were gasps and mutterings.

"Not a pretty sight, is it?" Maharla said coldly, her tone making it clear she wasn't seeking any answers. "Our city has been battered—no

House damaged as much as ours, but no House escaping loss, save perhaps Maulstryke. Notice—thank you for anticipating me, Galaerra, *this
once*—how little damage Maulgard has sustained. How few fallen lie before its gates, and in its grounds. Suspicious, is it not?"

The eldest crone paused, but there was silence around the table. If
she'd expected open agreement, she was now experiencing disappoint-
ment. Not that there was any hint of such in her voice, when she went on.

"Our rampants report much evidence of this attack coming from the
city of Ouvahlor, and so it did. Yet it is unlikely a city of blasphemers,
their faces turned so far from the favor of Olone, could accomplish so
much against strong, valiant Talonnorn without aid. I suspect treachery
on the part of *unscathed* House Maulstryke—and I want all Talonnorn to
suspect as much, as swiftly as possible, without any open accusation being made by anyone of Evendoom. See to it, sisters."

There was a faint stirring or rustling sound, as if those around the
table had all nodded or made some sort of gesture of assent, though
Orivon could see nothing.

"Yet I need you to do more. I need you to watch and listen—again,
without any overbold spying that takes any of you into places you would
not normally go, or deeds you would not normally undertake—for any
shred or hint of proof of Maulstryke involvement in this assault. Anything of this sort—*anything,* no matter how slight; a look, a tone of voice, a
smile—bring to me without delay."

Again the brief rustling.

"I need you to do even more than this. Our warblades were shockingly unprepared for what has just occurred. Our Hunt not flying the
moment the deepserpents reared up, our spellrobes not destroying them
before they could shatter our gates—and our servants and slaves not
hurled against the foe before that foe was inside our very walls! More
than this: Our rampants fought as *they* saw fit, seemingly without command. Our battlelords were absent from the fray. These lapses are not
only unacceptable, they are treasonous—and I personally can find no explanation for all of them occurring, and with such sweeping strength of
incompetence, other than our own Lord Evendoom intended matters to
be so."

There was a reaction to that, sharply indrawn breaths from many
places around the table. The eldest crone fell silent for a breath or two,
but no one spoke.

"Note that I do not accuse Lord Evendoom of being in league with

Maulstryke or Ouvahlor—yet." Maharla's voice was triumphant. "I have not the evidence—yet. You shall aid me in getting that evidence, or by your scrutiny ensuring that unprepared incompetence or laxity in defensive preparations shall never prevail in House Evendoom again. It seems our rampants are incapable of forethought, to say the very least, so we shall henceforth provide it for them. I shall hold all of you responsible for doing so. Lord Evendoom holds his title—and life—at our pleasure, of course. I have reminded him of that, and am personally displeased at his attitude. All of you, sisters, should beware attempts on his part to cast blame on us, and to seek to find traitors to Evendoom around *this* table."

There were murmurs, and even invocations to the Goddess, from the assembled crones. Maharla let them voice their anger until they fell silent of their own accord.

"However," she continued, "I'll not relieve Lord Evendoom of either title or life out of mere pleasure or spite, or to place blame that in some measure we all share. Not while we have a heir—and a Secondblood—who are so woefully unready to serve our House as befits a true Lord of Evendoom."

There was a brief, wordless murmur of disgusted agreement.

"It is my personal opinion that our Jalandral and Ravandarr will never be suitable for the lordship of this House. The one mocks all authority, and the other is weaker than the most broken-spirited of our slaves. So I have yet another task for you, sisters: Both of them must breed, several times and as swiftly as possible, to the *right* shes, of our selection. What we cannot make one way, we must create by another."

Another wordless murmur, ere Maharla continued, "I commend you for keeping silent, Taerune. Olone desires you to continue to do so." She raised her voice and said more briskly, "Galaerra, show us the Immur!"

The watch-whorl flickered, becoming darker, and the eldest crone said coldly, "Behold the Dark that lies between us and Ouvahlor. The raudren of Talonnorn are hunting at will, as you can see, and have devoured many of the fleeing forces of Ouvahlor—though it must be said that their meals are primarily slaves, gorkul and human, nigh mindless meat that Ouvahlor can replace in their Blindingbright raids of a few Turnings. We do not know, just now, who unleashed the raudren; I have heard both House Oszrim and House Oondaunt, but I stress that these are but speculations. I want the truth, and that is something else, sisters, that you shall uncover for me. Yes, I am going to be a very *wanting* Eldest of Evendoom."

Though she'd put mirth into that sentence, and now paused for laughter, only Galaerra—weakly and hesitantly, soon stumbling to silence—obliged.

Orivon smiled; it seemed as if one want this Maharla bitch was going to have was enthusiasm from her fellow crones, a little willing loyalty.

Maharla, it seemed, was not loved.

"Yet all of these tasks I set you, sisters," she said more coldly, obviously displeased by the reaction around the table, "pale before the greatest task we must all undertake. Those who attacked us used spells that were more powerful than ours. Both beasts like the dung-worms and near-beasts like the gorkul, as well as warblades in plenty, appeared *within* our wards in many places, somehow—and that 'somehow' can only be magical—bypassing our wards and alarm-spells and guardian spells. We must control our spellrobes very tightly, from this moment henceforth. We must know at all times their aims and loyalty to us, and their skills and what spells they have ready. We must spur them—with whips and the Scourge of Olone, if need be—to craft new and more powerful spells, so that no invader will ever be able to just 'appear' within our halls—inside the Eventowers, sisters!—again!"

Maharla was almost shouting now but suddenly her voice became calm, a silken calm that made Orivon's skin crawl, as she almost purred, "It is customary—as most of you are well aware—that we all speak at length, openly and freely, around this table. Yet this once, with a foe still at our gates and open butchery still adorning our halls, I ask—*command,* if you must have it so—you all to keep silent. I shall be calling each and every one of you to private audience with me—soon—to discuss these tasks I have identified, and other matters. This converse is now at an end, but I ask you all to remain for a *very* short time, now, as I attend to a matter that my predecessor neglected, against my advice, for far too long." Her voice sharpened. "Stand, Taerune of Evendoom."

Something moved, in the narrow column of view Orivon could see, and he dared to ever-so-gently pull the cloak over his face taut, so as to peer better through its weave.

What he saw was his longtime tormentor swaying up out of her seat, her obsidian face pale and set with pain—and no wonder! Her left arm was missing, just below the elbow, and where it had been severed, her leathers were melted and burned.

"You fought for our House as valiantly as any warblade," Maharla announced. "*More* valiantly than some, I'm told. When your arm was lost in the fray, you took it upon yourself to order a spellrobe of our House—Raereul, now our most senior and accomplished spellrobe—to sear your . . . stump so that you might continue to fight for Evendoom. When Raereul quite rightly hesitated to obey an order that came not from a battlelord or an anointed sister of this House, the heir of our House, the ever-irresponsible Jalandral, gave the spellrobe the same order. Thereby wasting a spell that could have slain more of the foe, and prolonging a life that had displeased Olone long enough."

"What?" Taerune's cry held more incredulity than fury—and more fury than fear.

"He will receive appropriate punishment soon," Maharla continued, as if Taerune had not spoken. "You remain, for us to deal with here and now."

"Are you seriously suggesting, before all the sisters around this table, that members of the pureblood Evendoom are no longer to be healed? So that they may continue to serve the family and Olone? Even if I am deemed unsuitable to become an anointed sister, I *am* breeding stock, to put matters bluntly, and therefore something valuable to the family, not to be disposed of on the whim of one crone, however exalted her rank! Family assets belong to the entire family, and the Rule—about which I should *not* have to remind you, Eldest!—is quite explicit: All of the crones of our House have a vote in how assets are used, and disposed of!"

"I am well aware of the Rule, presumptuous youngling," Maharla said, sneering, "but it seems *you* need to be reminded of something we all learn at an even younger age: that your, ah, *condition* is an affront to Olone, a stain upon this House that grows, bringing divine displeasure upon us all with every breath you take while it continues!"

"So heal me, as is my right as a pureblood Evendoom, and *your obligation,* Eldest, unless you renounce your office and authority here and now, to so serve the third-blood heir of Evendoom!"

"I regret," Maharla purred, the gloating tone of her voice making it clear she felt no regret at all, "to inform you, all-knowing little she, that all the healing magic of our House has been used, and our most powerful beneficial spells expended, just to keep the brains of the slain Telmoun, mightiest spellblade of our House, and Saharulae, Anointed of Olone, alive as they were taken from their butchered bodies and magically preserved in our precious healing font of the Goddess. Just now, there's no magic left to heal you. As Olone wills."

"That's your excuse, Maharla?" Taerune stood defiant, eyes glittering.

"Your way of getting rid of one of the two purebloods who's stood up to you, all these years? I suppose this 'appropriate punishment' you plan for Jalandral will be your way of ridding yourself of the other!"

"*Be still,* maimed and unworthy affront to Olone!"

"Oh, do you take that authority for yourself, too?" Taerune's voice was as strong and sharp as that of the Eldest.

Orivon shook his head in admiration, despite himself. So his Whipping Bitch stood proud under the lash after all, taking like harshness to what she'd visited on him!

"Sisters," Taerune snapped, "be wary of this viper in your midst! If you let her speak for the anointed priestesses, too, and decide what Holy Olone likes and does not like, she will become a tyrant indeed—and doom all of you, one after another, finding fault and treachery as you have heard her do here and now, around this table, until she and she alone is House Evendoom. Then the doom of our family *will* be complete!"

Maharla strolled around the outside of the table, and came to a stop right beside Orivon's closet, folding her hands as if she were a pious priestess. "You are not heard here, any longer," she intoned formally. "You no longer have a name. You are not of Evendoom!"

"I am *Taerune Evendoom.* My heritage, self-appointed tyrant, is not something *you* can take away from me!"

Maharla's smile was merciless. "Before we gathered here, I met with Chasra, Anointed of Olone, who admitted her treason to the Goddess and to this House, in failing to forewarn us of the attack. She accepted responsibility for what befell Saharulae, and accordingly threw herself upon the altar of the Goddess, naming, as she burned, myself as the Ruling Hand of Olone in Talonnorn. In the name of Olone, defiant youngling, I cast you out, and strip your name from you!"

"I see, Maharla. I see all too well," Taerune said softly. "Evendoom *is* doomed. So be it. So you have murdered Chasra, and now, I suppose, you'll murder me. In front of all the crones of our House, even after all the years I've served House Evendoom so well."

"No," was the cold response, as Maharla raised a hand, letting her sleeve drop. Everyone saw the scepter of Olone sheathed there—in the instant before it fired its bolt, and Taerune reeled and fell back into her seat.

A glowing chain of magic promptly encircled her throat, drawing her tight against the spired back of her chair, pinioned in place.

"It is because of your years of service, Maimed One," the Eldest of

Evendoom told her coldly, "that you've been allowed to live as one of us for so long, as grotesquerie has overtaken your arms—you bulge like a slave, Taerune!—and you fell farther and farther away from the favor of Olone. You were only a Turning away from being thrown out of Talonnorn even before these unfortunate events."

Maharla turned and strolled back to her own seat. "It is because of your years of service," she added in tones of gentle sorrow that fooled no one in the room, "that we've decided to grant you the mercy of taking your own life—rather than butchering you publicly, to the greater glory of House Evendoom."

Reaching her place at the table, she added with a smile, "You know the Rule. And you are strong, and serve House Evendoom so well: You know what is right. And will do it."

She turned her head and nodded to Galaerra, who rose and cast a knife onto the table in front of the trapped Taerune.

Then, her smile triumphant, Maharla raised both hands with a flourish, in the "I command you to rise" gesture used only by Ruling Hands of Olone.

The crones rose as one, Baraule and Klaerra both turning to face Taerune and drawing knives from their belts.

Maharla strode out, and all of the others followed, Baraule and Klaerra last of all, under Galaerra's watchful eye. Taerune could have struggled to turn her head and look at them, but did not, staring instead across the room, at nothing at all.

There came the heavy rattling of the door being locked. Orivon tensed. Then he felt at his belt for the reassuring weight of his hammer, and relaxed again. Even if the lock was enspelled, the backs of these closets were but wood—he could smash through them and get out into the attic, if he had to.

And so his Whipping Bitch had been delivered helpless into his hand, after all these years . . .

He smiled, and slid the cloak off his head to watch.

10

The Beast Remembers Its Name

All scores will be settled, and even I will learn shame.
Towers will totter, the hunter ride home at long last,
And the forest echo, as the Beast remembers its name.
—old Niflghar chant,
"When That Time Comes"

amn you, Maharla," Taerune whispered raggedly, on the verge of tears. The empty room around her seemed to be listening, so she choked back a sob, and said nothing more until she'd fought down the urge to burst out weeping. "Olone damn you!"

She could do nothing about the tears she knew were running down her cheeks. The spell was fading already—Maharla might wield a holy scepter, but she was very far from knowing how to use it properly, or being worthy to do so—and for a wild moment she considered sitting here until it was quite gone, and then taking the knife and doing a little Maharla hunting.

No. She'd never get anywhere near the bitch, and Maharla had the sense of humor that would have her spellbind Dral or Ravan to kill their sister Taera. Slowly.

Tears did flood then, but Taerune bit her lip and kept grimly silent, shaking as she felt her sorrow drip off her chin onto the table.

Then she reached for the knife with the only hand she had left. It was trembling.

It was a good knife, heavy and fitting her hand well. Taerune hefted it, and then held it up and peered at it.

"You made this, my Orivon," she whispered to the empty room, suddenly sure this was the work of "her" firefist. "Oh, Goddess, what will become of you now, my Dark Warrior? Are you even still alive?"

She shook her head, fighting back fresh tears. *"Olone,"* she cursed, and reversed the knife in her hand, tossing it and deftly catching it without looking, to plunge it into her own breast.

Which was when something large rose up from beneath the edge of the table, took her wrist in a grip of iron, and asked in a soft, deep, and unfriendly voice, "Want to live?"

Taerune's eyes flashed wide. In an instant she was past that astonishment and glaring at him. She hissed wordless fury—and fought, her arm astonishingly strong.

Astonishingly strong, but as nothing to Orivon's forge-tempered brawn. Disbelief warred with pain in her eyes, as they burned into his over the fading, pulsing spell-chain.

The knife trembled as she clenched her teeth, snarled, and threw all her strength against his, trying desperately to force the knife down into herself. Her breast heaved as she gasped, as if straining to meet the blade—and then, suddenly, she threw her strength the other way, trying to thrust the knife into Orivon's face.

He grinned at it mirthlessly—and held fast, withstanding all she could hurl, even when Taera sobbed and rocked her body wildly in the chair, again and again, seeking to overmatch him and force the warsteel where he was determined it would not go.

At last she fell back, shuddering and exhausted, pain as well as weariness on her face. Orivon kept firm hold of her wrist, expecting a sudden thrust if he let go, but she just shook her head at him and opened her hand, letting the knife clatter back onto the table.

"Will you listen to me, Lady Taerune?" he whispered, sweeping the steel well out of her reach with one long arm. "And not try to slay me, or yourself, or cry alarm to all House Evendoom?"

"S-slave, I will," she hissed back wearily. "What else is left for me but listening?"

"Nothing is left—here. For either of us. But what if we left Talonnorn?"

"*What?* Slave, are you *oriad?*"

"I'm *not* your slave, Nifl bitch. And I'm not oriad; only Niflghar have that luxury. We humans have to settle for going mad."

Orivon thrust his face close to hers—close enough to feel the warning prickle of the waning magic around her throat—and snarled, "And right now, I'm not far off from being mad. I'm a human who wants his freedom, and I'm mad enough to work with the Nifl-she who flogged and lorded it over me for *years,* to get free!"

Taerune's face twisted, incredulity ruling her. "What are you babbling of? Where would you *go?*"

"The village you nightskins snatched me from, when I was little. Up in the Blindingbright!"

"And what would *I* do there?" Taerune snarled back at him bitterly. "In my scant time of being raped by every man in your village, before you burned me alive?"

"Who said anything about you coming to my village? You could have a new life among the Ravagers!"

She stared at him, mocking laughter in her eyes. "The *Ravagers?*" She went on staring, and then gasped, "You're serious, aren't you?"

"Yes, Taerune Evendoom," he snapped, "I am serious—and despite being a human, I have a brain, and can think as well or better than most Niflghar. I'm not a beast, I'm a *man.* But once out in the Dark, I'm lost; I need you. If you'll be my guide and wits, knowing Nifl and the Dark as you do—or getting a map of the Wild Dark from somewhere in this castle, to serve us both—I'll be your brawn, and get you out with me!"

"You're oriad, man," she hissed, eyes blazing. "They'll catch us before we're even out of the Towers! Nor do I *want* to leave Talonnorn—or go anywhere with a Hairy One! You humans *stink!*"

"Well of course we do, seeing as you don't let your slaves bathe except when you want them doused in scents!"

The spell at her throat faded, and Taerune sprang from her chair like a striking snake, sinking her teeth into his wrist and lunging to reach the knife.

Orivon backhanded her, sending her flying across the table. The Nifl-she fetched up against a closet amid the wreckage of two chairs, hard enough to slam its door panel open with a shudder.

Shaking her head, she wriggled up from the floor like an angry eel, and raced for the knife once more.

Orivon sprang over the table and slammed into her, taking brutal advantage of her missing arm to get a hand around her throat and then step behind her, hauling her right off the floor to kick furiously but helplessly, strangling in his grasp.

"Will you *listen* to *me?*"

He shook her as he asked that question, hard enough to make her teeth clatter, and then threw her down onto the table and pinned her there, a knee on her hip and his hands holding her breasts like claws, pinning her down. "Well?"

"Kill me, man. Just kill me." Her breasts rose and fell, or tried to, as she fought for breath. "I've been tormented enough!"

"*Oh, no, you haven't.* You barely know what torment is! Why, if you'd felt the whip from *my* end, all those—"

"Orivon, there are whips in the end closet, by the door," she hissed up at him, through fresh tears. "Scores of them. Choose those you like, and cut me apart! I'll not resist you!"

Orivon looked up at the end closet, then back down at the helpless she under his hands. Something was uncoiling inside him that he couldn't name, something that broke his fury. "I . . . no. No."

"Then let me have the knife, or kill me with it yourself," the Lady Taerune whispered fiercely, staring up into his eyes.

Orivon let go of her, and stood back from the table. "I saw and heard everything," he said curtly, "of the crones' meeting, and . . . I—before Olone, do you *truly* desire to die more than you want to live?"

Taerune sat up, swallowing hard, and for the first time he noticed the spell had burned away the leathers at her throat, and seared the skin beneath.

Her eyes, as she stared at him, seemed to hold dancing fire, within the glimmering tears.

"N-no," she whispered at last, and burst out crying.

Orivon stood watching her weeping, frowning a little in thought. He hated her—Thorar, how he hated her!—but if he treated this bitch like a human woman, like a friend, comforting and praising her, she just might turn away from seeking her own swift death and be of some use.

Thorar, he hated her, but . . .

He set his jaw, stepped forward, and put his arms around her. The Nifl went as rigid as a sword, just for an instant—and then collapsed back into sobbing, burying her face in his chest.

Awkwardly, Orivon held her, stroking her shoulder—*the shoulder of the arm she'd lost!*

"Thorar!" he snarled aloud, snatching his hand away and flushing hot. "Give me the strength!"

"Suh-suh-strength," she fought to say through her sobs, clinging to his chest all the tighter, "you have, man. It's-it's everything *else* you lack!"

"Well, *thank* you, little bitch," he growled, nettled. He put his anger into violently thrusting her away from him. And holding her at arm's length, fingers sunk clawlike into her shoulders. Scowling silently, he watched her fight down her tears and master them.

She was still sniffling when he snapped, "So, again I ask: Will you work with me? To get us both out of Talonnorn? And win a new life—new *lives*—for us both?"

"Y-yes," she said, staring at him.

Orivon blinked at her.

His astonishment made her half-smile, and repeat a little tremulously, "I said yes, Orivon Firefist. Lady Taerune Evendoom accepts your generous offer."

Orivon snorted his own mirth. "There's hope for you yet. You're not as cold mad as all the rest of the nightskins in Talonnorn."

Those words swept away Taerune's smile; he saw fresh fire rising in her eyes. "There is no madness in what I say," she snarled. "The madness is *yours!*"

"Oh?" Orivon asked, tossing his head. "Ask one of the Ravagers who's mad and who's not of one who'll slay themselves because their uncaring kin ordered them to—and one who'll spurn them as they spurned you, and get up and go on!"

Taerune stared at him, fresh tears racing down her cheeks, and whispered, "*You* don't need a whip to lash me, I see."

She shook her head, turned away, and then sobbed, "But this is my *home*! This—this is the chamber *I* hoped to rule, uncounted Turnings from now!"

"So depart now," Orivon said, striding to where he could growl in her ear from behind, "and dream of returning someday to seize the rule here, when this Maharla is dust and you have spells or whatever you need enough to *take* what you want!"

Taerune whirled around to stare at him, their faces so close together that he could feel her breath, hot and spicy, on his face. Then she seemed to smell him, and her nostrils pinched with distaste, her lips drawing back from her teeth.

Orivon stepped back, face hardening in rising anger, and she flung out her hand to him and cried, "I was *not* trying to—to hand you anger! To scorn you! Please, believe me!"

"I—I do," he said deliberately, forcing himself to say that and only that, mastering his rage before asking, "So, will you go with me now?"

"Yes," she whispered, putting her head back against the wall and shuddering as if in release. And then she looked at him, as tense and anxious as ever, and hissed, "I am . . . at war with myself, but . . . winning. Yet there is one thing: my Orb. I cannot leave without my Orb!"

"Some bauble? A gem?"

"*Bauble?* Man, it is my *life*! All my spells, my prayers to Olone and the visions She sent me in answer; my soulguide!"

Orivon stared at the anguish in her eyes, his mouth tightening, and then asked shortly, "Where is it?"

"In my chambers, in the spell-locked coffer in my closet. A round stone, white, that fills my palm, in a wire cage—to make it a pendant; the chain's quite heavy. They can trace the coffer with spells, so leave it."

"And what will the locking spell do to me when I shatter it?"

"No need; just open it. It opens to—" She turned her head away, and whispered to the wall, "Your name."

Orivon stared at her—Thorar, that curving back, those hips!—in blinking astonishment, and then asked, "Just 'Orivon'?"

"Just Orivon," she echoed softly, and then added lightly, "My! The beast remembers its name!"

Orivon reached out a hand to Taerune's shoulder, spun her around, and said heavily, "As the maker of your Door of Fangs, I can get through it—and as a longtime slave, I know the way to that door, and can probably get there unseen, I hope. But what will I do with you while I'm fetching this Orb of yours?" He stared at her as if she was an unfamiliar plant or odd-looking stone. "Can I trust you?"

"I tell you yes, man," his longtime tormentor said quietly, "and mean it. Yet you don't have to trust me. Take the knife away, fetch whips from yon closet to bind me with, and leave me here bound and gagged. Or better: Take me a little back in these attic ways, and bind me there, in case Maharla sends crones back to clean up after the Nameless outcast's suicide."

Orivon nodded and went to the closet. When he turned from it, she was on her knees, holding out the knife to him hilt-first.

He shook his head a little, almost smiling, as he took it from her. "Thorar, you've fire in you, Taerune!"

"Oh? I was going to kill myself," she whispered. *"Bind me."*

"Later," he growled. "I'm not going to carry a bound Nifl around all those narrow corners. Walk with me—no, this way. Don't trip on the dead rats."

. . .

Luelldar chuckled down at the glowing whorl. "When the Talonar blow their precious horns to call their hunters back—and notice, Aloun: for all their snarlings about other houses being craven and foolish enough to loose the raudren, the Evendooms haven't blown *theirs,* have they?—they'll be very surprised at just how few return to Talonnorn."

Aloun nodded. "Yet Klarandarr's spells are all gone, yes?"

The senior Watcher nodded. "For now. Yet the raudren still left are more likely to pounce on marauding beasts of the Dark than find the last of our stragglers. *What* a blow we have struck!"

"Yes? Their crones still lord it over their city, sneering at Ouvahlor—and everyone else," Aloun said sourly.

"Ah, but who is left for the crones to rule? A few servants, not many, a handful of slaves; by the Ice, they lost nearly all! Of warblades and spellrobes, we took a goodly toll. All who are left, stand amid ruins; a constant reminder that the empty sneerings of the crones are just that: empty. *That* is our victory."

"You think they'll rise up and slaughter their crones? After generations upon generations of bowing down? Why, the crones will use this to make themselves tyrants, and strike down any who challenge them in the slightest!"

"You see keenly, Aloun; some crones already have. Yet our work is done, for the Talonar cannot fail to see how foolish and fallible their crones are. They will not forget."

"So, what will happen next?"

Luelldar turned from the whorl wearing a broad, smug smile. "Ouvahlor is going to sell off many slaves—and when the buyers are bound for Talonnorn, our price is going to soar."

Orivon approached the narrow passage warily. The cloaks were still hung up across it, just as he'd left them. Beyond, he'd laid Taerune on her front, her wrist lashed to the back of her neck, with two lashes crammed into her mouth and then bound around it in a wildly untidy gag he'd made sure her hair was caught up in. Then he'd bound her legs together at so many points that they seemed one great club, and pulled her ankles up to shelving well above her so only her chest and head were on the floor.

Helpless enough, to a first glance, but he had only her word that she needed this Orb to have any spells. Moreover, the only place on her he'd checked for weapons was her boots, and they'd been so full of empty dagger sheaths that it was a wonder she'd been able to walk at all!

And just where were those daggers? Could she bring them flying back to her with a whispered word?

He crept closer, hefting his hammer in his hand. It had felt good to use it, but it could do nothing against spells, and he'd been lucky–oh, thank Thorar, *so* lucky!–so far . . .

There was a faint, low sound from ahead, beyond the cloaks. Orivon froze.

Then it came again. He cocked his head to listen, stole forward a few more swift steps, paused with his nose almost touching the hanging cloaks, and–yes. Again.

He ducked past the cloaks and around the last corner in a rush, keeping low.

She was just as he'd left her, and she was snoring.

Orivon snorted. Well, she *had* endured a hard day thus far. Hmph. String a hundred more after it, without a break, and she might begin to have some idea of what she'd put her slaves through.

Without greeting or gentleness he thrust his hammer back through his belt, and started untying Taerune's legs. The snoring stopped in a sharp instant, but he didn't turn her over when her legs were freed. Kneeling on her back, he tugged out the gag–and more than a little of her hair with it–before untying her wrist. She made no protest, but flailed about so feebly trying to turn over that Orivon finally reached down and hauled her around and up to sit facing him.

Then he thrust what he'd retrieved into her face: her Orb, and the lash she'd used on him so often. Taerune blinked at the latter in astonishment.

Then she noticed that the Orb was slick with fresh blood, wherever a hasty swipe of a man's hands couldn't wipe it clean, and gasped, "What happened?"

"I had to kill to get this," Orivon told her curtly. "The shes of your House had already forced the Door, ransacked your rooms, and were down to arguing over the worst of your gowns. I left three of your loving sisters dead in your closets–so Maharla'll soon turn the towers upside down looking for us. We must move. *Now*."

"Right into the jaws of the raudren? Without trying to get some sort of map of the Wild Dark? Orivon, I've only been on three patrols out there in my entire *life,* and—"

The lash was still in Orivon's hand. He stepped grimly back from her and swung it across her face. Hard.

It snapped her head around and dashed her to the attic floor.

"Argue with me," he told the moaning Nifl at his feet, his voice flat and hard, "and die. I'm going *now,* and have no time left for dispute. Are you with me?"

Taerune's limbs were trembling, as she struggled back to a sitting position, shaking her head dazedly. Her stump, where the edge of the lash had caught it, had started to bleed.

Looking up at him through streaming tears, she hissed, "Yes! Olone take you, Firefist, yes!"

Orivon stepped back. "Well?"

"Well, help me up," she snarled, "or I'll not be going *anywhere.* You tied me too tightly."

Orivon hauled Taerune to her feet, and held out the Orb again. "Can I trust you with this?"

"Not to use it on you, you mean?" she asked wearily, closing her hand around it. "Yes. Can you *try* not to use the lash on me, in turn?"

She clung to a shelf of dusty coffers to keep upright, cursing softly under her breath. When Orivon reached down and caught up all the lashes he'd used to bind her, she murmured, "You won't be needing those."

"Oh? I have to sleep sometime. Trust must be earned, Taerune."

She stiffened, eyes blazing for a moment—and then nodded without saying anything and set off down the passage, stumbling a little.

"This way," Orivon commanded, turning into the labyrinth of dusty passages. So even the pureblood Evendooms, it seemed, had forgotten some of the back stairs of their castle.

He went on thinking that until they came out into a deep dungeon guardchamber, a swift eternity of descending dank stairs later, and found a line of well-armored warblades waiting for them, drawn swords in their hands.

"Halt," commanded the tall and strikingly handsome Niflghar rampant at their head, sounding a little sad.

"Halt and die?" Orivon growled, his hammer in his hand. "You nightskins offer your slaves such enticing choices!"

"Taera," said the tall Nifl, ignoring him, "it grieves me to see Eldest

Maharla's accusations proven, and behold you working with a slave of Ouvahlor."

"Uncle Faunhorn," Taerune replied calmly, "it grieves *me* to see you obeying that oriad tyrant, and believing—nay, even *listening* to—her lies."

"Your life is forfeit," he said quietly. "You know what we must do." The warblades raised their swords and took a step forward, in perfect unison—and Faunhorn stepped with them.

"I always loved you," Taerune whispered to him, and put her fingers to the Orb at her throat. "*Eyes,* Orivon!"

The stone winked once, there was a blinding flash in the darkness that Orivon didn't entirely escape, and the floor of the guardchamber was suddenly adorned with a line of twisted, motionless Niflghar.

"Dare we touch them?" Orivon asked, blinking hard in a struggle to see again. "Some of their swords may be of better size and weight for you than what I have. And they've scabbards, and belts and baldrics, too . . ."

"We can touch them," Taerune said shortly. "Leave . . . leave my uncle be."

They took what they wanted, working quickly as the faint, musky smell of burnt Nifl flesh grew stronger.

"How often can you make your Orb do that?" Orivon asked.

"Thrice more. Or to say it more meaningfully: not nearly often enough. Let's get out of here!"

"Lady Evendoom, I find I begin to agree with you!"

"What foolishness is this?" The Revered Mother's voice was sharper than usual.

Exalted Daughter of the Ice Semmeira whirled around. "Revered Mother! You're *well*!"

"Of course I'm well, child. I wish I could say the same of all of you. I await your answer, Semmeira."

The rebuke was mildly said, but the old eyes flashed a warning that even the haughty Exalted feared.

"R-revered Mother, your trance alarmed us. We were afraid that— that *monster* in your whorl—had done you some great harm, and that Lolonmae was involved."

"And so you trapped her in your ring and overwhelmed her, forcing your ways into her mind. That is *not* what I taught you that spell for—any of you. It is rape, Semmeira, nothing less, and can do far more lasting harm than a few minutes of humiliating discomfort under a rutting rampant. Believe me: I've endured both."

The Revered Mother looked at the frozen, fixedly staring novice in the center of the ring and said grimly, "All of you out of her mind, right now. Maurem and Tethyl, each of you put one of your arms gently under her armpits, and be ready to take her weight if she slumps. *Don't* let her fall! Right, now, all of you: Walk her gently to the altar, and let her down upon it. Cradle her head as gently as you know how. I'm watching."

The priestesses struggled under the limp, surprisingly heavy novice, but got her onto the altar gently—if ungracefully.

"Now stand back from her, all. Semmeira, tell us why you decided Lolonmae had in some way harmed me."

"Well . . . Revered Mother, I am so sorry for my error! It was done for love of you, truly, and—"

"Beg apologies *after* you obey," the eldest priestess said softly.

Exalted Daughter of the Ice Semmeira paled in embarrassment, went to her knees before the Revered Mother, and stammered, "F-forgive me, R-revered Mother, but I heard you speak to the raudren, naming it 'Lolonmae.' And then you fell into entrancement. I thought Lolonmae was the cause of that condition, and was somehow working with, or through, the monster."

"Good thinking," the Revered Mother said briskly. "Entirely wrong, but good thinking nonetheless. Know you this, Semmeira: Despite her youth, short time among us, and lack of rank, Lolonmae has been divinely chosen for some great task. I know not yet what it is—I may never be deemed worthy enough to know—but Lolonmae is intended to rise above all of us. Not displace you as Exalted, and not thrust aside any of us. Be aware that I will give my life, gladly, to protect her—the very same novice you fools have seen fit to try to punish and profane. From this moment forth, be aware that I shall slay anyone I so much as suspect of working harm, no matter how trifling, to Lolonmae—or letting her blunder into harm by herself while you smilingly stand by and do nothing. *Do you understand?*"

She had not raised her voice one whit, yet her last words rolled through their minds with deafening, roaring force that flung their heads back and left some of them bleeding from bitten lips and tongues, and all of them reeling with raging headaches.

"Semmeira, you shall soon undergo what I was intending to do with Lolonmae and this raudren, so I shall tell you what I was seeking to do.

I intended Lolonmae to learn the arts of contacting truly different minds, minds of power—in this case, a raudren—and learning to understand and control them. I chose this raudren's mind for Lolonmae to touch with her own, as I guarded her mind with my own, and I named Lolonmae to the raudren, to help it attune to her."

The elder priestess turned away. "Now get up off your knees and get over here, right by the altar. If you've driven her mad, I'll be needing your mind to put her into, while I go in and try to mend the damage."

"*My* mind? What will that do to me?"

The Revered Mother's gaze was dark and direct. "Well, now. That's something you'll just have to wait a few moments to learn, isn't it?"

11

Lord Evendoom Loses His Temper

To Olone I pray on bended knee
That never again shall these eyes see
Wrath so deep, deadly and storm-mighty
As Lord Evendoom's latest fell frenzy.
—from the old Talonar ballad,
"Lord Evendoom's Revenge"

"Orivon, if you don't mind my asking," Taerune murmured, after they'd walked briskly for what seemed a very long time in deep darkness, "when did you ever have the chance to learn our hidden ways?"

"At about the same time as you were . . . losing your arm," the firefist replied shortly. "I—sorry. I know no gentle way to say that."

They went on together in silence for a few strides before Taerune said, very quietly, "There *is* no gentle way to say that."

Silence fell between them again, and they walked on in it for a much longer time before Taerune asked, "This is the Hidden Gate, isn't it?"

"So a spellrobe told me—and a dying Maulstryke, too. They should both be just ahead of us, now, so: slow and quiet, Lady Evendoom."

"Taera," she murmured. "Call me Taera."

"*Quiet,* Lady Taera," he growled, giving her flank a gentle tap-tap with the coiled lash. She kept silent, and when he muttered, "Stay here," double-tapped his thigh with her hand, by way of reply.

Orivon drew the largest of the Nifl blades they'd salvaged—Faunhorn had borne a larger, grander one, a spellblade, but he'd left it untouched, as Taerune had pleaded—and took his trusty hammer into his other hand. Then he skulked forward, in a slow and careful crouch.

The tunnel—huddled bodies and all—was just as it had been when he'd last seen it. He stood just inside the door, peering and listening, for a long time, but saw nothing—and heard nothing more than two long, distant horn blasts, calling the raudren home. At last he risked going a little farther, to where he could be seen, but also see all around the tunnel mouth.

Nothing but the sprawled, silent bodies. Orivon listened to nothing for a long time before he turned and went back to his longtime tormentor.

Taerune was sitting in the tunnel, staring at the stump where her arm had been. She looked up quickly at his approach, hand going to the sword she'd laid on the tunnel floor—but then relaxed, her hand going back to cupping her other elbow.

"The way is clear," Orivon told her. "I want you to stay close beside me; I'm going to one of the clefts to recover some blades and tools I brought from the Rift. I'll bundle them in this spare cloak, and tie them into a bundle with the lashes."

Taerune nodded.

"You know where we're coming out, right?"

She nodded again.

"Good. So from the clefts, where do we head, to get out into the Dark?"

She shrugged. "Dozens of tunnels will take us there. Some are usually guarded, but now—who knows? When we're in the cleft, I'll point them out to you. You choose."

Orivon nodded, and they went forward together—walking slowly, Taerune a little ahead to give both of them room to swing swords freely. She paused by the open door and looked back in a silent questioning, and Orivon nodded and came up close behind her. If the Nifl noticed the point of his sword was almost touching her back, just where it met her behind, she gave no sign of doing so.

They came out into the great cavern that held Talonnorn, darting glances this way and that, but though the half-ruined Eventowers loomed dark behind them and they saw a distant darkwings with a rider on its back flapping across the huge cave, this little corner of Talonnorn seemed deserted.

Thankfully Orivon plunged into the cleft, clawed aside the stones he'd so carefully arranged, and bundled the swords and tools into the spare cloak. "Watch the entrance, behind me," he growled, busily knotting lashes.

"*Orivon,*" Taerune replied, warningly, and he spun around.

The local landscape was deserted no longer. Standing in the entrance to the cleft were a dozen warblades: a spellrobe; a Nifl-she wearing robes that bared her charms to every eye, in a lusty display that contrasted oddly with her coldly haughty expression; and an older Nifl rampant clad in black, who wore a cruel smile on his handsome face.

"Hello, little Nameless bitch," he drawled. "My, you're even lovelier than when you were Taerune Evendoom. It would have been frowned upon to force myself upon my own niece, but now . . . I'm going to *enjoy* this."

"*Are* you, Uncle Valarn?" Taerune asked, her question a biting challenge.

He laughed and drew his sword with a flourish; it kindled instantly into a ruby-red glow. Taerune touched her Orb and hissed something—and lightnings were suddenly leaping among the warblades like dancing snakes.

They avoided Valarn, the spellrobe, and the priestess of Olone altogether, and seemed to do no harm to the grinning, advancing warblades.

Valarn laughed again. "You're *that* much a fool, Taerune? To think we go into battle unprotected against lesser magics? Could it be that you fight unprotected? Oh, yes, of *course* you do; how forgetful of me! A pity you can't forget that missing arm for an instant, isn't it?"

Sword and hammer in hand, Orivon stepped past Taerune, curling his lip and saying to her contemptuously with a wave of his hammer in Valarn's direction, "*This* is a pureblood House Nifl?"

Valarn gave him a momentary—and withering—glance, and drawled one dismissive word: "Human."

Orivon replied, his voice an exact mimicry of Valarn's tone: "Niflghar."

Valarn stiffened and spat, "Slave!"

Orivon shrugged. "Slave-keeper!"

The warblades were only three strides away from Orivon now. "I weary of this," Valarn said dismissively. "Kill him. Disarm the former Lady Taerune, and prepare her for me—across that rock will do."

Then the leaping lightnings playing harmlessly around the Talonar changed—and warblades stiffened and screamed as their own swords and armor twisted and grew spikes in all directions, butchering them where they stood. The spellrobe and priestess shrieked as their metal rings and belt buckles did the same, severing most of their fingers and stabbing through their bellies. Even Valarn swore and shook a hand that shed fingers—and their rings, turned into vicious stars of bladed metal—as he did so.

"No, of *course* I don't think you go into battle unprotected against lesser magics, Uncle," Taerune said sweetly, watching everyone but Valarn die. "However, yes, I *do* know you're a fool. I have since I was old enough to mewl, as you like to put it."

Orivon stalked forward, and Valarn snarled and turned to flee. Orivon threw his sword—but it struck something unseen just before it would have bitten into the back of the Nifl's knee, and was hurled aside in a storm of sparks.

"His spellblade protects him," Taerune murmured. "Orivon, leave him to me. Please."

Orivon took one look at her face and stepped aside.

"Thank you, my Dark Warrior," she murmured, striding past him. She didn't seem to see him stiffen and give her a dark look; her hand was at her throat, fingers on the Orb.

It flashed once, and Valarn's quickening flight suddenly stopped. He was hurrying just as much, but going nowhere, walking—and then trotting—in place.

Then he looked back at her, scowled, and slashed all around himself with his glowing sword—and stumbled forward again, almost falling.

By then, Taerune was almost upon him, striding swiftly, no sword in her hand—the hand that was busy at the buckles of her leathers. "Why, Uncle," she said, "don't you *want* me?"

When he whirled around with a snarl, she pulled open the front of her leathers.

"Well?" she asked, challengingly. "Don't you?"

Taerune swept leather back off one shoulder, baring it, then the other, in a long, steady tug that bared her down to the waist. Her fingers dipped lower as she tossed her head, long hair swirling. "Uncle?"

Valarn snarled, *"Bitch!"* and swung his spellblade viciously. Orivon launched himself forward in sudden horror, sprinting and shouting—there was *no way* the he-Nifl could miss slicing her open!

Thorar, she's chosen this way out!

"Nooo! Taera, *no!"*

Spellblade and Orb flashed in unison, the sword raced through the space where Taerune's arm was missing and plunged into her, she threw back her head and screamed, the sword sliced on through, she turned as metallic all over as the blade was, the sword came out the other side of her and swept on, trailing silvery blood—and Taerune lunged forward, embraced Valarn, and bit his mouth, hard.

Valarn's arms flew up and started to flail, his spellblade whirling away to bounce and singingly clang its way to a skirling rest, on tumbled stones.

He went silvery, too, and made a sort of sobbing sound in Taerune's arms.

And then she arched over backward and threw herself away, kicking off from him as she went, metallic no longer. Orivon had just time to fling away sword and hammer and catch her in his hands, in an awkward collison that took them both to the stones, bouncing and winded.

Valarn Evendoom staggered back, agonized face raised to the unseen cavern ceiling above, and started to *really* scream. Smoke curled up from him as the metal melted into him, cooking him alive.

And then, cooking him dead.

Orivon watched him blacken, fall, and die, and swallowed down sudden nausea.

Then he realized that Taerune was lying face up on his stomach, in his arms, as unmarked as if that sword had never sliced through her. And he realized something more: just which smooth parts of her he had hold of—and snatched his hands away as if he'd been burned.

Taerune twisted her head around and grinned up at him, making no move to rebuckle anything. "That reminds me: We haven't brought along any food."

After a long, breathless moment of staring at her in astonishment, Orivon burst into shouts of laughter.

"Firstblood of the House, Secondblood of the House," the steward intoned formally, "I present to you Lord Erlingar Evendoom." He bowed deeply and withdrew, sealing the door. It caught cold and silent fire in his wake, to signify he'd activated the wards that bound the chamber into absolute privacy.

"Yes, Father?" Jalandral drawled. "Is all this grandeur truly necessary? Or is this something *else* Maharla's enjoying shoving down your throat?"

"Be still," Lord Evendoom snapped, in a coldly, venomously furious voice that drove Ravandarr into cowering openly and made even Jalandral flinch. "Know that I am beside myself with rage. Over the losses we have suffered, and even more because of, yes, our Eldest and her aims and decrees. I would tell the both of you what I truly think of you, and spend far longer bellowing to the very spires of our castle what I think of *her*—but I lack the time for such trifles."

He started to pace, his grand cloak billowing out behind him, the great voice that dominated any chamber and tamed assemblies regaining its dire thunder. "The Eventowers can be rebuilt, and I can raise flesh-rending magical fields to defend the breaches in its walls and cloak it against flying attackers until that time. However, I find myself in personal peril. To avoid being executed for allowing the honor of our House to be so stained, I must dramatically avenge all slights to that honor—and that means eliminating my maimed, mad, and disloyal daughter."

"*Taerune?*" Ravandarr burst out, too incredulous to keep silent.

"Taerune," Lord Evendoom confirmed gravely, "though the Eldest has now cast her out and made her Nameless. She alone did murder in our innermost chambers, spilling the blood of kin."

"What?" Jalandral raised an elegant, disbelieving eyebrow. "Taera? What lie of Maharla is this?"

"No lie," their father thundered, "and you risk your own necks— even here, with the wards up—for saying so. Ardranthra, Nelvune, and Qellarla lie dead on the altars of Olone right now, bound for the crypt; the rite is called for feasting-time. Ravandarr, you shall attend with me, in full mourning garb."

"Taerune killed . . . ?" Ravandarr said haltingly, staring at his father in horrified disbelief. Lord Evendoom, glaring hard at his Firstblood, never even glanced at his younger son.

Jalandral sighed theatrically. "Which means I must be attending to some errand or other, probably involving the bloodthirsty, vengeful, and very public slaying of dear Nameless Taera, yes?"

"Yes," Lord Evendoom said heavily. "Very shortly I shall be announcing your *aching* willingness to undertake this task. See that you play the part accordingly."

"Lo, in this hour of impending peril, Lord Evendoom sends forth the mightiest force he commands, his flippant and decidedly indolent heir, to do the dirtiest of misplacedly vengeful deeds ever ordered," Jalandral declaimed grandly, spreading his arms.

Striding past, Lord Evendoom jerked one of those arms sharply down, spinning Jalandral around, and snapped, "*Cease* playing the fool and behave as befits an Evendoom until you're gone! Then you can go back to being what you are!"

Jalandral sketched an airily florid salute. "Jalandral Evendoom stands ever ready to serve his family, his city—and every spiteful crone with a misplaced whim within them!"

"F-father," Ravandarr said then, stepping into Lord Evendoom's path, so that they almost collided, "let *me* go."

"What?" Lord Evendoom loomed over his son, swaying from his hasty halt. "Ravandarr, this is to be a *killing*. We're all well aware of your . . . closeness to Ta—to your sister, but she must be slaughtered, and her head brought back to be presented to the Eldest, as proof!"

His younger son was trembling, as pale as a sword blade, but he stood his ground. "I—I *will* do it, Father!"

"Bah!" Lord Evendoom whirled away, and stalked back across the chamber. "Look at you! You look *sick,* not capable! You picked a fine time to go rampant; pity you've not shown such spirit ever before!"

"Well, of *course* he's sick," Jalandral said soothingly. "Sick with disbelief—as we all are—and then revolted at Taera's treachery. See how he trembles with determination?"

Lord Evendoom whirled around again to face them both, cloak swirling. "Jalandral, *have done*! I look bad enough sending you, but at least it can be passed off as testing my heir and letting all see his true mettle! If I send *him,* the crones will openly accuse me of mocking their will, trying to see their decrees thwarted!"

"Ah, yes." Jalandral nodded, inspecting the backs of his fingernails critically, and dropping into mimicry of his father's strong, deep voice. "I see, I quite see. And we all know where *that* supposition of our dear crones would lead, don't we?"

Lord Evendoom burst into a wordless roar of rage that sent Ravandarr, already trembling on the edge of tears, into headlong flight. Then he found his voice again.

"Ravandarr, *halt*! And turn and stand your ground like an Evendoom, damn you, or by Olone and all Her temptations, I'll sword you myself, here and now! *Do this!*"

The power of his voice brought Ravandarr, already stopping and turning, cowering to his knees.

Lord Evendoom looked at them both, one after the other, and then said in a voice as cold as any crone's, "You will obey, and you will be-have so as to impress our Eldest and every crone of this House."

Ravandarr hastily stood up straight, still trembling.

Lord Evendoom gave him a curt nod, and added, "For if you fail, the crones will put us all to death. Go and prepare yourselves; this audi-ence is at an end."

Turning his back on them, he strode to the massive arched double doors that opened into the Long Hall.

Magics that had been old before Erlingar Evendoom was born made them open by themselves at his approach, grinding thunderously apart as the privacy wards flickered and died around them like ghostly flames. His two sons stood like statues, watching him go.

Out across the unbroken expanse of mirror-glossy tiles that stretched from the audience chamber into and throughout the cavernous Long Hall. A very long walk, even for a tall Nifl, to meet the Nifl gathered waiting there.

The heads of all the Houses of Talonnorn were standing inside a winking, glittering ring of multiple defensive magics. Between and around them were priestesses of Olone in full holy regalia, and many senior crones in simple robes, there to keep the peace between the Houses and to bear witness.

"We are gathered here in the House struck hardest," the softly lilting voice of Aumaeraunda, Holiest of Olone, rolled into every ear without being raised in the slightest, "to confer as to what Talonnorn should do now."

"Make war on Ouvahlor," Lord Oszrim snarled, ignoring the nor-mal precedence of speech; an effrontery that made Oszrim's Eldest and Oszrim's heir both pale in embarrassment. "What else?"

"Rebuild in a manner that forewarns Talonnorn against all attacks," Lord Dounlar put in.

"Attacks from without," Maharla, Eldest of Evendoom, added icily, "and from within."

"And who, exactly, are you?" the Eldest crone of Maulstryke asked in tones of sweet venom, a reminder to all of the suddenness and recent vintage of Maharla's self-appointed authority.

Maharla whirled, white with rage, but Aumaeraunda called upon a little of the Power of the magic ringing them all to render all crones in the ring momentarily frozen and voiceless.

"Lord Evendoom," she said, gathering the Power around her that none of them could withstand, "you have just taken private audience with your sons. The Will of Divine Olone Herself demands to know what orders you gave them."

Lord Evendoom gave her a little bow to signify that his obedience was a matter of his own assent as well as her coercion, and said with dignity, "In the strife just past, one of my daughters slew three of my daughters—in her bedchamber, not in formal combat—and fled. The Eldest of Evendoom has declared her Nameless, and I have just ordered my heir to hunt her down and slay her, to restore the honor of our House. My Secondblood requested that this duty be given to him, but upon him I ordered attendance at the death rites of our kin. I also ordered them both to behave befittingly, as Evendooms."

"He speaks truth to us all," the high priestess confirmed. "We are satisfied."

"*You* may be, Most Holy," burst out a tall, handsome young Nifl who stood a head taller than everyone except Lord Evendoom and Holy Aumaeraunda, his words a rudeness that made some of the elder crones emit indignant gasps that sounded like short, chirping shrieks, "but I am not. Your sons are widely known in Talonnorn—in *my* House, even our slaves know it—as disgraces to all Niflghar! The one a prancing, posing buffoon, the other a sniveling coward; *ordering* them to behave is easy enough, but will prove futile emptiness; Lord Evendoom, you should have *compelled* them to 'behave befittingly' many, many Turnings ago!"

"Maulstryke," Lord Evendoom said mildly, speaking to the father rather than to the son, "your heir is most . . . eloquent. Yet in Talonar society we cleave to customs of etiquette. Is"—he waved his hand gently in the direction of his cold critic—"*this* befitting behavior?"

"As my heir, what Shoan has said is both rude and out of place," Lord Ohzeld Maulstryke replied, his voice somehow both silken-sharp and deep. "Yet I rebuke him not, nor will do so, because he spoke then not as my heir, but as the battlelord of Maulstryke, quite rightly identifying weaknesses in House Evendoom—the House most damaged in this strife, let all remember; something that speaks more tellingly of their preparedness than all the words we may care to utter here—that affect all Talonnorn. To be blunt, Evendoom, Shoan points out the obvious, and we all know it is something you should have addressed long ago. Your eldest daughter—Taerune, is it not?—is thrice the warrior your heir and Secondblood put together will ever be. So—"

"The one to whom you refer is now *Nameless!*" Maharla hissed. "Speak not of her!"

"Ah. I find myself unsurprised," Lord Maulstryke observed coldly, well aware of the enjoyment glittering in the eyes of most of the gathered crones. "She no doubt acted out of rage at the behavior of her kin in this time of Talonnorn's need. I understand that rage."

"If the head and heir of House Maulstryke are so deeply concerned about the competencies of my sons," Lord Evendoom said calmly, "they are welcome to accompany my heir, to see for themselves that the honor of Talonnorn is ably defended."

"I *will* go," Shoan Maulstryke snarled, "and shall begin to ready myself this instant!"

He stormed out of the ring, the high priestess hastily working its barrier magics to let him pass unscathed.

In silence they watched him stride off down the Long Hall, cloak streaming in his wake.

"Unlike Lord Evendoom," Lord Ohzeld Maulstryke said then, "I am aware of my duties, and cannot undertake vengeful escapades when Talonnorn stands threatened. There is much to do, and overbold talk and dispute will get none of these needful things done. I take this opportunity to gift Lord Evendoom with a promise—some might call it a warning—that dire consequences will follow if his decision to send his heir on such a fool's errand is revealed to have been mistaken or if any treachery is worked against *my* heir. May you all enjoy an excellent converse, hereafter."

And with a nod to the Holiest of Olone, Lord Maulstryke followed his son out of the ring, his cloak trailing sparks of its Power as he began the long walk.

Orivon frowned down at the weapons he'd brought from the Rift. "All of these are too long to fit you with."

Taerune held up her stump. "Just a dagger, perhaps? We've plenty to choose from, now."

There arose a sudden crackle behind them, and they both whirled around.

Close enough to tug at their limbs as it snarled into eerily blue, humming life, a wall of glowing air they could see through was rising, building slowly up from the stones by their boots into the darkness high overhead. Magic was now cloaking Talonnorn.

Orivon stared at the humming blue fire rather grimly, watching it lick and dance across the tunnel, around the door that was still ajar. "The wards."

"Yes," Taerune said softly, and let out a great sigh. "Protecting Talonnorn from dung-worms and attacking Niflghar of Ouvahlor alike. Walling us out, too."

Orivon shook his head. "You Nifl are so . . . dramatic. Overblown. Everything's so—florid."

Taerune's smile was as sad as his words had been wry. "And I had to teach you eloquence, didn't I? Just to have a slave who could appreciate my own cleverness."

Orivon gave her a hard look. "Is that why you did it?"

She went pale, looked away, and then said quietly, "This probably isn't the best of times to tell you, but I've almost no magic left. This Orb isn't . . ."

Orivon sighed. " 'Magic,' you were going to say? Or 'useful'?"

12

Glee Among the Ravagers

When there is glee among the Ravagers
Prices will be high, and selection short.
—old Niflghar traders' saying

"Took a lot of rockfalls, that did," the Nifl everyone knew as Old Bloodblade commented, looking down from the high ledge at a crew of younger Ravagers busily clambering over (and through) the huge skeleton of a raudren, scraping and hewing flesh and hide into baskets for the cooking fires and the tanning cauldrons. "Yet we slew it in the end."

Gruffly pointing out the obvious was what Old Bloodblade *did,* so the one-eyed Ravager lounging beside him didn't bother getting irritated. Instead, Blind Lharlak transferred the strip of raudren hide he was chewing on from one cheek to the other with his tongue, and through its movements made the grunt that signified agreement. His eye patch and ever-present curved sword made him look villainous indeed, and he did nothing to discourage that image—though his mustache was far tidier and more slender than the bristling foliage of his ledge-mate.

Needing no further encouragement, Old Bloodblade growled on. "Heard only six raudren flew back to Talonnorn, when they blew the horns, and one of them was so sorely wounded that it flew headlong into a castle tower and got itself killed—smashing the top off the tower, too! Crushed a lot of Haraedra, that did!"

"Unfortunately, they were Nameless," Lharlak replied. "Servants, warblades—*our* sort of Nifl. Not the purebloods and spellrobes, priest-esses and crones."

"Hmph," Old Bloodblade commented. "Those sort of Nifl never get killed—except on the sly, by their own kind. Rat eating rat, you might say."

"And many do," Lharlak murmured, a favorite saying that Old Bloodblade heard all too often. "And many do."

Orivon thrust his sword into the narrowing crack at the end of the ledge, where it grew too small for his body to go farther. The steel bit into noth-ing, and he heard and smelled no beast. "I *think* it's safe," he muttered. "We sleep here?"

"You're the one with the lashes, and I'm the one who gets tied up," Taerune reminded him softly. "You must decide."

Orivon's mouth's tightened. "We sleep here."

She promptly nodded, let out a long sigh, and sagged back against the rough rock. "Good. I'm . . . more than weary."

"And we have no food, nor anything to drink," Orivon said grimly, "and no map. With Talonnorn shielded against us."

Taerune nodded silently, eyes on his.

"Well?" Orivon growled. "Aren't you even going to say anything?"

Taerune shrugged. "We'll both be happier about this disaster after we've had some sleep?"

Her longtime slave snorted. "*Thank* you, Lady Evendoom."

"This isn't going to be comfortable," she complained. "Can't you dump the weapons out on the ledge and give us both another cloak to put under us? This stone is very . . . hard."

Orivon snorted again, amused despite himself at her brilliant obser-vation. "Any more requests?"

"Yes. Could you bind me faceup, this time? Just tie my wrist to my side."

"As my Lady commands," he said sarcastically, getting out the lashes.

"Ho, luggards," the new arrival on the ledge greeted Old Bloodblade and Lharlak casually.

"Ho, Daruse," they mumbled back, waving at an empty stretch of ledge in an invitation to sit down.

Daruse accepted. He looked even more like the Talonar view of a Ravager than his fellows: dirty, clad in tangled scraps of weathered, salvaged armor, and hung about with a fearsome arsenal of rusty, well-used weapons. He looked battered, with the edge of one ear torn and gone, his not-so-obsidian skin sporting more than a few scars and nasty-looking scaly areas. He wore several gaudy things seized from the bodies of Nifl he'd slain that he believed were amulets, and an eye patch. Unlike Lharlak, Daruse's eye patch was for show, and when the whim took him, he moved it from one eye to the other, or dropped it down around his neck to dangle and leave both his eyes free.

"Barandon," he said, using Old Bloodblade's real name because it irritated the stout old Nifl immensely, and because doing so got him Bloodblade's immediate attention, "I've been thinking."

"*Oh,* no! Gird yourselves for battle, all! It'll be raining spellrobes in a bit, and Olone Herself'll be down to personally kiss our backsides! Daruse has been *thinking*!"

"Gently, gently," Daruse drawled amiably. "My ire's a terrible flame when aroused, you know!"

"So the shes have said," Lharlak jested, "but they were giggling something fierce when they said it!"

"Chortle, chortle," Daruse replied with a yawn. "*Any*how, listen: Talonnorn's badly weakened, yes?"

"Yes," the other two chorused, having heard many vivid descriptions of the Eventowers half-collapsed, fires and corpses everywhere, and towers fallen all across the city.

"*Well,* now! Stands to reason this is a great chance for us to raid, and do some *real* damage! Raudren almost all slain, their Hunt and their warblades both cut to tripes and every House eyeing every other House; all suspicious, and wanting to keep their blades at home to use on each other . . . and once they start to rebuild, and everything is chaos and confusion and supplies heaped everywhere for the taking . . ."

"I'm hearing you," Old Bloodblade grunted. "And nodding for once, too."

Lharlak saved himself the effort of speaking, and just nodded.

"So what say, brave blades? Do we sit here, camped out in the Wild Dark, waiting for the next creeping monster to gobble us? Or do we seize this *ideal time to attack,* and *really* loot and pillage Talonnorn at last?"

"Me for looting," Old Bloodblade growled.

"Me for pillaging," Lharlak chimed in laconically, shifting his chew back to the other cheek again.

"Oh, you *luggards!*" Daruse growled disgustedly. "I might have saved myself a lot of breath—"

"By asking us straight out if we'd already agreed to muster a raiding party," Old Bloodblade told him. "Which we have."

"Well, why didn't you *say*—"

Blind Lharlak turned on Daruse, pouting his lips in a parody of a lusty wanton Nifl-she, and said, "Because we so *love* to hear you cajole, Ruse, we do! You could cajole a crone to lick your behind, you could!"

"*Oh,* now," Old Bloodblade rumbled, "that's something I'll be wanting to see him demonstrate, once we're lording it in some Talonar castle! Could you spare a crone for me, Ruse, old friend?"

"For you, Lord Barandon, no less than four—if your aging heart can take it, that is!"

"Olone *rut,*" Old Bloodblade snarled, making the lewd hooked-fingers gesture that went with that oath.

He made it again when the others on the ledge both chuckled mockingly at him.

It was rare indeed for Lord Ohzeld Maulstryke to stand in this particular chamber of Maulgard—and rarer still for him to be there without a silently waiting cluster of servants.

They were all just beyond the outer doors, of course. Neither father nor son wanted them closer, and the scrying-foil glows of both their wards warred soundlessly in the air around them to keep subtler spies—the crones of their own House—at bay. The castle of House Maulstryke, for all its habitual silence, was a place of energetic spying and vicious betrayals, and none of the Maulstryke rampants were eager to cross their crones more than they had to. So by all the magical means either Nifl could muster, this was, and would remain, a strictly private meeting.

Disdaining any of the chairs his son seemed to think must crowd a robing-room, Lord Ohzeld stood like a statue of icy anger on the largest clear expanse of gleaming black marble. "You have said and done many stupid things in your life, Shoan, but this surpasses all. I am appalled. More than that, I am disgusted and disappointed. That a son of mine should let a dolt like Evendoom goad you—goad you like a child!—into declaring you'd set boots outside Talonnorn in the company of that grin-ning fop Jalandral—as lazily a poison-using murderer as this city has ever held—hunting some matter-nothing Maimed One, who when she was whole was fit only to flog slaves, at that!"

The Firstblood of House Maulstryke was just as angry, but his ire was hot forgefire to his father's ice. He strode around his marble cham-bers with swift, abrupt whirlings, anger in his every movement, slapping on armor and fetching forth his best weapons with impatient rattlings.

"Father, I have my own honor to avenge. She once struck *me* with her lash. In . . . a private moment, something too small and shameful to de-mand redress in the normal way of things. Yet it's fitting that if Taerune Evendoom be struck down, my hand be the one to grind her face into the rock and make her beg vainly for mercy, through her own blood!"

Ohzeld stared at his heir in expressionless silence for too long a time for either of them to be comfortable . . . and then nodded, slowly and curtly. "Fitting, yes. This, I was unaware of. Because you kept a secret you should not have kept. Secrets, Shoan, are weaknesses; take care you not carry too many, lest your best armor become a cloak full of holes."

Jalandral Evendoom moved around his chambers with unhurried, lan-guid grace, buckling on the last of his sleek black armor, and flexing its sliding plates experimentally by swinging and bending his arms thus and so.

Ravandarr was certain that if he hadn't been present, Jalandral would have been *humming*.

Oh So Holy Olone, why was Dral always so *happy*? Was he . . . oriad?

"Dral," he snapped, unable to keep silent any longer.

His older brother looked up from the array of weapons laid out on his bed. "Hmm?"

Ravandarr was leaning against the door frame, scowling, not even trying to keep the bitterness out of his face and voice. "*I* should be the one to hunt Taera down," he grated, bouncing a fist morosely off the un-yielding stone beside him. "I was the one she was closest to. The one who has been most betrayed."

"Nay, brother," Jalandral said dryly, sighting along the glossy edge of a favorite blade with every evidence of satisfaction, before sliding it back into its scabbard. "Our dead sisters have been the most betrayed."

"Perhaps." Ravan's scowl deepened. "No, you speak truth. Yet they *are* dead, and so feel no scorn-fire. Whereas I—"

"Seethe and bubble like cauldron-simmer, brother." Jalandral shook his head, turned from equipping himself, and wagged one long, elegant finger. "Cloak that rage, gather it within, and *master* it, Ravan. When you have mastered it, you can forge from it whatever you need . . . to see your aims fulfilled, your whims made deeds . . . your battles turned to triumphs." He scooped up an evidently succulent amraunt from a handy pedestal dish, smiled and winked at it, and ate it with impish grace.

Ravandarr swung his hand angrily, as if slicing the air with a sword he did not have. "But that's just it! *What* battles? Father never lets me so much as—"

"Ah, but he will. Soon after I depart. His own neck is at risk in this, and he sees me as far too much the self-minded, pert little puppy. *You* are his burningly loyal back-blade. He will send you off after me with a force of your own, to strike if I fail or falter or just decide to do something other than slay Taera and bring her severed head back here for him to parade before the crones."

" 'Something other'?" Ravandarr frowned. "Such as?"

"Such as rape her—now that she's maimed, and thus no longer our kin. I've wanted to taste her charms for a long time, haven't you?—and then help her get to the Ravagers, to find a new life there."

Ravandarr gaped at his brother, aghast. "But-but-*why*? Every moment she still breathes is an affront to Olone! House Evendoom can't help but sink into divine disfavor, and be—"

"Nay, brother," Jalandral interrupted jauntily, "every moment she still breathes is an affront to the crones, as it reminds all that their power isn't absolute. Olone cares nothing for what we do to others—or haven't you been listening to the holy chants?"

He turned back to the bed, took up the sword they'd both known he'd choose, and began buckling it on. "Olone cares only about our personal quests for perfection—'beauty,' if you will. Needlessly putting a sword through a Maimed One does nothing at all to make us more perfect."

Settling the sword belt in place with a nod of satisfaction, Jalandral took up another sheathed dagger and chose the best place to strap it on. "A Maimed One, moreover, who is outcast—and out of Talonnorn to stay, probably soon to perish out in the Dark if we did nothing about her at all. No threat to us, and no threat to the city."

Sliding home another dagger into its sheath and gracefully patting his amulets in swift succession to make sure they were where they should be, he murmured, "See to yourself, as I do, and obey Father and the crones carefully and attentively—and as little as possible. Let their mistakes be their mistakes, not yours. You'll live longer, that way."

Flicking fingertips in a jaunty farewell across his younger brother's chest with a backhanded wave of his hand, the Firstblood of House Evendoom awakened the amulet at his throat, the one that turned aside daggers. As its faint singing rose around him, he strode out, leaving Ravandarr staring after him.

Imdul ran a swift hand down the front of his favorite serving-she, who gave him a wink and a smile before adroitly twisting away. Grinning at her amiably, he fell into his usual chair.

"Gates still down?" Urgel grunted, by way of greeting.

"As well you know," the poisoner murmured. "My, but their lack makes the street seem different."

"The street *is* different," Clazlathor said flatly, cradling his goblet of aehrodel. He was seated facing the doors. Not so long ago, whenever they opened, he would have seen the great, now-fallen gates House Evendoom had raised to guard their Forgerift, looming mere strides away across the street. Now, when the doors of the Waiting Warm Dark opened, there was nothing but the forlornly empty anvil and table of Orivon Firefist, and the angry glow of the Forgerift, beyond. "Evendoom's talons no longer hold it in an unshakable grip."

"Ho, ho," big Munthur agreed, from his end of the table, "and won't all our lives be interesting, these next few Turnings? Will it be House against House in the streets, d'you think? Or just a few swords drawn in alleys?"

Urgel shrugged. "We'd best keep low and silent while the Houses snap and snarl and settle things—or they'll quite happily turn on *us* to vent their fury. And if they do that, no matter how ridiculous their claims about our treasons are, we'll all be a little too dead to scoff—or care overmuch about the future of Talonnorn."

Tarlyn shrugged. "As to that, they could have slain any of us whenever they wished, all our lives. The High Houses have always done as they pleased in Talonnorn. *We* should all be pleased whenever they don't get their every idle whim fulfilled—such rarities are their only reminders that Olone's the Goddess, not each and every one of them." He drained the last of his aehrodel, sighed as he savored it, and added, "If nothing teaches them even a little prudence, we're all doomed."

"True," Urgel agreed, "but if Houses fall and war erupts *within* Talonnorn, as opposed to being brought to us by invaders from without, all of us around this table are threatened, even if we *somehow*"—his tone made a mocking point of just how likely that would be—"fix it that every last pureblood in all the Houses think we're the most marvelous of Niflghar and their best friends and most valuable allies! We thrive with things as they are now; large and permanent changes could doom us!"

"Correct," Imdul said firmly. "And I'd change that 'could,' which after all is but stating a truism that has always held sway across the Dark, to 'will probably,' and add 'here in Talonnorn.' We have seized opportunities and done well by them while the Houses stood in uneasy balance, and therefore relative peace. If things fall apart, how can we continue to demand and receive gems for what hundreds of other Nifl will be doing for free, out of desperation or to redress wrongs done to them, or just out of sheer blind blundering? We do the unpleasant with swords and slyness in the alleys; if it comes to open war, *everyone* in Talonnorn will be 'doing the unpleasant.' We may hate the Houses and complain about them every time we sit down at this table—but we need them to stay right where they are, lording it over us, seemingly eternal and sneering down at us and paying us no more attention than that! Leaving us to scurry past their noses like rats, and make our stones!"

"Why is it," Clazlathor asked, apparently addressing his own goblet, "that I *hate* it when you point out truths? Absolutely hate it?"

"So what do you think," Tarlyn asked with a frown, leaning forward on his elbows to look at Imdul and then at Urgel, "of the latest: this Evendoom-ordered hunt across the city for their vanished firefist? Orivon the Hairy One, Maker of Many Mighty Spellblades?"

"Can't blame the slave for running," Munthur rumbled unexpectedly, waving at the Waiting Warm Dark's front door to indicate the empty forge floor they all knew could be seen outside, right across the street. "It's what I'd have done, in his place."

Clazlathor shrugged. "Of course. Fell a few sneeringly overconfident Evendooms who're used to slaves cowering under their whips and make his escape—well, that's what humans *do,* if you let them see their chance.

If you haven't beaten all the life out of them, they'll leap at any scent of freedom. Every time."

"Saw his chance and took it, that's just what he did," Urgel agreed. "The Evendooms are fools to spread word. It's as if they think another House took him in, and are trying to threaten them into revealing by their blustering. Even if he was their best firefist, he was *only a firefist.* Rather than keeping quiet about it and raiding to gain replacement fire-fists, the Evendooms are bolstering this human's importance—and parad-ing their own obsessions and weakness of character before all the city."

"So we must soothe where they inflame," Imdul murmured, "but how?"

"Too late to stop word of the firefist's escape spreading," Urgel said, frowning down at his drink. "So we already stand in peril of slaves all over Talonnorn drinking deep of hope, and trying their own uprisings. Olone *spew!*"

"We must spread our own words," Imdul said, dropping his voice and leaning forward over the table. "Hinting that the Evendooms are speaking of this to hide something darker. This *wasn't* a slave escape, and Orivon Firefist never fled out of Talonnorn. Instead, he's been snatched into the Eventowers and chained there, hidden from all, because . . . why?"

"The bored Evendoom crones want to breed with him?" Clazlathor offered, mockingly.

Urgel snorted at *that* old gibe. "No, they want to breed him with something else, to produce—what? Remember, this lie of ours has to *soothe,* not thrust Talonnorn closer to swords-out!"

"So no mightier monsters, and nothing at all to do with Olone or her priestesses—or the Ever-Ice, for that matter," Tarlyn mused aloud. "What . . . what if they're using spells to alter his looks, and more spells to control his mind? So as to make him look like a different human, so they can send him up into the Blindingbright to spy for them?"

Urgel shook his head. "That'll have the other Houses hurling all they have at the Eventowers, to try to get this Orivon dead before he can be used to gain whatever advantage they fear the Evendooms will be able to achieve with him. We'll *cause* war in Talonnorn."

Tarlyn shook his head slowly. "Not if the tale we spread insists that their use for him is merely to cloak their own shame."

"Sending him to try to find a wayward Evendoom who fled with a lot of family magic," Clazlathor suggested. "Perhaps a crone with a . . . heir under her wing? I'm sure in all the fighting the Evendooms lost *some* purebloods, so other Houses, hearing our falsehoods, can believe them if they want to."

Imdul smiled, softly and slowly. "And they *will* want to believe. Oh, by the Burning Talon, they will."

Tarlyn and Urgel nodded eagerly.

"Now *that*," Urgel said, leaning back with drinking horn in hand, "I like."

"Slake throats, all, and let's be out and a-whispering," Tarlyn urged, chuckling.

"I know *just* where to begin," Imdul purred.

"Careful," Munthur rumbled. "Must be sly, so no hint this is false."

Imdul gave him a withering look. "I was born sly and careful—and by the time I was old enough to walk, I'd learned to be *thoroughly* false."

Munthur stared down the table at the poisoner, frowning in thought. Then, slowly, he started to chuckle.

The roar shook the rock all around them, hurling Orivon and Taerune up off the ledge and awake even before they crashed back down onto it, bouncing hard on rock still quivering amid a hard rain of gravel. Shouts rang through the pittering of stones all around them. Nifl shouts.

Dust was swirling in the air, but not thickly enough to entirely cloak what had happened. Across the cavern, a Nifl spellrobe was standing atop a high horn of rock, hands still raised in the aftermath of the spell he'd hurled—a magic so strong that the fitful, dying glows and drifting sparks of its blossoming were still clinging to him.

Other Niflghar in war-armor were ranged along lower rocks, hurl-bows strapped to their forearms, peering where the spellrobe was look-ing: down into the bottom of the cavern, where the roiling dust was thickest. They were obviously working with the spellrobe, and both Orivon and Taerune saw an Arc of Eyes, the targe of House Raskshaula, on the breast of one warblade ere there was a deep, groaning roar—and another great hanging tooth of rock tore free and plunged down to shatter on the cavern floor below.

This large Outcavern was angled like the arm of a giant, turning just beyond their ledge, the spellrobe's horn of rock rising on the inside curve of the angle. A plentiful stone forest of stalactites stretched away into un-seen darkness, thinned only slightly by the six or so huge stone fangs the spellrobe's magic had already brought down.

One of the Talonar warblades pointed into the dust-shrouded depths, and he and several fellows aimed their arms and triggered their bows, firing down into the roiling dust.

Taerune drove her chin hard into Orivon's arm and then nodded frantically, in a clear plea to be ungagged. Throwing an arm over her to hold her prone on the ledge, Orivon tugged her gag most of the way out, enough to let her choke, husk, and hiss, "Release me! If we must fight—"

Orivon thrust her gag back into place and shook his head, holding her firmly down. "And have you shout out," he whispered, "and betray me to these Nifl? Lie quiet a bit, and we'll see if unbinding becomes needful. I have your Orb ready."

Taerune's eyes blazed her fury at him, but that was all she could do. She couldn't call on the Orb without touching it.

Or could she?

13

No Orb Too Mighty

In the striving of spell against spell, priestess against spellrobe, house against house, city against city, No Nifl lady can have an orb too mighty for her needs, for there will never be an end to her mighty needs.

—**Talonar crones' saying**

*J*alandral Evendoom was unsurprised to find a priestess of Olone waiting for him at the gates. One who looked as young and agile as he was, and wore armor as sleek and fine as his own, the slender sword scabbarded at her hip doubtless a spellblade. Stunningly beautiful, unfamiliar to him, and—of course—coldly haughty, her eyes gleaming a frosty challenge.

"Firstblood of Evendoom, I shall accompany you until your task is accomplished."

He cocked an eyebrow. "My father ordered me to do a slaying for the honor of House Evendoom. A purely family matter, one would think. I was unaware that the Consecrated of Olone indulged in prurient curiosity about such matters—or have you a better reason?"

"None that I see need to share with you, Heir of Evendoom." Her tone was noticeably colder. "Other than to warn you that many in Talonnorn shall be watching you—and judging your behavior. Your father is one such. Consider me an ever-present gentle reminder."

Jalandral gave her a casually elegant salute. "Welcome along, then. Have you a name, gentle reminder?"

"None that you need know."

"Well, then, Gentle," the heir said affably, "know you that I am Jalandral—or Dral, to my intimates—and that our time together can be as pleasant or otherwise as you choose to make it. I am cordial fellowship itself . . . when I am allowed to be. Choose your gambits shrewdly."

She kept silent, and in that silence he regarded her from gleaming boot tips to crown of hair. "Are you expecting me to feed you, along the way? And have you chosen some role for yourself, beyond that of watcher? Do you give back rubs?"

"I do not," the priestess said shortly, the faint paleness of a blush spreading along her jaw.

Jalandral smirked and watched that betraying hue spread.

"I will require no food nor drink from you," the priestess added stiffly, "and am to assist you by guiding you to . . . the one you seek."

"Ah. Well, it's certainly heartening to know that Olone doesn't want Talonar rampants stumbling around the Dark thinking for themselves," Jalandral observed jovially, and waved a languid gauntlet at the gate, which the impassive guards had drawn open. "Shall we hence?"

The priestess gave no reply, but strode into the entrance and then stopped and turned, awaiting him—almost as if she suspected he'd order the gate slammed behind her and then turn and depart by another way. Jalandral grinned; her suspicions were quite correct.

However, he could see Shoan Maulstryke and another priestess waiting in the street outside. They would make sure to misconstrue such a prank, and enthusiastically spread false report of it across the city— cowardice and insolent renunciation of Olone, all at once—handing a pretext to the crones that might well cost both Lord Evendoom and his Firstblood their lives.

And as Jalandral happened to be the one and did not want to become the other—not for a long time, and not in such circumstances as prevailed now in Talonnorn—he ordered nothing, but merely waved cheerful farewells and salutes to the Evendoom warblades, who returned them with grins as broad as his own.

Jalandral's smile turned wry. Well, it was nice to stroll out to probable death knowing *someone* understood and appreciated you.

To me, center of my power. Come to me. Taerune bit down on the gag savagely, willing her Orb to answer her. *Respond, by Olone!* Some of the oldest crones, their wills tempered over lifetimes, were reputed to be able to call their Orbs swooping to their fingertips across half Talonnorn, or send their Orbs flying off to do their bidding, even to spitting forth spells when they were nowhere near.

Yet when she wasn't touching her Orb, Taerune had never been able to do more than make it change hue, glow or cease glowing, or flash with a sudden flare of light—and then only when she was within easy reach of it. Glaring now at where she knew it to be, gathering her will with such fierce force that her head began to pound and sweat started to run into her eyes and drip from her nose, she felt . . . nothing. Nothing at all from her Orb. Again and again she thrust out her will, reaching, probing.

Without result, until she collapsed, exhausted, and rested her chin on the rough rock, trying not to weep around the rough gag.

She was—had been—a spoilt lady pureblood, not a priestess or crone blood-offered to Olone, which meant her Orb stored a handful of spells, and with them gone it was no more than a toy and not a formidable weapon. She should have let Orivon plunder a spellblade. Yet not Uncle Faunhorn's, or Valarn's, or any Evendoom blade, for those they could trace with ease.

If they ever got a chance to pluck a blade belonging to another House, though . . .

Let her Dark Warrior wield it and strut with it—and see if she and her Orb couldn't quietly assume command over it, while he did so.

The gag prevented her from smiling, but she no longer felt like crying.

"So, Coward of Evendoom, your escort of Olone shamed you into setting forth at last," Shoan Maulstryke sneered.

Jalandral yawned. "I'd hoped, yet not expected, an insult *slightly* more creative, Shoan, but I suppose that until House Maulstryke does something about its breeding habits, I should put such hopes aside."

The eyes of the Firstblood of Maulstryke went flat and hard with hate.

"I see you, too, have acquired a Gentle Reminder," Jalandral observed conversationally, ignoring Shoan's fury. "I believe I'll call mine 'Gentle'— for I hope she will be, when we've time to know each other rather better— and yours 'Reminder.' Unless, that is, you two Eyes of Olone will deign to favor us with your names?"

Jalandral's current collection of unfriendly stares grew, as two stony Nifl-she gazes joined Shoan Maulstryke's burning one.

The heir of House Evendoom grinned. "I bask in your warm, deep love. Lead on, holy guides. Shoan, I see we're both arrayed for battle. These vigilant priestesses by their very presence prevent us from slaughtering each other right away, but at the same time make a certainty of our trading cutting words—threats, insults, and the usual condescending observations—with each other. So have you anything truly colorful memorized that you'd like to share with us at this time, or shall I seize the moment?"

"You are an oriad *child*," Shoan hissed contemptuously, "as wild-tongued as Maulstryke younglings just after they learn to *walk*."

Jalandral yawned again. "So, no, nothing memorized. I suppose the burden of entertainment must therefore fall to me."

He drew his spellblade, and laughed at the triple whirlwind of leaping back and drawing steel this evoked. "The Outcaverns, it seems, are an even more dangerous place than I'd heard. Ladies?"

His elaborate gesture of courtesy was as flawlessly ornate as it was archaic.

"We are *not* ladies—we are Consecrated of Olone," Reminder corrected him severely, but the priestesses did move forward. Three long strides, ere they turned in smooth unison and beckoned the two heirs to stride past them.

"But of course," Jalandral replied, starting his long walk out of Talonnorn. A moment later they were all walking, bound for the Outcaverns with weapons at the ready, a careful distance apart.

Orivon hid a grim smile as he turned away from Taerune's furious face to watch the battle. Slaves have their desires denied at every turn; it was time, and more than time, that she knew what that felt like. And she *would* see this as probably her last chance to call on other Nifl, and so get free. If these were all Rakshaula, they might well aid her in return for what she could tell them that would let them defeat Evendoom, and—

Under his arm, Taerune started wriggling energetically, bobbing and squirming. Orivon turned back to her, anger flaring.

She was struggling to move forward to the edge of the ledge. Orivon lifted his arm to let her travel—but brought it down again to grasp her belt firmly. If she wanted to see the Nifl fighting, well and good; she might well see or learn something he wouldn't understand . . . but if she sought to hurl herself off the ledge to her death, and managed it, he'd lose his guide, his envoy to talk to Nifl, and his possible bargaining bait, all at once.

When Taerune's chin reached the edge of the ledge she stopped moving, and gave him a look that might be angry thanks or might mean "So there!"

Orivon nodded and turned his attention back to the fray below. She'd used her lash on him for years, and accomplished little; how long would it take him to train her?

The oldest, deepest chamber in Coldheart was also the coldest.

Of the ring of priestesses standing around the huge scrying-whorl, gazing into its many moving, winking glows, only the Revered Mother of the Ever-Ice was wearing anything: her gown of Ice crystals.

The other Nifl-shes tried to stand tall and quell their shiverings under her watchful gaze: Lolonmae Daughter of the Ice, trying to seem serene but with trembling lips and clenched fists that shook at her sides; the chastened but still sane Exalted Daughter of the Ice Semmeira; and six senior priestesses of lesser rank. No holy abbey of the Ever-Ice was as old and respected as Coldheart, and few in Arnoenar would have dared even try to spy on this chamber with spells—though every last Nifl of the city knew of this place, where the holy shes of the Ever-Ice spied on *them*.

Under the Revered Mother's brisk bidding, Trusted Tongue of the Ice Ithmeira had just reluctantly and tentatively ventured her opinion as to what Coldheart should do, in light of what could be seen in the scrying-whorl. She was now trembling almost as violently as the priestess beside her, Trusted Tongue of the Ice Darraeya, whose thin build shielded her not at all against the chill of the chamber—but Ithmeira's shivering was as much fear as discomfort.

"You are quite correct, Ithmeira," the Revered Mother said softly, and waited for the priestess to let out her almost violent sigh of relief before adding, "We *must* become involved. Ouvahlor has succeeded not only in wounding Talonnorn deeply, but stirring up the Ravagers—and Imbrae and Yarlys, too; see, here and here? The Immur is now one great battlefield—and if Klarandarr starts hurling the spells around that I fear he's itching to, he'll awaken That Which Sleeps Below, and all Niflheim will again know *real* war."

She turned her head and said calmly, "Semmeira, we will need the mindbolt spell you've been perfecting."

The Exalted Daughter's jet-black skin went a sickly yellow-white. "The–?"

"The spell you've been practicing in secret, to use on me, Child of the Ice," the Revered Mother said flatly. "Did you *really* think you could do such things here without my knowing? I feel every pulse and shift of magic from the topmost spires of Coldheart down to the rock beneath its roots. Go now, Semmeira, and meet me in my chambers as soon as you can. We must alter your spell together, to make it a lance to slay Klarandarr of Ouvahlor."

Semmeira was trembling, almost white from head to toe, her eyes very dark. "H-how?" she whispered.

"Using some of his seed, of course."

"Revered Mother," Darraeya asked shakily, as she and Ithmeira eyed Semmeira as if the Exalted Daughter were going to die in an instant, right in front of them, "how will we ever get any of that?"

The Revered Mother sighed. "From my stock of such handy necessities, child. I didn't go to all that trouble seducing the rampant when he was much younger and fiercer than he is now—and win all the bites and bruises he gave me, too—for nothing."

And she turned and swept out without another word, reacting not at all to the gasps of jaws dropping open all around her.

It was impossible to tell if the huge stalactites had crushed any foes when they'd crashed down onto the cavern floor. Atop his horn of rock, the spellrobe was bending and peering almost frantically, trying to see through the dust down there.

Then he sprang back as if stung, almost falling in his haste; something too small for Orivon and Taerune to see had come hurtling up at him from below. The warblades back along the cavern were cocking and firing their hurlbows in swift, deft earnest, firing at some foe below, some—there!

Taerune caught a glimpse of a dark, slender figure that was somehow *shimmering* . . .

Another, yonder, and another. Nifl were dodging among the tumbled stones down there, swords in their hands. One of them began the unmistakable movements of whirling a stone in a sling and then letting it fly at the spellrobe.

The Nifl scattered across the cavern floor were clad in all manner of mismatched armor, and hung about with sheathed weapons and flasks, packs and—Taerune's eyes narrowed—ah! There: those rolling stones! Dislodged by a boot that her eyes told her was well over yonder. The shimmering . . . of course!

They were all using magic to make themselves seem in one place, when they were in truth standing off to the side. Ravagers? Probably, for no Talonar warband—and probably none of Ouvahlor, either—would make war in such motley armor.

By the way he moved his head, Orivon had seen them too, but Taerune had only a moment to glance sidelong at him; the spellrobe was casting something.

And no wonder. The Raskshaulan warblades must be running out of arrows, they'd sent so many sleeting down, yet she'd seen only one Nifl struck, twisting and toppling over amid the rocks strewn across the cavern floor.

Crouching low as he tried to avoid slung stones, the spellrobe finished working his spell, its light flaring around him. He'd chosen haste over the precision that would have poured all the power he'd called up into the magical effect alone.

The rock overhead glowed, and Orivon's grip on her belt tightened. There came another deep, yawning groan, and another stalactite fell.

Just one, this time. They watched it break free—huge and brown-gray and hoary—and fall, slow and ponderous. Below, Nifl were running and clambering frantically, as doom came down to greet them.

Orivon rolled back from the edge, clawing Taerune with him . . . but the heavy, rolling crash, as the stalactite smashed and the cavern shook, still almost flung them both off the ledge.

Someone screamed in pain and terror—a long, falling wailing that came from across the cavern, not below—as Taerune came down hard and helplessly atop Orivon, driving the breath out of him. Grunting, he lost his grip on her, as she twisted and arched, trying to roll along the ledge and away from him—and not off the ledge into a deadly fall.

She was managing it, gag still firmly in place and bound arm throbbing from all the bruising it was taking, when the bare stone end of the ledge she was rolling toward blossomed into a fell radiance.

At the heart of which appeared the spellrobe who'd been standing on the horn of rock, crouched with hands raised to hurl more magic, gaze bent on the cavern floor below.

As the glow of his magical journeying faded, he saw Taerune tumbling along the ledge and Orivon scrambling to his feet beyond her. His eyes widened in fear and anger.

And a moment later, in recognition.

They'd all seen each other before, across the Rift. The firefist and his tormentor were sharing this ledge with the watcher House Raskshaula had often sent to spy on House Evendoom's prize slave.

The cruel young spellrobe Ondrar of Raskshaula—who was now moving his hands in the first framing gestures of a spellweaving, even as he gaped at them in disbelief.

He was casting a slaying spell.

Lord Erlingar Evendoom poured the last of his best elanselveir into a goblet that matched his own in grandeur, and held it forth, smiling a genuine smile. "I never thought I'd see you alive again."

Faunhorn Evendoom took the wine with a nod of thanks. "I am similarly surprised. By the grace of Olone—or Taerune's own intent and precise unleashing—the magic that felled me burned me inside, marring my skin not at all. The priestesses and our crones both saw this as a mark of Olone's favor, not a sin before her. Wherefore the Waters."

Lord Evendoom nodded. Faunhorn's near-lifeless body had been submerged in the Waters of Healing in a hidden chamber of the Eventowers, a family secret known only to Evendooms and a handful of Talonnorn's most senior priestesses of the Goddess. In the healing pool Faunhorn had drifted from ravaged weakness to unharmed and vigorous far faster than most the Waters had aided. Another mark of Olone's favor.

Lord Evendoom savored the familiar ruby heat of the elanselveir, thoughtfully—and expressionlessly—regarding the only Nifl in all Talonnorn he trusted.

Faunhorn had gone into that pool because he was trusted by everyone. Some called him the most honest and honorable Niflghar in Talonnorn, and it was no secret the priestesses of Olone saw him as an ideal Lord of House Evendoom. That he'd escaped all scarring or mutilation just made their decision easier; they wanted Faunhorn alive to give them the freedom to sweep away a certain Erlingar Evendoom and both his sons, if the desire—ah, pray pardon, *Olone's* will—took them.

Yet Faunhorn could be trusted, and was capable. No treachery would make him act against the rightful ruler and heirs of Evendoom, and henceforth no mercy would make him hesitate in striking down

Taerune—no matter how fond he'd been of her—now that he knew she bore her Orb, and that her treason was blatant and extended to unhesitatingly trying to slay *him*.

Not if the Lord of Evendoom ordered it.

Erlingar sipped again, swallowed, and said formally, "As Lord of Evendoom, I order you to hunt down Orivon Firefist and my now-Nameless daughter, she who we both knew as Taerune—and slay them both. Do you accept these orders, Faunhorn Evendoom?"

Faunhorn frowned, but nodded. "I do."

Lord Evendoom sighed—he'd not realized until that moment how much he'd feared a refusal and the fight to the death that would have had to follow, given what the Evendoom crones had told him of why they were allowing Faunhorn to be brought back from slow and lingering death—and drank deeply. When he'd recovered from the raging ruby fire of the elanselveir, he said roughly, "Taera's using her orb to mask her whereabouts—but we have a means of tracing her scent out in the Dark. A gorkul."

He reached down with the walking stick he'd brought with him—the stick both of them knew held many slaying magics of the House, enough for a Lord of Evendoom to blast any number of Faunhorns—and with its tip slid aside an ordauth plate in the stone floor beneath their boots.

"This is why we met here," Faunhorn said. It was not a question.

Erlingar Evendoom nodded, and pointed with his stick down through the revealed grating—at a chained and naked gorkul looking balefully up at them from the depths of a cell below.

It knew better than to do anything but keep silent.

"We've already used it to trace her into the Outcaverns, to make sure she didn't try to hide here in the city and betray us to a rival House. This is one of the first gorkul she personally trained; she named it 'Grunt Tusks.'"

"I see. So this Grunt Tusks had been overseeing other slaves working at the Rift?"

"Indeed."

"So just what's going to make a he-gorkul we've lashed and goaded into lashing and goading other slaves want to hunt down this Orivon for us? What are we going to offer him?"

"His life."

·   ·   ·

Orivon sprang over her, arrow-swift, a dagger flashing in his hand. Taerune tried to shriek a warning around the gag, even as Ondrar's wards flared—and the human froze in midair, caught and held in the shimmering, swirling force of the spellrobe's defensive magics.

More than held; the magic would be searing his innards, cooking him alive!

Taerune spun around on the ledge, pivoting on her bound arm and kicking out viciously, sweeping the spellrobe's ankles from under him before he could even start to shout.

Ondrar of Raskshaula toppled like a smashed turret, arm and shoulder slamming down onto the edge of the ledge with bone-shattering force, bouncing him back up into the air like a thing of rags—to start the long, shouting fall down to the cavern floor.

And snatching his wards away from the Hairy One who'd come leaping to slay him.

Freed, Orivon Firefist landed and ran forward on wobbling, collapsing legs. As he fell obliviously on his face, plumes of smoke streamed from his mouth and staring, sightless eyes.

The cavern around them trembled, ever so slightly, even before the distant echoes of thudding falls reached them.

"Ho, now!" Old Bloodblade rumbled. "Those were short and sharp, with no groaning of rock before them, only after. Battle."

Daruse nodded. "Battle." He looked back over his shoulder at the grim, motley Nifl behind them. Two dozen veteran Ravagers hungry to raid Talonnorn were walking with the slow, sure-footed ease of dark elves used to traversing wild ways as quietly as possible. "So, do we go to see who's fighting?"

Beside Daruse's other shoulder, Lharlak shook his head. "Not off that way. That's the Immur, and apt to be crawling with warbands of Ouvahlor, slowly returning home. The wounded and the wise."

Old Bloodblade swung around, to squint at him hard. " 'Wounded and wise'? How so?"

"Two sorts travel slowly in the Immur: those who can only manage slow travel thanks to their wounds, and those wise enough to move quietly and warily. Those who go faster meet their dooms sooner." Lharlak pointed. "We go this way, to the Outcaverns *not* between Ouvahlor and Talonnorn, and come around to approach the city on another side, where sentinels and ready defenders are less likely. Me, I like to survive my raids."

For once, there came no dispute.

On her knees on the hard ledge, bending over Orivon, Taerune peered at him. Was he dead? Was she alone here in the Outcaverns, with murderous Talonar all around her?

He moaned, softly, and started to move, hands feebly seeking his eyes.

Alive.

Taerune's mouth tightened. Her Dark Warrior, her brute who'd so eagerly—gloatingly—used her own lash on her.

It would be *so* easy to slay him now; the nearest of the daggers on the ledge was an easy crawl away. Once she sawed through the lash binding her wrist to her side, it would be the work of but a moment to slit his throat or sink the dagger hilt-deep in one of his eyes . . .

And then she *would* be alone; even something slow and mindless like a cave creeper could slay her whenever she fell asleep. Shouts and warsteel ringing on warsteel from below sharply reminded her of dangers far faster and smarter than cave creepers. Dangers who might want to . . . enjoy her before slitting her throat. With no one to stop them.

No one to talk to, no one to guard her back—or flank, with but one arm—Olone! No one to help the Nifl with the missing arm even *climb*.

She dared not kill him. She needed him too much.

Yet how alive *was* he? The Orb could do many things, but powerful healings were not among them, and even if she'd had a dozen Orbs aglow with power and obedient to her command, she didn't know *how* to restore blinded eyes. Oh, where was a spellrobe when you needed—

Taerune swept that thought away with a grim grin and put her arm over her Dark Warrior much as he had done to her, to keep him low and unmoving on the ledge should he start to writhe. Then her lip curled in distaste, and she wriggled hastily away from him, nostrils flaring.

The wards had scorched him, making his human stink sharper and stronger. She was used to his reek from the brandings, but still . . . With the gag in, she'd choke if she spewed. If she cut it free, spewing her guts all over him might well rouse him, but she doubted he'd waken in a kindly mood. Not to mention that he'd then smell far worse.

Taerune drew in as deep a breath as she could around the gag, and dared to thrust her head out and look down over the edge of the ledge at the battle.

Nifl were busily slaughtering Nifl, blade against blade down in the drifting dust and tumbled rocks. With their spellrobe gone and nothing left for their hurlbows to bite with, the Talonar warblades were faring poorly—and dying swiftly. She watched them thrust desperately at empty air, aware by now that their foes weren't where their eyes told them they stood—and she watched them fall, spitted before they could wound what they couldn't see, blades falling from spasming hands to clatter on rocks.

The Ravagers—they had to be Ravagers—would very soon kill the last warblade, and have time to peer up at high ledges in search of the missing spellrobe, to make sure he wouldn't lurk awaiting the best moment to drop stalactites on their heads. Taerune rolled over onto her back, away from the lip of the ledge, and lay there staring at the rough rock high overhead, listening to the clangor fading.

When it ended, there was a brief mutter of low voices—Nifl rampants, uttering a few words she caught: "our noise heard far off" and "must *move,* now" and "raid Talonnorn, not fight Talonar idiots." Then there came the thuds and scrapings of armored Nifl clambering over rocks, moving in the direction of Talonnorn . . . then, silence.

Taerune lay for a long time listening, seeking not the stretching silence but the faint sounds of cave creepers or anything else cautiously approaching. Out in the Wild Dark, noises meant battle or the rare yawnings of the earth . . . which meant possible food. Dead, injured, or pinned and helpless creatures to feed on.

A wounded, senseless human and a bound and maimed Nifl on a ledge, for instance.

14

The Fear of the Hunted

Taste it as your blade comes out,
The fear of the hunted,
The despairing shout.
Mercy is for fools,
Hesitation for the weak.
Spilling blood makes every sword sleek.
—old Nifl warblade drinking chant

Orivon groaned. Taerune rolled over hastily and sat up.

He groaned again, one outflung arm twitching. Taerune threw herself into worming her way past him to the swords. The blade that was lying the right way up, allowing her to easily trap it between wrist and hip and slice through the lash binding her, was right . . . here . . .

The lash parted and fell away, freeing her, at about the time she saw Orivon's eyelids flutter. Hastily Taerune crawled back behind him, and put her arm down against her hip as if it were still bound.

She watched him lift a hand to his face, trail his fingers across it, and tap lightly at his eyes. He let his hand fall, sighed, and felt around in front of him, patting the rough stone of the ledge, less than a finger length from his dagger. The dagger he seemed to be searching for . . .

He can't see!

"Taerune?" Orivon asked quietly. "You're behind me, aren't you?"

She drew in a long, slow breath, saying nothing. So the wardfires had blinded him. This changed everything.

And nothing.

She watched him snarl a soundless curse and feel for the dagger again. He was going to find it, his fingers almost on it . . . there. Even as he cautiously closed his hand around it and then snatched it up, Taerune replied calmly, "Yes. Yes, I am."

He turned slowly, dagger in one hand and tracing the stone in front of him with the other.

"You can't see, can you?"

"No," he said shortly. "Your doing?"

"No. The spellrobe's wards."

"Ah. And he's—?"

"Dead." Taerune drew in a deep breath. "I kicked him off the ledge. It sounded like a long fall."

Orivon nodded. "And his friends?"

"The others—Ravagers, I believe—slew them all. And moved on."

Orivon nodded again. "If I try to climb down, I'll probably fall too."

"Not . . . not if I go first, and tell you where to reach. The climb wasn't that hard."

Her Dark Warrior grinned bitterly. "Can you tell me the movements of foes, fast enough for me to put a sword through them before they kill me? If I can kill one with a map, you'll have to read it."

Nettled by his calm, Taerune burst out, "Aren't you *afraid*?"

Orivon turned to look at her, as if he could see her. His eyes looked unharmed, but stared through her, at nothing. "Slaves breathe fear, eat fear, drink fear. Fear is in every thing we do. We have no time to indulge it, for there is always the work. Waiting. And the punishment, waiting if the work gets not done. I learned—very long ago—not to have time for fear." He was silent for a moment, and then added expressionlessly, "You taught me that."

A breath later, as she wondered what to reply, he spoke again. "I can see shapes, a little."

"Good," Taerune sighed, her relief strong and swift. "Hopefully the spellrobe's wards merely clawed at the darksight spell we cast on you, and as its chaos calms, your sight will ret—*Nooo!*"

Her shout was startled and despairing.

Orivon turned toward the faint, somehow familiar rippling sound Taerune was shouting at, pawing at his eyes in a desperate attempt to see.

And then, a moment before cruel Nifl laughter began to sweep down on them, he heard the deep, wet burbling of an eager darkwings, and knew.

The Hunt of Talonnorn was flying, and here, and swooping down at them!

For the first time, Jalandral Evendoom and Shoan Maulstryke exchanged meaningful glances that held mutual exasperation, rather than sneering scorn or open hatred.

Their escorts had halted again, hands raised against them in preemptory "halt" signals, to cast another tracing spell. Reminder had woven the last such magic, so Gentle cast it this time. Grounding their swords, the two heirs swallowed sighs, glanced around at the nigh-featureless cavern, and then watched the priestesses work. Both knew they'd have little chance of finding the fleeing Nameless one and her slave without these castings, but that knowledge did nothing to make them enjoy being treated as disobedient—and stupid—children by holy shes whose hauteur far outstripped their own.

And the Olone-exalted shes took so damned *long* in their castings, adding wholly unnecessary implorings of the Goddess and little "face this way, and pose just so" rituals to add an air of mysterious power and importance that fooled no one, and afforded them many opportunities to coldly make clear their disdain for the two Firstbloods. All of this preening, moreover, was presumably being paraded before an unseen audience of worthies back in Talonnorn.

This particular Outcavern was lofty, bare, and of purple-white stone; aside from its choice of two tunnels at the far end from the one they'd entered it by, even a casual glance could tell it held nothing of interest. So Jalandral and Shoan had plenty of time, as the manyfold gestures, elaborate positionings, and ever-holier prayers droned on, to gaze into each other's eyes and wordlessly agree on certain matters.

Their hatred was mutual; each was seeking a chance to slay or at least wound the other—but both were also awaiting opportunities, even if seizing such would mean they must work together, of slaying their infuriating escorts and winning the freedom to fight each other.

The Consecrated of Olone seemed to sense this, or to have learned the Firstbloods' thoughts through magic. From the moment they'd stepped outside the main cavern that held Talonnorn, they had taken care never to get too close to either heir, turn their backs, or allow one rampant to block their view of the other.

"Merely helping us hunt Taerune, my left dancing eyeball," Jalandral murmured under his breath, smiling coldly at the last elaborate flourishes of what should have been a simply muttered, over-in-two-instants tracing spell.

The flourishes ended at last, and Gentle closed her eyes, her slender fingers cupping air in an attitude of devout prayer.

As she contentrated, trembling, Reminder warily watched the two heirs. Her needle-slender spellblade was aimed oh-so-casually at Jalandral Evendoom—and Gentle's blade, temporarily in Reminder's other hand, was coincidentally trained upon Shoan Maulstryke.

The Firstbloods' own spellblades could hurl spells but were real swords, not dainty near-needles. Those borne by the Eyes of Olone—as they were so unsubtly being warned—must be delicate arsenals of deadly spells.

So Jalandral and Shoan calmly ignored the swords aimed at them, leaning on their own blades in elegantly posed silence, and waited for Gentle's playacted trance to end.

Which it eventually did, with a gasp and a shiver, a murmured prayer to Olone, and a straightening and sudden turn to point dramatically at one of the tunnel mouths. Whereupon Gentle frowned sternly and commanded overloudly, "We go *that* way."

"Fair hearing," Jalandral and Shoan replied in rough unison, nodding. As Reminder returned Gentle's spellblade to her, with the priestesses watching the heirs steadily, the Firstblood of Evendoom drawled, "A question, holy guides: just what, precisely, are you tracing? I understand the magic of the Nameless hides her from you quite effectively, so . . . ?"

"Olone's secrets," Reminder informed him stiffly, "are just that. And must remain so."

"Ah," Shoan Maulstryke said brightly then, "but Aumaeraunda, Holiest of Olone, has told us the Goddess has ordered her Consecrated *to inform the Houses fully* of all they learn that is vital to the honor or interests of Talonnorn. And as the Holiest herself confirmed this task to be vital to the honor of our city . . ."

He spread his hands, one eyebrow lifting, his gaze a clear challenge.

Reminder scowled at him, but Jalandral murmured, "Talonnorn watches. Talonnorn *expects*."

The priestess went pale, eyes glittering in fury, but Gentle came to stand beside her, and said quietly, "You are correct, twice: we are not tracing the Nameless one, whose magic indeed masks her whereabouts from us, and that we should impart truthful answer to you as to what we are tracing. Know, then, that our spells trace tokens built into the boots of the escaped slave we believe to be accompanying her. The Nameless was neither a crone of her House nor a Consecrated, and so was unaware—as I believe both of you were, until this moment—that such tokens are put into all slaves' boots for just this purpose."

Jalandral decided it was time to arch one of *his* eyebrows. "Really? And how many other tokens are we all carrying around, for you to use for other secret purposes whenever it suits you?"

"Ah," Gentle said with the most fleeting of smiles, "as to that, I fear I must remind you that Olone's secrets *are* Olone's secrets—and must remain so."

Like a hurtling shadow of talons and great leathery wings, the foremost darkwings of the Hunt raced down upon Orivon and Taerune on the ledge, its bulk blotting out the rest of the cavern, its long neck undulating as it thrust its head out and to the side, poised to scour along the ledge with jaws agape.

"By Olone and Talonnorn," its rider cried out, hauling it back from that scouring in an angry flurry of flapping wings that slapped the very lip of the ledge, "*these* aren't Ravagers! It's the slave and the Nameless we're seeking! Keep their faces intact, remember; the Eldest wants to see the heads!"

As if in reply, but before any of the other laughing riders on the line of darkwings behind it could shout a word, there came a sudden burst of bright magic in the air—a blast that made the head of the darkwings vanish, and its spasming body, neck flailing blindly and bloodily, crash into the cavern wall just below the ledge.

Again Taerune and Orivon clung to each other, bouncing helplessly as the rock shook under them. Neither of them saw the Nifl dashed to broken-limbed death, or rider and steed rebound off the wall and tumble limp and lifeless down to the littered rocks of the cavern floor below.

Depths from which angry Nifl cries arose, even before the astonished Hunt riders started shouting.

"Bloodblade, what're you *doing*?"

"Oriad-head! Are you *trying* to get us all killed?"

"Ha-ha!" Old Bloodblade roared, stepping away from the overhanging cavern wall into full view of the Hunt above, and triggering his wand again to blast the next darkwings. "I always wanted to do this!"

His target burst into bloody spatters, rider and all.

"By the Ghodal Below and the Blindingbright Above, the wand works!" the aging Ravager roared. "Alathla promised me I could bathe *armies* in flame with this, and she told the *truth* for once! Ha-*ha*!"

Amid his delighted shouts, the third wandburst missed its darkwings but struck the cavern ceiling beyond—bringing a rain of rock onto the heads of the rest of the Hunt, that dashed them down, down to a rolling, buried death far below.

Blinding, roiling dust shrouded the ledge, and in the heart of it Taerune rolled herself hard against Orivon—and awakened her Orb.

It burst from his hiding into her hand, even as she thrust her face against his, and forced her tongue into his startled mouth. She slapped the Orb against their locked-together lips and held it there.

[*DON'T move*] she ordered, her mind-voice—boosted by the Orb—sliding into his head like a slicingly sharp silver dagger. [*I'm magically keeping us from coughing or choking, so the Nifl below don't find us. Just—lie here. Please.*]

She convulsed against him. *What—what's wrong?* Orivon thought, and heard his mind-voice, anger and apprehension warring, roll around both their heads loudly enough to make him wince as swiftly as she did.

[*Ignore me. I'm just gagging.*]

"*Just gagging*"? *Why?*

[*Take this not the wrong way, Orivon, but to Niflghar, humans reek.*]

Orivon was silent for a time. *I see. Well, to humans, Nifl-shes smell, too. But they taste quite nice.*

Taerune squirmed and wriggled on the ledge, seeking to keep their mouths together but to thrust her body as far from him as she could.

Take that not the wrong way. His mind-voice was mocking.

It had been good to watch the Hunt wheel and laugh, chasing each other around city spires and flourishing their blades in salute. Yet after they'd flown forth from Talonnorn for the first time since the battles, winging out of the great cavern into the Dark beyond, Ravandarr Evendoom had turned away with a surprisingly heavy heart.

The ramparts suddenly seemed a cold and unfriendly place. Jalandral was out there, somewhere, and so was . . .

Savagely Ravan put all thoughts of his sister Taera out of his mind, his head swirling as wildly as his cloak, and stalked down through dark and deserted passages, seeking his own chambers. There to brood, perhaps summon some Nameless shes to dance for him, or whip each other while he watched . . . *yes*. None of them would be Taerune Evendoom, but–

Something moved in the darkness ahead; something that was blocking his way. Ravan's hand went to his sword hilt out of habit, even as his wards flared. He let his real, rising anger put sparks into his frown. "Who–"

His wards faded away before a stronger radiance, a ruby-red glow that outlined a dark and slender figure. Shorter than he was, curvaceous . . . and all too familiar. Astonishment made him blurt out, "Maharla?"

"The same," the Eldest of Evendoom purred, even before he could curse himself for not greeting the most senior crone of the House properly. "I am very pleased to have found you so swiftly, Ravandarr . . . and alone."

Deepening astonishment. Friendliness? From *Maharla?* He was speechless as her hand–tingling with power, surging magic that swirled sparks from the hilt of Ravan's blade that almost certainly marked it being magically bound into its scabbard–took his, soft and warm and strong, and drew him toward the wall.

It parted before her, a door opening soundlessly to reveal a chamber awash in moving, surging red glows of her magic. Prepared beforehand, obviously; Ravan's bracers tingled with life of their own as his wards tried to awaken again, but were overwhelmed.

Maharla drew him firmly inside the room, her magic sealing them in together, and murmured, "Be not alarmed, Secondblood of Evendoom. You stand in the favor of Holy Olone."

Ravandarr blinked. "I–I do?"

The Eldest was towing him, ever so gently, across the room of billowing red smoke to a chased oval coffer. It stood up out of the swirling smoke atop a plinth of smooth-carved, upswept stone, that was shaped like a frozen wave of water.

"You do," she confirmed softly. "The Goddess has sent me a vision. A vision of you."

She stopped beside the coffer. "You were walking alone, sword in hand, through the caverns of the Wild Dark–and you were pursuing your Nameless sister."

"I . . ." Ravandarr realized he knew nothing safe to say, and so said merely, "I know not what this might mean, Eldest. Guide me."

Maharla nodded, satisfaction in her solemn eyes. "You must go forth into the Outcaverns in secret, telling no one, and do what Jalandral will undoubtedly fail to do, and so prove your true worth to your father."

"I must hunt T—ah, the Nameless."

Maharla nodded and put her hand on the coffer. Her slender fingers slid into some of its carved grooves; using them as a handle, she lifted the top half of the oval, revealing its bowl-like base. Dipping her other hand inside, she lifted out a small stone threaded on a long, fine neck chain, and held it out to him.

"This," she whispered reverently, "is the most precious thing in all Talonnorn!"

They gazed at it together as it swayed slightly, her fingers spread above it to hold the chain apart and let it dangle. No matter how hard Ravandarr stared, it remained a small, rough, nondescript stone. A thumb-sized fragment of cave rock, not a gemstone.

"This was once touched by Holy Olone herself," Maharla told him, her voice still a whisper of excitement, "and holds great power. You shall wear it around your neck, and through it I can mind-whisper directions to you from afar, guiding you unerringly after . . . the one who must be slain. With this, you cannot fail."

Dumbfounded, Ravan blurted out, "But I thought—you—"

"Despised you as a weakling? I did. Yet Olone is all-seeing, and Her will guides us all. Ravandarr, I despise you no longer, but admire you—for Olone has chosen you, which makes you greater than us all."

Setting the lid back down on the coffer, the Eldest of Evendoom raised the necklace in both hands, stepped forward, and put it around his neck.

"Hurry, now!" she murmured, as they stood face to face. "It may take time to do Olone's will, but you must begin now."

Then, as Ravan gazed at her in deepening disbelief, Maharla Evendoom took his head in her hands and kissed him.

Whereupon, as the old Nifl tales put it, it was too late.

Ravandarr stirred under her lips as her spell flooded into him, awakening the pendant's mind-link, and flooding him with waves of love, pride, and admiration.

Erlingar Evendoom himself could not have withstood that conquering—and Ravandarr was young and frustrated and weak-willed, a yearning rampant, not a wise and hardened foe.

He stiffened, against her, and moaned into her mouth in rapture, and threw back his head wearing the widest smile it had ever worn, eyes a-glow. "Eldest, command me!" he gasped. "Hurry where, exactly?"

"Back to your chambers—speaking to *no one* of this—to properly arm yourself, and take pouches of food and water. Then go, seeking the Out-caverns by any path that will get you out of Eventowers unseen. Call on me—in your mind—for guidance if you encounter difficulties, and call on me again when you reach the Outcaverns, for the right way to take onward. Go."

"Eldest," he gasped, bending to kiss her open hands in reverence. Then he spun around and departed in eager haste.

Maharla did not allow herself to smirk in triumph until her mists had quite hidden the door that had opened before him and closed behind him again by its silent self and without Ravandarr Evendoom even notic-ing it.

What a fool.

When Lord Evendoom discovered his second son gone, his rage would be terrible. Whereupon it would be trifling ease itself to goad him into saying or doing something that would let her bring down Olone's doom upon him.

Then *she* would choose the pureblood who would rule the Even-dooms. In her name, of course. In her bed it would take but moments to drift into the mind of that new Lord Evendoom and put it in thrall—probably, if she did it at a moment of rapture, without him even noticing.

Ravandarr could serve her as that Lord. *If* he returned. Even with one arm, Taerune could probably slay him in moments—and if Shoan Maulstryke hadn't managed to fell Jalandral, Ravandarr would be her sacrificial dart, hurled at his own brother heedless of what harm he took, to wound that laughing fool as sorely as he could.

No, Ravandarr was as good as dead already.

Ah, Olone was *such* a hungry goddess.

"What can you see?" Taerune asked cautiously.

Orivon opened his tightly shut eyes, tears swimming, blinked, swiped at his eyes with his forearm, and blinked again. "You," he growled at last, trying to ignore the blurring that kept creeping back in long after he was sure the tears had gone, which his knuckling and grimacing had brought on. He shook his head several times as he strode up and down the ledge.

"Aye," he said at last. "I can see." He said nothing about his weak, sick feeling inside, and the searing pain down his left side. Wizards' wards, it seemed, were . . . painful things. Next time, he'd throw a rock.

"So let's be moving," he added. "It seems half Talonnorn can't help but find this ledge."

Taerune smiled—the first time he could ever recall seeing a smile on her face that hadn't held a sneer, or cruel excitement, or pain. It changed her face completely.

His lingering stare made her flush—that creeping paleness Nifl got— and turn away. "Yes," she agreed, her back to him. "Let's . . . be moving. The Ravagers are quite gone. On to raid Talonnorn."

It was a shapely back. Looking at it, Orivon could forget the sting of her lash. For a breath or two.

"We need to find a cavern, or some crevice, where we can hide," he growled. "One where we can roll a stone across like a door, or some such. A place we can rest without the Hunt being able to see us if they swoop past."

Taerune opened her mouth to tell him she didn't think there was enough of the Hunt left, now, to fly anywhere—and then shut it again, without saying a word. What did she know, really? There had always been young rampants eager to join, lesser flyers scorned by the veterans— and the riders of other Houses forbidden or unwilling to fly under Even- doom command. Talonnorn was different, now. Too badly ravaged to merely forget a day of battle, rebuild and shrug aside sharp lessons and pretend it had never happened. Talonnorn had been changed, leaving her knowing . . . nothing.

"Rest would be good," she agreed instead, watching Orivon collect blades and whips back into a bundle. He must have noticed that her gag and the severed ends of the lash were thrust through her belt, revealing that she'd freed herself, but he said not a word.

Over many, many Turnings of plying her whip, she'd noticed that some humans did that. Watched and smoldered, where a Talonar Nifl would have coldly confronted. Or perhaps being a slave taught that slow, patient anger.

The firefist turned and straightened. She'd forgotten just how *large* he was, how . . . muscled. Hulking. "Right, we're seeking a cavern where we can hide from the Hunt and rest, and I can affix a blade to your stump. So, Lady Evendoom, give me your wisdom," he said formally. "Whither?"

Taerune shrugged. "Deeper into the Wild Dark; where else?"

He pointed at the lip of the ledge, silently ordering her to climb down first. She shrugged again, nodded, and swung herself over the edge.

The climb was easy, even under the tiny stingings of the little stones his boots dislodged onto her, the drift left behind by the dust of the spells that had smashed stalactites off the ceiling. Taerune was soon down in the tumbled stones, surrounded by bodies. Swift gouging-beetles were already swarming over some of them, eating holes in leather and flesh alike.

Orivon joined her with a grunt of distaste—and then waded into the gnawing frenzy, bringing his fists down like hammers on the beetles until he could reach flasks and pouches and belts, and tug them free. Food, and drink, and—

"See anything that might be a map?" he asked, waving a hand to indicate all the dead, across the cavern. There was nothing approaching hope in his voice.

"No," Taerune told him truthfully. "I can tell you now that there's nothing here. Unless the Ravagers are more different from Talonar than I've been told."

Orivon gave her a frowning look. "Oh? Different how? Couldn't there be a map on every dead Nifl here? A scrap of cloth? A folded parchment in a pouch?"

His longtime tormentor shook her head. "Maps can't be flat."

"What?" Orivon's growl was disbelieving. "Of *course* they can. Why, in Ash—in my village, the elders scratched them in the fireside dirt with a stick. And the grand maps, the ones that lasted, were burned into tabletops with fire coals. They held the coals with tongs, and marked the rivers, the . . ."

His voice trailed off under Taerune's sad smile.

"The Blindingbright," she half-said, and half-asked, "is land with sky above it, and nothing below—yes? Except graves you dig, and caves, and us." She swept her hand through the air, as if running it along a gently undulating ledge or tabletop.

Orivon nodded.

The Niflghar shook her head. "So simple. Here in the Dark, there is always something above you, and something below, not just what lies this way or that way. Flat maps are useless, unless perhaps in assigning bedchambers to guests in the Eventowers."

"So what does a Nifl map look like?"

"In Talonnorn, either a . . . a volume of air enspelled so colored sparks float in it, marking the locations of features—or a sphere made up of stacked layers of metal discs, graven with features of the Dark. The layers are held apart, thus, by spines of metal they slot into, but it can all be pulled apart and collapsed into, ah . . ."

"A thick heap of metal discs, like shields stacked on a forgefist's 'done' table," Orivon growled. "So, not flat."

"Not flat," Taerune agreed, smiling that real smile again.

"So how do merchants—and armies—find their ways through the Dark, then? I can't see the Hunt flapping along trying to fit together a metal ball in midair!"

"Nor can I. Mainly, they stick to ways they know. In their heads."

"So, if we find, say, some traders, and follow them . . ."

"We'll reach wherever they're heading for. Talonnorn, Ouvahlor, or wherever. Two 'ifs' arise. If there are any traders to find; I fear all this fighting has driven them away until they hear it's over. And, if traders go to the Blindingbright, I've never heard of it. *Ravagers* go there. All we have to do is find some Ravagers—and somehow avoid having them kill us. We're from Talonnorn, and they're raiding Talonnorn just now, remember?"

"While warbands from Talonnorn and Ouvahlor swarm all over the Immur trying to kill each other," Orivon growled. "Would any of them have one of these metal maps?"

"Possibly," Taerune said dryly. "If you see to the trifling detail of killing them all, I'll take care of trying to read the map. What say you to that?"

15

For the Greater Glory of Olone

Uncounted thousands I have slain, and will again,
For the greater glory of Olone.
—Ashardyn's prayer

The way was narrow, and there was much tension among the four Talonar clambering cautiously up through the rocks; Shoan foremost, Reminder behind him, then Jalandral, and behind him Gentle, all warily carrying spellblades that glowed more brightly than the glimmerings of their personal wards. Then the tunnel abruptly opened out into one of the largest caves Shoan had ever seen. A little smaller than the one that held Talonnorn, perhaps, but this one didn't have a city filling the middle of it.

It looked like the rib cage of a slaughtered pack-snout, lines of ragged ridges curving down into the sides of a great stone bowl, the stalactites few but gigantic, some of them meeting the far more numerous stalagmites jutting up from the ridges, to form huge columns. A few inky pools of water lay tranquil here and there down the cavern, as it stretched away to the right, curving out of sight, and the eerie glows of candlemoss clung to cracks and ledges high on the cavern walls. There was no sign of habitation or even a trail, but every Talonar knew this cavern's name, even though most of them had never been there: Longdeath.

The size and location of Longdeath had made it a frequent battleground, where Nifl armies clashed to decide the dominance of faiths, cities, and rival rulers. Longdeath was where the Outcaverns ended and the Wild Dark began.

Shoan Maulstryke had never been this far from Talonnorn before—it was rare for Houses to risk their heirs in forays this far from gathered family might, with so many scores to be settled and murderous Nifl ambition even among kin—so he climbed a nearby spur of rock that let him look far down the cavern. Lazy mists were drifting above some of the larger pools, but he could see nothing else moving . . . or of interest.

He shrugged and rejoined the others, who'd halted at the lip of the tunnel.

"Alerted every watching thing of our arrival?" Jalandral asked lightly.

Shoan ignored him, turning to ask Gentle, "Still no trace of the Evendoom traitor?"

It was Reminder who shook her head. "Her magic still hides her from us. The slave, we can sense clearly."

"Near, now? Far?"

"Near. So no shouting—and quell the glowing of your blades, Firstbloods."

" 'Near' as in: here, in this cavern?" Shoan asked sharply, hefting his spellblade and dulling its glow not a whit.

The two priestesses looked at him expressionlessly, then at each other.

"We shall go a little apart—up there—to work a certain ritual that should give us all clear answer to that," Gentle announced. "*Try* not to slay each other, House heirs."

Shoan and Jalandral looked at each other across perhaps six strides of broken rock, faces carefully blank, and lifted their blades in brief and casual salute to each other. Then they turned in smooth unison and saluted the priestesses.

Who trudged up to the height they'd indicated, a long-shattered stalagmite right beside a bulging column that had broken off horizontally to form a level platform of sorts. There they turned to watch the two heirs, spread their hands and then touched their breasts and then spread their hands again in the customary prayer to Olone. Unbuckling their spellblades, the two laid them aside, quelled their wards in unison, and together began to cast a long and complicated ritual.

They were well into it, incantations flowing as their hands shaped fluid gestures in the air and their fingers sprouted fleeting flames and glows, when a dark figure suddenly burst into view high above their heads, swinging around the flank of the great stone column on a line.

The two Firstbloods lifted their spellblades—and were blinded by sudden wand-blasts that made their wards and spellblades flare into full raging radiance as their magics struggled to stand against the fury sent against them. Rooted to the spot with sparks swirling around their knees, they could barely see what happened next.

The Nifl on the line hurtled around the pillar, spiraling down. The taut cord in his wake quivered and came free, trailing a few rocks—and then, with a deep and suddenly growing roar, a great avalanche of rocks fell from a hitherto stone-choked rent high in the column, thundering down to smash the two priestesses flat, and then burying them.

"Ha-ha!" a rampant's voice roared out, from somewhere high in the column. "*Beautifully* done, Sarntor! Olone's short two Holy shes, for sure! I've yet to find a ward that can defend against being landed on by the weight of a thousand Niflghar!"

"Bloodblade, will you stop *gloating?*" another male Nifl spoke, from about the same spot, exasperation riding his voice. "There're still two House heirs standing there, protected by wards and spellblades and Olone only knows what-all else! *Two* of your precious wand-blasts they took, yet stand untouched!"

"Untouched for now," Sarntor called, from the stones at the base of the pillar, untying the line he'd sprung the stone fall with. "*I've* never yet found a wardshield that can hurl back shaft after hurlbow shaft! You *did* bring your hurlbow, Lharlak?"

"I *wear* my hurlbow, youngfang. Ho, Daruse! Did you remember yours?"

"I do believe I did," another, deeper voice replied pleasantly, from the mouth of the tunnel the two heirs had taken to reach Longdeath.

Sparks dying away around their ankles, Jalandral Evendoom and Shoan Maulstryke whirled to see who'd spoken—and found themselves gazing at a grinning, ragtag Ravager with an eye patch, who lifted one hurlbow-adorned arm lazily to indicate the rocks behind the two heirs. They turned to look where he indicated—in time to see Ravagers bob up into view from behind various rocks, in a long arc of ready bows and ruthless smiles.

"Olone spew!" Shoan gasped—as Jalandral sprang past him, in a hard and desperate sprint right up the heap of boulders where the priestesses had stood.

Shoan stared after the Firstblood of Evendoom for only a moment, and then started running too.

"Ha-*ha!*" Old Bloodblade bellowed joyously. "*Get them!*"

Hurlbows sang and twanged, and heirs' wards flared as shaft after shaft struck—and was slowed until it hung motionless . . . and then fell harmlessly in the wake of the sprinting Firstbloods, as the two heirs moved on and their wards moved with them.

"*Well,* now! I've got to get my hands on one of these fancy wards!" Old Bloodblade said. "Perhaps after one of these purebloods is too dead to need it longer . . ."

Loose stones spinning and clattering underfoot, Jalandral reached the sudden tomb of Gentle and Reminder, and was unsurprised to see a ribbon of bright blood wending its way out from under some of the largest boulders. If luck was with him, no Ravagers would be waiting on the far slope of this now-buried height, or beyond.

"Wait! In Olone's name, I beseech . . ."

The thin, sobbing voice seemed to come from the very stones at his feet. Not slowing, he vaulted another boulder—and saw Gentle lying crushed and half-buried under a great flow of stones, blood spewing from her mouth and pleading agony in her eyes. "Aid! I beg you, Evendoom!"

Jalandral ran on, giving her a merry smile and wave. "I'd tarry," he called back, "but Olone's stern orders forbid. We're on a divine mission, remember? Olone expects!"

"By the Ice!" Aloun gasped, staring wide-eyed into the bright whirling of the whorl. "It's . . . it's *magnificent!*"

Luelldar nodded in grim satisfaction, saying nothing, devoting himself wholly in these beautiful moments to being a Watcher of Ouvahlor. He had already murmured the magic that would sear these moments unfailingly and vividly in his memory, to be called forth whenever needed.

Or whenever he just wanted to see again what was unfolding in the whorl before his eyes right now: Klarandarr, the mightiest spellrobe of Ouvahlor and of all the Dark—possibly the greatest wizard ever—standing stern and tall in black, flapping robes, hands caressing and intricately weaving the very air as they trailed trembling lines of glowing flame, shaping a titanic spell.

A slaying magic, of many rings within whirling rings of teeth, all facing the same way and made of pure magic, intended to bite through stone, wards, and flesh alike. A spell that Klarandarr let build into a shrieking frenzy . . . and then hurled, as a Nifl child throws a stone, into a waiting whorl-maw, a vortex he'd raised earlier that would spit it out—Luelldar turned his head to look at the second whorl he'd raised—into the very wards of the old, dark-spired abbey of Coldheart, rising almost to touch the cavern roof above it, in the great cave that held the city of Arnoenar, falling away in its own magnificent myriad spires and domes in all directions from the holy high place of the Ever-Ice.

Purple and then crimson those wards flared as Klarandarr's unwelcome bolt of magic sheared into them, biting deep. The whirling rings slowed, melting visibly as they shed bright tatters of magic—but bored on, the wards flashing brighter and brighter as they . . .

Broke and failed, letting Klarandarr's striking magic slice into the spires within the wards, and bite even deeper.

Chortling now despite himself, Luelldar bounced up and down in his chair, watching those old dark spires start to topple and shatter.

"This one," Shoan Maulstryke snarled, "is yours!"

Jalandral grinned savagely and spun away from the Ravager whose throat he'd just slashed open, in time to drive his moaning, flickering spellblade into the armpit of the Ravager Shoan had crotch-kicked in his direction.

That Nifl shrieked, hacking at him vainly with a sword that was too short to reach the Evendoom heir—unless he pushed forward, impaling himself more deeply on Jalandral's blade.

Which Jalandral now twisted, causing the Ravager to sink down, squalling in agony, to where he could easily receive Jalandral's boot in his throat. Jalandral kicked hard, but didn't trigger the toe-blade that would have ended the young Nifl's life in an instant. A crushed throat and broken neck slew just as surely as steel, and he didn't want Shoan to know he had toe-blades . . . just yet.

Only the youngest five Ravagers had been fleet enough to chase down the fleeing Firstbloods, so when Shoan and Jalandral had been brought to bay some six side-caverns beyond Longdeath, they found themselves facing the least experienced, most reckless Ravagers. Younglings lacking wards and spellblades, with poor armor and worse training. Enthusiasm only forges so far.

Wherefore this gargling, dying Ravager was the last, and the two Talonar heirs now found themselves gazing at each other across a few strides of smooth rock, in an unfamiliar cavern out in the Wild Dark, with no foes or escorting priestesses to keep them apart. At last.

"Slaughtering time," Jalandral whispered, eyes bright and eager.

Eyes locked in menacing promise, the Firstbloods of Evendoom and Maulstryke grew slow, mutual grins, like bloody-jawed wolves. Hefting their spellblades, they stepped slowly toward each other.

Whereupon Aumaeraunda, Holiest of Olone said commandingly inside their heads, the voice of her will stone-strong and steel-sharp: *OH, NO, YOU DON'T, HEIRS OF EVENDOOM AND MAULSTRYKE.*

Jalandral and Shoan stiffened as one, swaying as they fought against the sudden steely presence in their minds. They were being forced to lower their swords, to step back . . . their jaws worked as they tried to curse and snarl, and were prevented even from that.

FOOLS AND RAMPANTS YOU MAY BE, BUT YOU ARE ALSO REACHING SWORDS OF TALONNORN–AND TALONNORN HAS NEED OF YOU YET. FOR THE GREATER GLORY OF OLONE. YOU WILL DISCOVER THAT YOU HAVE NO CHOICE BUT TO OBEY ME UTTERLY. WHICH IS AS IT SHOULD BE.

Jalandral fought with all his strength to raise his spellblade and step forward again, to break the tightening control in his head. Shoan was doing the same, he saw; the Maulstryke's body was also trembling, his face also frozen in the first creases of pain but prevented from twisting into a full grimace.

It'll be our eyes next, Jalandral thought. Or our lungs, if she tires of our defiance and just wants us gone. He was lurching along at her bidding, muscles burning and spasming in protest as the distant Aumaeraunda forced him to sheathe his spellblade and begin to walk on down the unfamiliar cavern, Shoan at his side.

Around a bend, stiffly stumbling, and up a rocky slope–more easily, as both of the heirs abandoned their struggles against her–to stop and stand silently on a high vantage point: a lip of rock overlooking a larger, wider cavern.

The Firstbloods could still move their heads and eyes with perfect freedom, and did so, watching small slithering things moving furtively in the rocks around them–and two much larger creatures trudging quite openly along the cavern floor below.

A hulking human, and a one-armed yet still beautiful Nifl-she: Orivon Firefist and Taerune Evendoom.

"Klarandarr struck at Coldheart *not* out of any challenge to the faith of the Ever-Ice," Luelldar explained patiently, "but purely because the

Revered Mother—and other senior priestesses of that abbey, too—regarded him as a threat to their personal power and influence, and took it upon themselves to craft a spell to slay him."

The priestess facing him grew a sneer, but the Watcher threw up a hand to forestall comment, and hurried to add, "Despite the vital importance to us all of his matchless power, in our battles with the cities of Olone, they desired to eliminate him, straying from regard for all Nifl of the Ever-Ice to promoting their personal power—a sin all religious Nifl must constantly guard against. Though many will not see it this way, Klarandarr has done the Consecrated of the Ice—and all of us who dwell in cities where our true faith holds sway—a great service this day, by removing those who had begun to stray, striding onto the path of tyranny and away from that of holy service."

"We see it differently, Watcher." Exalted Lady of the Ice Naerbrantha's voice was even sharper and colder than her initial greeting had been.

· Luelldar inclined his head. "Respectfully, Holy One, let me observe: of course you do. Let me also remind you that I *am* a Watcher, and our office was established by wiser Revered Mothers, in time long gone, *precisely* to 'see all,' and to do so a step removed from holy office or ruling power—or unconstrained wizardry, for that matter—so as to perceive and understand unfolding events most clearly, forming opinions about them and their implications that are not bound by self-interest or creed or training."

He drew forth the blue-white shard of the Ever-Ice that he wore against his breast, and held it up, cupping his hand around it. At the sight of its glimmering murmurs arose among the underpriestesses, who had never seen such a holy thing anywhere but on—or frozen within—an altar.

Naerbrantha was unimpressed. "Grand terms, to be sure, for what I deem 'spying.'"

"Priestess, you blaspheme," Luelldar snapped, precisely matching the cold precision of her tones. "Before the Ever-Ice"—he grasped the shard, and raised it higher to show everyone that it did not sear him as he spoke on, so that his words were true—"we are *not* spies. We are guardians of all Ice-revering Niflghar."

"Yet *Klarandarr* is not. What was *he* doing, that he—as you claim—had learned the most private intent of our sisters of Coldheart to magically slay him, that he could know to strike at them first?"

"He was learning all he could before acting, as all responsible spellrobes must do, so as to avoid unwittingly drifting into the ways of tyranny himself. Devout worshippers of the Ice seek to know the beliefs and intents of Holy Ones of the Ice, so as to act in accord with them—or to perceive corruption and straying, so that they be not led into ill deeds or thinking."

"And I suppose he spied upon *me,* also—and that you 'watch' over me constantly, too?"

"I dare suppose nothing about Klarandarr or any spellrobe, but I believe he often employs scrying magics to learn all he can about the Dark around us. I can speak for my own watchings, Exalted Lady, and so can say that I have not watched over you save incidentally, on seven occasions that I can recall, when you were a participant—one among many—in rituals conducted by the Revered Mother or other Holy Ones. Those were my only watchings upon you."

"I find that difficult to believe."

"Do you doubt the Ever-Ice?" Luelldar asked softly, holding his shard up before her as if warding something evil away. "That's a serious failing in a Holy One, Naerbrantha."

"Dabble not in holy opinions, Watcher! Presume to judge no priestess!" Exalted Lady Naerbrantha hissed, eyes glittering in real fury. "I ask you again: How many times have you watched over me, and when, and what did you see?"

"You participating, alongside many fellow Exalted, in the Melting that Cleanses, the Ordeal, the Triumph of the Ice, the Doom of the Dead—and other holy rituals. As I have just sworn on the Ever-Ice, priestess!"

"I—" The priestess waved her hands impatiently. "You did, but I can scarcely believe that if you watch so diligently as you claim, you have seen so little of me."

"Exalted Lady of the Ice Naerbrantha," Luelldar said gravely, "please understand that I invite no quarrel with you, think no ill of you, and have no wish to offend or humiliate you. Yet you press me, before all, for an answer, so know that—forgive me—your station and deeds, until the loss of the Holy of Coldheart, did not place you highly enough to merit more attention. Or to put it more gently, you were not as dangerous as many Nifl whose activities *demand* diligent watching, so that we Watchers can properly anticipate change, and be ready to properly advise Ouvahlor. I fear that—"

"Watcher Luelldar!" Aloun said urgently, pointing. "The whorl!"

Everyone looked where the junior Watcher was pointing, in time to see Klarandarr, standing tall, slender and dark in the whorl's bright depths, atop a height with his cloak billowing, throw up his hands with lightnings crackling between them—and fall on his face, exhausted, lightnings still spiraling and coursing.

Luelldar flung himself at the whorl, plunging both of his hands into it. Lightnings raced up his own arms and made the shard of Ice glow and sing, he grunted in pain and flung his head back, eyes closed and the flesh of his throat sharp-ridged and trembling . . . and the scene in the whorl changed.

"Watcher Luelldar has bound our scrying to the spellrobe's spell," Aloun explained, with something approaching awe in his voice. "So we'll see the target of the magic, wherever and whatever it is, and the effects of Klarandarr's work on it."

The whorl, spinning strangely, was showing them a haughty Nifl whose beauty was breathtaking, and who hovered upright in midair in a large but dark stone chamber, her arms arched and raised, a glowing robe playing gently about her otherwise bared body. Her eyes were closed and her face raised, wearing a serene sneer. Her toes were well above a pulsing symbol set into black stone, and that symbol was—

"Olone!" priestesses hissed, all over the chamber, raising the backs of their hands in shunning gestures.

"Behold," Luelldar gasped, straightening up out of the whorl with his skin mottled and pale, sweat drenching his face like a cavern waterfall, "Aumaeraunda, the Holiest of Olone of the city of Talonnorn. She is working magic on someone distant—and Klarandarr's spell, likewise from afar, is directed at her."

"He's working with a priestess of *Olone*?" Exalted Lady Naerbrantha snarled. "*This* is the craven Nifl you *dare* to defend to us? Why, firedeath is too merciful for you! And as for *him*, I—"

The hovering figure's eyes opened wide with alarm. Her beautiful mouth opened to shout something . . . and a bright and crawling *something* struck her from the left and swept over her like a hungry wave, a whiteness that devoured and gnawed, leaving only bones in its wake.

Bones that hovered for a moment, toes still together and pointed and arms raised—and then slumped, melting into dust and nothingness even as they tumbled. Another Nifl-she came running into the whorl-scene from the right, waving her arms in alarm, sobbing disbelief on her face—and plunged into the whiteness, becoming bones in midstride and collapsing in turn.

"Just as Klarandarr's mighty magic allowed us to humble hated

Talonnorn and leave its ruling Houses fighting among themselves to supplant shattered Evendoom," Luelldar said in weary satisfaction, indicating the bright whiteness that now blotted out everything else in the whorl, "he has now destroyed that city's Holiest of Olone—ensuring that the priestesses of the Twisted Goddess will devote their efforts to eliminating each other for a time. Time that I am certain Exalted Lady of the Ice Naerbrantha will use well, to rebuild and lead all Holy of the Ever-Ice to clear and everlasting supremacy!"

It was Aloun who started the shouts of joy and the chant of "The Ice! The Ice!" It was the priestesses who joined in, with loud and excited enthusiasm. It was Naerbrantha who favored Luelldar with the first real and welcoming smile she'd given anyone in a very long time. And it was Luelldar who mirrored it, while thinking inwardly: *Or use well to slaughter all possible rivals and establish a tyranny as futile as it is small-minded, that will drag Ouvahlor down to doom—unless Klarandarr gets to her first.*

"You . . . sent for me, Lord?" Maharla asked softly, eyebrows raised, smiling that little smile of menace and warning.

"*Maharla,*" Lord Evendoom barked, rising from his chair like a surging darkwings. "I mean, Eldest!"

Maharla inclined her head graciously, and then looked pointedly around the room, reminding him that a throne-servant and a dozen warblades were present, and would be better dismissed.

Lord Evendoom took the hint and swept his arms about curtly in impatient wavings toward the doors that left no doubt at all as to the rage riding him.

"My warblades," he told Maharla loudly, while they were still bowing and marching out past him, "tell me my son Ravandarr is nowhere to be found in Eventowers."

"And they took it upon themselves to tell you this why, exactly?" the priestess asked silkily, strolling past unconcernedly to seat herself gracefully in Erlingar's own chair. After all, he was going to storm and pace, so she might as well seat herself in comfort . . . dominant comfort . . .

"Took it upon themselves, *nothing*! I set them to searching, crone, after I sent for him and his servants reported him gone from his rooms! Leaving blades and clothes strewn about as if he'd been arming to go off to war! *You* can use the wards to tell you if he's here, somewhere, in hiding–bedding a she, say! You can even tell me if he's out in the Araed, drinking or wenching or up to something!"

"I can indeed," Maharla murmured, discovering that she really enjoyed this. Erlingar's raging was . . . exciting.

"Well? *Do it!*"

His shout rang back from the ceiling, and rolled around the room.

Maharla basked in it for as long as she dared. Then as Lord Evendoom loomed up over her, his face almost white and his eyes dark and terrible, she said gently, "There's no need. I know where he is, and what he's doing."

"And you told me *not?*"

"Erlingar, how can your Secondblood ever grow to be the Evendoom we both want him to be if he does nothing without permission or reporting in beforehand–like the lowest of your Nameless servants?"

She stood up, thrusting her face and bosom almost into him, to startle the Lord of her House out of the roaring reply that was about to burst out of him, and added brightly, "Besides, this time he is doing *nothing* he can be faulted for! He's following and obeying a holy vision sent by Olone herself!"

"Olone doesn't slime-slithering know who Ravandarr Evendoom *is!*" Lord Evendoom snarled. "Have you any *better* lies to hand me, Eldest?"

"Well, perhaps the vision was sent by the Holy Ones of Olone here in Talonnorn, rather than by the busy Goddess herself," Maharla said smoothly, "but it *was* sent. I received it myself, and took the opportunity to advise young Ravan when I saw him. He saw his duty immediately, Erlingar. You should be proud of him; he's growing into a son any Nifl lord should take true pride in. Without hesitation he rushed to obey, arming himself and setting out into the Dark."

"*WHAAAT?!*"

Maharla sighed theatrically, and smoothly slid around behind his throne, to put it between them. "I warned him you'd not be pleased, that your first concern–after House Evendoom itself–was for your heirs, as it must always be. Yet the visions were clear about the vital urgency of his duty, and he–"

"He went *alone?*"

"Yes, as I–"

"And am I to know, as Lord of this House, what this vision was? And just *what* he's out there doing, or seeking to do, or thinks he'll achieve?"

"Slaying his Nameless sister; the vision showed him walking alone in the Outcaverns, drawn sword in hand, a-hunting her."

Evendoom plucked up his heavy desk and hurled it aside as if it weighed nothing, to get at the throne—and at her, behind it.

"Jalandral's out there already!" he roared. "Stupid she, you've thrown away the future of our House! They'll *both* be lost, all so you can see the little scourge-tongue who dared to stand up to you die for it!"

Maharla pretended fear she did not feel, shrinking back and putting a hand over her mouth so he'd not see her lip curling in contempt. "*I* sent no visions!" she wailed. "Hand your fury to the Goddess—or her holy priestesses! I merely stressed that scorning a divine vision would plunge his life into misfortune and a swift ending, and our House with him! Take your quarrel to them—and perhaps their magic can snatch Ravandarr back to us, *if* you can convince them!"

"Oh, I'll convince them, all right," Lord Evendoom snarled, voice dire and eyes like two fire coals. He snapped out the word that brought his spellblade down off the wall, unsheathed and glowing, into his hand. It had to fly after Erlingar Evendoom to get there, as he strode across the room to the door, flung it open with a violence Maharla could feel, and stormed out.

The Eldest of Evendoom calmly sat back down in the throne again, propping her crossed ankles on one of its broad arms. Passing her hand over the glow-plate that would summon servants from the wine cellars, she let her face—at long last—acquire a triumphant smirk.

If the priestesses or their guards didn't slay him out of hand, his rude raging would give her all the pretext she could ever need to do anything she wanted to Erlingar Evendoom. Over and over, calling on Olone to drag him back to life so she could torment him anew, for the next thousand-thousand Turnings. Or so.

16

Swords, Spells, and Scheming

*For I have yet to find mightier means of swiftly causing
many deaths than swords, spells, and scheming.*
—The Words of Dounlar

There was a momentary shriek of fear, a moment of sobbing despair that drove him to his knees in sick pain, as the Dark seemed to fade into dimness and die away all around him—and then the steely presence of Aumaeraunda, Holiest of Olone, was gone from Jalandral's mind.

Utterly gone, vanished as if it had never been, leaving him back in this cavern in the Wild Dark, blinded by tears. Frantically blinking them away, Jalandral Evendoom hefted his spellblade in his hand and looked for the Firstblood of Maulstryke.

His hated rival was also on his knees, a bare three strides away on the lip of stone—and looking for him.

Without a word they sprang up and raced at each other, spellblades singing to life.

The first magics pouring forth from each blade met in a savage shower of sparks between the snarling, fiercely grinning heirs, and flung them apart even before their darting swords could meet.

Whirling helplessly away across hard stone, Jalandral momentarily glimpsed his sister and the slave staring up at him from the larger cavern below—before he called on his spellblade's ability to fly, and snatched himself away from what would have been a bone-shattering meeting with the cavern wall.

As he soared off the lip into the larger cavern, he saw Shoan Maulstryke doing the same thing, a golden plume of magical radiance to his own ruby-red flaming.

Jalandral took hold of his hilt in both hands to strengthen his grip, and brought his spellblade up and back, as if to rest it on his shoulder—whipping his aerial flight back on itself in a turn so tight it nearly snatched his arms from their sockets. Teeth clenched, he fought his blade around in a second tight turn—to bring himself swooping up at Shoan from behind and below.

The Firstblood of Maulstryke had lost sight of him, and was slowing to look around—so he'd time for only a frantic parry as Jalandral came racing right at him.

Jalandral called another spell out of his blade, to spit lightning at his foe, triggering it just before their impact. Which meant his power of flight ended and he plunged under Shoan's parry, grazing a Maulstryke boot with his shoulder and sending his foe cartwheeling helplessly across the cavern, wreathed in lightnings that struck and struck, causing Shoan more pain than real injury—but ravaging his wards down to feeble flickerings.

Grinning ruthlessly, Jalandral awakened his spellblade's flight again, snatching himself away from a crash into the cavern floor not far from his sister—who'd flung up the one arm she had left to hold back her human slave from running to hack at a handy passing Firstblood—and went after Shoan again, letting his sword tow him along so he hurtled across the large cavern point-first, like a gigantic hurlbow arrow.

Shoan was standing on a large rock bathed in surging spell-glows, calling magic out of his spellblade to heal himself and mend his wards. He cast a swift glance at his onrushing foe but set his jaw and kept at it, waiting until the last instant to spring aside and—

Get struck by a swerving Jalandral anyway, in a long slash that made his wards flare blinding-bright and then go down entirely, overtaxed as he was flung back hard against rocks at the same time as Jalandral's spellblade was slicing deep into Maulstryke magic.

The backlash left Shoan hissing a curse and watching Jalandral fight his racing blade around in another tight turn, coming back for the kill.

Shoan bent to his boots, plucked forth a dagger, and threw it, murmuring a word that made it flare into a baleful drifting crimson glow that Jalandral had to swerve to avoid—and found himself followed by.

Then the Maulstryke heir leaped into the air and made his blade fly again, to get himself away from the Firstblood of Evendoom. The power of flight was one of the fastest-awakened spellblade magics, and Shoan found himself racing back across the cavern about a sword length ahead of Jalandral.

Who drew a dagger from his sleeve and awakened *its* power of flight, to hurl himself along even faster. He climbed, to get above and behind the Maulstryke heir, swerving from side to side as Shoan twisted his head around, trying to see just where Jalandral was.

Jalandral obliged him with a mocking grin and a roll in the air, slipping to one side as he came out of it. He only had to distract Shoan for a moment or two longer . . .

Shoan Maulstryke snatched a glance back at where he was heading, saw the jagged edge of the stone lip where he'd stood with Jalandral under the Holiest's control rushing up to meet him, and swerved desperately.

Or tried to. Jalandral pushed his speed to the utmost, and used it to slam hard into Shoan, lacerating his foe with the spellblade but also glancing him back in the direction he'd been swerving away from.

Shoan Maulstryke slammed full-tilt into the unyielding stone ledge, lacking even time to shout.

Banking sharply away to avoid a similar meeting with the cavern ceiling, Jalandral heard ribs snap behind him, and a grunt of pain. Fighting his way through yet another tight turn, he saw the Maulstryke Firstblood tumbling back up into the air, wincing and groaning, blinded by pain and blood—

Which made it Olone-blessedly easy to race back, spellblade held sidewise, and almost delicately slice through Shoan Maulstryke's no longer ward-shielded wrists.

The severed hands spun away, still gripping a spellblade—and the rest of Shoan, sobbing incoherently, fell toward the waiting cavern floor.

Smiling bleakly, his eyes as merciless as stone, Jalandral swooped around and down, almost grazing stalagmites as he raced along the floor, angling up . . .

Tumbling helplessly, the Firstblood of Maulstryke impaled himself on a waiting Evendoom spellblade, as Jalandral flew viciously upward and into him, hilt-deep.

Shoan's sobs ended in a great gasp and gout of blood. He slumped against Jalandral, arms and legs spasming.

Only then did Jalandral allow himself to laugh in triumph.

So he was laughing when Shoan died—and spells that had waited a long, long time burst into life, causing the Maulstryke heir's various hidden amulets and daggers to explode in shards and flame, that no enemy might come to possess them.

Jalandral's ward failed almost instantly under the onslaught of so much whirling steel, and he hadn't even time to roar in pain before it was all over, and he was flying along raggedly, burned and bleeding.

His innards felt wet and loose and . . . dangling. Goddess, he should have known . . .

His wounds were bad, probably fatal if he didn't see to them swiftly. He could barely see, his face was so twisted with the pain. Rolling over in the air to give Taerune a salute that began as an airy wave but ended in a spasm of pain, Jalandral called on his blade to translocate him from this place.

His long-unvisited dire-doom cache, with its healings . . .

Jalandral winced at the pain he was feeling—and at the much greater pain he knew was coming.

He was still wincing when he vanished.

"Ithmeira!" The hiss came from between her boots; the priestess stepped back so swiftly she almost overbalanced and fell among the jagged, blackened spars.

By the Ice, she'd almost stepped on Semmeira's face! No wonder the warning hiss had been so sharp.

Ithmeira knelt without a word, and started plucking aside the wreckage of Coldheart from around the Exalted Daughter's grim and furious face.

All around them was heaped and tumbled wrack—blackened stone and riven, splintered wood—amid scudding drifts of smoldering smoke. The abbey that had been Ithmeira's home for as long as she could remember was . . . gone.

And the vivid memory flooded her mind again: the Revered Mother exploding like a star, shouting out frantic spells to the last. She shuddered, and shook her head, trying vainly to banish what would not go away.

"Exalted Daughter of the Ice," Ithmeira asked, as she struggled to heave aside a broken-off length of column that was larger than she was, "are you . . . whole?"

"I know not. Free me, and we'll see." Exalted Daughter of the Ice

Semmeira might have meant to say more, but thick smoke swept over her, and she burst into a fit of helpless coughing.

Grimly the scorched, wounded priestess worked on. It was *so* tempting to just go, and leave Semmeira and her ruthless ambition to die here, buried and helpless . . . but this was a holy place of the Ever-Ice, even as desecrated and ruined as it was now. The Divine Ice would know what she'd done, and punish her accordingly.

Forever.

Wherefore Ithmeira dug and clawed and heaved, until at last a stiff and wincing Semmeira staggered to her feet, refusing to groan or whimper, felt her arms and legs with reluctantly probing fingers, and asked curtly, "Are we the only two living?" Then the coughing claimed her again, and she doubled over.

"No," Ithmeira replied wearily, dragging her upright and pointing across the streaming smokes that had been Coldheart. "There's Lolonmae."

"Of course," Semmeira said bitterly. "Well, not for much longer."

She fumbled through the tatters of what was left of her robes until her fingers reached the searingly cold dagger of enchanted Ice that all devout priestesses of the Ice wear against their thighs. She drew it forth and started through the wreckage, falling on her face almost immediately.

"No!" Ithmeira caught her by the shoulder and hauled her upright and around, so as to hiss in her face: "Try to slay her, and I'll see that *you* perish first!"

Semmeira gave her a look that would once have made Ithmeira tremble and shrink back, begging forgiveness.

This time the priestess stood unmoved, and it was the Exalted Daughter who looked away first—and then turned again to gaze upon Lolonmae.

Ithmeira felt her stiffen, and knew why. She'd seen that Lolonmae had been changed by the titanic magics in some way. The young holyshe stood dazed but physically unmarked, on a little patch of surviving abbey floor tiles, peering about vaguely—and her sightless eyes were spitting little lightnings.

"See?" she hissed to Semmeira. "Either by the foe who struck us all down, or by the Divine Ice, Lolonmae may have become the mightiest weapon in all the Dark. If we can but learn how to wield her."

. . .

Orivon kept his sword ready in his hand. "Do you know who it is?"

"It *was* Shoan Maulstryke," Taerune told him. "It's no one, now."

The body was blackened and twisted, the arms ending abruptly without hands, the torso slashed away to bare bone here and there, the face frozen in a grimace of disbelieving agony that would last until some cave slitherer ate it away.

"No weapons," Orivon growled, and lifted his head to look across the cavern to where the spellblade lay flickering, severed hands still clutching its hilt like two gnarled spiders.

"No," Taerune said warningly. "Spellblades can be traced from afar. Any Talonar who knows how can find you—and the spellrobes of House Maulstryke can probably awaken the blade, while they're still standing in their chambers back in Talonnorn and you're swinging it at someone, to harm you. If this hadn't been a Firstblood—if I didn't think Maulstryke was watching—there might be a chance to snatch a spellblade. Here and now, we dare not."

Orivon gave her a frown and knelt down to peer at what still adorned the corpse's ruined forearms: the ward-bracers.

They'd both seen feeble glows arise from the metal bands earlier. They'd watched those dim radiances dance, flicker, and then fade away again, and Taerune had told the firefist that meant their wearer had died, and his last deathbound magics were spent. She'd also admitted that the bracers had their own magic, that yet survived.

Orivon reached for the nearest bracer.

"No!" his former owner hissed, striking aside his fingers. "Spellrobes can trace ward-bracers! If any Maul is scrying their heir, or thinks to seek his whereabouts, they'll find you!"

Orivon gave Taerune a grim look.

"Good," he told her softly. "I *want* them to find me."

Old Bloodblade waved at the many bright glows ahead in a mincing mockery of a sophisticated Haraedra Nifl's flourish, and declaimed grandly, "Behold Talonnorn!"

"Why, *thank* you, Barandon," Lharlak replied sarcastically. "Once again your aged wisdom rescues us all! Such is my blindness, I would *never* have noticed it without—"

Lharlak was lacking an eye, but hadn't lost it by being slow in a fray. Wherefore he turned his head and reared back even faster than the hurlbow shaft came streaking out of the darkness—so it snatched away his eye patch rather than bursting through his head.

The Ravager standing next to him gurgled around a shaft suddenly sprouting from his throat, and toppled. His fall took him hard into Daruse, driving the amulet-festooned Nifl into a swift stagger aside.

Which left Old Bloodblade alone to face the warblades rushing out of the darkness.

Or, if one preferred, gave him a clear field of fire to cook them in.

He seized his opportunity, well-used sword in one hand and wand in the other, bathing the Talonar in bright, blinding flame before anyone else could aim a hurlbow at what was, after all—before Olone, even he admitted it—a large and imposing target.

Their screams were so loud that the Ravager leader had a hard time hearing Daruse say warningly, "There'll come a moment in some battle or other when you'll boldly unleash that toy, and discover Alathla's magic has run out. And it won't be a pretty moment."

"Ah," Old Bloodblade growled, "but *this* one is! Aye?"

They stepped back around a stalagmite bigger than both of them and watched the flames fade, many licking along the limbs of staggering, falling blackened things that had been warblades of Talonnorn a breath earlier.

"D'you think we got them all?"

"No," said Lharlak, Daruse, and Sarntor, all together.

"Well, then, all you experts on the defenses of Talonnorn, d'you think we blundered into one band out on a foray, or is this part of a ring of defenders?"

"Doesn't matter which," Daruse replied. "A city ruled by rival Houses, all of them rich in spellblades; if these were but warblades out on a foray, we have to think they've now managed to tell everyone we're—"

"Which *means*," Lharlak interrupted urgently, "we shouldn't *be* here, longer! We should get gone—along there—and come at Talonnorn by another way."

"A brilliant plan, Lord Bloodblade!" Sarntor said enthusiastically, and darted off down the passage Lharlak had indicated. There was a rush to follow.

"I didn't—" Old Bloodblade snarled and found himself addressing empty air.

With a smile and a shrug, he stopped talking and lumbered hastily after the band he thought he'd been commanding. 'Twouldn't do, to find himself standing alone against a score or more Talonar warblades. 'Twouldn't do at all.

The glow around his feet told him he'd arrived.

Which was good, because he could barely think through the shrieking pain . . . and even through his agonies he could *feel* blood pumping out of him. Olone *damn* Shoan Maulstryke!

Well, now . . . she undoubtedly had. Jalandral started to chuckle at that—unwisely. The fresh pain left him sagging helplessly against the nearby stone wall, groaning.

Do it, Dral. Do it or die.

He told himself that, again and again, as he fumbled along the ledge. The flagon, the vial . . . and Goddess, yes, the row of little hollows with dusty gemstones in each. The healing stones, the spells on them his deliverance. He'd need at least three . . .

He almost dropped the vial getting its stopper off, but managed to empty the hissing acid it held into the flagon instead. This was going to hurt worse than anything he'd yet felt on this little journey . . . and for a very long time before that, perhaps ever.

With trembling fingers he dropped the gemstones in and watched the smoke rise and the hissing intensify as they dissolved.

It soon died again, and the Firstblood of Evendoom lifted the flagon, murmured, "Hail, all you crones," and—tossed it down his throat, letting the flagon fall and sinking to his knees before the burning agony could choke him.

He made it, or thought he did, before the eternity of moaning through a ruined mouth and throat, their burning agony like swallowing coals. It went on searing him long after soothing relief had spread slowly—oh, so slowly—out through the rest of his body.

His torture sank down into a dull aching at last, and Jalandral found himself curled up on his side on the cold, hard stone floor. He was whole again, or nearly so, and had best be up and out of this place before some busynose tried to trace him with spells . . .

With a sigh of relief at finding the agony gone, leaving only a tightness in his limbs where he'd convulsed and fought against collapse, like a remembered echo of unpleasantness, Jalandral stood, stretched, and—froze as he became aware that someone was watching him.

It was a Nifl face he knew—a she of his own House—and it was wearing a grim smile.

As Evendoom crones often did, when they weren't looking haughty or coldly displeased.

Klaerra Evendoom.

Jalandral straightened as swiftly as he'd ever done anything in his life, plucking and hurling a dagger from his sleeve. Lightning-swift he threw another, spinning right behind the first—and watched them both come to a sudden halt in the air, to hover in front of her throat and breast.

Her wards were up and waiting, and they were stronger by far than any he'd yet seen. Those blades bore runes that carried them through most wards as if those defenses didn't exist . . .

Klaerra lifted her hands between his motionless daggers and then casually spread them apart, thrusting the steel fangs aside—whereupon they regained their former swift spinning in an instant, and flashed past her to crash and clang off the stone walls behind her. Her smile never changed.

"We must talk," she said softly.

Sarntor turned to the rest of the Ravagers and pointed, saying not a word. He didn't have to.

By the glow flooding down it, they all knew the cross tunnel opened into the great cavern that held Talonnorn. His manner of pointing told them the tunnel didn't *seem* to be guarded.

Lharlak and Daruse held up their hands to the other Ravagers in clear "stand and stay" commands, and went with Sarntor.

All three returned almost immediately to signal "clear, come!" and the Ravagers started forward—only to be jostled aside by a puffing Old Bloodblade, who'd been hurrying along in their rear. Spreading his arms wide to hold everyone back, he aimed his wand down the cross tunnel at the waiting city and triggered it.

Bright flame burst forth—and then rebounded back at the Nifl leader, even as it raced outward in all directions, to form to a huge sheet of roaring flames that filled the tunnel, and made more than one Ravager whirl and run.

The heat smote their faces, and unlike the wand-bursts they'd seen their leader hurl before, the flames crackled on hungrily, fading only slowly.

Old Bloodblade turned, inclined his head to them all in the manner of a vindicated House lord regally forgiving those who've doubted him, and growled, "We older, wiser Nifl have our uses."

Sarntor frowned, and nodded at the flames. "So what is that, exactly?"

"The wards of Talonnorn. If you waited until all the flames are gone and the air looks empty again, you'll still be dead if you stepped forward too far."

"What?" Lharlak asked disbelievingly, watching the flames die.

Old Bloodblade nodded. "To reach Talonnorn, we'll have to wait until the Talonar open a breach in their wards, to let some of their own in or out, and try to rush through—and by the Dark, we'll have to be quick! Some of those crones don't care how many of their own warblades they slay, so long as they fell any foes and get their way in all things!"

"I've spied on Talonnorn before," Daruse said suspiciously, "and the wards *glowed* then. And hummed. A sort of blue sheen that was always in the air . . ." He waved at the air in front of him, up and down, as if shaping a wall.

Old Bloodblade nodded. "Those are the everyday wards, a wall of glowing air you can see through, that's solid and blocks arrows, flung stones, prowling monsters, slaves seeking to run out—and Nifl like us. They stop some spells, but let others through." He waved at the tunnel, and the glow of the castle-filled cavern beyond. "These, here, are invisible wards, that stop all magic"—he pointed at the flames—"and slay creatures blundering into them. Including Talonar, which is why they're so seldom used."

Lharlak sighed. "Should we feel honored?"

"It takes six or so spellblades quite some time to raise this sort of ward," Old Bloodblade told him. "Longer than it's been since we came within sight of Talonnorn. Unless a sentinel saw us way out in the Dark, and somehow came to believe we were a huge army, they don't even know we're here."

"That last band of warblades know," Daruse said. "Now." Around him, Ravagers chuckled mirthlessly.

Lharlak hefted his curved sword. "So, do we tarry and wait for a way in to open, or work our way all around the wards, testing them at every tunnel? Or turn away, and try again another time?"

"We turn away," Old Bloodblade growled. "We came to raid and make ourselves richer, not launch a war. Every moment we stay here makes it more likely they'll see us and send out warblades enough to overwhelm us. No, we go back. Out into the Dark, and hope to find traders coming in or one of their fighting bands coming home—so we can pounce. Or if the band's too strong, skulk after them and see if we can learn the way in. A signal, or a token they carry, or sentries and a pass phrase . . . it must be something simple, or no Talonar would be able to understand it, aye?"

"You," Orivon growled accusingly, "just don't want me to get my hands on spellblades or bracers—or any other Nifl magic I can use!"

Taerune shook her head. "No, Orivon, I just don't want us to be hunted from now on, by foes who know exactly where to find us! Do you *want* to spend all the life you have left—and it'll be short, believe you me—doing nothing but fighting and running and fighting, against foes who never, ever stop attacking?"

Orivon shook his head. "You'll say anything to stop me getting any Talonar magic!" He reached again for the bracers—and when Taerune made an exasperated sound and thrust her hand in his way, whirled around and slapped her hand away, glowering.

She glowered right back.

17

No Cause for Doom-Crying

Bloodshed among the Holy Ones is no cause for doom-crying. When they're truly in peaceful accord, then should Niflghar tremble.

—**The Words of Dounlar**

The Place of the Goddess, beautiful though it was, seldom saw Lords of Houses striding through its halls. Even less so, a Lord in everyday garb, with naked sword in hand and anger riding face and utterances.

"Out of my way or die," Erlingar Evendoom snarled at the guardians of the gate, two Holy-shes chosen for their looks and clad in armor designed to ensnare the eye and warm the loins of rampants, not protect the sleekly rounded flesh beneath against anything. Yet the magic throbbing in their gauntlets, bracers, open helms, styled pectorals, thigh-high boots, and the various blades and whips sheathed and scabbarded at various locations about their bodies made them formidable holy defenders indeed. Moreover, they wore two invisible armors: All Talonnorn knew their every word and deed was backed by the ready spells of the Holy Ones of Olone, and they acted with the cold, certain hauteur born of the approval and authority of the Goddess Herself.

A lone, angrily striding Nifl seeking to enter the temple with a drawn sword would customarily have been ordered to withdraw, and lashed with a pair of long, spell-crackling whips if he kept coming. No matter what rank he declared, nor urgency and right to passage he claimed.

Not that Lord Erlingar Evendoom knew this would be their customary reception of such visitors—wherefore he was unaware that something within the Place of the Goddess must be amiss indeed, when the guardians murmured something he didn't bother to listen to, and stepped back to let him pass between them. He heard the alarm gongs they rang in his wake, but paused not, nor cared; all servants seemed to get excited when he arrived anywhere.

"Aumaeraunda!" he shouted, as he strode down a grand hall lined on both sides with tall statues that upon another occasion he might have paused to examine appreciatively. "Where are you? And why have you snatched my Secondblood from me?"

Answer came there none, nor hastening priestesses, despite the gongs ringing on and on—and that *was* unusual. He slowed, frowning. "Aumaeraunda?"

A face peeked momentarily around the edge of a doorway ahead, then hurriedly withdrew. Taking another stride on, toward that door—there were many on both sides of this stretch of the vaulted hall, most of them closed—Evendoom spotted something else unusual.

A large scorch scar on the polished stone floor ahead . . . and a little way beyond it, something that was unmistakably a large pool of blood. Nifl blood.

Had they not cleaned up after the attack? For some holy reason, perhaps? The blood looked wet, freshly spilled, but might not be. Everyone knew the temple was a-crawl with spell upon spell, many of them preservative, to keep beauty at its perfect peak. Yet surely—even with the legendary pride of the Consecrated—Aumaeraunda would have said *some*thing about the fighting she and her Holy Ones had done on Talonnorn's behalf, the losses the Holy of Olone had suffered, to win respect among the Lords and Eldests of the Houses that would have made things much easier for her during that little council gathering that had probably cost Ohzeld Maulstryke his Firstbrat.

Still no priestesses. No, something was very wrong in the temple of Olone. He reached the doorway where the peering priestess had been, and looked inside rather warily, sword at the ready.

The great chamber beyond was shrouded in darkness, its customary braziers unlit. Dead priestesses—many of them—lay strewn about the floor and the exquisitely curved couches.

Lord Evendoom blinked at them in astonishment, dimly recalling this as a brightly lit room of ostentatious splendor, clearly intended to show any visitor that the Holy of Olone were wealthier and more beautiful than even the haughtiest of the city's Houses, and had taste and reach to outmatch even House Evendoom.

"Olone forfend," he muttered, seeing sudden radiance kindle far, far away—through a gaping hole at the far end of the chamber, that let him look through a wall into an even larger room beyond. Powerful magic had been hurled about here, to blast that hole and hurl and tumble bodies and furniture and even the magically floating aerial plants the priestesses so loved everywhere.

The glow he was watching outlined the busily weaving hands of a priestess casting a spell; the glow was the mustering power of her magic. By her pose and the way she moved, she was angry, hurrying—and gazing at a foe or target Evendoom couldn't see.

A bright bolt of magic suddenly burst into his view, from a part of that distant room hidden from him by the wall that still stood around the jagged hole, and struck the priestess.

Evendoom had a momentary glimpse of her, silhouetted against the ravening light that was slaying her, as she arched back, convulsing, as magic stripped flesh and all from her bones—and then the bolt faded, its deadly work done, and he was blinking as her skeleton collapsed, tumbling from view.

"Olone *spew!*" he cursed, ducking back out of the room and along the passage before whoever had hurled that deadly magic might think to seek targets in his direction. Had the Holy Ones gone mad?

He hadn't reached the next door before a priestess burst through it, sobbing and running hard, with another Consecrated hard on her heels. They both rushed past the Nifl Lord and his raised sword as if he were invisible, and as he watched, the pursuing priestess caught the other one up, trod hard on her heels so she stumbled and crashed down—and pounced on her, stabbing repeatedly and viciously with a long dagger that was wet to the hilt with Nifl blood after its first strike, and dripping by the last one.

"By Olone, you deserved that, Narazmra!" the murderess hissed, rising from the sprawled body of the priestess she'd just slain. "Now to see to Paerille!"

She dashed away down the passage, ignoring Lord Evendoom as if he were just another of the statues, and raced up the stairs just inside the gates. The Nifl Lord sighed, wondering if he should follow. Or venture on—carefully, mind—into the other great chambers of the ground floor of the temple. Or, by Olone, turn and flee out of the Place of the Goddess while he still could.

"Die, traitor to Olone!" an unseen priestess shrieked, from somewhere in the chambers beyond, and there was a sudden roar of magic, a booming that shook the walls and made tiny pebbles bounce and hail briefly around him. In its wake, dust curled—and an eerie silence fell.

Lord Evendoom frowned, drew a dagger to keep his spellblade company, and strode on down the passage, stepping through the first door that stood open on his right.

Where he almost tripped over a Nifl-she he knew: Draurathra, Eldest of Raskshaula, who lay on her back, blood running from her mouth and her legs gone—melted into what looked like black tentacles, that had then been hacked and diced like runthar-meat on a cook's board, leaving a dark pool of most of her blood.

Her eyelids flickered. "Hail, Erlingar," she murmured, voice faint, slow, and slurred. "What brings you here, to this pit of she-malice?"

"Demanding an answer of the Holiest of Olone," Evendoom told her grimly. "Who did this to you?"

"Askrautha of Dounlar, but it was the last thing she ever did. I caught her with whirlblades, and she was headless before she could even stop gloating." Her voice faded. "Go, Erlingar. Go while you still can. I always liked—Olone damn it, I always fancied you. I'd plead for a kiss, but you don't want to be near me when my death-spells go off."

She waved one hand bonelessly. "Go! You won't get any answers out of Aumaeraunda. Ever again."

"Oh?" Erlingar asked, backing away and frowningly anticipating the answer he was about to receive.

"She's dead, Erlingar. All this chaos you see is the fight to succeed her, just beginning. We go through this every time, and learn *nothing*. Pah! It's *all* nothing to me, now. Farewell, Erlingar. I loved you a little, but took care you never knew it . . . I took sufficient care, didn't I?"

"I—you did, Draurathra," Lord Evendoom said, surprised to find his throat thick and his heart heavy. "You did."

He never knew if she'd heard him. That weakly waving hand fell as the first word left his lips—the explosions and wraithlike billowings were well underway by the time he finished speaking—and spun around to flee as fast as he'd ever run in his life.

As he sprinted out of the Place of the Goddess, between the saluting gate guardians, he heard an agonized scream from somewhere above and behind him—and from somewhere deeper in the temple, another spell blasted through what sounded like another wall.

"Truly," he muttered sarcastically, pausing in the street—the surprisingly empty street—to catch his breath, "yon's a testament to Olone's beauty."

The temple shook again, and a plume of smoke burst out between the two beautiful guardians.

Lord Erlingar Evendoom shook his head, turned away, and started back toward the Eventowers.

The struggle to succeed Aumaeraunda had more than begun.

The Eldest of Evendoom casually kicked a flow-sculpture that had been old before the Eventowers were built off its pedestal, ignoring the servants' frantic dives to save it, and propped her boot heels on the vacated pedestal. Three cushions had served to make Erlingar's throne fairly comfortable to a Holy-she reclining languidly sidewise upon it, and Erlingar's best wine was *very* good.

Maharla sipped again from the Lord's own grand goblet—Olone, it was heavy, but then if Erlingar could wave it about, so could she, and the more she drank the lighter it would get—and smiled as she contemplated just how to make herself the undisputed head of House Evendoom without having to slaughter too many of her kin and senior servants, and anger the rest of them, in the process. Fear forged the best loyalty, but not if she left strong foes alive to band together against her, and—

The searing pain in her head was as sudden as it was blinding. Maharla shrieked despite herself. Wine splashed across her face and lap as she clutched the goblet against her breast, hugging herself against the stabbing agony.

Nothing but a temple-summons should be able to reach her through the House wards, and Aumaeraunda could hardly need aid urgently enough to call on the newest Eldest in Talonnorn, that she clearly despised . . . yet neither was the Holiest of Olone stupid enough to try to spell-harm Maharla Evendoom just now, with Ouvahlor still on the prowl and—

Sickening pain flooded through her mind, swirled and washed away, and then returned again, stronger than ever. What was going *on*?

The servants, drenched with relieved sweat as they looked up from righting the unshattered sculpture, saw the Eldest make the swift, impatient gesture of a simple spell.

Then they saw her go very pale, mouth falling open at about the same time as her hand did. The great goblet plummeted, unregarded.

"Oh, *no!*" she gasped, her voice a ragged whisper almost lost in the goblet's bounce, musical clang, and loud splash of spilled wine. "Oh, flaming, blood-spewing Olone!"

Orivon and Taerune warred with their glares, as sharp and bright as if they'd been thrusting at each other with swords.

"*You're* wearing magic bracers," Orivon told his longtime tormentor, his frown fierce. "Or rather, *one* bracer, now."

"Thank you for reminding me," she said coldly. "And I have my Orb, which masks this ward-bracer—and *only* this bracer—from anyone trying to magically locate it from afar."

"There's much you're not telling me about Talonar magic," Orivon growled.

"Yes," she replied flatly. "There is."

They traded glares again, and then the Nifl sighed and said quietly, "We need to get far from Talonnorn. Quickly. I think you know that."

Orivon's nod was grim and grudging, but they turned away together from the blackened thing that had been Shoan Maulstryke, and walked off side-by-side.

They were two caverns away before something quivered and started, very faintly, to glow.

Something that lifted a little, trailing one severed Nifl hand that held it in a death grip, and another that was on the verge of falling away.

Silently, with no living thing in the cavern to see it, the spellblade that had belonged to Shoan Maulstryke rose into the dark air.

"Lord!" one of the warblades said urgently, pointing.

Faunhorn Evendoom made the gesture for silence rather sharply. Olone have mercy, if Tersarr couldn't see things until he was about to stumble over them . . .

He strode over to the warblade until their wards touched, flaring slightly, and let their magic carry his nigh silent whisper to Tersarr's ears. "Take Goraun and Imbrel down this side of the cavern, and around. Peer carefully; expect hidden foes. Only when we know no one is about to pounce on us will we examine . . . the remains."

Without waiting for a reply he turned to look at Lorand, at the head of the ring of warblades holding the gorkul's chains. Grunt Tusks gave him a baleful sidelong glance that he ignored; if that collar had been around his neck, and the chains held by a ring of foes, he'd probably have felt far less than friendly, too.

Faunhorn jerked his head in an order; Lorand nodded and urged the chained gorkul forward, seeking the slave's trail. He was unsurprised to see it sniff loudly, lower its head briefly, and then start right down the center of the cavern in a rattle of chain. Taerune and the slave had been in some haste.

And no wonder. Spellrobes can trace things they've helped enchant across a very great distance, even in the Wild Dark.

If this cooked carrion wasn't Jalandral, it was Shoan Maulstryke. And those severed hands, yonder, held nothing, though they'd recently been clutching something.

The spellblade that should have been there was gone.

Lord Evendoom sagged in his seat, asleep even before the servants could finish filling his favorite goblet and hold it out to him.

Behind a locked door in a chamber not far away, Maharla smiled. The spell she'd left on the throne had sent Erlingar into slumber and opened his mind to hers in two swift and silent instants. Sometimes the simple traps are the best ones.

His thoughts were a whirlwind of anger, fear, and excitement; he eagerly wanted to watch as priestess murdered priestess, to enjoy their struggle to succeed the slain Aumaeraunda as Holiest of Olone. Seeing the temple so weakened had been a joy as well as a shock to him.

Maharla watched, drifting through his welter of memories, pleased to see old foes lying dead and the spell she'd cast on Erlingar earlier—the one that would let her transport him at will from wherever he stood to wherever Taerune was, keeping herself hidden from both of them—still intact.

Olone's kiss, but this had been fast. The temple had gone from the haughty fist of true power in Talonnorn to a shell fought over by mind-wounded or junior Holy-shes in a trice.

Handing Maharla Evendoom her own chance.

Yes, it was time.

Not letting herself begin to gloat yet, not even for a moment, the Eldest of Evendoom strode around the chamber, carefully preparing to cast the most intricate spell she'd ever tried. Yet.

Its glossy length gave off no glow, now, for any eye to see as it raced through the air, point foremost.

The spellblade flew in utter silence, sliding through the air as it flew, quite by itself, back through the Wild Dark to Talonnorn.

Maharla trembled, her heart pounding. If Askrautha were still alive, or Draurathra, or old Amedra, she'd never have dared do this.

Using her consecration-stone to link with everyone who wore such a stone—every crone and priestess of Holy Olone in Talonnorn—left her mind open to anyone who had the right spells and a more powerful stone.

Yet the spell was done, and nothing had come storming into her mind! Maharla fought down a surge of excitement so strong it almost sickened her. She'd done it! Olone be *praised*!

"Faithful of Olone, hear me," she said, keeping her voice gentle and welcoming. Her voice thundered around the sealed chamber like the boom of a spellblast and rolled back at her, almost deafeningly. All over Talonnorn, now, crones and priestesses would be hearing her.

"Maharla am I, Eldest of Evendoom, and I stand now in Olone's favor. The Goddess who guides us all has sent me a vision, of the champion of my house who shall fittingly slay the murderers of Aumaeraunda, Holiest of Olone. I say 'fittingly' because a traitor Nameless of Evendoom and a runaway slave belonging to that traitor killed the Holiest. I have sent that champion forth in obedience to Olone, who has made my reward clear to me. That the bloodshed that now afflicts Talonnorn may cease, I invite you all to watch what this my magic shows you as the champion confronts the murderers. You know I can deceive you in no way, with my magic linking our minds thus. You shall see what you see, in accordance with Olone's wishes. Watch now, and heed."

It had not been hard to find some of Taerune's blood, and kindly old Orlarra had been more cunning than any Evendoom had guessed: She'd used a spell Maharla had never suspected existed, to trace every last Evendoom Orb when she wanted to.

That spell was unfolding glowingly in front of Maharla right now, and so she knew Faunhorn was very near to Taerune, and Ravandarr was close behind.

She couldn't lie to all the crones and priestesses, but she could hide things in her mind from them, and one of the things she intended to keep hidden was just who the champion was.

Faunhorn, Ravandarr—and if need be, an awakened and spell-hurled into the Dark Erlingar—could all try to slay Taerune and the Hairy One. She could triumphantly claim the glory no matter who succeeded, and deem any failures not Olone's champion.

She could feel the weight of them in her mind, all the crones and priestesses. Watching; unable not to watch. All across Talonnorn, despite themselves, they'd stopped whatever they'd been doing, and were watching.

Folding her arms across her chest, Maharla allowed herself to smile.

"*Well,* now," Lharlak murmured, sliding his eye patch out of the way to peer with both eyes at the moving figures far below. "Talonar warblades hunting someone with a gorkul's nose. Curious."

"How so?" Old Bloodblade rumbled, as quietly as he knew how.

"Warbands from Ouvahlor lurking everywhere, their city in turmoil, and they go hunting? In numbers so few? They're hunting *someone,* or one beast, or a pair at most. Now, who could be so valuable to warrant such attention just now? Such quiet, *private* attention?"

"A Nifl fled with the treasury of his house?" Daruse offered, joining them. "That's an Evendoom, down there, and those are Evendoom warblades."

Old Bloodblade shrugged. "I'm intrigued. So we follow them for a bit before slaying the lot of them, to see if they unfurl their little mystery for us."

Daruse showed his teeth. "I *like* Talonar treasuries."

It was not unusual for crones to slip out of the grand fortresses of their noble Houses from time to time, to taste the pleasures of the Araed. By unspoken agreement, crones who recognized each other among the

Nameless pretended not to, and because what a Consecrated does to other Consecrated is quite likely to be done back to that same Consecrated, it *was* unusual for Eldests and other crones to spell-reach from their towers out into the Araed after them.

Wherefore the almost bare Nifl-she dancing atop a table in the Waiting Warm Dark—who none in that tavern knew to be Naersarra of House Dounlar—was shocked indeed when Maharla's spell rolled into her mind, dashing aside the warm happiness born of her favorite wine and the eager caresses of low rampants.

She stiffened and gasped, "What *madness* is this?"

One look at Naersarra's face had the Nameless carters and pack-snout tamers hastily letting go of her thighs and ducking away, even before she raised her hands to cast a spell.

The tavern master reached under the bar for his slowsleep-tipped darts—and then swallowed, drew his hand back, and awaited his doom. More Turnings than he cared to count ago he'd seen a furious Ruling Hand of Olone clear a street with a spell that hurled, tumbled, and shredded Nifl, gorkul, and pack-snouts alike—and he knew what he was looking at now. No dart he could hurl was going to save the Waiting Warm Dark, if—

The barefoot, sweat-bedewed Nifl-she atop his corner table finished her spell with an angry flourish, her eyes blazing. She turned slowly in the tense silence that had fallen around her, met many frightened gazes, and snapped, "Watch and listen, all of you, to what the Eldest of Evendoom has the effrontery to show every crone and priestess in Talonnorn. I want you *all* to see an arrogant and dangerous attempt to claim the mantle of Holiest of Olone over all of us. For your hands are the ones that may have to clean up the rubble of our fair city in Turnings soon to come—or your backs may well feel her lash. *Behold!*"

Naersarra of House Dounlar flung her arms wide, heedless of her last scrap of garment falling away—and the ceiling of the room above her became a great window into the Wild Dark, a cavern lit by the flaring wards of noble Talonar.

Everyone in the Waiting Warm Dark was now seeing exactly what Maharla was showing the minds of the crones and priestesses. In silence they stared up at warblades with drawn swords trudging forward in that unfamiliar cavern, tightening a menacing ring around a one-armed Nifl-she in dusty battle-leathers and a Hairy One who stood tall in motley garments, bracers strapped to his upper arms, forearms, and lower legs.

His muscled bulk showed clearly through the too-small cloak clasped around his shoulders, and long, wicked-looking blades gleamed back ward-glows in both of his hands. There was a glimmering heap of swords at his feet, and a bleak warrior's look on his face that promised death to anyone who came within reach of his warsteel.

Tarlyn and Clazlathor shook their heads grimly, Munthur gaped, and Imdul and Urgel just stared frowningly. Like all the rest, they said not a word.

Not a wager was spoken in that room, but Nifl who often bet and blustered about duels and Hunt takings leaned forward eagerly, and grew bright smiles.

It seemed they were about to see a death-duel, large and clear, wherein Nifl would butcher a large, formidable, and well-armed human. It didn't get any better than this.

Taerune and her uncle stared into each other's eyes briefly, as Faun-horn's arc of silent warblades became an encircling ring, but they said nothing at all to each other. Everyone's face was grim.

"Orivon," Taerune murmured, out of the side of her mouth, "this Orb of mine has nothing much left in it that can be of help in a fray. We're going to die here."

"This is it, then," Orivon said grimly—and sprang at the nearest war-blade who danced aside almost contemptuously from the Hairy One's wildly slashing sword, only to be astonished by the human leaping to keep pace with him—and drive the second blade through his throat.

Orivon whirled away to meet a second, onrushing warblade even before the first started to fall.

There was a shout from behind him as Taerune flung herself at the ankles of the warblades closing in around her, and toppled one over. She had only the one arm to stab him with, so the warblade escaped with his life as she sprang up, behind him, and raced around his back as he whirled. The Talonar cursed, spinning around to follow her—and then spat blood in mewing disbelief as a sword burst through him from be-hind, and Daruse announced calmly, "First blood to me, Old Blood-blade."

"Second!" Sarntor said a moment later, as another warblade started to slide moaningly off the youngest Ravager's sword. From across the cavern there came a snarling, a wild rattle of chains, shouts—and a shriek that ended abruptly.

Groaning, another warblade went down as Daruse tugged his blade free of the dark elf's ribs.

"Ravagers!" Faunhorn spat. "Lorand! Imbrel! To me!"

"I'm afraid," rumbled the fattest Niflghar the Evendoom Lord had ever seen, as Lorand fell like so much dead meat and his slayer rose ponderously out of the shadows behind him, "'tis me you'll have to greet instead!" He winked at the astonished Faunhorn, and his bristling mustache twisted in what might have been a grin. "Old Bloodblade himself, Sometime Scourge of Talonnorn!"

A filthy Nifl wearing an eye patch and mismatched tatters of armor now stood where Imbrel should have been, bloody sword in hand. He waved that sword meaningfully, and Old Bloodblade cast him a glance and continued, "Er, me and Lharlak here, I should have said! We've been strolling along behind you for three caverns now—and that's two caverns too many for Talonar to be tolerated, out here in *our* Dark."

Faunhorn gave them a cold smile. "You'll find the price of my death rather high," he promised, bending to pluck a poisoned dagger from his boots.

A rock the size of an Evendoom Lord's head crashed into the side of his face before he could straighten, and he collapsed silently to the stones underfoot.

"That," Daruse of the Ravagers told the senseless Talonar with a grin, "is why we don't want to cross blades with you. We'll probably all throw stones at you from a distance, so all your death-spells will hurl themselves at nothing, after we deal with—"

He swung around to face the Hairy One, who now stood back-to-back with the maimed Nifl-she, ringed by wary Ravagers now that the Talonar had all fallen.

"Ravagers, spare us!" the Nifl-she cried, her hand at her throat, where something glowed. "Down steel, all!"

"Spare you?" Old Bloodblade grunted, frowningly watching the Talonar she calling on her Orb. "Why?"

Taerune used the Orb to make her voice loud enough for every Nifl there to hear clearly, and cried, "Behold the Dark Warrior! Foe of the decadent Houses who practice misrule over Talonnorn! One who seeks peace between Ravagers and the City of the Spires! Nameless

Nifl, Ravagers, and all who are oppressed by Evendoom and Maulstryke, Dounlar and Raskshaula, Oszrim and Oondaunt—*this* is your champion!"

WHAAAT? Orivon mind-shouted, his back firm against hers.

[I'm trying to keep us alive], Taerune mind-spoke to him fiercely. *[Play the part, PLEASE.]*

Through the Orb, she felt his amusement. *So you've discovered you want to live, after all . . .*

18

Dark Champions, Going Cheap

Yet when our follies at last we reap,
Foes pressing hard our every doomed fray,
Many dark champions, going cheap,
Shall rise, mar their moments, and fade away.
—from an anonymous Nifl tavern song,
"A Lament for Talonnorn"

*I*n a sealed chamber in the Eventowers, Maharla Evendoom
seethed, her rage making the mind-sending briefly flare ruby-
red. The little bitch Taerune thrusting forward her *slave* as
Olone's champion? And aiming him like a hurlbow shaft right at House
Evendoom and the other houses? How had she even *known*—

Impossible. She hadn't. She didn't. She didn't even know the crones
and Holy-shes of Talonnorn could hear her. This was a desperate ploy
to keep the Ravagers from killing her, no more.

A ploy that seemed to be working, thus far. They were lowering
their weapons, not closing in and hacking.

Now Taerune was taking off her Orb and dropping it to the stones,
and the Hairy One was grounding the points of his swords.

And the Ravagers—bah!

Ravagers couldn't be trusted!

Ever, and in anything!

Fighting down her rage—the headaches of carrying on multiple
mind-magics at once, and shielding one from the other always made her

angry, even before *this*—Maharla clenched her fists and bent her will on Ravandarr.

It helped to visualize stepping through a door, firmly closing it against the heavy mind-weight of the link that was showing what befell in that cavern in the Wild Dark to all the watching priestesses and crones of Talonnorn, and casting endless tapestries across her wake as she sped along a passage to the pale white light of Ravandarr's stone.

Ravandarr, Champion of Olone, she thought crisply—and a veil in her mind drew back, and she was suddenly on a ledge high up on the wall of a dimly lit cavern, looking down upon the heads of a cluster of armed Nifl and a lone human through rising anger that was not her own. Ah, yes; Ravandarr had liked Faunhorn. Seeing his uncle felled, but not obviously slain, would enrage him.

Mahar—uh, Eldest? Ravandarr's mental reply was as weak and tentative as ever.

Maharla's lip curled, but she was careful to keep the tone of her mind-voice warm and encouraging. *Ravandarr, it is time. The escaped slave and the Nameless stand just below you, within easy reach of daggers you hurl. Your sister's wards will deflect your steel, but a rock can down her, just as that Ravager's stone struck down Faunhorn. Shout out that she's famous for slaying Ravagers, and is readying a spell to use on them right now. I feel Olone, watching through me. She wants to see this dangerous human and this disgrace to our blood dead, without delay. Kill them both. Kill them NOW.*

She could feel his reluctance, his quivering distaste.

You're afraid, she mind-told him scornfully. *Afraid of a few Ravagers, and what they'll do. Afraid to obey Olone. What is a stinking human Rift slave to you?*

Ravandarr shook his head. *Taerune,* he said miserably. *I can't.* His resolve and resentment flared together. *I won't.*

Maharla fought down her own rush of fury, and managed to make her next mind-speech stern rather than snarling. *Ravandarr? Olone is watching you, judging you. To restore the honor of House Evendoom and make yourself favored, lifelong, you must do this thing. Two swift, simple slayings. Ridding us all of a dangerous Hairy One and an even more dangerous Nameless traitor—a proven, self-admitted traitor to our house, Talonnorn, and all we hold dear. Now find a stone, draw your daggers, and make an end to them both.*

Ravandar's mind shivered, its turmoil and deepening misery making her feel sick. Maharla fought to keep from being swamped in his rising dislike, the swirling fear, the old, old resentment at being told what to do by cruel, ruthless crones . . .

Ravandarr! She tried one last time, making her voice a disapproving, searing command.

That met dark defiance of sudden strength. *Get back to Olone, and share your schemings with Her! I doubt She wants this senselessness—I doubt even more you've told Her about it at all! And if She does, then I don't want HER! You're not telling me the TRUTH, Maharla! I can feel it, I can—*Her own anger was letting his mind-shouts leak into her sending; it was going red again.

Maharla Evendoom suddenly found herself right out of patience with this mewling weakling, this sullen waste of wine and food and air. *Talonar* wine and food and air. He wasn't going to risk his own skin by attacking with Ravagers all around, and he wasn't ever going to harm his beloved sister.

With a sudden surge of satisfaction—that she knew would be all too short-lived—Maharla whispered the word that would make Ravandarr Evendoom's necklace explode.

She had just time to set her teeth in a wide and cruel grin, to ride out the shrill-shrieking mind-storm that followed.

Headless, spattering the rocks around him involuntarily, Ravandarr clawed the air as Ravagers below spun around and sprang aside, and fell back down the narrow way he'd come, guts and blood and everything exploding wetly.

Maharla turned back to her sending almost gleefully. Culling the rampants, purging weakness . . . "Ravandarr Evendoom, whose death was as futile as his life," she murmured aloud.

Thinking of which, it seemed Erlingar Evendoom was going to be undertaking a little kin-slaying expedition after all.

"But Bloodblade," Sarntor said frowningly, "a *human* to be our champion? To lead us to—what? Striding openly into war with the ruling houses of a dozen Nifl cities, so as to get ourselves swift graves just as fast as it takes us to reach them? I *like* skulking in the Dark and raiding. A slaying here, a slaying there, coins and blades and"—he gave Taerune a leer—"other spoils to enjoy, when we can."

"If that's what you want," Taerune told him, tugging meaningfully at her bodice, "take it." She turned, her gaze a quiet challenge. "All of you." She shrugged. "I'd do better washed and rested, and with two arms—but I'm hardly standing here in strength, to command such things."

Silence fell, in which the Ravagers around her shifted uneasily. It was Old Bloodblade who ducked his head and said gently, "Lady, 'tis no secret we . . . have our hungers, and welcome all Nifl-shes who'll have us. But not surrendering in fear or anger, hating us. Where's the satisfaction in that?"

"Aye," Daruse leered, shifting his eye patch from one eye to the other. "We likes 'em *willing.*"

His grotesque parody of a drooling tavern rampant made Taerune snort with mirth.

"If you don't want a human to rally around," Orivon said then, his voice deep and firm, "there was a gorkul hereabouts a moment ago. It's even trained to flog Nifl."

"It fled that way," a Ravager said, pointing with his sword down the cavern, into darkness. "I can't see it lasting long. There'll be all too few meals it can catch, locked into that collar and dragging half its weight in chain."

"Do you truly want to break the ruling Houses, Dark Warrior?" Lharlak asked quietly.

"I am Orivon Firefist, and the forge is where I've done my fighting. What I truly want is to get back to the Blindingbright, to the village I was snatched from," Orivon replied. "I want to go home." He looked around the ring of Ravager faces. "And so do all of you."

"The homes we seek no longer exist," Bloodblade said heavily. "Not since the priestesses and the grand Houses became open tyrants, and we were cast out or deemed dead if caught, each one of us."

"And we do well enough raiding and harrying," Lharlak said calmly, "without a champion–figurehead or no, human or no–strapped to us. Nifl know who and what we are. Need we take on the hatred some– most–will have for a human?"

"A human'll certainly get us noticed," Bloodblade growled.

Daruse chuckled. "*That's* truth. Noticed by every last priestess of Olone, with the crones to echo 'em, that an unholy and accursed *Hairy One* is coming to despoil their daughters in their beds!"

"I don't want to despoil any Nifl, shes or otherwise," Orivon said wearily. "I just want to go home."

"Aye, and I believe you, man," the Ravager agreed, plucking off his eye patch to look at the human with both eyes. "But how are the Haraedra Nifl ever going to hear you say that, to have any chance at believing you?"

. . .

The hall around him was cold, dark, and empty. Long abandoned, by the look of it, cracks and fallen stones and the faint speckles of ancient slime trails. It was tall and elegant, but deserted and old.

"What is this place?" Jalandral asked curiously, gazing all around. Through a shattered window he could see several cave mouths, crowded like the frozen maws of blindfish on a platter; they were somewhere out in the Dark.

The Evendoom crone came closer, as silently as drifting cavern mist. "Once this was a proud Niflghar city," she said, "Evennar by name. Our family came from here—this hall we're standing in—fleeing to found Talonnorn when Evennar was torn apart by battling Houses, with the priestesses of Olone urging them on to strife rather than constraining them. It all ended in death, for those who stayed to fight."

Jalandral turned to face her. "As you believe it will in Talonnorn, right now."

Klaerra shrugged. "I believe we should both be . . . unfound by anyone, until there is a new Holiest and House Evendoom, at least, has finished tearing itself apart. Taerune has just done something that may yet bring civil war to Talonnorn."

"So silent absence is prudence for both of us, just now," Jalandral agreed. And sighed. "I'm going to grow dreadfully bored."

Klaerra glided closer. "Ah, now, *that* I should be able to prevent." She did something to her robes that made them fall open.

Jalandral let his gaze fall slowly from her smile to her ankles and back. Real admiration grew upon his face—for a crone of the age he knew she must be, Klaerra was magnificent—but he remarked pleasantly, "I've seen—and more than seen—friendly unclad Nifl shes before, you know. Even within the family."

Klaerra smiled, and her empty hands were suddenly holding a decanter of superb wine and a cluster of amraunt, the succulent mushrooms so sought after among Nifl. "Ah, but think of the fun of the chase," she purred. "If you don't find and catch me, you don't eat."

And she winked out, leaving only a cold and empty hall—and a glow at its far end, wherein she'd reappeared, beside an archway.

Jalandral shrugged, smiled, and started running lightly toward her. Laughing, Klaerra ducked through the archway, and was gone.

. . .

"Spewing *Ravagers!*" Maharla Evendoom snarled, beating her fists against the nearest wall in frustration. "Kill the human! *Kill him!*"

But no, they were smiling now, and clasping forearms, the lot of them, relaxing like friends at a tavern, moving companionably together to plunder the Evendoom fallen.

Squawking in wordless fury, Maharla shattered her spell, saying the words and inhaling the powder that would instantly break her mind-link.

The powder exploded behind her nose and down her throat, just as it was supposed to, leaving her staggering—but in and through her mind the Ravagers and the slave and Olone-utterly-cursed Taerune paraded on, chatting, their every word making it more likely that the watching Talonar would think Maharla Evendoom had utterly failed, or even that the *human* was the champion she'd crowed about!

How could it still be going on? She'd *ended* the spell, its magic was fled and gone from her mind and limbs!

How could—? Not Holy Olone, surely?

Maharla cast a frantic quelling-spell on the air before her and charged into it, not quite daring to cast it directly on herself and so leave herself powerless for more than a Turning . . .

The scene that every crone and priestess in all Talonnorn was seeing still proceeded in her head, bright and clear.

Maharla went to her knees, howling in frustration.

"*Oh,* no," Naersarra Dounlar murmured, standing naked atop her table in the Waiting Warm Dark. "Oh, no you don't."

She'd always been one of the fastest spell-hurlers of House Dounlar, and she used all of that swiftness now. The rising anger in Maharla Evendoom's mind had warned her, and she'd already cast the bridging spell—slowly and carefully, too—that would link her to all the crones and priestesses. She left its other end hanging, the incantation unfinished and slowly fading, rather than link herself to Maharla. She needed Maharla's link to that cavern full of Ravagers . . .

To Taerune Evendoom, it must be, or—no! Taerune's *Orb!*

That was it! It had to be!

Yet she'd no way of linking to that Orb directly; she had to find Maharla's link and bind herself to it, without Maharla noticing . . .

It had been like wading in hot, stinking ooze, that slow and subtle drift through the Eldest of Evendoom's dark, nasty, raging mind, seeking the thread of magic at the center of those swirling emotions without getting noticed.

"Fight! *Kill* the Hairy One!" someone in the Waiting Warm Dark had shouted disgustedly. "Olone *drench us!*"

"Aye!" someone else snarled. "Are outlaw Nifl rampants so lonely desperate for pleasure they're cuddling *humans* now?"

But those had been the only shouts, ere eager silence had returned. No one had departed the tavern, or even taken their eyes from what they were seeing on the ceiling.

And in the wake of those angry shouts, Naersarra had found the thread she sought, and—slowly, softly—*melted* into it.

She was in it, but not yet bound to it, when Maharla had said words that echoed like thunder around her, heavy and hard, to shatter the thread.

And that was when Naersarra Dounlar needed her fabled quickness. She hissed words that were hooks to pierce and cling to the thread around her—and then finished the incantation in a glib-tongued rush, a bare instant before Maharla's mind went white-hot and powder blasted all around her, and she whimpered atop her table, trembling, and clung as hard as she knew how, throwing back her head and gasping in blind pain.

And the link held.

And the spell went on.

Leaving Naersarra shaken but able to blink swimming eyes and behold the Waiting Warm Dark around her once more. A room so full of eagerly watching Nifl that no one had yet laid hand on her, or roared out something lewd, or thrown anything.

She bent over languidly to retrieve her gauzelike shift—and then changed her mind and plucked up several drinks instead, to sip at her leisure. Their owners ignored her theft completely, intent on what was unfolding in that cavern out in the Wild Dark.

At one of the tables, the large Nifl named Munthur was still gaping, his open mouth becoming as dry as rock dust. Tarlyn's eyes were narrow with suspicion and forboding, an expression echoed more faintly in the sourness on Clazlathor's face. Imdul and Urgel just watched, now, making no judgments. Yet.

·　·　·

"I care not what Haraedra Nifl think of me," Orivon said slowly. "To the Talonar, I was but a slave–a valued slave because I was good at the forge, but nothing more than a slave. I have seen nothing worse in my time in Talonnorn than what is done in the name of Olone. The constant cruelty, the . . . the Houses lording it over the Nifl they call Nameless, who do all the work and risk their skins daily so the crones and pure-bloods can stay unblemished. I was a slave, so of course they whipped me. Yet I saw more Nifl whipped than slaves, some of them struck aside with casual insolence in the streets of the Araed for no greater sin than being in the way of a Lord or Lady of a ruling House, or irritating such a personage, sometimes for no reason I could see. How is that wise, to goad those whose work permits you to stand, exalted, above them? How soon will they cast you down? In an 'accident,' perhaps? And if a true ac-cident *does* befall one who rules, just whose hand do they expect will aid them?"

"I never knew humans could *talk* so much," Daruse murmured. "And all of it wiser than a priestess!"

"I never knew humans could *talk*," Lharlak said ruefully. "When did we start teaching them?"

"*I* am most impressed that you care about how things are ordered among Niflghar at all," Old Bloodblade rumbled, peering keenly at Orivon. "I'd have thought you'd want us all dead–speedily."

The tall, hulking human shrugged. "I hate not your race, but only a few, specific Nifl. I imagine most Nifl, when they hate, do so likewise. Even when you're taught and expected to hate those of another city, I'm sure in truth you truly hate no one who hasn't done you personal harm, or that you've been told hurt you."

"If we take you in as one of us," Sarntor asked, "d'you think you can possibly avoid talking so much?"

Orivon turned and said two heartfelt words in reply: "With plea-sure."

Eyebrows went up, among the Ravagers, and someone chuckled.

Someone else asked, "So do we hunt down this chains-trailing gorkul? Or is it time, and past time, to eat?"

"So, now," said an older Nifl, slapping the table. "Is this Hairy One our doom, once he's finished mustering all the Ravagers? Or will he be just a human among them, one more ragtag misfit trying to raid us?"

"If he brings down the Houses, I care not if he's human or escaped slave or prancing Olone herself," someone else muttered.

"Hah!" an off-duty warblade snarled. "You complain about the Houses because they provide all. Were you not standing in their shadow, as they shield and defend you, you'd be too busy fighting every Nifl in this cavern—or dying—to complain about anything! The Houses are what make us strong, so we rule the Dark and not the motherless, uncounting and uncountable gorkul!"

"The Houses make *themselves* strong," a traveling merchant said bitterly. "You prattle about what the Talonar Houses do without ever having seen other cities, and other ways! You'll not want to hear it, warblade, as no one likes to know they've been duped, but 'tis your blade, and those of your fellows in arms, that keep Talonnorn strong! Someone must command, aye, but why *families?* And if families, why this one and not that one? Why should one blood sit thrones forever, clearly making decisions for their own gain, and retaining those thrones, rather than for the good of Talonnorn?"

"Well, but the good of Talonnorn *is* their good, too," the warblade said triumphantly, with the air of a Nifl who's proved a point to a dim-witted opponent.

"It is if you think it is, I suppose," the merchant responded. "To me, it seems that is not thinking, but letting the ruling Houses think for you, and believing them when they say what is good for them is good for all. When was the last time *you* lounged for days on end in bed with enslaved shes, drinking the best wine and having splendid food brought to you without waiting for the next table over to be served first, and having to lay down hard coin to get the platters to come at all?"

Several other warblades chuckled, turning from admiring Naersarra Dounlar's unclad beauty, as she sat down on her table to accept several goblets of wine and the return of various garments.

"Hah!" one of them said. "He's got you there, Larravyn!"

"As for me," another merchant said, "I *like* this Dark Warrior. Even if he's a fool, or a human lying to us who just wants to stir up trouble so he can do harm to those who flogged him—what of it? If he does the stirring, who cares why? I want the Houses to have to start behaving, to feel themselves again beholden to the rest of us! If he was Niflghar, I'd have to worry about embracing a tyrant, come to sweep the Houses away so he could step in and treat all of us as slaves! But he's a Hairy One—there's not a chance in all the Dark he'll end up ruling us! So he can be the hand that shakes the cauldron without ever snatching the cauldron for his own!"

"I hate humans," another warblade put in. "They stink, and they make my skin crawl. Yet I like what that one says—and you're right: He'll be dead in less than a Turning if he ever tries to seize power. Let him talk, and muster swords, and raid the Houses. If he takes the sneer off the face of one Eldest or one Lord of a House, he'll have done us all good."

At the next table, a listening Nifl exploded.

"I-I can't believe I'm hearing this," Tarlyn spat, white to his very lips. "Niflghar admiring a—a *Hairy One!*"

He thrust himself upright, eyes blazing.

"Tarlyn, *listen,*" Urgel began. "I—"

"Listen to *what?* Sick love for a—a beast?"

"A *useful* beast," Imdul snapped, his voice raised for the first time any of them had ever heard. "This firefist is a goad and blade for change, who could keep Talonar and all other Nifl unsettled, and *thinking.* If he keeps crones from the sneering certainty of their righteous and unchallenged authority, and so moves them to doing things to help Talonnorn instead of just scheming as they wait for the next Eldest to die so everyone's backside can shift one place closer to the high seat—he'll be worth any strife and fighting off Ravagers we have to do."

He rose from his seat, too, to wag a finger and say firmly, "We need this human—we around this table, who make our livings dancing along the dark edges of Nifl society, and *all* Nifl, too, to keep the tyranny of Olone and the crones from becoming absolute, and all of us as enslaved as the humans and others we crack our whips on."

Eyes blazing, Tarlyn hurled his goblet down on the table by way of reply, and turned amid its bouncing and clanging to storm out of the Waiting Warm Dark, snarling, "Olone take you! Olone take you all!"

Aloun had whooped his delight aloud, and was now laughing excitedly. Luelldar had said merely, "Well, now. *Well,* now," but was sitting slumped back from his flickering whorl with a broad smile on his face. "A champion, Maharla Evendoom says—and what a grasping, overeager Eldest *she's* made. A 'Dark Warrior,' and she makes him a *human.* Behold my puppet, ye of the Dark!"

The Watchers of Ouvahlor turned and grinned at each other, Luelldar shaking his head. Maharla's sending had faded from both their whorls, but Luelldar's arc of lesser whorls had captured it thrice over, for later study. Where precisely was that cavern in the Wild Dark? What did any of the faces betray, as they spoke? Had Maharla revealed anything more than her bare words, by the way she said them?

Ah, but this was . . . delicious. Talonnorn, tearing itself apart before their eyes.

"My grand schemes unfold, so they do," Luelldar chuckled—and was forever after grateful he'd said those words when he did, and not a breath later—at the moment when Exalted Lady of the Ice Naerbrantha burst in on them, eyes flashing in excitement.

"You heard and saw?" she almost shouted. "Senior Watcher, I demand your wisest counsel: Is this Ouvahlor's best chance to finally destroy Talonnorn?"

Wearing a smile to match what was dancing in her eyes, Luelldar said gravely, "With regret I must say, Holy Lady, no. As the Talonar priestesses of Olone claw at each other and their city slides toward strife in the streets, we must wait and watch, to see if this Dark Warrior gathers an army that can threaten Talonnorn and keep its warblades and attention occupied. The moment he does, *that* will be the time to strike at Talonnorn's unprotected backside."

19

Burning the Talon

If ever the Turning comes when one proud Lord
Is so desperate-driven or plunged into fear
As to burn the Talon
Then I shall cower and weep
Mourning lost Talonnorn.

—anonymous Talonar lament,
"All Niflghar Die in the Dark"

How can she *do* such a thing, at a time like this?"

Auree was pale with rage, her white lips making the dark red of the fresh sword scar down her cheek even more stark.

Drayele shrugged, and reached again for a goblet she'd already emptied.

Across the table, Quaeva saw and pulled the chime for more wine, before making a bitter answer: "She cares nothing for the Goddess or for Talonar. Blind with power, drunk on it, she thinks not a moment about how Talonnorn will be smashed and diminished—as long as she ends up with more power."

Priestesses nodded around the table, faces pale with anger or fear—and all of them looking weary. Auree wasn't the only one bearing a scar; every one of the five Nifl-shes crowded into the curtained-off alcove of the Proud House had fled in headlong desperation from the bloodshed still raging in the temple. They owed their lives to luck, agility, and sharing low station among the Consecrated. As near novices, they were casual targets rather than deadly foes of the most ambitious upper priestesses.

Desperation had brought them here, to a private club in the Araed they'd have scorned—and felt unwelcome in—at another time. The Proud House catered to crones of the ruling Houses of Talonnorn, and rampants were shut out of it. In all Talonnorn, it was the only refuge of Niflshes they knew.

"Maharla Evendoom is hardly the only crone reckless-hungry for power," Zarele said tiredly, "not that I needed to remind you." There was a fresh and bloody bandage on her arm, and a long streak down her flank where her robe and her skin looked melted together, her flesh frozen in clusters of bubbles that the priestess beside her, Velle, could not seem to stop looking at—though Velle's darting glances made her lips visibly tighten in nausea.

"I feel like hiding here until it's all over," Drayele sighed. "Which may be when our fair temple is a smoking heap of rubble."

Auree snorted. "Hide *here*? In the midst of the Holy One alone knows how many crones?"

"Better we spend our waiting hunting Maharla Evendoom," Velle said suddenly. "I could at least take some pride in that."

Zarele nodded, and then snorted, her mouth crooking into a wry smile. " 'Dark Warrior'! I quake, I cower, I quail!"

"A *human*! Surely she meant it as some sort of sick jest!"

"She's sick, all right," Zarele agreed heavily. "If I'm to die, I might as well do so rending Evendoom's Eldest as drinking my lifeblood away at this table. So, does anyone know any Maharla-slaying schemes?"

The curtain parted with more violence than a young winemaid would have done to it, and the priestesses looked up, blinking in sudden apprehension.

"No, but I'm willing to help you craft some!" the unfamiliar crone standing over them said fiercely. She was tall, dark brows framing large, dark, and imperious eyes. "May I join you?"

"You've been listening to us with a spell, haven't you?" Zarele asked dully. "I *knew* it was a mistake to come here."

"Who *are* you?" Auree asked sharply, drawing back her hand as if the empty air she was cupping were deadly fire she could hurl.

The crone smiled at her rather pityingly, shaking her head to let

Auree know she knew all battle-magic must be long spent. "Baerone am I, of House Raskshaula!"

"So, Baerone of Raskshaula," Quaeva asked carefully, "who else on the far side of that curtain has heard our words? And why are you so eager to help us? Is House Raskshaula running low on dupes to be blamed for their next attack on Evendoom?"

Baerone's smile widened into real mirth. "No one; I want to help because I am as appalled as you are by Maharla Evendoom's oriad idea; and House Raskshaula knows absolutely nothing about this. Yet. Though if any of you shout any more loudly, someone out in yon room won't be able to help but hear you—and you know how crones gossip."

"*Oh,* yes," several of the priestesses said, in wry unison, as the curtain parted again and two anxious-looking winemaids looked in.

"Olone's mercy, I beg," one of them began, "we're fair run off our feet out he—"

"Just put the wine on the table," Zarele told them without looking up, "and go and fetch more. A decanter for each of us, I'd say—including our just-arrived friend, here." Not waiting for them to reply, she turned her head and told Baerone, "Sit down, and tell us precisely what you want to work together with us on."

The winemaids set down their wine and hastened out, not wanting to hear one word of whatever reply the crone might make.

Baerone smiled after their swift and deft vanishings ere turning to the table, sitting down, and saying briskly, "First, we must slaughter this *dangerous* Maharla Evendoom. Then we must eliminate the most cruel of the surviving upper priestesses of your temple. Please don't misunderstand me: I'm not trying to sweep away all Consecrated—I want you to decide which of your sisters must be brought down. My intent here is to make it possible for us all to survive the fighting that you've so wisely fled from."

Priestesses looked at each other around the table. "Will you submit to a truth-reading spell?" Drayele asked quietly.

"Of course."

More silent looks were traded, and this time some of them were accompanied by nods.

"We are agreed," Auree told the crone. "Welcome."

"Start scheming," Zarele said simply, reaching for the nearest decanter.

. . .

Erlingar Evendoom's shoulder hurt. Swimming slowly up from the drowsy dimness of a slumber somehow *heavier* than he'd felt in a long, long time, he became aware of two things: that he was slumped over in his own chair, all his weight on one arm that must be as numb as its shoulder was aching—and that excited voices were chattering in his head. Familiar voices; Nifl-shes he . . .

Kryree and Varaeme! But what were they—?

Never, in all the many, many Turnings of his tramping off to the depths of the Araed to take his pleasure with them—or any of the willing shes of the Waiting Kisses where they dwelt and worked—had he so much as breathed their names here, in the Eventowers. So what, by Olone's blinding beauty, were they doing *here?*

In anger, Lord Evendoom came fully awake, and found himself sitting alone in a silent chamber. Kryree and Varaeme's converse was spilling into his head from the ring by which he always bespoke them from afar, to tell them to be ready for his arrival.

He stared thoughtfully down at it now, the plainest of the massive rings he wore on every finger—the only one not adorned with a knuckle-sized gemstone. He hadn't been aware its magic could awaken without him willing it to, or carry anything to him but the replies they thought at him after he'd contacted them.

Erlingar started to frown. Across the room, a wall sculpture of polished silver spheres orbiting endlessly, silently around a central sword, had broken apart into wild orbits that flung spheres well out into the room, and back again. And this heaviness still creeping along his limbs . . . somehow that had the smell of magic about it, too; he could *taste* it, at the back of his throat.

What was going *on?* Letting out a sigh that was more a snarl than anything else, Lord Evendoom thrust his attention to listening to the voices of his mistresses.

They weren't talking to him . . . had no idea he was listening. So something *was* twisting the magic of his ring.

Kryree and Varaeme were excitedly discussing something they'd seen—something that had been seen all over the Araed, they'd just been told. Something about a Dark Warrior—a human—a champion, Maharla Evend—*Maharla?*

He must have shouted that as loudly in his mind as in the room, for the door was banging open and a warblade was looking in, sword drawn. "Lord?"

Evendoom raised an imperious hand to tell the guard to stay where he was, and keep silent, as he listened to the startled voices in his mind, asking him if he was himself.

I am Erlingar, whom you both know well, he said firmly in his mind. *Kryree—Varaeme—what is this matter of a Dark Warrior and Maharla Evendoom? You saw it how?*

A spell, it seemed, Maharla's spell, intended for crones and priestesses and seen by them all over the Araed and presumably Talonnorn. A spell that the magical wards of their pleasure-house, ironically intended to block magical prying and scrying, had captured—and were now repeating, presenting it over and over again for anyone inside the front room of the Waiting Kisses to see. Mistress Tarlarla was sending for a spellrobe right now to purge the wards and banish it, but until then there'd be no escaping this Dark Warrior, this forge slave standing in a cavern with . . . with . . .

Taerune? Lord Evendoom's mind-shout made them cower. *Tell Tarlarla to leave those wards alone until I get there and see this magic of Maharla's! If she does not, I'll bring the Waiting Kisses down on her head! Tell her that!*

Minds tremulous, they agreed, but Erlingar barely heard their reply. He was striding across the room to snatch down a spellblade he hadn't used for as long as he could remember, the dangerous one that—

"Raelaund!" he snapped at the guard. "Fetch me a score of warblades, armed and armored and in the front hall by the time I get there! I want double-strength guards on our gates, and the rest to come with me! *Go!*"

"Lord!" the warblade snapped back, whirled away, and was gone.

Erlingar strode after him, and then came to a halt. Now where was the *other* really powerful spellblade, Olone damn it?

"Ice and Beauty, but I'm getting old!" he snarled. "I can't even storm out of the Eventowers properly anymore!"

Orivon had never eaten cave-sleeth before, but it was *good.* The dark, tendon-crowded meat, not just the steaming sauce the Ravagers had boiled it in and then ladled over it. Everyone had crowded around the carcass and gone to work with their daggers, Taerune clumsily with only one hand. Nearly getting the point of her dagger in his eye, dripping sleeth impaled on it, Orivon had reared back, looked for the Ravager he'd noticed earlier with the belt bristling with forge tools, and asked if he might borrow some briefly.

"Why?" had been the blunt response.

"To fit one of my blades to the stump of her arm. In payment, I offer one of the other blades I've brought. I made them; they're good warsteel."

The Ravager had turned and looked at Old Bloodblade, who had slowly nodded.

The sleeth had vanished down to bones in a surprisingly short time, and everyone had drunk much. There was much telling of crude tales, of ambushes in dark caverns and creeping beasts and pratfalls of blundering Talonar patrols, and then the yawns had begun. When the Ravagers started to disperse, some plucking forth sleeping-cloaks from their packs, Daruse and Lharlak were among many who were already slumped over, drunk and snoring. Old Bloodblade pointed, here and there, and Ravagers who'd drunk much less quietly went around covering their sleeping fellows with cloaks.

Ravagers, it seemed, slept by finding smooth rock, laying down a cloak in it, rolling themselves in a second cloak, and lying on the first cloak. It also seemed they fell asleep the moment they were down, still in clothes and boots.

Old Bloodblade kept standing. He was busy at his pack, unrolling and laying out tunic after tunic on a rock as tall as he was. "Wrinkle," he muttered often. "They all wrinkle."

Taerune stared in fascination at the badges adorning the garments. "You have tunics with the badges of *all* the major Niflghar cities?"

Bloodblade crooked an eyebrow at her. "Of course! Doesn't everyone?"

Then the Ravager with the tools came up to him. Bloodblade watched Orivon's blade traded for the loans of the tools, nodded, and then pointed at the human and then off into the darkness at a particular cave mouth. "Do your work yonder, as quickly as you can, and come back, after," he said. "Yon cave goes nowhere, and we'll be using it for other things."

Orivon and Taerune nodded, trying to stifle their own yawns, and headed off to the cave mouth.

The moment they'd vanished through it, Daruse and Lharlak abruptly stopped snoring and sat bolt upright to look at Bloodblade.

He nodded, and they shed their cloaks to steal silently off after the Dark Warrior and the outcast Evendoom.

. . .

"I-it repeats, Lord, from here." Kryree's voice quavered.

"So I've seen it all?" It took Lord Evendoom some effort to keep his own voice level; fury was almost choking him.

At their nods, he said curtly, "I thank you both," and started to stride away.

Kryree could move quickly when she wanted to. "My lord," she murmured, nose to nose, her arms around him and her breath as sweet as ever on his chin, "you are troubled, and this pains me. Lord Erlingar Evendoom should be happy and content whenever he departs this house, and—"

Iron-hard but precisely careful Evendoom fingers lifted her under her elbows and set her aside, and their owner's burning gaze looked past her to still the nimble fingers of a voluptuous and smiling Varaeme, in the midst of their task of unlacing her own bodice to offer her charms to him.

"Fondly though I'd love to tarry and dally with you both, who play 'lady' immeasurably more than the titled shes of my own blood and give me far more love and loyalty, I must now depart in haste to attend to the safety of my House and our city. Be assured I'll return when I can, and accept these as payment for the service you have just done all Talon-norn."

Lord Evendoom plucked two rings off his fingers without looking at them, handed one to each pleasure-she, and whirled away.

He was long gone while they were still gasping at what sparkled in their palms. Bristling with gems, the rings were by far the largest payment either of them had ever received.

Erlingar Evendoom was half a street closer to home by then and striding hard, the warblades who'd stood outside the doors of the Waiting Kiss now trotting to keep up with him.

"The Lords of the other Houses will soon be arriving," he snapped to Taersor, the most senior of his guard, "with guards of their own. Greet them with courtesy and escort them with all honor to my chambers; there is to be *no* fighting or turning any of them away."

"The Lords of all the Houses?" Taersor echoed. "With priestesses and Eldests, too?"

"I doubt it," Lord Evendoom said grimly. "I'll be burning the Talon."

Faces went pale all around him, and guards shrank back.

Erlingar Evendoom paid them no heed, but rushed on, passing through his own gates like an angry whirlwind.

Aloun of Ouvahlor frowned down into his whorl. "Burning the Talon? What's that?"

Luelldar lifted his head from his own whorl and said as gravely as any intoning underpriest: "At the founding of Talonnorn, the lords of the great Houses who'd fled from Evennar established a means to summon each other aside from their crones and the priestesses of Olone. Each has a claw fashioned of ordauth. When plunged into flame, it alerts every other lord; no matter where he might be, his head fills with a vision of the burning talon. By this oldest law and tradition of Talonnorn, those ruling lords are compelled to attend that summons as swiftly as they can, with heirs and bodyguards if they wish, but without priestesses or spellrobes."

He leaned forward to examine the arc of smaller whorls floating in front of him, around the larger central eye. "They're rushing to the Eventowers right now," he added, pointing down at several of the smaller whorls. "See?"

Taerune's face tightened. "Hurts," she murmured.

Orivon nodded. "Unavoidable. If it doesn't clamp tight, it'll chafe and cut, and rot will set in. Remember the gorkuls I fitted with carry-hooks?"

She nodded, almost impatiently, and ran her hand again along the underside of her forearm, feeling the straps that now led to her elbow, and around her arm just above it.

"I'll alter the buckle so you can fasten it by yourself," he told her shortly, reaching for the little tap hammer again, and guiding her arm to the stone that was serving him as an anvil. Taerune winced in anticipation. "Is your Orb shielding us well enough, d'you think?"

Every hammer blow, as precise and dainty as they were, made the outcast Evendoom flinch in pain. She set her teeth, and through them hissed, "Yes."

"Good," Orivon growled, lifting her arm to peer closely at the flange he'd fashioned of its hilt, that would cover the tender end of her stump, "because I want you to know just how furious I am with you, Taerune Evendoom!"

"Why are you furious?" she sighed wearily, face white with pain as he set her arm back down and struck again, more firmly this time. Sweat was starting to drip off her chin.

"I wanted to just skulk through the Dark and find a way up to the Blindingbright, to get home—and you neatly made that impossible. 'Dark Warrior,' my *fist*! A name, nothing more! You've lauded a hollow champion, and these Ravagers will see that soon enough—and they'll slay us just as dead as the Talonar hunting parties would have done! *You* can perhaps find a life among them, but you've trapped me, good and proper!"

Orivon's hammer came down hard enough to make her jump in his grip and cry out. In its wake, as he pulled Taerune's arm upright to examine it again, she hissed, "They would have killed us right there and then, like they killed Unc—my uncle Faunhorn, and the rest! My words kept us both alive—and while we live, you still have a chance at reaching the Blindingbright. More than that: we're among the Ravagers, not hiding from them or being chased by them as well as patrols from the city! Only by being here can you prove your worth to them—and only with their help will you ever have Olone's own hope of ever finding a way to the world above!"

"So you have said," Orivon said shortly, unbuckling the blade and drawing it off, to work almost impatiently on its growing network of straps and buckles. "I should make two of these harnesses, so cut or broken straps can be replaced in moments."

Cradling her stump, Taerune nodded silently.

He cast a glance at her tear-streaked face. "All right?"

"I'll live," she murmured. "There is . . . much pain, but I'm grateful for this."

"Good," Orivon said tersely. "I'm still angry at you."

"I . . . understand. Yet please believe I meant to aid you, and keep us both alive. You can trust me."

Plucking up her arm again to put the blade back on, Orivon crooked a disbelieving eyebrow at her.

"You saved my life," Taerune told him, almost pleadingly. "I am . . . grateful. And have always been . . . fond of you."

"Fond," Orivon echoed furiously. Letting the blade fall with a clatter, he snatched out one of the whips from the bundle still lashed to his thigh, and thrust it under her nose.

Taerune sighed wearily, clumsily tugged open the bodice of her leathers with the hand she had left, and turned as she sat, to present her bared back to him.

"You have too many Turnings for me to count, in which to lash me," she said over her shoulder, "if we are ever to find any equal measure in dealing pain to each other. So strike now. I'll try to get used to it."

Orivon hefted the whip, his face stony. Then he let fly, letting it crack hard across her back. She flinched, curling over in silence and biting her lip.

Her former slave flung the whip down and aside disgustedly, as if it were a snake, and said roughly, "I've no stomach for slicing you like meat. Cover yourself."

She turned, her half-smile a challenge. "Or you'll—?"

Orivon growled, caught hold of her stump with one hand and her throat in the other, and muttered, "I don't know. I truly don't. Some of me would *love* to break your neck right now. And more of me thinks that'd be too swift and easy a passing for you, by far. And . . . and a little of me would die with you, if ever you fell. And a little of me judges you too beautiful and smart and spirited to ever harm, for any reason. And part of me never wants to see your face again."

"It seems you have many parts to you, Orivon Firefist," she murmured. "May I choose which part I deal with, henceforth?"

They stared into each other's eyes for a long time before she started to chuckle.

It was even longer before he chuckled, too.

They ended up leaning chest to chest, shaking with laughter they were trying to stifle. It took some time for their mirth to die away before Orivon managed to growl, "I must return these tools."

"And *I* must sleep," Taerune replied, yawning.

Orivon nodded, fitted her blade back onto her, and growled, "Keep it on. You have to get used to it."

Then he reached down to one of the bracers he'd taken off his arms and legs when he'd started work, thrust it against her chest, and tugged the bodice of her leathers together over it. "Here. It might do you some good, in a fight."

"But . . . why don't you just put it back on?"

Orivon gave her a wry look as he shoved the other two bracers down his own front. "Didn't you watch what I was doing? Where did you think I got the buckles and straps from? The bare stone around us?"

Taerune flushed, and then tossed her head. "The pain left me not thinking clearly about much of anything. Now spare me the bitter comment about how poor a slave I'd make, please."

Orivon regarded her expressionlessly for a moment, and then bowed his head, sweeping his arms about in mockery of a haughty servant's flourishes. "As my Lady Evendoom wishes."

While she was still thinking of a reply, he sprang up and reached down a hand to haul her up to her feet. She swayed for a moment, unused to the weight of warsteel on her left arm, and then said briskly, "Right. Back to join the others. What should I carry?"

Neither of them noticed two Nifl rising like silent shadows from behind nearby rocks, and exchanging winks to tell each other that they'd both heard every word passing between the human and the Talonar she.

Lharlak and Daruse then sank back down to wait, knowing that Orivon, at least, would almost certainly turn to look back before leaving the cavern.

Ravagers didn't grow old by making mistakes.

"Ouvahlor *invades* us, and you burn no Talon," Lord Oszrim growled. "So now the priestesses go mad and butcher each other—something I see as Olone's will, and just fine, besides—and *now* you summon us. Why?"

Lord Evendoom crossed his forearms and scowled, but before he could say anything, Lord Raskshaula leaned forward and said, "Easy, Erlingar. I'd have put it more gently than Lorloungart, but I wonder the same thing: why this, and why now? Surely the battles of the Holy Ones are just that: the battles of the Holy Ones, not our affair."

"If it was just the Consecrated, inside the walls of their temple, I'd agree with you," Lord Evendoom said heavily. "Olone governs those of Olone, and all that. But it's more than that—much more." He held up both of his forefingers, regarded the one on his left hand, and said, "The Eldest of my House has made it *much* more, oriad bitch that she is." He waggled that finger. "She cast a spell right across this city, that every priestess and crone saw—and so has dragged every crone of all our families into it. The fighting won't be staying inside the temple walls. It's erupting within all our walls, whether they've drawn dagger yet or not. If your crones—or yours—don't hurl their holy spells first, someone will hurl holy spells at them . . . and we'll have Talonnorn ablaze."

He folded his left forefinger down, and turned to look at his right forefinger. "All of you know of this spell Maharla Evendoom cast, do you not? What she said?"

"I do not," said Lord Raudreth Oondaunt, but he was the only one amid the murmurings of the other lords.

"Every priestess and crone across our city heard and saw Maharla's spell—and believe me, Lords, when I catch up to her, her life will be swiftly and painfully brought to an end! They saw my daughter, whom Maharla made Nameless and outcast, and a human forge slave who escaped during the Ouvahlor attack, standing together in a cavern of the Wild Dark with some Ravagers. They heard Maharla declare this *man* a champion of the oppressed!"

Lord Maulstryke, who'd kept stonily silent up until that moment, snickered and said, "I tremble. Erlingar, are your wits wandering lately?"

Lord Evendoom didn't even bother to look at his longtime rival. "As some of us seem unable to comprehend the seriousness of this one spell, let me repeat the words Maharla used when declaring this Dark Warrior her champion. She called him 'Foe of the decadent Houses who practice misrule over Talonnorn! One who seeks peace between Ravagers and the City of the Spires! Nameless Nifl, Ravagers, and all who are oppressed by Evendoom and Maulstryke, Dounlar and Raskshaula, Oszrim and Oondaunt, this is your champion!' "

Up and down the table, lords blinked and frowned. "This *is* serious," Lord Oszrim rasped, and there were nods.

Maulstryke chuckled again. "It would be, if anyone were ever foolish enough to think of heeding Maharla Evendoom. Erlingar, they laugh and ridicule her—almost as much as they do you, for not slapping her oriad head off her shoulders when she had the temerity to strip your Taerune of her name! You should have waded into your unhousebroken shes then, swording any crone who dared stand up to you, defied them all, and kept your daughter! Then you'd still have an heir!"

Lord Evendoom rounded on Lord Maulstryke so swiftly that every lord at the table flinched. "*What* do you mean?"

In the tense silence that followed, he asked very quietly, "Just what do you know of the fates of my Firstblood and Secondblood, Ohzeld?"

Lord Maulstryke drew himself up in his seat, as pale as his questioner, and said with a smile that held no love nor mirth, "I know nothing certain, Erlingar, and assure you that I have taken no hand in anything touching on either of your heirs. Yet was it not this same Maharla who banished your daughter, and then sent forth your Secondblood into the Wild Dark, *after* your Firstblood had set forth with mine? And has the Dark delivered any of them back to you, or even any word of them?"

"No," Lord Evendoom said shortly. "Yet I take your warning. Maharla is a danger to us all. Yet I burned the Talon not over her, but for what she's unleashed on all of us: this Dark Warrior. A powerless figurehead, perhaps, but a rallying point regardless, and so a danger."

Lord Naerlon Dounlar laced his fingers together, and said with a touch of weariness, "We are beset with so many dangers. Evendoom, I accept that this is a threat more immediate than most—and that even if he musters a puny force, Ouvahlor can turn around and thrust at us once again while we're dealing with him. What I would hear from you, before I say yea or nay, is what you want from us."

Evendoom nodded. "Fairly said. I want us all to arm for battle. Warblades assembled, our most difficult crones and spellrobes ordered out on patrol with them into the Wild Dark—and the moment they're gone, we send a dozen warblades each to the temple, and swiftly scour it out. Then each of us decides which of our crones could best serve Talonnorn by meeting with personal 'accidents,' and forthwith arrange those accidents. Let Maharla Evendoom be on all our lists."

There was more than one grin around the table, as Lord Evendoom swept on. "Then we meet again, and set our spellrobes to working together—to thoroughly farscry the Wild Dark for the Ravagers, any creeping forays from Ouvahlor, and this Dark Warrior.

"I like it," said Lord Raskshaula. "Count Raskshaula in."

"Thank you, Morluar." Lord Evendoom looked around the table. "Naerlon?"

Lord Dounlar shrugged. "I think this Dark Warrior is a ruse, but I like your scheming in the name of dealing with him. Dounlar stands with you."

"I," Lord Oszrim rasped, "have a question."

Lord Evendoom spread his hand in a "say on" gesture.

"Why can't our crones just pray to Olone the right way—and snatch this human slave out of whatever cavern he's currently despoiling, and hurl him into our laps?" Oszrim demanded. "My best spellblade rides my hip, here; I can bury it in him as often as you need me to. Why all the mustering and the spellrobes? What are you *really* up to?"

"Arousing your suspicions, of course," Lord Evendoom sighed. "I've told you what I intend, Lorloungart—and I've told you *all* I intend."

"I still don't see why the spellrobes. I mistrust spellrobes working together, for any reason. What if they take it into their heads that Talonnorn would be better off without Lords, and turn and blast us all? How would we stop them?"

"How indeed?" murmured Lord Oondaunt. "I must confess, Erlingar, the spellrobes worry me, too. Could we not strike that element from your scheme? Or discuss it again at this next meeting you propose, after we've rid ourselves of our troublesome crones and the worst of the priestesses?"

"We could, Raudreth," Evendoom replied. "I withdraw my suggestion about the spellrobes."

"I have another concern," Lord Maulstryke said flatly. "I want it understood that with the lone exception of Maharla Evendoom, no one is to strike down any crone not of their own house. I want no feuds arising out of this. Moreover, we must be very careful when in the temple, and at all times when dealing with priestesses. I *don't* want the wrath of Olone flattening Talonnorn, and all of us with it."

"Well said," Lord Oondaunt murmured, and there were some nods around the table.

"One more thing," Lord Maulstryke added.

"I am unsurprised," Lord Raskshaula murmured.

Maulstryke's gaze turned very cold. "Do you *mock* me, Morluar?"

"I mock everyone, Ohzeld, including myself. For hundreds of Turnings I've done so, now. Try to get used to it."

Lord Maulstryke shook his head, sneering dismissively, and added icily, "I wish to point out why our host's stated reason for assembling the spellrobes is either mistaken or a ruse—and in either case, must never happen for the reason he has just stated."

The glance Lord Evendoom gave Maulstryke then was inquisitive, not hostile. Lord Maulstryke met it for a moment, and then looked around the table and said flatly, "*No* wizard can touch this Dark Warrior with their spells, or anyone, at a distance out into the Dark. Or even perceive where he is. The Wild Dark has its own crawling magics, that twist and confuse when one gets sufficiently far from one's foe.

Moreover, the Evendoom traitress has her Orb with her, to shield them both."

"She can *do* that?" Lorloungart Oszrim snarled. "Breasts of Olone! What have my crones been hiding from me, I wonder?"

Several Lords rolled their eyes.

"Well, it's never too late to wonder, I suppose," Lord Raskshaula murmured to the ceiling.

20

Not Dangerous Enough Yet

Am I not dangerous enough yet?
Or must I slay all of you, to impress?
—The Deeds of Raularr, Hero of the Niflghar

Old Bloodblade lifted one eyebrow. "Well?"

Lharlak and Daruse shrugged and smiled in almost perfect unison.

"Yon Hairy One knows not what he wants to do," Daruse said. "He's none too happy she told us all he was a champion called the Dark Warrior; 'twas news to him."

"So much I'd gathered for myself," Bloodblade said, his voice dry.

"Yet we do have a certainty for you to chew on, Barandon," Lharlak put in, adjusting his eye patch. "This Orivon certainly isn't some cunning schemer who already has some dark plan up his sleeve, and intends to use us without telling them what he's up to."

Daruse nodded. "One thing: we can trust this human. He means what he says."

"That might not be a good thing," Old Bloodblade grunted, but he was smiling.

Lords stiffened around a table in the Eventowers, and looked sharply at their host—who looked just as alert and alarmed as they were. They could hear distant shouting and a rising, jangling singing sound that all of them knew was the cry of a magical ward under sudden great strain.

"If you've secondary wards," Lord Evendoom snapped, "awaken them. Those are some of my spellrobes, doing the shouting."

Glows and singings erupted around the table, errant sparks racing through empty air to shape auras about swiftly moving arms. Someone screamed just outside the room, the whistle of the wards rose into a wail that was part moan and part earsplitting shriek—and the doors of the room all burst open, evoking curses and the flashes of hurriedly drawn spellblades.

Through one door, out of a whirlwind of howling ward-magic, a spellblade streaked into the room, flying point-first. It flashed up to Lord Maulstryke, reversed itself smoothly in the air, and slapped its hilt into his hand.

As the screams and howlings died away, leaving an eerie silence in their wake, five of the Lords of Talonnorn watched Ohzeld Maulstryke reel in his seat, as white as the fangs of a darkwings.

Trembling, his mouth working, he managed to say, "My Shoan is no more."

In deepening silence he sat, struggling to control his face. It seemed to take a very long time before it settled into a calm mask that looked at Evendoom and asked gently, "Do I have your leave to butcher Maharla Evendoom as I see fit?"

Lord Evendoom nodded grimly. "Yes."

Without another word, Ohzeld Maulstryke rose, bowed to Evendoom, and strode out, the spellblade pulsing in his hand.

Klaerra's ward flickered as some prowler in the Dark blundered too near—and then hastily scuttled away again.

Staring up at its glow, they lay together on their backs, bare and sated, on stone made soft and warm by the ward beneath them.

Jalandral smiled. "You're scheming again; I can tell by your smile."

That smile widened ere Klaerra murmured, "There are many spells I must teach you yet, to make you truly a blade to change and rule Talonnorn, and to cleanse House Evendoom into true greatness."

"I'm not dangerous enough, yet?" Jalandral's tone was mocking.

"Not quite," she replied with a smile.

In a swift, lithe surge he rolled atop her, putting his hands lightly around her neck, both his thumbs hooked under her Orb just enough to lift it away from her throat.

"Aren't you afraid," he asked, his eyes very large and dark as their noses almost touched, "that once I've learned the magic I want from you, I'll just . . . remove an old crone who now knows me too well, and might want to leash me for the rest of my life, and use me as her sword on others?"

"Afraid, no," Klaerra told him calmly. "Disappointed if you serve me thus, perhaps."

She put her hands over his and pushed on them, tightening his grip on her throat.

"I was old and tired," she whispered, "when you were a drooling toddler. If I can see Maharla gone and our blood on the road back to greatness, I'll be happy to breathe my last. The tenderness you've shown me this Turning has been a delight I'd thought never to taste again. Jalandral, kill me whenever you feel the need. Only let me make you stronger first. Much stronger."

Jalandral gently thrust her hands away, releasing his grip on her throat. He shook his head gently, in bemused wonder. "You are so much deeper in your scheming than I'd thought. So tell me why I must be 'much stronger.' Is it to humble scores of Talonar crones? Impress every warblade, so none will dare stand against me? Hmm?"

"If it even seems possible that you may unite and rule Talonnorn, there will be some who will hurl everything they have at you to prevent that. Klarandarr of Ouvahlor, for example."

"And who is Klarandarr of Ouvahlor?"

"The greatest Niflghar spellrobe the Dark has ever known—perhaps the greatest we ever will know. Yet he's not the greatest threat."

"Oh? Ah! Olone, of course."

"No. Olone aids those who triumph, and only watches all others. The greatest threat to you are the oldest crones of the rival Houses of Talonnorn. Not the Eldests in rank, mind; I mean the old and wrinkled wise ones. Like me."

"Oh? You mean they'll teach spells to their own champions, to send forth against me?"

"They're already hard at work on that; you're not seeing their champions in battle yet only because they don't know it's you they have to defeat. I spoke rather of the hidden weapon they can wield to doom us all. The weapon they alone know how to awaken."

Jalandral crooked an eyebrow. "Are you going to tell me?"

He moved his hips as if to thrust into her, but Klaerra did not smile.

"That Which Sleeps Below," she whispered.

"The *Ghodal?* You're trying to frighten me with a *nursery* telling?"

"I'm trying to shatter the jaunty arrogance you believe armors you, Jalandral Evendoom. The Ghodal is *real,* and some of the crones of our city know how to summon it. Haven't you ever wondered why we hadn't all erupted over this or that insult, with the Hunt and our spells and so many warblades and all the feuds, and butchered each other in the streets, long before you were born? 'Twas the Ghodal, and knowing that other Houses could take you down with them, if ever they felt threatened enough."

It was Jalandral's turn to whisper. "You're serious."

Klaerra nodded. "You have *so* much more to learn. Don't kill me quite yet."

Taerune looked younger when she was asleep—younger and terrified, as if some monster were clawing at her in her dreams. Her eyes moved under closed lids, roving desperately this way and that.

Orivon reached out a hand to rouse her, and then drew it back without touching her. If he robbed her of slumber, it was gone for good, and for all he knew she might always sleep this way.

Yawning, he peered again at her blade, half-protruding from under the cloak that was draped over her. He'd thrust it into one of her own boots, wadded up the House Evendoom robe he'd had from the spell-robe, and stuffed the boot full, around the blade, so (he hoped) the steel would stay in, and she'd not harm herself or anyone else while sleeping.

"She'll do no harm," Daruse murmured in his ear. "Be at ease—and stay that way, please; we'd speak with you privately, yonder."

" 'We'?" Orivon muttered—and reared back, startled, as Lharlak was suddenly grinning at him from inches away, the eye patch-wearing head rising up almost out of his lap.

"We mean you no harm," Daruse muttered. "We just want to know where you stand on certain things—and what you know of this Evendoom lady you travel with."

"As to that second question, you could just ask *me,*" Taerune said flatly from below them, her eyes suddenly wide open and fixed on him.

Lharlak and Daruse drew back, spreading their empty hands to show they intended no harm.

"And as to your first question," Taerune added calmly, "I'll listen to Orivon with interest."

Her Dark Warrior grinned at that. Through another yawn, he asked the two Ravagers, "Can't this wait until I've slept?"

"It can," Daruse said simply, retreating.

Taerune gazed steadily at both Ravagers, something approaching defiance in her eyes. As Orivon rolled himself into his cloaks beside her, she stretched her arm out over him protectively.

Daruse gave her a grin and made the Ravager signs for "acceptance" and "self on guard watch." Turning away, Lharlak at his shoulder, he sought the deeper darknesses.

Taerune watched them go, the Orb at her throat glowing slightly, and mouthed a silent curse. Or two.

"Remember," Taersor said sternly, "sword *all* but the most junior priestesses—and every one of them who defies us, too."

"What? But the temple cooks are the bes—"

"You can spare the cooks," Taersor snapped. "Hurlbows ready? Right! Forward and *fire!*"

The two armored guardians flanking the tall and splendid gates of the Place of the Goddess wore armor that showcased their striking beauty more than it protected them. Yet that armor met the sudden hail of streaking shafts with the sudden glows of powerful wards, that turned aside onrushing death even as it ate away at the shafts, so only drifts of dust struck the ground and temple wall.

The warblades had expected no less, and trotted steadily forward, reloading the bows strapped to their forearms. The two armored Holy-shes exchanged terrified looks, and cast swift and longing glances back into the glow of the open temple behind them. Death was coming for them—but the wrath and damnation of Olone awaited if they fled from it . . .

Hurlbows hummed again, the shafts driving the two still-unharmed guardians back against the wall by the sheer fury of their arrival. Doggedly they drew their swords, heads bent against the shafts leaping at them. Then the warblades reached them—and streamed past, straight on into the temple. The guardians tried to block their way—and got driven back against the sides of the tall entry arch, pinned by the onslaught of dozens of thrusting blades. Taersor calmly took the heavy stone he'd been carrying from its sack, swung it back and forth underhanded to get some momentum—and hurled it at the face of the nearest guardian.

Her wards flared blinding bright, but had been made to yield before stone so their wearer could walk and fit through doorways—and the guardian jerked once, spasmodically, and then slid bloodily down the wall, her dislodged helm clanging and bouncing. There was very little left of her head.

The other guardian saw the fate of her fellow, and a warblade bending to retrieve the bloody stone sack—and whirled away to flee into Talonnorn, tearing at her armor as she went.

Warblades started after her, and Taersor barked, "*Don't* lose her! Get after her—and silence her!"

By then, screams could be heard from inside the temple.

Naersarra Dounlar was waiting for old Baransa's spell to warm the waters. Sitting in a loose robe in the upstairs bathing chamber shared by all the Dounlar crones, she was flexing her feet and wincing.

Yes, as much as it hurt to admit it, she was getting just a little too old for dancing all night on tables, and the drinking had left a truly terrible taste in her mouth. Perhaps it was time—

Something that was shrieking and sobbing incoherently burst into being in midair above the soaking pool, and fell into it with a great splash.

Walls of water drenched several crones and brought others to their feet, eyes flashing in alarm and hands rising to hurl spells, the moment a foe—

Came floundering up out of the pool, weeping, and flung wet arms around Naersarra. "S-sister, *save me!*"

Aelrabarra Dounlar was much changed, but Naersarra knew her sister's eyes—even red and wide with staring terror and grief—and so had stayed the slaying magic she had been about to hurl.

"Aelra," she said, embracing the sobbing priestess tightly, rocking her slightly as she hugged. "What's—"

"Warblades! Swording us all in the *temple!*"

Wrinkled old Ranauthra Dounlar was so infuriated she tore off her mask to snap, "*Another* attack by those Olone-cursed Ouvahlans? Is there—"

"No," Aelrabarra wailed, "not Ouvahlor! *Talonar* warblades, of all the houses!"

"Oh! The young she's gone oriad, she's so upset! Someone—"

"*Enough,* Ranauthra!" Naersarra commanded, loudly enough to cut through Aelra's weeping and the angry gabbling of the older crones. "Danthra, spell-calm the water! Braerambra, use them for a scrying-whorl the moment they're smooth enough—we'll *all* see for ourselves what's happening at the temple!"

"Hmph," old Ranauthra told the room sourly. "It's not as if *some* of us haven't spied on the goings-on there before!"

Lharlak looked over his shoulder and saw that three Ravagers were all talking to Old Bloodblade at once. Well and good.

He steered Daruse around a stalagmite larger than them both, and when they reached its far side said quietly, "I'm worried about this Dark Warrior. What if all the Haraedra get scared enough to unite, and come looking to slaughter us before we can do them harm? Patrols, even the Hunt, we can handle—armies, no."

Daruse nodded. "So what do we do? Kill the human?"

Lharlak shrugged. "Easily enough done. Yet the Evendoom outcast has her Orb, and wits as sharp as blades, too. With the one, she knows how to use the other. You saw how she came awake."

"She's the real danger," Daruse murmured. "I saw that from the start. He's but her dupe."

Lharlak thrust a finger under his eye patch to rub an itch in his empty eyesocket. "And if ever he realizes it, 'twon't be *us* she'll have to fear."

"Olone's Bloody Burning Tears," Naersarra Dounlar cursed, dropping every word slowly, loudly, and deliberately from her lips as she fought to ride her temper back down under control.

The vivid scenes of butchery they'd seen in the pool were fading, but no one in the room was forgetting them. The only sound in the chamber was Aelra's muffled sobbing, as she clung to Naersarra and wept into her bosom. Naersarra stroked her sister's hair in comforting that she knew was ineffectual, and tried to think through her fury.

Lords of Houses would *die* for this. Slowly, and knowing why.

The blasphemous effrontery of *daring* to use this pretext to rid themselves of difficult Consecrated and their own kin! The danger they courted for all unwitting Talonnorn, of bringing down the righteous wrath of Olone on the entire city!

"It's happening all over the city," Braerambra said flatly, looking up from the dying glow of a collapsing spell. "Some of the crones of Raskshaula and those of Oondaunt are out in the streets and saying very much the same thing: warblades are happily butchering priestesses in the Place of the Goddess, sparing only a few of the youngest. At least a dozen got out as Aelrabarra did, into the arms of crones in most of the Houses—and the crones are as angry as we are, and telling everyone the Lords have gone mad, are insulting Holy Olone, and doom will surely—and swiftly—befall Talonnorn if they aren't stopped."

"That doesn't just mean blasting a few fools of warblades out of their boots," Ranauthra said sourly. "That means stopping the Lords of all our Houses, who're giving them their orders."

An uneasy silence fell.

Into it, Naersarra said softly, "Sisters, it very much looks to me as if it's up to us to stop them."

Lord Maulstryke looked more like a perching sunderbeak than ever as he peered around the room, tall and dark, hands clasped behind his back. Every spellrobe of his household stared back at him, from rank novices to his most highly regarded spellslayers, who posed as his personal envoys and wore ward-crowns at all times, to keep their minds free of the prying of the Maulstryke crones, and so preserve as many of their secrets as possible.

Those same crones were temporarily forbidden to enter this tower of Maulgard, and kept from stealthy approaches not only by the strongest wards Maulstryke's row of carefully clamped, long-unused breastplates and the spellblades of dead ancestors could generate, but by ward-helmed warblades posted at every door. He'd sent only the young and expendable blades off temple-raiding, expecting grim fates for participants in that particular folly.

Ohzeld Maulstryke knew he'd spoken plain truth to his fellow Lords: the natural magics a-crawl in the Wild Dark made hurling spells of any sort into it from afar chancy at best. Yet he had only one Shoan Maulstryke, and had devoted many, many Turnings to making him a fitting heir.

"You know why you're here," he told them now, staring at many Nifl faces painted with glow-runes and set in habitual sneers. "I want to know the location and fate of the Firstblood of Maulstryke, believed to be somewhere out in the Wild Dark with a Consecrated of Olone escorting him. So long as you tell me what you're trying, do nothing to hamper each other's work, and nothing to ruin the future spells of others, I want you to try *everything*. This is Shoan Maulstryke's spellblade, here on the table before me; arranged along it are items of his clothing, as recently worn as could be found, brought here from his chambers. Alive or dead, I want him found."

Lord Maulstryke paced along the table, his eyes bleak, his face expressionless. "I order you to find my heir, the future and hope of this greatest House of Talonnorn," he told them, and then stopped, turned, and added coldly, "I will, if necessary, cajole, plead, and threaten. *Accomplish this thing.*"

"We've arrived where every parley does, eventually," Lord Raskshaula observed. "The time when we begin to talk again and again about matters that have already been argued over. It's time for this conclave to end, Lords, and all of us to return to our own homes and get to work. The Turning ahead is not going to be pleasant, but we can't stop what's coming by sitting here longer and—"

For the second time at that gathering, a pair of the tall, splendidly carved Evendoom doors burst open, wards swirling in sudden bright drifts of menacing magic.

Helmed warblades stood anxiously in the doorway, bloodied swords drawn, ignoring the spellblades hissing out of Lords' scabbards all over the room.

"My Lords!" the foremost gasped. "Urgent news!"

"It had better be," Lord Evendoom growled. "Say on, Raelaund."

The warblade bowed, stiff in his armor. "The city is plunged into armed uproar! Crones of all Houses are felling warblades with spells! There's fighting in the streets, and many dead! Scores are being settled, and priestesses and crones in all of your towers, Lords, are crying vengeance upon you!"

"Evendoom," Oszrim roared, "if this is some trick of your doing—"

"I hardly think that's possible," Lord Raskshaula snapped, using some trick of the rings on his fingers to make his voice louder while keeping it calm and level. "Warblade Raelaund, how do you know this?"

The Nifl shook his blade. "This blood came from Nifl of this House, that I was forced to fell to keep them from charging in here. Spells of Evendoom crones had hold of their minds, and as we chased those crones out and down from this tower, I saw out a window many warblades of the same Houses at battle in the streets, crones pointing and shouting among them. Dare look out a window, Lords, and you can all see for yourselves!"

"Goddess and Talon!" Lord Oondaunt swore, rising so swiftly his chair crashed over behind him. "How are we to even get home safely?"

"Can't your spellblade fly you?" Lord Dounlar asked, a trifle wearily. "Evendoom, have I your leave to have this good warblade of yours find me a window? Preferably when he's *not* holding a ready sword in his hand?"

"Well, *try* it! Slaughter every pack-snout in the stables if you have to!" Lord Maulstryke snapped, striding over to a stammering spellrobe in a frenzy that made the young Nifl cower.

Others, busy at the tables all around, winced, looked away, and tried to pay no heed. None of them wanted the mad Nifl Lord roaring in their face next. The air was full of smokes, drifting powders, the fading glows of runes that had been drawn on empty air, and the mutters of gesturing spellrobes.

Tirelessly Lord Maulstryke stalked among them, crossing his chambers time and time again, coldly goading them on.

"They all got away safely, Lord," Raelund gasped, as they hurried along a dark passage in the Eventowers together. "But you must get into armor now; the house is full of—*eeurraaah!*"

Lord Evendoom turned in time to see three swords that darted and thrust by themselves—plain working weapons, not spellblades, but aswirl with the glow of a spell as they flew and flashed in the air—drive deep into his faithful warblade's throat, leather breeches in the momentarily exposed gap between thigh-plates and cods, and armpit, racing up along the underside of Raelund's sword arm.

The dying warblade started the stumble that would end in him crashing to his knees, and Evendoom didn't wait to see those blades slide back out of him again, dripping blood, and start their menacing turns in his direction.

He could see the crone behind them, grinning at him bloodthirstily—old Opaelra, who'd never liked him; nor he, her—and behind her a crowd of servants with old swords and spears and kitchen knives in their hands. They let out a roar as the warblade's fall let them see their Lord staring at them, and surged forward.

Erlingar Evendoom turned away from them and hurled himself into a lumbering run, crashing bruisingly off sculptures and wall reliefs, too winded and suddenly afraid to even think of an oath to bark.

Was *this* to be his ending? Hacked apart by an angry mob of his own Nameless servants, led by crones of his own blood?

He reached a flight of unfamiliar back stairs leading down—the sweeping, curving ramps he was used to seemed in short supply in the servants' corners of Eventowers—and took them five and six at a time, stumbling and roaring in pain when his heels caught on the edges of steps, but not, for the love of Olone and the skin of Erlingar Evendoom, slowing down one whit.

Enthusiastically, Evendoom servants streamed after him, waving their weapons clumsily and howling for their Lord's blood.

That noisy parade of pursuit raced past many a dark and open door in the part of the Eventowers given over to dust, darkness, and storage, and someone came to one of them, after the hue and cry passed, to look after them and laugh softly.

That someone was Maharla Evendoom, and her fingers were tracing the deeply graven letters of the name "Ravandarr" as she hefted the spellblade that bore it in her hand.

"An Orb! My spell has found a Talonar Orb!" a spellrobe cried excitedly. Lord Maulstryke turned at the far end of the room and almost flew across it, to stand over him. Several wizards crowded around.

"There!" the excited spellrobe said, pointing into the tangled glow that floated in the air right in front of him. "Closer . . . closer . . ."

A crowd was all around him now, leaning forward eagerly, not wanting to miss anything. The glowing lines started to writhe and brighten, as if sharing their excitement.

21

Trust, Fell Magic, and Hunting Traitors

In the end, my every war has come down to these:
Trust, fell magic, and ahunting traitors.
   —The Words of Dounlar

Klaerra stiffened under him. Jalandral's sword was in his hand in an instant. "What is it?" he hissed.

"A spell . . . probing for me," the crone hissed, her hand darting up between them to the Orb at her throat. It flared under her fingers, brightly enough to blind him into cursing and looking away, and then faded just as quickly.

"I'm sure that was needful," he snapped, one hand cupped over his sightless eyes. "Are you going to tell me why?"

The soft movement under him was almost certainly a shrug.

"It was necessary," Klaerra replied calmly. "I had no time to build to lethal force. Just lie still, and your sight will return. As you well know, there are times when one must be . . . ruthless."

The spellrobe shrieked as his spell flared up in his face like a windblown candle. Then it was gone, leaving those crowding around blinking at empty air—and the spellrobe slumping lifelessly, smoke curling from his ears and scorched, bubbling eyes.

The wizards around drew back from the strong reek of cooked Nifl flesh, even before an older spellrobe clear across the chamber said quietly, "Lord, I've found something you should see."

There followed a general rush across the room, the more prudent spellrobes ducking out of the way of Lord Maulstryke, who came to a sudden, silent halt in front of a scene floating in the air, that the spellrobe had already turned away from.

It was a view of an uninhabited cavern, somewhere in the Wild Dark, wherein lay a blackened, twisted Niflghar body—little more than a skeleton cloaked in charred flesh. The forearms ended in stumps, hands missing.

"Whose body am I seeing?" Ohzeld Maulstryke asked with a terrible gentleness.

The spellrobe finished his second spell—and the spellblade on the table started to glow.

The wizard sighed, and then looked away as he whispered, "Shoan Maulstryke, Lord. The spellblade confirms it. I'm sorry."

The spellrobes crowding around Lord Maulstryke all carefully looked away, and edged as far from the Talonar Lord as they could, expecting him to rage and weep and smash things.

Lord Maulstryke gave them silence. Long silence, during which he drew himself up, if possible, even taller and straighter.

Then he remarked calmly, "Orbs, I'm told, can leave a trail when very strong magic is called forth from them. Is there such a trail leading out of this cavern?"

All around him, wizards broke into a frenzy of spellcasting, and it seemed no time at all before one—and then, very quickly, another—said excitedly, "Yes!"

"Follow it," Maulstryke told them, in that same gentle voice, and the feverish spellcasting began all around him again.

Taerune was asleep at last, her long slow breaths threaded with the faintest and briefest of soft, gurgling snores.

Orivon lay awake, staring at the jagged cavern ceiling high above, very aware of the slender Nifl arm draped across him.

How did he truly feel about Taerune Evendoom?

She'd been tender, even loving, she had—yes—saved both their lives. More than once.

She'd refrained from killing him when she clearly could have, and . . . could he trust her? Truly trust her?

With a sound that was half groan and half gasp, the fifth spellrobe toppled forward in his seat, smashing his face on the unyielding smoothness of the stone table. Another swayed, biting his lip.

All of the nine remaining spellrobes concentrating on tracing spells were now pale and beaded with sweat.

The lesser wizards who had no spells underway eyed the nine anxiously, looking from one to the other. Lord Maulstryke stood like a patient statue, silent and expressionless as he watched, only his eyes moving.

Abruptly another spellrobe toppled forward, convulsing, his flailing arms striking aside a row of his own vials.

A novice wizard plucked them up as they started to roll, that none might shatter and be lost. Another looked up at Maulstryke's set face and said anxiously, "Lord, they're doing all they can! Such tracing is *extremely* tiring, even when concentrating on ways near at hand, and not through the strange magics of the Wild Dark! This is why items and—and wanted persons aren't traced all the time by magic, and—"

"Thank you, Clael," Lord Maulstryke said gently.

Clael gasped, astonished that his Lord even knew his name.

"However," Maulstryke added calmly, "this trail *will* be followed, and the bearer of the Orb at the end of it found. Or not one of you will leave this room alive."

[Orivon, you can trust me. And I'll prove it.]

Orivon stiffened. The whisper in his mind was Taerune's. He turned his head, in time to see her open her eyes. She looked at him, not smiling, and then rose, tugging her boot off her blade and putting it on.

Leaving their cloaks and the robe he'd stuffed her boot with lying tangled, she took his hand and started leading him silently through the sleeping Ravagers. They were heading toward the side cavern again.

.   .   .

A spellrobe reeled, bright-eyed, and blurted out, "I–I've found it! Many magics, Orb-cloaked, but–yes!"

Maulstryke was suddenly standing over him, and turning to calmly command one of the junior wizards: "Map."

The wizard nodded excitedly, waved a hand, and the floating spell construct drifted smoothly to a spot just above the desk of the spellrobe who'd made the trace.

Smiling, he plunged both hands into the wraithlike sphere of caverns and winding tunnels. It flared red around his fingers as he and the junior wizard locked gazes, smiling, and the spellrobe felt for control over the map-spell.

The floating map wavered, sank and drooped for a moment as if about to collapse, and then glowed more brightly as the spellrobe's fingers started to trace new caverns and passages, drawing them with his forefingers and extending the map rapidly.

The junior wizard started to sweat and tremble, and a spellrobe beside him took his shoulder and drew him down into an empty chair. The map steadied, growing new caverns and passages more rapidly–and then, suddenly, was done, the spellrobe withdrawing his hands and pointing at a large cavern that was still glowing.

"There!"

Maulstryke nodded curt thanks, and then turned to look at all the other spellrobes. "Do all you can," he ordered, "to see if anything of my heir lives. His sentience trapped in a gem or a cage-worm, his brain kept alive by an enemy spellrobe hoping to learn all he knows; you know the possibilities."

The junior wizard grimaced, and then dared to ask, "And if . . . if he does not?"

"We destroy everything and everyone in that cavern. Of course."

"*Now* what?" Daruse muttered to Lharlak, as they watched the Evendoomshe leading her human off into the side cavern, and rose to follow. "Don't humans ever *sleep*?"

Lharlak had only one eye to wink with, but he knew how to use it, and did so.

.   .   .

A pale spellrobe ran hands that trembled with weariness over his face and said reluctantly, "Nothing, Lord. No trace at all."

Lord Maulstryke nodded, his face still expressionless. Again he looked around at all the spellrobes looking silently back at him, pointed at the glowing cavern in the floating map, and said softly, "You know what to do."

Across the chamber, spellrobes nodded, moved apart from each other to gain enough space, arranged their powders and vials, wriggled their fingers, drew deep breaths—and began their castings.

The most junior wizards were already clustered around the spellrobe who'd traced the cavern, aiding him in expanding it to float high at one end of the room, where all the spellrobes now weaving death could see it, and concentrate their spells on it.

"Maintaining the focus will consume much magic," Clael stammered, fear in his eyes as he looked at Maulstryke questioningly—and extended his hand to one of the old spellblades that had belonged to a Maulstryke of Turnings long, long ago.

Lord Maulstryke nodded, his eyes two holes of darkness, and the junior wizard shivered as he shakily smiled his thanks and turned hurriedly away, to put the sword delicately into the hands of the tracing spellrobe. Where it flared into a bright glow—and started to melt away, slowly but steadily.

Lord Maulstryke stood as unmoving and watchful as a sunderbeak perching on a high ledge waiting for prey, as battle spells took shape and sizzled, thundered, and flashed past him, into the glowing image of the cavern, where they were swallowed.

Great tumbling spiked boulders of wraithlike force, crackling nets of stabbing lightnings, hungry tongues of fire . . . spell after spell, the Maulstryke wizards shouting their incantations and waving their arms in wild flourishes, with no foes to hurry or menace them.

Soon enough the flurry ceased, as wizard after wizard ran out of deadly spells, and slumped down in seats, or wandered wearily aside from those still hurling death.

"Lord," one said at last, lowering hands that still flamed, "we're done."

Maulstryke nodded slowly, and turned to look a silent question at the spellrobe who'd made the trace. The spellblade in the wizard's hands looked more like a long, thin dagger now.

He lifted the still-diminishing sword as if to offer it to a spellrobe standing near. That wizard stepped forward, grasped it, and cast a careful spell with his other hand.

The air in front of Lord Maulstryke grew a dark eye, floating at about the level of his chest. It grew as large as the Lord's torso, blinked once, and then opened, showing everyone in the room a silent scene of chaos: a cavern strewn with fallen stalactites and sprawled bodies, where Nifl were running back and forth amid crackling lightnings and a few fading, fitful bursts of fire.

"Ravagers," one wizard offered.

"Many still live," another added grimly, as if the Lord had no eyes of his own.

"Have my thanks. You are all dismissed, save Clael and Aumryth, who must remain here and maintain the trace. Touch no spellblades as you depart, upon pain of death."

The spellrobes blinked at him for a moment, and then turned and started for the doors.

Leaving an astonished Clael standing before Maulstryke, and asking fearfully, "Lord?"

Maulstryke drew his spellblade and put it hilt-first into the astonished wizard's hand. Taking up Shoan's spellblade from the table for himself, he said, "Come. We have a Hunt to go on."

"A Hunt? For whom?"

"Traitors."

"Traitors?"

"Anyone who crosses me, causes me loss, or hampers my plans is a traitor to Talonnorn," Lord Maulstryke said softly. "Even if that anyone is my own flesh and blood, another Lord of a House, or Undying Olone Herself. You are quite right to fear me, Clael."

There was no warning.

The air above the sleeping Ravagers suddenly glowed, every hair of those on watch stood on end, they opened their mouths to exclaim—and the air sprouted lightnings.

Bright bolts washed over the cloaked sleepers, tumbling some of them and hurling others stiff-limbed into the air—in time for them to be caught in sudden spheres of bursting flame that spat streamers of fire in all directions.

By then Ravagers were shouting and scrambling all over the cavern—

but by then their own swords and daggers were rising up in deadly whirl-winds, the air was disgorging whorls of little disembodied fanged jaws that came into being in one moment and flew in all directions the next, snapping at still drowsy Ravagers, biting down hard, bone on bone.

Fresh lightnings washed across the cavern, Ravagers death-dancing in their wake, and then the air was full of shadowy drifting shapes that swooped menacingly at Ravagers, plunged into disbelieving Nifl faces—and melted them away to bare bone, screams fading swiftly.

Some Ravagers were up and running, hacking desperately at the snapping jaws pursuing them.

Old Bloodblade came awake in his cleft in the rocks at one end of the cavern, tried to shake awake a Ravager who knew some sorcery, cursed when he found that Nifl now had no face left, and scrambled hastily along the cavern wall to another Ravager, who'd trained as a spellrobe once, before a miscast spell slew his patron's favored son and forced his flight out into the Wild Dark.

That Ravager was already awake but cowering. Bloodblade roared into his face, shook him like a helpless child—and then thrust a sphere of ordauth into his hands.

It was Bloodblade's greatest treasure, and the spellrobe gaped at it for all the time it took one lightning bolt to stab across the cavern at him—and blast the magical thing he held into full arousal.

And from it a ward rose like a black and sighing wall, all around the cavern, rising into a great dome overhead that sealed the Ravagers off from the rest of the Wild Dark.

It did nothing at all to the fire, lightning, life-sucking wraith-things, whirling blades, and hungry jaws still raging around inside it.

The black wall brought utter silence as it entombed them; the snapping lightnings, bursts of flame, and shouts and screams were all suddenly—gone.

Taerune and Orivon blinked at each other, and then rolled over. The outcast Evendoom rose a little unsteadily from where she'd been ly-ing flat on her face on cold stone and called, "Daruse! Lharlak! I know you're hiding behind your usual rocks, to listen in on all we do. Well, what we do is going to be nothing until we know what happened back there."

She turned and waved back at where the main cavern full of sleeping

Ravagers had been, and a solid, smooth black wall that looked like or-dauth was now. "So, what happened back there?"

Daruse and Lharlak rose into view rather sheepishly, drawn swords in their hands, and shrugged.

"Sudden tumult," Lharlak offered, "and then—a full ward, just like that."

"Something bad," said Daruse. "That looked like a family of wizards attacking. Never seen the like."

Orivon got up. "So what do we do now?" he asked, trying not to sound as angry as he felt.

"You're asking *us?*"

Taerune shrugged. "We hope to learn things even from clever Ni-flghar."

That made the two Ravagers grin. They came a little closer, their swords still ready in their hands.

"Suppose," Daruse suggested, "you tell us what you so purposefully—and stealthily—came into this cavern to do. You who were so yawningly tired such a short time ago."

Taerune put the only hand she had left on one hip, and the flange of her new hand-blade on the other, and regarded them, lips narrowing. "I'd prefer that this have remained a private matter between Orivon Fire-fist and Taerune Evendoom, but perhaps it's better that there be wit-nesses, at that, to tell Orivon that this is no ruse on my part."

Daruse inclined his head like a priestess saluting a crone. "Here we are: witnesses, two by number. What's no ruse?"

"An oath-swearing, before the Goddess, of my loyalty. So he'll trust me."

Orivon looked at Taerune, and then at the two Ravagers. "What is this oath?"

"A blood pact that binds Niflghar upon their honor, before the God-dess," Lharlak replied. "Among Nifl, it's believed that breaking such a promise angers Holy Olone, who soon strikes down dead the offending Nifl, or twists them forever into beast shape, Nifl no longer."

Orivon looked at Taerune. "This matters to you?"

"Very much. If it will make you believe you can trust me."

"Then let's do it."

It had been some time since the High Ledge had heard boasting and tri-umphant laughter; the surviving Hunt were scared young Nifl terrified of the next orders they might receive, that could send them out into the Wild Dark to their deaths.

Wherefore they were sitting glumly, trading quiet gossip about the tumult they could see unfolding in the streets below, and hoping it would mean no summons to do anything before their shift ended, when a sudden spell-glow blossomed on the empty ledge in front of them, and out of it stepped two unfamiliar Nifl.

The Hunt members rose, frowning, their hands going to their swords. Unfamiliar the two arrivals might be, but they bore glowing spellblades in their hands, and the Three Black Tears of Maulstryke on the breasts of their splendid robes. The tall one had the manner of one used to being obeyed.

"You will take us," this tall Nifl commanded, "to a certain cavern out in the Dark, that my companion here will direct you to."

The leader of that shift of the Hunt did not trouble to keep the sneer on his face out of his voice. "No *Maulstryke* will ever order the Hunt what to do and what not to do!"

The air flickered, and a third figure was suddenly standing beside the other two, also holding a spellblade. This arrival was disheveled, but had a face every Hunt rider knew.

"That's why the order to take Lord Maulstryke out to this cavern he seeks is coming from me," he said calmly. "And I'll be accompanying him and his pet spellrobe. I'm missing some heirs, too."

The Hunt found themselves gaping at Lord Erlingar Evendoom.

"Before Olone I swear this," Taerune whispered, as softly as a kiss, and bent her lips to the blood filling Orivon's palm.

"You do the same, with hers," Daruse muttered, from beside him.

"Before Olone," he said roughly, "I swear this." And he kissed the blood in her palm. It was sweeter than he'd expected, with none of the iron tang of his own.

Taerune smiled at him. "'Tis done," she said lightly, "but your blood must not be wasted." And she bent her head and lapped it.

Orivon shuddered. *I feel . . . aroused.*

[Of course.] Taerune's whisper was warm in his mind. *[It always feels thus. Drink mine in health, and welcome.]*

Orivon growled as he bent over her hand to do so, and Daruse and Lharlak both chuckled.

"You know," Lharlak remarked, "it really was terribly interesting over behind yon rocks. Did you not find it so, friend Daruse?"

"Now that you mention it, I *did*. Let us return thither for a time, and leave these two misfits from Talonnorn to their own devices. I'm sure they'll find *something* to do, while we all wait for Bloodblade to turn his little toy off again."

The din was deafening.

Nifl shouting, snarling insults, screaming in agony, and slamming every sword, dagger, pot, tool, or stool they could find into each other and everything that stood in the way of lashing out at every other Nifl who stood near. The streets of Talonnorn were choked with Talonar hacking at everyone—crones, priestesses, and each other.

"*Die,* motherless Olone-kisser!" a drover snarled, towering up suddenly over her with a snout-goad in his hand. He swung it viciously, splintering the door frame Naersarra Dounlar ducked back through, and roaring with rage as he shouldered through that opening and swung again.

Naersarra had found herself in a kitchen, its floor littered with broken crockery and slick with fresh blood. The first things that came to hand were the jagged shards of a huge, shattered bowl, so she snatched them up and flung them in the drover's face.

The second thing was a cleaver, and she flung it into his throat while he was still cursing, half-blinded by the shards.

He gurgled and started to die, kicking at the air as he went down. Naersarra clung to a pillar and sobbed for breath. A sudden roar of jubilation rose outside, and she heard raw-voiced rampants nearby take it up, laughing as they called, "Hear that? They got Oszrim! Hacked apart, Lord high and bloody Lorloungart Oszrim! Dead as dung! Ha-*ha*!"

There was a splintering crash in another room, a scream, and then a panting crone reeled into the room, disheveled and bloody, and Naersarra found herself staring at Baerone Maulstryke.

"Don't—" Baerone gasped fearfully, fighting for breath. "Don't kill me!"

"Won't," Naersarra assured her, just as breathlessly. "This has— the city's gone *oriad*! All this . . . must be stopped!"

Baerone stared at her, nodding, and then seemed to crumple. "They'll butcher every last one of us!" she sobbed. "They care not who they slay! I've even seen armed *gorkul* in the streets, hacking and hewing! We *must* stop this!"

"Agreed! But how?"

"Maharla's champion?" Baerone asked bitterly. "The Dark Warrior, striding the streets?"

"And where is he? Or his army?"

"He's a fiction, and no more than that!" Baerone stormed, her eyes wild. "And Maharla Evendoom is to blame for all this! She moved the Lords from shaking their heads at the oriad Consecrated, a-slaying each other inside their temple, to being afraid they'd lead an uprising, and had to be butchered!"

"And they were right, weren't they? This *is* an uprising! I'm just afraid that the Lords will gather their wizards around them, and hurl death at us all, using spells to heap the Araed with our bodies!"

"And destroy Talonnorn? Just what do they think they'll have left to rule?"

"That's just it, Baerone: they're Lords. They *don't* think."

"I don't like the look of that," the Hunt rider muttered, as the darkwings beneath them squalled and tried to flap away. He fought it down to a claw-skittering landing in front of the smooth black barrier. "Stinks of magic."

Lord Maulstryke looked at Clael, saw his miserable nod, and said crisply, "This is the place. Set us all down."

The Hunt rider nodded curtly, and waved his hands to signal the other riders. Then he waved at the barrier. "What is it?"

"Magic, of course," Maulstryke said flatly, and looked at Clael again. "Any of our doing?"

The spellrobe, who was white to the lips and busy licking his lips and peering at the dark caverns all around, shook his head. "N-no. This is beyond anything we can do."

"Are you saying you have no spell to shatter it?"

"Yes," Clael whispered reluctantly. "That's what I'm saying. This is *old* Nifl magic, beyond what anyone of Talonnorn can do now."

"Then we'll wait." Maulstryke turned back to the Hunt rider. "Return to the High Ledge, and await our call."

The Nifl lifted a cold eyebrow, and pointedly turned to Lord Evendoom, who nodded and said calmly, "Be guided by Lord Maulstryke's suggestion as if it was an order from me."

The Hunt rider inclined his head. "Then good hunting." He made a sound in his throat like a muffled screech and the darkwings sprang into the air, its great claws slicing air just in front of their chins, and was gone, the great beats of its wings—and of the other darkwings, flapping in its wake—hurling up dust and small stones that stung their faces.

They all turned away, to face the black barrier. Only Clael looked back at the distant, dwindling Hunt.

He looked back several times, each glance more wistful.

"And now?" Lord Evendoom asked Lord Maulstryke calmly.

"And now, we wait." Maulstryke strolled a little way along the black wall and then stopped, turned, and added, "Erlingar. Fear no blade of mine until we're both back in Talonnorn."

"Likewise," Evendoom replied.

Clael looked from one lord to the other, suppressed a shiver, and then peered fearfully into the darkness all around them. Not for the first time.

22

Important Things Happen

It always seems to involve bloodshed
And much tumult and breaking of things
Whenever important things happen.
—The Words of Dounlar

The smoke drifting down the street was thick now, quelling some of the roared insults and ranting. The screams came just as often though, amid the clash and clang of swords and tools and kitchen knives.

"Imdul!" Urgel called, as he smashed a House steward across the side of the head with the hilt of one of his blades, driving the rampant's jaw down to meet his upthrusting knee. The steward crashed to the stones unregarded.

"Gel!" his slender friend called back, out of the gaping hole that had been a shuttered window. "Out in a trice!"

The mask maker nodded, gasping for breath, and whirled around to look in all directions for approaching trouble. It had been a desperate fight just to stay alive in the rioting mobs. Everywhere in the Araed Nameless were looting and burning—and raping in the brothels, too; Urgel had passed one where pleasure-shes were frantically hacking and stabbing rampants in the ruins of what had been their front display windows.

Urgel was well beyond being sick of it all, but there was nowhere safe to hide or get clear of the fighting—and at least in the streets he and Imdul could try to kill every crone and priestess they saw. That would be *some* good, out of all this mess.

Imdul came out staggering, his arms wet with blood to the elbows.

"All right?" Urgel asked.

"Oh. Aye, none of this is mine." The poisoner shook his head wearily. "It's going to be a long time mending Talonnorn—if Ouvahlor leaves us alone to try."

"A long time," Urgel agreed grimly—and then set his teeth and lifted the blades he held in both hands, as a fresh mob of howling, running Nifl came around a corner and swept down on them.

"Inside!" Imdul snapped. "Back inside, where I was! They'll trample us, out here!"

They hastened, ending up fighting like oriad Nifl against a veritable whirling forest of swords that caught up to them before they could get through the door.

And then the mob swept on, leaving behind only a few reeling, shouting Niflghar hacking angrily at each other.

"No fit place to stay, in there," Imdul said. "It's afire, down the far end. We'd best get on."

They had to hack and thrust their way to the next corner, where it seemed a dozen duels were all going on at once where the streets met. In the midst of that frantic fray the two friends came face to face with Tarlyn, who shouted, "Ho! What price soothing rumors now? Or Hairy Ones as conquering champions! I hear Lord Oszrim's dead, and Lord Dounlar, too!"

"Olone take us all," Urgel growled, wearily—just as someone ran Tarlyn through from behind, a bright sword bursting out of his chest.

The handsome Nifl stared at them, aghast and dying, spitting bubbling blood as he tried to say something—and failed.

As he slid forward onto his face and into oblivion, Urgel and Imdul roared their rage and burst over his sagging body, to hack apart his slayer.

It was a fat shopkeeper; their blades thrust and slashed at him at will as he sobbed and whimpered his way to his knees.

"*Why* did you do it?" Urgel roared into his face. "Why slay a fellow Talonar?"

"H-husband," the shopkeeper coughed, trying to raise a pointing finger to indicate Tarlyn's sprawled body. "He 'n' my wife. Olone-dung, him . . ."

Rage draining away, Urgel and Imdul stepped back, looked at each other—and then were flung aside, screaming, as a wall of ravening magic blasted down the street, hurling all Nifl before it.

Their longtime comrade Clazlathor came down the blood-slick way, the glows of that ravening spell still curling around his hands, and the giant Nifl Munthur strode with him.

"Imdul? Urgel?" the spellrobe called at the gaping windows and doors all around. "Has anyone seen the mask maker? Imdul?"

Clazlathor's spell had heaped a great mass of broken bodies against the front of one building at the street-moot, and they trod on limbs and torsos to get past, never knowing that some of the remains were those of Imdul and Urgel.

Far down the street behind them, there came a great groan that slowly grew into thunder, as a building collapsed. The great crash drowned out a few feeble screams.

The last of the deadly magics faded away at last. After the silence started to stretch, and a dagger flung across the cavern awakened no lightnings or gliding wraiths, a wincing, staggering Old Bloodblade dared to come out of the cleft, lift his head, and call, "Anyone still alive? Anyone?"

Far across the cavern, Sarntor struggled to his feet, spitting blood, and mumbled, "For now." Two other Ravagers managed to rise, and the four gathered in a grim little ring, looking around at all the dead.

"Are we trapped here, doomed to starve?" Sarntor asked, waving a weary hand at the black dome. "One last magical thrust at us?"

"No," Old Bloodblade replied, touching three deeply-set buttons in the ordauth sphere he was cradling.

The black dome faded slowly away.

"We must go," he added. "Someone obviously knows we're here, and will probably be along to finish off any survivors—and that'd be us."

"Indeed," said Lord Maulstryke pleasantly, striding forward out of the darkness beyond the cavern, with a spellblade beginning to glow in his hand. "That finishing off doesn't look like all that formidable a task, either."

There were two other Nifl behind the robed Talonar Lord. The Ravagers saw Lord Evendoom give the third Talonar a meaningful glare, and the spellrobe acquire a look of real fear as he reluctantly advanced in Maulstryke's wake.

"Mine," one of the Ravagers mumbled, and limped forward to face Maulstryke, drawing a dagger and a battered sword as he went. Sarntor made as if to follow, but Bloodblade laid a restraining hand on his arm.

The other Ravager was too far away for Bloodblade to reach, and also set off across the strewn dead toward Lord Maulstryke.

Who strolled to meet the first Ravager, and then did something swift and deft; the Ravager barely had time to cry out before he was falling. The second Ravager charged, and was greeted with a stone-cold smile and the words, "Greetings. I am Ohzeld Maulstryke, Lord of my House—and I am your doom. In the name of Shoan Maulstryke . . ."

That last word had barely left his lips by the time the spellblade in his hand burst through the Ravager's throat and neck and withdrew again; the outcast Nifl toppled in a welter of blood.

"Well, now, Talonar Lords, you're a long way from home," a new voice observed jauntily. "Have you run out of slaves to butcher at last?"

Daruse gave the three Talonar a mocking smile as he came out of the side cavern, with a human, an Evendoom she, and the eye-patch-wearing Lharlak right behind him.

"Daughter!" Lord Evendoom cried, extending his arms welcomingly.

The stare Taerune gave him was cold. "I *was* your daughter. Until you spurned me. I suppose it's the hand of expediency that turns your heart my way again now—yes?"

Maulstryke chuckled. "Ah," he said pleasantly, as the badly wounded Sarntor broke free of Bloodblade and charged. The spellblade left Maulstryke's hand to fly and fight by itself, striking aside Sarntor's swift and deadly lunge so Maulstryke could almost leisurely draw and thrust a belt dagger up through Sarntor's jaw from beneath. "I may enjoy this after all."

Bloodblade was turning the sphere in his hands over and over, pressing buttons rapidly. Sidestepping Sarntor's clawing, dying hands as the Ravager fell, Maulstryke pointed at Bloodblade and snapped, "Clael!"

The spellrobe raised his hands and wove a swift spell—just as Bloodblade did something that made the sphere click loudly and stepped back from it, leaving it hanging in midair.

Lightnings streamed from each of Clael's fingers, leaping at the sphere—and vanishing, swallowed by it. A part of the sphere glowed green, and spat out a tongue of white radiance that grew into an upright, glowing white door floating in midair.

"Clael!" Maulstryke snapped again, sounding angry this time, and the pale-faced wizard frantically worked another spell, leveling a pointing finger at Bloodblade.

A crimson beam sprang from that shaking finger and hissed across the cavern at the stout Ravager. Just before it reached him it was plucked aside, curving sharply around to race right into the glowing door. Wherein it, too, vanished without a sound.

"Very pretty," Daruse commented, hurling a dagger hard at Clael. Lord Evendoom pointed his spellblade and triggered a beam of magic from its tip that melted the whirling knife in midair. Lharlak had flung a dagger of his own, just behind Daruse's but arcing higher; it flashed past the beam—and plunged home in one of Clael's eyes.

Screaming, the spellrobe fell.

Mouth tightening, Lord Maulstryke hefted his spellblade and advanced purposefully on Old Bloodblade.

The Ravager leader drew his own sword, and then a dagger to match, kicked aside a fallen Ravager's arm to give himself clear footing, and waited.

"I have never seen such a fat, ugly Niflghar in my life," Maulstryke observed with a sneer. "No wonder you're outcast; Holy Olone must find you revolting."

"Whereas I," Bloodblade replied calmly, "have never seen such a twisted, decadent city as Talonnorn, where a few Nifl enslave the rest, exalt themselves as Lords or priestesses, and devote their lives to the pursuit of beauty—and thinking up new ways to be nasty to their fellows. Fortunately, we're not in Talonnorn now. You stand in *my* domain, Ohzeld Maulstryke."

"You know my name. Interesting." The spellblade lifted out of Lord Maulstryke's grasp, rising point-first to menace Bloodblade, and Maulstryke calmly reached his now open hand back behind him to receive his own spellblade. It slid free of the fallen Clael to come streaking through the air.

"I knew your mother—twice or thrice," Bloodblade replied with a grin. "And she was twice the rampant you'll ever be."

He moved his empty hand deliberately from left to right—and the glowing door slid through the air and swallowed the spellblade that had belonged to Shoan Maulstryke. "Are you ready yet to face me blade to blade?" the Ravager asked mildly. "As *true* Nifl fight?"

The spellblade reached Lord Maulstryke's hand—and he snarled and sprang forward, the blade singing and flaring into a fell glow as it swept down viciously. Darts of glowing magic raced from its cutting edge at the Ravager—only to be snatched aside into the door.

Blades met, Bloodblade's shrieking with the strain as the spellblade flared red-hot—but the Ravager swayed back to let the bound blades carry to his right, and reached over them almost delicately to slice the fingers of Maulstryke's sword hand. Sparks spat as the dagger struck rings, Maulstryke screamed—and when he hauled his blade free and brought it back across in a slash that forced the Ravager to step back, two severed fingers tumbled in its wake. Their rings flared, spun free—and raced into the glowing door.

Orivon strode steadily across the cavern, to get between Evendoom and Maulstryke—but Taerune's father made no move to help Ohzeld Maulstryke. He stood watching, spellblade grounded, looking past the human as if Orivon did not exist.

[NO, Orivon. Leave him be!] Taerune's mind-voice was frantic, almost a shout. He nodded to let her know he'd heard, and heeded, giving Lord Evendoom a glower that was cooly ignored.

Face twisted in pain, Maulstryke stepped back and switched hands, wringing his wounded one. Blood flew. Bloodblade stepped forward—and the Talonar lord rushed him, swinging the spellblade in a wild flurry of slashes, its magic flaring brightly around them. Bloodblade stood his ground, the two blades clashing and crashing together.

Sparks showered from the ringing spellblade, and seemed to swirl and gather as if about to build into something—but drifted inexorably to Bloodblade's glowing door, and were swallowed.

"You were . . . *lucky,* Ravager!" Maulstryke snarled, as their blades rang and rebounded, clashed again and whirled. "I was trained by warblades who'd not have trusted you to fetch their boots!"

"That would have been wise of them," Bloodblade grinned, though he was starting to gasp for breath—and caught the darting Talonar spellblade on his dagger. This time it was his sword that slashed in, to sever more fingers.

"Still," he added jovially, as Maulstryke staggered back, shouting in pain and shedding more fingers, "I can't help but wonder *what* they trained you in. It certainly wasn't blade-work."

More magical rings drifted toward the door. Maulstryke made a clumsy grab for them, but Bloodblade's thrusting blade forced him into a frantic parry, and drove him back, out of reach of the rings as they reached the door and . . . vanished.

The door started to sing; it was growing larger and brighter. "It seems my little pet here is hungry," Bloodblade commented, pressing forward. "Let's see if we can't feed it more of those pretty rings of yours . . ."

He lashed out, Maulstryke grimaced and brought one arm up to shield his maimed hands—and Bloodblade's thrust sank down under it to skitter off a concealed Maulstryke codpiece and plunge deep into a thigh beside it.

Maulstryke groaned and started to sag, smashing Bloodblade's sword away with desperate back-and-forth parries that he retreated behind, still doubled over.

Lord Evendoom smiled at that, turned, and started striding purposefully back out of the cavern. Orivon started after him, breaking into a trot—but Daruse and Lharlak burst past the human, running like vengeful gales after the fleeing Talonar. Evendoom heard their onrushing boots and looked back. His face tightened—and a jet of flame sprang from the tip of his spellblade. He swung it around behind him and kept it there, propelling himself into the air and away.

The jet of snarling flames carried him swiftly out of sight and far beyond their reach.

Puffing, the fat Ravager took two running strides and launched himself at Maulstryke from above, sword and dagger held ready before him. He came crashing down on the wincingly held spellblade and bore it to the ground, Maulstryke sobbing in pain, and then rolled, forcing the Talonar lord apart from his weapon. Then he rose, plucked up the spellblade, and threw it into the glowing door—which promptly doubled in size, shooting up with a roar.

"The problem with Haraedran Lords," Bloodblade told Maulstryke slowly, between panting breaths, "isn't killing them. It's dealing with all of the magics they wear and carry and drag around, that avenge their worthless carcasses after you've rid the Dark of them. Now, I see you still have some fingers . . ."

Sobbing, Maulstryke drew a dagger and stared vainly at the few rings he had left. Those that had evidently held means of escape were gone, and he stared at Bloodblade in despair as the fat Ravager lumbered forward.

Then he turned to run, slipping and stumbling on the Ravager corpses. Bloodblade drove the tip of his sword into Maulstryke's behind, hooked his dagger through Maulstryke's belt, hauled the sobbing, feebly kicking Talonar lord around to face the glowing door—and rushed him forward at it, freeing his sword to slice Maulstryke's throat just before the Talonar half-stumbled, half-fell through it.

And the door exploded.

. . .

In a deep cavern walled in glistening ice crystals larger than Nifl heads, priestesses chanted, their fervor gaining speed and force as Lolonmae of the Ever-Ice embraced a column of ice taller than she was, thrusting her bare body against the ice as mist curled up from her, meltwater ran down her limbs, and the deep glow of the Ever-Ice brightened beneath all their bare feet.

The Ever-Ice was coming, the Ever-Ice was heeding, its great slow and chill power flowing into them, the might of all Niflheim becoming theirs—

And then Lolonmae, holiest of them all, broke off in the midst of her gasping prayer, to fling back her head and stare around with her sightless eyes.

Priestesses stared at her, startled and aghast.

Lolonmae waved impatiently at them to remain still and silent. She seemed to be listening to something they could not hear, *feeling* something.

"Blessed of the Ice," Ithmeira dared to whisper, "can you tell us—?"

Lolonmae looked at her with eyes that could not see her, and murmured, "Something's happened! Something important!"

She turned then, striding briskly away from the ice column she'd been embracing, and commanded, "Semmeira! Cast a farscrying! It's Talonnorn again—the Wild Dark near it! *Old* magic!"

"But Exalted, the ceremony! We—"

"Semmeira," Lolonmae said mildly. The Daughter of the Ice leaped to obey her.

"Run!" Orivon shouted desperately at Taerune as she flung herself down among the Ravager corpses. What seemed to be a towering ball of sparks leaping in all directions expanded above and behind her, and the fat, jangling, trinket-shedding bellowing ball that was Old Bloodblade Barandon came hurtling down the cavern, waving arms vainly, and—crashed into Orivon.

Snatched off his feet, the human awkwardly tried to cradle the Ravager, wrapping himself around Bloodblade as they struck stone, skidded along, found air again, crashed bruisingly down again, bounced up—and came to a solid, bone-jarring halt against the stump of a scarred old stalagmite.

"Ohhh," Orivon gasped, wincing, as he straightened himself, still lying on his side with Bloodblade wedged against him on one side, and the un-yielding stone fang on the other. Nothing *seemed* to be broken, but . . .

Bloodblade rolled away and up to his feet, swaying unsteadily, and then reached down a hand to haul Orivon up. "Thanks, Firefist. You make a better cushion than a lot of shes I've . . . ahem . . ."

Taerune waved at them. She was standing unscathed among the corpses, grinning at them both. "Bloodblade, come see what madness your magic toy has wrought now."

Daruse and Lharlak were already tramping past them. "Hmmph," the Nifl with the eye patch commented. "We go chasing Talonar Lords at great risk to ourselves, and you two lie down for a little nap. Think yourselves decadent Haraedran Lords or suchlike?"

Then they saw where Taerune was pointing, stopped, and started to chuckle.

On a blasted-clear ring of stone floor, a faint shimmering glow re-mained, and at its heart lay a Niflghar battle kit: gleaming armor, boots, and all manner of weapons, neatly laid out as if on a Lord's wardrobe bench.

They gathered to stare at it. "Well, *that's* new," Bloodblade muttered. "And that battle plate won't fit me." He looked at Orivon. "Or him."

Daruse and Lharlak looked at the armor, and then at each other, and shook their heads. "Not interested," said Daruse.

"Prefer what I'm used to," Lharlak added. "Besides, that armor might come with spells on it that force me to go and do something, or hate all gorkuls, or something."

They both looked at Taerune, who just shook her head—and then reached down and plucked up one weapon: a Niflghar battle-whip, three braided wire tails about as long as two Nifl stood tall, tipped with barbs that looked like daggers. She smiled, and purred, "I've always wanted one of these."

Daruse smirked, and murmured in Orivon's ear, "I'd be glad you just did the blood-swearing, if I were you."

"Looks like a pack-snout drover's whip, with blades where the club ends should be," Lharlak said, peering at Orivon's broad shoulders. "Aye, it's going to leave marks."

"Will you two jesters leave off?" Taerune growled, in mimicry of Bloodblade's usual tone.

"Aye," Bloodblade echoed her perfectly. "Will you two jesters leave off?"

They all laughed, and then Bloodblade growled, "Let's just leave everything else right where it is. I've about had enough of magic; I'm getting too old for surprises."

"So what do we do now?" Taerune asked, looking from one Ravager to another.

"Get far from here, deep out into the Dark, and start over," Bloodblade growled. "If I know Talonnorn—and Ouvahlor—they'll be all over this cavern, and scouring the Dark around it, before long. Coming with us, Dark Warrior? I know two ways up to the surface, and we'll be going right past one of them!"

Orivon stared at the fat Ravager. "So you know," he said slowly.

Bloodblade gave him an amused look. "I'm an outcast Nifl, not a stupid one, human. And thanks to these two skulkers"—he waved at Daruse and Lharlak, who obligingly bowed and struck preening poses—"I have very long ears. Armies! Throwing off oppressors in Talonnorn! Dream-spew, lad; pure dream-spew! They're probably sitting in the city sipping wine right now, with a gleaming army or two of their own standing ready to greet us!"

He trudged away—and then topped, whirled around, and pointed at the corpse-strewn cavern floor behind them. "Grab some blankets. At least three each. Oh, and a cookpot or two; it's hard to feed this many cooking out of a codpiece! Firefist, make yourself useful! Pretend you're a slave again!"

Maharla Evendoom passed her hand over the flickering glow of her scrying-spell to end it, and sighed. "Erlingar almost back here, all the crones of the city thirsting for my blood . . . my time as Eldest of Evendoom is done."

She strode across the spell-sealed chamber to the long table where she'd laid out most powerful magic items of House Evendoom, and made some swift selections.

"I must flee Talonnorn," she mused aloud, tapping her chin with a scepter that winked warningly, "and that means hiding in the Dark. And *that* means becoming a Ravager, at least until the temple is stable again, and I can slay whoever rules there and replace them with my shapechanged self."

Biting her lip, she pondered, frown deepening. "If I can take the shape of a Ravager slain in that cavern . . ."

Suddenly brisk, she strode to her robing room. "I must get there and find a body that's not too damaged, to shape myself on . . ."

"Thorar, this is hot and heavy!" Orivon complained, hefting the huge load on his shoulders. Pots swayed and chains jangled. "Do all Ravagers go loaded like pack-snouts?"

"Yes," Lharlak told him sweetly, so hung about with salvaged water-skins that he looked like a gigantic sphere of hide. "Who's Thorar?"

"What? Why, Thorar's the god of—uh, a human god. Of storms and rain and . . . lightning . . . night . . ." Orivon caught sight of the mocking expressions Daruse and Lharlak were wearing, and growled, "Well, I was young when I was . . . dragged down here."

Amid their chuckles he heaved, swung, and set down his gigantic lashed-together assembly of rolled blankets, pots and pans, rope and tools (with sad, silent thanks he'd taken those he'd used to make Taerune's blade from a Ravager who was now far beyond needing them again). Off came his robe with the bracers stuffed into it, and the tunic, to be thrust through the ropes binding the load together. Stripped to the waist, he swung the huge load back up onto his back and shoulders, snugged the buckled-together baldrics into place, and growled, "That's better."

"Good to hear," Bloodblade replied, from behind a stalagmite up ahead. "Are we ready to see all too much of the Dark?"

"We are," Taerune replied, putting herself between Bloodblade and Orivon. Daruse went on ahead, Lharlak fell to the rear—and they set off into the Wild Dark.

"Do we have a map?" Orivon asked, as the passage narrowed and the stone floor under their boots started to rise.

Bloodblade looked back at the human incredulously. "Map?" He tapped his head. "*This* is my map!"

Aloun took another sip of his elanselveir, and yawned again. "Ahh, but this is good! Why can't we have whorls-off times more often?"

"We can, if those who lead Ouvahlor and its foes take more time off from trying to destroy each other," Luelldar replied, leaning back in his chair with his feet up on a sculpture and the arc of scrying-whorls in front of him dark and silent. It was the first occasion Aloun had ever seen them that way. "However, as long as they're hurling armies and patrols and fly-ing Hunts and Klarandarr-only-knows what else at each other . . ."

"Oh! Klarandarr—where do you think he'll spell-smash next? Glow-stone?"

" 'Spell-smash'? Wherever do you pick up these clumsy expressions? Really, I—*no,* he won't strike Glowstone just yet. Not until after our army has passed through."

23

Glowstone and Beyond

And I've fared far into the deadly Wild Dark,
As far as lawless Glowstone, and beyond.
—**The Words of Dounlar**

Daruse was waiting for them as they trudged up a slippery passage and around a bend into a low-ceilinged, foul-smelling cavern.

"This is about close enough," he said, and Bloodblade nodded.

"Pack-snout dung?" Orivon asked, sniffing. The stout Ravager nodded.

"Traders often pen their snouts up here."

"Traders? Who trades hereabouts?"

"Ravagers. Up ahead is a Ravager-moot, a market. Glowstone by name. Which is why you're going to have to walk tethered from now on."

"'Tethered'?"

"Remember the blood-swearing, Orivon," Taerune said quickly. "Trust us, please. We have to make you look like a slave. A rope around your neck, Bloodblade holding its other end, leading you long—and I'll have this whip out. If I crack you a time or two, act as if you're used to it; *don't* turn on me, or we'll have half the Ravagers in Glowstone charging at you, trying to 'help tame the uppity slave.'"

Orivon glared at her.

"Please?" she asked quietly. "I still stand in your debt, for saving my life—or so I see it. Trust me."

"Aye, but these Nifl with us don't," he growled.

Bloodblade laid a hand on Orivon's arm. "Firefist," he growled in almost identical tones, "we're *Ravagers,* not Haraedra. Doesn't matter to us if you're human, or gorkul, or Holy Olone herself: you've fought Talonar alongside us and dealt with us fairly. You're one of us. Now trust us, and perhaps we'll all get through Glowstone alive."

"And we can't go around?"

"Firefist, have you seen any heaps of handy food in all the caverns we've walked thus far? In Glowstone we'll trade some of those swords and boots that're weighing you down so heavily for food. Our friends are too dead to need the boots and warsteel longer, but we can use the meals."

Orivon sighed and set down his load. "Put the rope on me."

Lord Oondaunt turned. "Naraedel, I need you to deliver these words to her: 'Come now. The time is right.' She will know their meaning."

The envoy bowed low. "Of course, Lord. 'Come now. The time is right.' I shall not fail you."

Raudreth Oondaunt smiled. "You never have—and never will."

Naraedel gave his Lord a grateful smile, whispered his thanks as ardently as any lover, rose and turned in one smooth movement, and hurried away to where his darkwings was waiting.

Never will, indeed, he thought. She'll slay me as soon as I speak those words; you've agreed on it. I KNOW that smile, Raudreth Oondaunt. And she'll cast her spell and step right into your chamber—and from there into the Place of the Goddess. She'll seize rule over the temple ruthlessly—and between you, you and she will do the same to Talonnorn. I think NOT.

Secure against the ever-probing Oondaunt spellrobes in the mindshield he'd bought in the Araed, Naraedel strode on. This was the last time he'd ever see these walls—Olone spit, this *city.*

This would be the first—and last—message he'd fail to deliver. And no one trusts an envoy who decides for himself which messages to impart, and which to bury. So, how much could he get for a tamed darkwings in, say, Arnoenar?

Once past the hard-eyed sentries with their racks of ready bows and longspears, Glowstone was a crowded, noisy place.

Orivon looked around in astonishment; there were a *lot* of Ravagers dwelling out in the Dark, if this place was any indication. It was a large cavern—not as big as the one that held Talonnorn, and much lower-ceilinged—crowded with stone storefronts, pens, carts, hurrying and haggling Nifl of all descriptions, few of them unblemished enough to have been tolerated in Talonnorn at all. An unending market.

They'd passed only the first few stalls when someone called, "Ho, Bloodblade! Where're the rest of you?"

Old Bloodblade grinned, waved, and made no reply.

About then, a Nifl rampant looked up from what looked like small blocks of pressed dung, but were probably dried fruits of some sort. He peered hard at Orivon, grinned in recognition, and said, "Good disguise!"

Orivon blinked, and so (he saw) did Bloodblade.

They crossed a street, and another Nifl said the same thing. A stall later, someone looked up and jeered, "Ho, Dark Warrior! Lost your army?"

"I don't recall anyone standing in that cavern but us," Lharlak murmured, from close behind Orivon, and Taerune hummed a wordless, puzzled agreement.

They came to another cross street, and a shrine to Olone so small and simple that it would have been sneered at in Talonnorn, or thrown down as an insult to the Goddess. A Nifl priestess swaying there in quiet personal prayer broke off her chant to cry, "Hail, Orivon Firefist, sent by Olone!"

"What?" Taerune's murmur was bewildered. "*I made all that up! Or . . . did I?*" She stared at the face of the Goddess, sculpted above the altar of the open shrine.

"We'd already figured as much," Bloodblade muttered. "Yet decided we liked you enough to spare your lives, regardless."

"*Thank* you," Taerune told him. "I . . . misjudged you. All of you."

"Many do," Lharlak intoned. "Many do."

"May the favor of Olone find us all," Daruse said piously, bending to kiss the hands of the priestess and leave the tiniest gems Orivon had ever seen in them.

The Consecrated smiled as if delighted, and thanked him profusely as they walked on.

"Yonder's the trader whose food I prefer," Bloodblade said, pointing ahead.

"Whose *wine* you like, you mean," Daruse teased. "Try to remember to buy something solid, this time."

"Consider yourself expendable," Bloodblade growled.

"As long as you never have to run anywhere," Daruse agreed, "or think about anything . . ."

Jalandral sighed. "Klaerra, dearest, are we fated to tarry in Evennar *forever*?"

"No. We'll depart soon, now. Yet patience, my bright young blade, patience. Some things you learn all too slowly."

Jalandral winked, grinned, and struck a pose. "Would your teaching preferences have anything to do with that?"

"Of course. A crone's hard life has to hold some rewards."

Jalandral snorted. "Let me know when to start noticing the 'hard' part." Then he saw her eyes start to twinkle. Rolling his eyes, he sighed, "I can't believe I just *said* that."

"Yes, you're tired, and yes, they have soft sleeping beds—for outrageous fees—but I never tarry in Glowstone long," Bloodblade answered a complaining Orivon, four caverns past the market-moot. "It gives sneak-thieves and a few personal enemies time to prepare something unpleasant for us. In and out, before they can tear themselves away from the business of the moment. We'll turn off the main passage soon, and take a side way I know, and then sleep in a tight place we can wall up with rocks."

"I—" Orivon started to say, and then fell silent because Daruse was hurrying back toward them, his face grim.

"There's an *army* ahead, scouts far that way and right along *that* far, too. Heading this way," he snapped. "Ouvahlor."

Luelldar swung his feet down and waved one hand across the arc of whorls. They flashed into spinning life in an instant.

Aloun stared. "What—?"

"They're about to attack Glowstone, by now," the Senior Watcher replied crisply. "Awaken your whorl."

"But how do you *know* that?"

"I watch, and learn, and so I know. You'll get used to doing so, too. In about a thousand thousand Turnings from now, at the rate you're going."

He pointed down at the junior Watcher's whorl. "Watch. See. Learn. And don't glower at me: most Ouvahlans never learn to, all their lives long."

"Hurry," Bloodblade snapped. "Taerune, unlimber that whip. Orivon, she'll lash the load as much as she can, but you're going to get stung. Bah! *Where's* that Olone-blasted Ouvahlan tunic? At the bottom, the one you want's *always* at the bottom . . ."

"What're we—?"

"Pretending to be Ouvahlan slave-traders, with one slave. You."

Orivon glared at the fat Ravager. "This'd *better* not be a trick . . ."

"Firefist," Lharlak said quietly, "this had better *be* a trick, and one that works well. Or we'll all be dead very soon."

"Be glad we're out here," the Talonar patrol leader grunted. "Beasts prowl out here, aye—but *everyone's* killing each other back in the city."

"What I want to know is what comes and gnaws on dead Nifl like this," a warblade said bitterly, using his sword to turn over a corpse that was more bone than flesh.

"Nothing's touched them, over here," another warblade called—and then sprang back. "Hoy! *This* one's not dead!"

The patrol rushed forward—as Faunhorn Evendoom struggled to sit up and menace them with his sword.

"Easy, Lord, easy!" a warblade said quickly. "You're of Evendoom, right?"

"Yes." The reply was grim. "What's this about killings in Talonnorn?"

The patrol leader took a deep breath. "Lord, I know not if you'll believe this, but . . ."

"Not much of a slaver," a battlemar smirked. "*One* slave."

"Ah, but it was big one!" a lanceshar joked. "No, Arlarran, he just sold them all off in Glowstone, see?"

"Arlarran," the Ouvahlan commander snapped, silencing the banter. "Small that slaving band may be, but kill them for me."

"Lord? He *was* of Ouvahlor."

"What of it? He's one more tongue that can wag about our presence. Take some warblades back to silence him. Mind you witness every death; you'll be describing them to me. If you hurry, you might not miss the slaughter."

"No more Glowstone," the lanceshar murmured.

On a ledge high above the Talonar patrol, Grunt Tusks lay very still. The knotted-together chains made a crude but mighty flail, but metal moving on stone would make a noise the Nifl below couldn't miss. Their dooms would come, but not here and not now.

It had been a slow, hard job to batter that collar off; Grunt Tusks intended to live a long, long time. And kill a lot more Talonar Nifl than just one patrol.

She'll betray me. This is all just an excuse. They've got me where they want me, now, a slave again, and that's where they'll keep me.

[Orivon! Stop this! We're blood-sworn, remember? Don't you know ANY-THING about Nifl?]

Aye, that they enslave humans. Get out of my mind, Nifl bitch.

[Your trust doesn't run very deep, does it?]

Taerune's lash came down for the hundredth time, its strike burning and stinging. Orivon had no idea how she was managing to wield it so he didn't get cut by its blades, but that bespoke only her skill, not friendly intent. If she sliced up the only slave she had, she'd have to carry all this heavy gear, wouldn't she?

"Watch out!"

The shout was as sudden as it was loud—and was more of a scream than a shout, at that.

Bloodblade spun around. "That was Lharlak!"

He stared past them, and then snapped, "Lots of Nifl, back there! Firefist, drop the bundle! Tarerune, help him! *Run!*"

"Run where?" Orivon snarled, heaving his huge load sideways and ducking to get out from under it. Taerune was already clawing at the baldric buckles.

"Up ahead! *Ruse?*"

"I'm here! Lharlak?"

"Dead—that's his arm there, dangling! Is the Throat within reach?"

"Aye, but *look!* They're *right* behind us!"

"So we fight and run—thank Olone they're Ouvahlan: no hurlbows!" They ran.

Laughing now, waving their swords, the Ouvahlan warblades sprang down the tumbled rocks and sprinted after them. One waved Lharlak's severed head around—and then hurled it.

It fell far short of them, thudding wetly on rocks, and Bloodblade snarled, "Crone-schooled *bastard.* I'll remember that face, I will . . ."

Then he was huffing and puffing too hard to say more. Stones turned and tumbled underfoot as they ran up a steeply rising, narrowing passage, ducked around a sharp bend, and came out into a tiny cavern.

"The Throat," Daruse panted. "We stand here, and strike at the Ouvahlans as they come along the narrow way."

Orivon stared across the cavern, at a wider passage running on. "Won't they just circle around and come at us from that way?"

"Of course, but it's a *long* way around, if they know it at all. Any tricks to help us, Bloodblade?"

"Nothing that's any use in a battle. One healing-stone."

"Huh," Daruse grunted dismissively. "Right: we fight!"

"My turn," Orivon growled, hefting his sword and glaring at Taerune, daring her to say anything against him.

Gravely, she nodded, kissed her dagger, and gave him an Evendoom salute with it.

"Firefist," Bloodblade grunted, "if they blind you or wound you, or you start to slip, back out *fast.* In this direction, if you can, so we can jump in past you and hold the way."

"I hear," Orivon grunted, stepping forward—and then staggering, as the first hard-running Ouvahlan charged right into him, striking his sword aside and trying to bull his way on, into the cavern. A second Ouvahlan warblade was right behind him.

Orivon kicked the blade right out of that second warblade's hand—and Taerune hurled herself forward like a spear to put her sword tip into his face. The force of Orivon's kick slammed the warblade he was grappling into the wall where the narrow way started to widen into the cavern—and the flat of Bloodblade's sword slammed into the warblade's sword, pinning it against the stone. Orivon dared to let go of his own trapped blade long enough to punch the Nifl's throat as hard as he could, and managed to catch hold of his sword hilt again before the gagging, gargling warblade started to fall.

Another two Ouvahlan warblades slammed into their dying fellows from behind, driving everyone out into the cavern—and suddenly the room was full of hacking, thrusting Niflghar, Daruse was roaring in pain, and Bloodblade was snarling out a flood of curses as two or three Ouvahlans drove him back, clear across the cavern and into the passage beyond.

Then Taerune swung her whip, shouting, "*Down,* Orivon!"

Deadly blades sliced Nifl all around her; warblades shouted in pain all around the cavern. Someone threw a dagger that caught in her hair and another that struck her bodice and was turned away by the bracers Orivon had thrust into them—and then Orivon was up and hacking furiously at any bloodied, startled warblade he could reach, crouching as low as he could. Something icy sliced across his back, he heard Taerune cry, "*Sorry,* Orivon!" and then more Nifl screamed.

"Motherless, Ice-loving sleeth!" Bloodblade snarled, sounding faint and far away—and then Orivon was too busy killing Niflghar warblades who were trying to kill him, to notice anything else but the frantic thrust, turn, twist, leap, and hack of his own fighting.

He was vaguely aware of bodies underfoot, and thought he saw the staring face of Daruse among them, but really couldn't be sure—as he panted for breath, whirled to look for a warblade he was sure had ducked past him, found that Nifl sinking down as Taerune's whip tore out his face, and caught sight of a puffing, blood-drenched Bloodblade staggering back into the cavern.

Then Taerune's whip entangled the legs of one last warblade, he toppled, she ruthlessly drove the blade her left arm now ended in into his throat . . . and silence fell.

There were no more Ouvahlans standing in the cavern, though the floor was heaped with them. Bloodblade peered down the passage that led back to Glowstone, swore, started to run—and then stopped, sighing. "One—their commander—getting away," he panted. "Back to tell—"

"I'll take him!" Orivon snapped, and launched himself into the passage. He could hear Taerune gasping behind him as he ran, shoulders slamming bruisingly into this side wall and then that one, hurling himself along.

Soon they'd come to the steep slope down, with the loose stones, but it was a long way before there'd be side caverns and other passages, that the Nifl could choose to take. He had to run down the Ouvahlan before then, or the rest of the army would be guided, patrol after patrol, until—

A dagger came hurtling right at his face!

Behind it, the Ouvahlan was rushing forward, sword up.

Orivon slipped.

The dagger flashed over him as he started to fall, and he heard Taerune grunt, and then sob.

Thorar, no! She's been hit!

The grinning warblade thrust at him. Still falling, Orivon kicked desperately, slashed back and forth with his blade, and flung up his free hand to try to slap the darting Ouvahlan blade away.

His kick struck only air, his blade clanged off the Ouvahlan's sword but drove it past his shoulder—and his hand slammed into the Ouvahlan's sword hand. He shoved at it as he slid on past, slamming into the Nifl's legs.

The Ouvahlan fell on him, hard. They both cursed, and Orivon saw a Nifl hand plucking at a sheathed dagger. He slammed the hilt of his sword into his foe's head, heard the warblade grunt, and—was flung sideways as Taerune hurled herself along his body, blade-first, to bury her steel in the Ouvahlan's neck and throat.

The Nifl went limp, and Taerune crawled on them both, using the warblade's own dagger to make sure the Ouvahlan was dead.

Then things went very quiet, save for their hard breathing.

"Are they all dead?" Orivon gasped.

"Yes," Taerune gasped back, her knees and elbows bruising him as she turned atop him.

"Are you hurt?" he managed to gasp out—before her lips found his.

They were hot and hungry, and were all the answer he got until Bloodblade grunted, "Could you two couple in a slightly roomier spot, d'you think? Taerune, you're bleeding something fierce, and should be cuddling my healing-stone, not this huge hairy human!"

Jalandral smiled as the glow that had claimed him faded away again. Drawing his sword, he stepped forward confidently into an unfamiliar passage, deep in the Wild Dark.

He was walking into danger again, and that was just how he wanted it.

. . .

Orivon's bundle was much smaller now. Taerune walked ahead of him, her painful healing done, and Bloodblade trudged along behind. No one mentioned Lharlak or Daruse, and no one dawdled. There might be many more Ouvahlan patrols looking for travelers to butcher.

"I'm sorry you got hurt," Orivon told Taerune. Again. "That dagger should never have got past me."

Taerune sighed and turned. "Don't be. It was *battle*. Behave cruelly more often; you'll find it gets much easier."

Orivon gave her a dark look. "That's *precisely* what I fear."

"Enough, you two," Bloodblade growled from behind them. "We're almost at the way up into the Blindingbright—and there's always beasts lurking thereabouts to deal with."

By the time he reached the Hidden Gate and found its guards gone, Lord Evendoom was more than tired of burning Nameless rabble, crones, and Evendoom servants. Moreover, spellblade magic doesn't last forever, and he did *not* want to end up beset by Lord-murderers in his own bed-chambers, defending himself with nothing but a dagger and a no-longer-magic sword. So he had to remember all the places battle-magic had been hidden in the Eventowers, and hope by Olone that the crones hadn't gotten to all of them first.

Trudging down the long tunnel that served as the back way into the Eventowers, he passed the time thinking up new curses.

"I'll wait down here in the Dark for you two to kiss and slobber and all of that," Bloodblade grunted. "Don't go throwing any temporarily discarded clothing down on my head, now."

Orivon and Taerune both gave him withering looks; he just grinned and waved them up the narrow, winding way that led up into ever-brighter light.

Despite Bloodblade's dire warnings, there'd been no beasts, though they'd seen gnawed and scattered bones in plenty. Taerune shivered as they stepped up into a boulder-strewn cavern whose far end was one blinding wall of light.

"The Blindingbright," Orivon said roughly. "My home."

"Another world," Taerune mumbled, trembling.

Orivon put an arm around her. "It's just light. Nothing to be afraid of."

"For you," she hissed, her fingers over her eyes. "Humans slaughter Nifl, remember?"

Orivon stroked her hair awkwardly, drawing her against his chest. "I hated you so much," he muttered, "for so long."

She sighed. "I didn't hate you," she said, in a small voice. Then she added firmly, "Have my thanks, Orivon. I owe you my life. Dark Warrior."

Orivon looked over her head at the sunlight. He could just see green leaves, now. "I won't forget you," he said, suddenly very weary.

"I know that. We're blood-sworn . . . and you're Olone's Dark Warrior."

"And what is Olone, but a name priestesses threaten other Nifl with?"

"Be not so sure of that." She shivered violently, and then hissed, "If ever you are in need, get back down into the Dark, away from this light, fill your hand with your own blood, and say my name. I will hear."

"And?"

"And come to this place, if I can. I stand in your debt, Orivon Fire-fist."

"For lashing you? And turning your city into a battlefield?"

"Oh, Olone damn you, human, don't make this *harder!*" Taerune's finger caught hold of his ear, she dragged his face down and kissed him fiercely, her tongue like a sword—and then tore free and strode away from him.

They gazed at each other in silence, and then Taerune slowly drew her dagger, gave him an Evendoom salute, and turned away.

"Taerune—lass—" Orivon blurted out, and she turned to face him, already two strides down the cleft that led down into the Dark.

"Keep safe," he said roughly. "And may we meet again as friends, by Thorar. And Olone."

Taerune gave him a smile, blew him a kiss, and was gone.

Orivon stood for a long time staring at where his last sight of her had been, remembering those eyes staring at his, wet with tears.

And then he sighed heavily, felt for the hilt of his sword, and started the walk out to the waiting sunlight.

. . .

Taerune wiped her eyes and stood still in the gloom, with the light of the Blindingbright behind her and the deep and familiar darkness ahead.

She was an Evendoom no more.

Whether Maharla or her father were alive or dead, no matter who was Eldest and who ruled the Place of the Goddess, the family she knew—and knew her place in, a place she still sorely wanted—was gone. Gone to her. No one-armed Nifl-she could stand in the favor of the Goddess.

This one-armed Nifl-she no longer wanted to. Merely thinking of the cruelty and endless striving, blood against blood, family against family, city against city . . . no.

Not for her.

Nor was she truly a Ravager, embracing their endless skulking to survive. It was still fighting, always fighting.

Something she'd had a taste for when she was a pampered Lady Evendoom, able to sneer at so many, take what she wanted, and never fear danger nor hunger. Something that held no glee at all now, when she would have to struggle to seize everything, from her next meal to freedom from a slave chain or the pawings of every Nifl-he stronger than she was, who had two arms to defeat her one.

"I am alone," she murmured to the waiting darkness. "Loyal now only to myself, and those who've proven their loyalty to me."

She stood silent for a long time ere adding in a whisper, "Like the hairy beast who just left my life. Olo—no, *Thorar* damn you, Dark Warrior."

Her sigh trembled almost into another sob. Tossing her head angrily and sweeping her surviving arm through the darkness as if she could hurl Orivon Firefist and Talonnorn and every last Talonar Nifl away from her, she set off back down into the darkness.

It was a very short time before she reached the jutting edge of rock. Beyond it, when she turned the corner, fat Bloodblade would be waiting to greet her with some smart remark about the lovemaking of humans, no doubt.

She went around the rock. Someone else was standing there, with a grin on his face and a drawn sword in his hand.

"Sister," Jalandral purred, "I've been hunting you for a long time."

Taerune stared at him, open-mouthed.

Her brother took a slow, smiling step toward her.

Behind him, Old Bloodblade stepped silently out of a dark side cleft, sword and dagger raised.

Epilogue

Coming home is seldom as easy as the tales have it.
—saying of the priests of Thorar

Two strides out of the cave, Orivon started to cry.

He'd been so afraid he'd find unfamiliar countryside and villages full of folk he didn't know, who'd see him as some sort of marauder to be slain or driven out.

But there were Old Larthor's fields—all overgrown, mind—and the roofs of Ashenuld below him. He hurried down the slope.

Birds called and flitted, but there were no shouts, no beasts in the fields . . .

Nothing but silence and empty homes, their stones tumbling into an overgrown street.

Ashenuld was an abandoned ruin.

"A welcome?" Orivon bellowed, loudly enough to set birds shrieking up into the sky to wheel squawking overhead. "Anyone?"

No voice replied.

Orivon drew his sword. Jaw set, he tramped to his home. Its door was open, the inside dark and empty, nothing greeting him but the faint reek of mold. No one had lived there for a long time.

The next house was the same.

And the next.

Silently raging, fresh tears almost blinding him, Orivon sought the holy hut.

It was fallen and gone, trees standing thickly where its door had been. He could see the worn threshold, between some roots, but . . .

Ashenuld was gone. These were but its bones.

Orivon looked back at the cave, hefting his sword in his hand, and then shook his head.

He looked slowly all around at what had been his home, shook his head again, and then whispered, "Farewell, Mother. I hope you died well, and lived better."

The same empty words he'd heard the old aunts say so often, at one death or another.

"Thorar be with me now," he whispered—and set off down what had been Ashenuld's main street, the way that led down out of the hills to the village of Orlkettle, and then on to the market-moot of Blard's Brook, and then a long, long way to the fabled many-kings' city of Orlpur.

Orlkettle was almost a day's walk, and—he looked up at the sky—he had less than a day left, before nightfall.

When the wolves and worse came out.

Orivon smiled mirthlessly, and strode on. That "worse" would now be him.

It did not seem to him that he'd walked all that long before he saw the plumes of smoke climbing the sky. Three or four; the thin ribbons that rise from chimneys. Orlkettle. That largest, darkest plume would be the smithy.

He strode to it, ignoring the cries of fearful children and goodwives running for the fields to fetch their men.

There were shouts, and someone came to the door of the smithy before he reached it. Someone old, and scarred, and bristle-bearded, who fixed him with a hard gaze.

"Who be you, stranger, and what want you here, with drawn sword and all?"

"Orivon am I, of . . . a far place. What befell in Ashenuld?"

"Nightskin raids, until none were left but old Ralla and her kin, who tarried in hopes that her son would return."

"And where are Ralla and her kin now?"

"Dead, all of them, in the hard winters and the jaws of the wolves and nightskin raids."

The smith eyed Orivon's scars as if he recognized them.

"Now I've given answers, and it's your turn. Where'd you come by that sword?"

"Made it," Orivon said simply.

The smith nodded, looking not surprised in the slightest. "New to these hills?"

"Old and of these hills."

"So how is it you knew Ashenuld? As small a place in these uplands as any?"

"I was of Ashenuld, once."

Men were creeping up behind Orivon now, with shovels and pitchforks and rakes in their hands, but he kept his back to them, and his eyes on the smith, who raised his voice a little, so that all could hear it, and asked, "Want work here, and a roof and bed? I'm getting no younger."

Orivon smiled slowly and said, "Why not? Back to the forge. An anvil was my life for long years; I can rebuild that life at yours. Aye, if you'll have me."

The smith nodded, and smiled too. "I will."

"Can you fight nightskins?" a man called, from behind Orivon.

He turned slowly, lifted his sword a little, and said firmly, "No nightskin will ever take me alive again."

There was a murmur; women were joining the onlookers now, peering at him curiously from between the men.

"And if you dwell here and work our smithy," a raspy voiced man asked suspiciously, "will you take that sword of yours to us?"

"Only to someone who attacks me. Yet hear this, folk of Orlkettle: I will not be driven from here. This will be my home."

Orivon took a step closer to the watching villagers, and raised his sword on high. "I am Firefist, the Dark Warrior," he shouted, and it seemed to them that flames rose in his eyes.

Lore about the Dark Below has always been both scarce and suspect. To this day scholars cannot agree about the true nature of That Which Sleeps Below, the Ghodal so feared by Niflghar, whose awakening presaged the Great Doom.

Yet it is clear that in the winter after the Second Summer of Araum, the greatest Niflghar spellrobe of all, Klarandar, rose to prominence in the city of Ouvahlor. In the Fourth Summer of Araum, Ouvahlor made war once more upon its traditional foe, the city of Talonnorn.

Whereas Talonnorn, greatest of the cities of Olone, had prevailed in previous strife between the two cities, such was not the case this time. The city of Talonnorn was shattered by the attack, and whereas some sages assert that the Talonar hurled back their attackers, most read the more reliable accounts to mean that the armies of Ouvahlor withdrew and let the Talonar fight among themselves, bringing their own city down around them.

What is certain is that the city of Talonnorn fell into turmoil at this time, its temple of Olone riven and the grasp of the Goddess on the city broken. Much murder was done within the houses, most Eldests and ruling Lords perishing, and House Evendoom, long dominant in Talonnorn, fell far from ruling might.

It is from this time that the legend of the Dark Warrior rose, the scourge of Niflghar whose adventures are so vividly told and retold. Most sources agree that he was of, or from, Talonnorn, and name him Orivon, or Firefist or Forgefist. Some say he was a renegade Nifl, others an exiled Lord or heir of a fallen House. Perhaps, as some of the wildest tales claim, he was no Niflghar at all, but an escaped human slave. Some even claim the Dark Warrior was an Evendoom she who turned against her house and brought about its fall. Inevitably, the holy writings of the priestesses of the Ever-Ice claim the Dark Warrior was the Ice itself, thrust into the body of a mortal, to walk the Dark Below and cleanse all.

All that can be said for certain is that the Dark Warrior rose, and the Dark Below was changed forever.

–from *Dynasties of Darkness,*
penned by Erammon the Elder,
published the Sixth Summer of Urraul

Afterword

Of Dark Elves, Wonder, and Danger

It all began a long, long time ago.

How long ago, no one knows. Probably the first humans, daring to duck into caves for shelter, had legends of dark-skinned, evil beings dwelling in the darkness at the back of the cave . . . and below, under the earth.

Long before the Mines of Moria, long before Menzoberranzan—well, let's dispense with a lot of the "long agos" and stop at Snorri Sturluson (1178–1241), an Icelandic historian who wrote:

> There are many magnificent dwellings. One is there called Alfheim. There dwell the folk that are called light-elves; but the dark-elves dwell down in the earth, and they are unlike the light-elves in appearance, but much more so in deeds. The light-elves are fairer than the sun to look upon, but the dark-elves are blacker than pitch.

Snorri called those "blacker than pitch" beings *svartálfar* ("black elves") and *dökkálfar* ("dark elves"), as he sorted through and summarized Norse mythology. They may or may not be the same beings as the *duergar* (dwarves), but they are certainly dark-skinned creatures who dwell under the earth, and are regarded by humans as evil (whereas the light-elves may be proud, magically powerful, and capricious, but are fair and essentially good).

Both light and dark elves appear in hundreds of fantasy stories; to pluck up just one example: the "svarts" of Alan Garner's classic children's fantasies *The Weirdstone of Brisingamen* (1960) and *The Moon of Gomrath* (1963).

In part this modern popularity of "light" and "dark" elves in literature is due to the elves of J.R.R. Tolkien's epic, phenomenally influential *The Lord of the Rings,* but in part it's also due to the same root tradition Tolkien borrowed from: the elves (or faeries) of European folklore, who lived under hills or burial mounds (or within trees, springs, or wells). Many English fantasy writers, from Kipling (*Puck of Pook's Hill* and *Rewards and Fairies*) to Enid Blyton (too many titles to list), drew on this tradition. Creatures who grant wishes, or dance with humans as hundreds of years pass in a single night, or play tricks, or are proud and terrible in their dealings with humans—these populate the fairy tales all fantasy writers grow up with, and become inspired by.

As Brian M. Thomsen puts it in his book *The Awful Truths* (Collins, 2006): "J.R.R. Tolkien did not invent Middle-Earth," which "predates Tolkien by over a thousand years." Skipping over the scholarship, Thomsen summarizes matters thus:

> Middle-Earth is another name for Midgard which is the domain where men dwell in ancient Norse mythology which was the source for the original Beowulf tale. It is located somewhere between the realm of the gods and the realm of the underworld (more simply in Judeo-Christian terms heaven and hell). Midgard/Middle-Earth is also the setting for Beowulf (mentioned specifically in the text no less than six times), a manuscript that Tolkien spent many hours studying, and as it turns out being inspired by.

Indeed, Thomsen's anthology *The Further Tales of Beowulf, Champion of Middle Earth* (Carroll & Graf, 2006) includes the stirring tale "Beowulf and the City of the Dark Elves" by noted fantasy writer Jeff Grubb. In this story, Beowulf travels to a far place, discovers that the local human trade with the elves who dwell under the mountains there has ceased because those elves have revealed their grim preferred diet: the meat of human children. As might be expected, a heroic adventure ensues.

Interestingly, Tolkien has his dark elves, too, although the main epic bypasses them, and most readers know nothing about them: the

Morquendi (the Elves of Darkness) are elves who chose not to journey over the sea to Valinor.

In his book *The Real Middle Earth: Magic and Mystery in the Dark Ages* (Sidgwick & Jackson, 2002), Brian Bates reminds us that when Celtic tales mention the *sidh-folk,* this means "creatures of the burial mounds," and there is a long tradition of humans treating with elves and giving them gifts or feasting in their honor, to stay on their good side. Gaelic calls these elves *daoi-sith* ("dark elves") and *du-sith* ("black elves").

Celtic traditions include many tales of humans who danced with elves for a night, only to discover that years upon years had passed and all the folk they knew were long dead; humans tricked by elves or who managed to trick elves; and tragic romances and fatal bargains between humans and elves. The fey faeries are never lurking far beyond the firelight of human encampments, as they dance in their faery rings and glide or fly through their forests.

If *The Lord of the Rings* was the first great stir in modern fantasy, founding today's commercial fantasy genre and spawning countless imitators, the second great stir was Dungeons & Dragons®, the fantasy role-playing game released in the 1970s. It, too, spawned many imitators and made new fantasy fans by the thousands, drawing imaginative people into participating in new fantasy storytelling rather than just reading fantasy stories.

Gary Gygax, cocreator of the game (joined in the final adventure by cowriter David C. Sutherland III), introduced dark elves to D&D® gamers as the "drow," in a classic series of "adventure modules" that began with an above-ground trilogy wherein game players' characters battled different sorts of giants in high, cold mountains. A second trilogy took the characters through a rift down into the depths of the earth, into a vast subterranean realm known as "the Underdark," where the action reached a city of the dark elves, in *The Vault of the Drow.*

The D&D® dark elves were obsidian-skinned and pointy-eared; sophisticated and cruel slavers and merciless slayers who worshipped a spider goddess, Lolth (or "Lloth"). In *Queen of the Demonweb Pits,* the adventure saga took surviving adventurers onto another plane of existence, the abode of that fell goddess. Gygax's drow were warring families or merchant clans, akin to the Borgias and their rivals in historical Venice under the Doge. In these adventures, the matriarchal clergy of the spider goddess were ruthlessly destroying priests of an unnamed "Elder

Elemental God" that was obviously losing the battle for religious supremacy in this drow city.

It was a setting that fascinated players, myself among them. In 1986, the drow adventures were revised and collected into *Queen of the Spiders,* which a 2004 *DUNGEON*® magazine poll voted *the* "greatest D&D® adventure of all time."

Mr. Gygax almost certainly took the name "drow" (rhymes with "cow" and not "show") from the evil drow (dark elves) of the Shetland Isles (related to the "trow" of the Orkney Islands; both are likely local versions of the Norse *dökkálfar*). The drow he presented to gamers back in 1978, in the *Descent Into the Depths of the Earth* adventure (white-haired and black-skinned, elegant and agile and cruel, with male fighters and wizards ruled by female priestesses), are essentially the drow of fantasy fiction today. After the D&D® game itself, they are arguably Gary Gygax's greatest, most influential fantasy creation.

A year after *Queen of the Spiders* appeared, gamers saw the first Realms-lore outside the pages of *DRAGON*® magazine. The Forgotten Realms®, the fantasy world I'd created as a child, had been adopted as the setting for the D&D® game. One of the many modifications of my original made in the published Realms was sweeping aside my nebulous subterranean kingdoms, the "Realms Below," to bolt on the Underdark of D&D® (drow and all).

A flood of Realms novels from many pens appeared. Among them was *The Crystal Shard* by R. A. Salvatore, featuring a band of heroes that included an outcast drow, Drizzt Do'Urden. "The" dark elf was then just one adventurer among equals, but caught the imagination of readers, soaring swiftly to prominence as a major character in fantasy fiction.

Salvatore's second trilogy began with a book now rightly regarded as a classic: *Homeland,* the story of Drizzt's coming of age in the drow city of Menzoberranzan. Readers were thrust into the heart of life and politics in a city ruled by the cruel faith of Lolth, where betrayals among family were as icily keen as the attacks of foes, females ordered males about, and those females (from the matrons who rule each House downward) engaged in an endless struggle for supremacy. This was "real life" for drow, brought vividly alive on the printed page; I loved it, and eagerly accepted a role in detailing Menzoberranzan in D&D® terms, detailing its spells, food, customs, and minutae in a boxed game set.

Drizzt's saga has continued for book after book, many of them departing the Underdark for surface adventures, and other writers have been welcomed aboard to tell stories of the drow, from Elaine Cunningham's highly regarded Liriel Baenre series to the recent multiauthor *War of the Spider Queen* saga.

I share the fascination many readers obviously have for the drow of the spider goddess, and yet . . .

I have always wanted to explore *my* dark elves, my conception of a nearly-but-not-quite-human subterranean obsidian-skinned race. The elves I imagined before D&D was created and before Gary Gygax gave us his superbly realized drow culture.

Drawing on the Moondragon character of Marvel Comics® and Eartha Kitt femme fatales, on dozens of pulp tales of sensuous deadly vampires and ghosts, and on fantastic art from Erté to Virgil Finlay, I had already envisaged a long-fingered, deft, elegant, sophisticated (even jaded) race of tall, slender, ruthless elves. A ghost story told to me by my grandfather gave me jet-black skin—and fingernails—to go with those long, reaching fingers.

Yet my dark elves weren't called "drow," and they dwelt in a world that held no trace of a spider goddess. I wanted to explore dark elves without Lolth and her faith determining every aspect of dark elven existence, where religious obedience took a backseat to personal moral choices and necessity and state law. I had a writer's problem with the vicious society of the D&D® drow: Those ruthless strivings and sharply defined roles made for plenty of gaming adventure opportunities and a race of readily recognizable villains, but restricted opportunities for dark elves to be individualistic, to argue (without someone dying in a hurry!), to pursue different goals and philosophies, and to display hobbies and gentleness and playfulness (as something more than a glimpse or a perceived and ridiculed weakness).

And of course, I wanted to tell stories of human dealings with such elves.

So in this book, at last, you'll meet *my* dark elves, in my Underworld. I've stepped back to Norse mythology, and entered Niflheim.

Why Niflheim, a world of mist, chill, and ice (the realm of the frost giants in many Scandinavian tales) when in Norse tradition the dark elves dwelt in Svartalfaheim?

Well, Norse mythology tells us that there are nine (linked, coexisting) worlds. There's an upper level of three worlds: Asgard (the land of the gods or Aesir), Alfheim (abode of the elves), and Vanaheim (home of the Vanir); a middle level of Midgard (the "Middle-Earth" of humans),

Jotunheim (land of the giants), Svartalfaheim (where the dark elves dwell), and Nithavellir (home of the dwarves); and a lower level of Muspelheim (a realm of fire) and Niflheim (the home of the dead, the dark, cold and misty lowest region of the underworld). The World Tree, Yggdrasil, holds all of them together—although Niflheim is home to the adder Nidhogge (darkness) who gnaws ever at the roots of Yggdrasil.

In the beginning, there were only fire (Muspelheim) and ice (Niflheim), with a great chasm, Ginnungagap, between. Where the heat met the frost, the frost melted and formed "eitr," a substance that kindled into life and became the giant Ymir, the father of all Frost giants. In the Norse story of creation, Odin killed Ymir, whose outpouring blood killed all but one of the frost giants, and whose body Odin shaped into Midgard.

I'm skipping quite a lot here, but Niflheim remains dark, cold, and misty, and ends up depopulated of frost giants. It's the home of the dead, and is often seen as an endless series of caverns. (It also acquired the name Hel, which in early Germanic mythology became the name of the goddess who ruled the dead in Hel/Niflheim.)

I don't want to offend anyone by cleaving closely to mythic traditions and *then* twisting or gainsaying or embroidering them, so that some will be angered because I "got it wrong."

Rather, I want to explore a fictional Niflheim of darkness and the dead (ghosts and undead). I chose Niflheim rather than Svartalfaheim for my dark elves because of the cold and mist. I have plans for that cold and mist. Dark plans.

What dark plans? Well, as many tale-tellers say across dying fires: In the fullness of time more will be revealed.